# CHILLWATER COVE

**Also by Thomas Lakeman**

*The Shadow Catchers*

# CHILLWATER COVE

Thomas Lakeman

 ST. MARTIN'S MINOTAUR 🙶 NEW YORK

F
LAK

CHILLWATER COVE. Copyright © 2007 by Thomas Lakeman. All rights reserved. Printed in the United States of America. No part of this book may be used or reproduced in any manner whatsoever without written permission except in the case of brief quotations embodied in critical articles or reviews. For information, address St. Martin's Press, 175 Fifth Avenue, New York, N.Y. 10010.

www.minotaurbooks.com

Library of Congress Cataloging-in-Publication Data

Lakeman, Thomas.
    Chillwater Cove / Thomas Lakeman.—1st ed.
        p.   cm.
    ISBN-13: 978-0-312-34800-7
    ISBN-10: 0-312-34800-2
    1. United States. Federal Bureau of Investigation—Officials and employees—Fiction.
2. Kidnapping—Fiction. 3. Tennessee—Fiction. I. Title.

PS 3612.A53C48 2007
813'.6—dc22            2007032238

10   9   8   7   6   5   4   3   2

MY   '08

For my mother

# Acknowledgments

In completing my second novel, I'm deeply grateful for the continuing support of all those who helped me through the first book, as well as some new well-cherished friends.

FBI Special Agent Volney Hayes (retired) was my principal adviser on Bureau-related matters. He was the one who taught me how to format an FBI memorandum, the correct way to pronounce all those acronyms, and why so many brave and talented men and women (including him) have chosen to devote their lives to federal law enforcement.

Johnny Smiley, proprietor of Epiphany Computer Services, helped me avoid many embarrassing mistakes in my depiction of computers and information technology.

Anything I persisted in getting wrong is my fault, not theirs.

I owe thanks to all those who offered insight on the manuscript: Dr. Randall Davis, Mark Tapio Kines, Kelley Lackeos, Victoria Lakeman, and Dr. Mary Leah Lowe. The creative input of my colleague Keira Mallinger, on matters large and small, was valuable beyond telling.

Admiring thanks to my agent, Marian Young, for challenging me to do my best, and for letting me know she believed in me. Sincere appreciation to my editor, Kelley Ragland, for guiding this book swiftly and safely to publication.

A special note of gratitude to my father, the Reverend Ed Lakeman, for introducing me to Volney; and to my mother, Dr. Patricia Burchfield, for introducing me to Melungeons. Anyone wishing to learn more about these people and their fascinating past, present, and future is invited to visit www.melungeon.org or read any of the many fine books on the subject.

The Melungeons of Chillwater Cove—not to mention the residents, faculty, and students of Avalon College, Tennessee—are solely inhabitants of the author's imagination. Any apparent resemblance to people or places in the actual universe is superficial and mostly accidental.

*Had I the eloquence of Orpheus, my father, to move the rocks by chanted spells to follow me, or to charm by speaking whom I would, I had resorted to it. But as it is, I'll bring my tears—the only art I know.*

—Euripedes, *Iphigeneia at Aulis*

*I like women. I don't think there is anything wrong with that.*

—Timothy McVeigh

# ONE

*Storytime has seen better days*, the woman in the red Lamborghini thought as she pulled up to the old schoolhouse. Once upon a time, sending your toddler to Storytime Children's Academy was something to brag about in Philadelphia. Now the place was a rathole. On that chill April night, the only other vehicles in the lot were a green Eldorado, a van from Propeller Hedz Computer Services, and a blacked-out panel truck with Jersey plates. It was the last one that troubled her: the truck's tag number had checked out fake, and the driver's description wasn't on her prep sheets.

The woman's business cards read *Renée McDormand, Importer-Exporter*—as did several other pieces of identification, none of them more than a few hours old. Her real name was FBI Special Agent Peggy Weaver. Somewhere in the darkness, men with automatic weapons waited for her command.

Peggy briefly checked herself in the mirror: thirty-seven, auburn hair, hazel eyes, light freckles on a nose that she'd never liked. That night her eyebrows were freshly tweezed and she wore a killer black suit that made the SWAT team boys grin at their final briefing. Peggy wasn't sure if the getup made her look more like an executive or a trophy wife, but that was precisely what the subject's profile demanded. She sure as hell didn't look forward to chasing anyone on those stiletto heels.

"Stop primping. You look fine." A cocksure male voice spoke over her in-ear receiver. "I see you decided to go with the black bra."

"My eyes are up here, Yeager." She raised an eyebrow at the cable van down the road, where her partner Mike Yeager was running tactical. "Yoshi's in place?"

"Roger that. We've got thermal and audio surveillance working. Awaiting visual." He paused. "Sounds like they're still debating whether to trust you. You sure you want to go in alone like this?"

"I'm not crazy about it. But until we confirm the victim's status, this has to be a soft-target entry."

"Yoshi just texted us. The panel truck driver's carrying a semiautomatic, maybe a forty-five. He's brought at least two friends along." Mike's voice lowered; he'd put her on closed comm. "Make an excuse and get out, Peg. This smells bad."

She didn't answer. Someone was watching her through the blinds. Peggy stood from the car, smoothing her jacket to make sure her Glock 22 was still within easy reach. *Please God, don't make me use this tonight*: the prayer she breathed every time she armed herself. *Don't let anyone die because I missed something important.*

The door opened before she could knock.

"Hello!" Peggy was all bright smiles and handshakes. "I'm Renée Mc-Dormand. Thank you *so* much for meeting me this late."

**"I have to admit, my** wife didn't like your people sending a woman." Dr. Barry Cooke, the school's pastry-plump codirector, escorted Peggy through dark and empty playrooms. "She thinks I'm a pushover for pretty girls."

She smiled. "Actually, Dr. Cooke, I own the company—well, I and our mutual friends."

His eyes flickered south of her neckline. "You obviously do well. What is that out front, a Lamborghini Diablo? Magnificent. What did it cost, if you don't mind?"

"Oh—a buck and a half?" She was glad she'd remembered to ask the attorney who lent her the vehicle. "I didn't get overcharged, did I?"

"A hundred and fifty thousand dollars? Please." He chuckled. "You practically stole it. Time was I could have driven a car like that right off the lot. Not today. Not with all the troubles Dr. Barry Cooke is having lately."

Dr. Barry Cooke often referred to himself in the third person—as did his wife, Dr. Clara Cooke. Peggy knew that the degrees were bogus—just as she knew that, in their native Ukraine, their true names were Vasyl and Kalyna Kohut. The Cookes' troubles began when one of their employees was arrested on possession of child pornography. Thanks to a ruinously expensive defense, they beat the rap—barely. The prosecutor told Peggy he'd been barred from presenting evidence that suggested the photographs not only belonged to the Cookes, but had likely been taken by them on school property.

"The scandal destroyed us," Barry told Peggy as he led her into an office decorated with purple dinosaurs. "Our kids were the finest. Three-year-olds speaking French! And now it's all dust and ashes."

"Has my old fart of a husband been flirting with you again?" Clara Cooke looked at Peggy with gimlet eyes. "It's a wonder a pretty girl like you still isn't married."

Barry had been an easy sell. It was his wife who'd insisted on references and background checks. Renée McDormand's marital status had never come up in conversation—but Peggy had carefully planted the information in her bona fides, just in case Clara decided to dig deeper. Evidently she had.

Two men were waiting for them on the sofa. She recognized the fidgety teenager as the Cookes' son, Adam. The middle-aged man, tough and blunt, was the driver of the panel truck. As she glanced beneath his jacket, she realized that Yoshi was wrong about the gun. It wasn't a .45. The shooter carried a .357 Magnum Desert Eagle, a gas-operated semiautomatic. It would tear her in half before she could get anywhere close to her Glock. He stared at her torso, but not with pleasure. He was noticing her lack of body armor.

"How much longer will this computer nonsense take?" Clara asked the technician crouched behind a desktop PC. "We're trying to do a meeting here."

"Actually, we're good. Almost." According to his Propeller Hedz jacket, the spiky-haired young man's name was Scotty. That was an in-joke around the Philadelphia field office; a tribute to his favorite TV show, *Star Trek*. Peggy knew him as Special Agent Yoshi Hiraka, someone who could work miracles with technology—even rig video surveillance under the pretense of upgrading the Cookes' computer network.

"Peg?" Mike's voice on the comm. "There's two other targets guarding the basement. I think that's our play. We're pulling Yoshi back so he can knock out their security system. Maybe you could give him a little nudge out the door."

Yoshi was meanwhile chatting about server protocols and needing to get behind the firewall. Peggy could tell he was trying very hard not to look her way.

She turned instead to Clara. "Should we reschedule for another time? Things seem a little disorganized."

"This was supposed to be done hours ago. I'm not paying for this incompetence." Clara snapped her fingers at Adam. "Go give this boy whatever he needs in the computer room. Shut the door when you leave."

"Why can't I stay?" Adam's eyes darted nervously at Peggy.

"Because, because, because. Out." Clara's features hardened as the door closed. "Enough chitchat, dear. What can you do for us, and for how much?"

"I understand you want something moved out of the country," Peggy answered. "As I'm sure you know by now, my associates and I have secure channels across the Mexican and Canadian borders, as well as through all major U.S. ports. No delays, no inspections. I can make you disappear."

"Dr. Barry Cooke likes to fly first class." Barry tried to laugh, but he was sweating. "As long as he doesn't have to take off his shoes at security."

Peggy threw Clara a sympathetic look: *I see what you have to put up with.* The woman didn't respond.

"We do have contacts at LaGuardia, LAX, and Atlanta," Peggy replied. "There's additional risk involved. It'll run the costs a bit higher."

"How much higher?" Clara folded her arms.

Peggy tapped out a number on a pocket calculator and showed it to Clara.

"Too pricey." She shook her head. "Sorry you came all this way for nothing, dear. You're looking at people on a fixed income."

Barry cringed. "Maybe she'll take a percentage?"

"A percentage of what?" Peggy noticed that the question made Clara frown. "We generally work on a cash basis."

The shooter laughed and said something to Clara in a foreign tongue: his voice rang like thresher blades, keen and remorseless.

"It's Ukrainian," Mike said. "Hang on, we're getting the translation. He said . . . 'I told you your husband was thinking with his dick. This bitch is full of shit.'"

Barry started to answer—then Clara cut him off in the same language.

"Clara's telling her husband to make the call," Mike translated. "She says that if he's wrong about you, they're going to be digging some holes in the basement tonight."

Peggy cleared her throat.

"Dr. Cooke." She stared right at Clara. "You and your husband need to understand, I'm not a travel agent. If you want to cheap out, go hire some coyote with a false-bottom eighteen-wheeler. I personally think you'll run straight into ICE. But if you want peace of mind, you're going to have to pay for it."

"And you don't even ask what we're moving." Clara snapped her fingers. "Drugs, bombs—you just want your money."

"Not unless it keeps me from doing my job."

Clara glanced at the shooter. He raised his hands as if to say: *It's your mess, you clean it up.*

"Let's show the girl how much we trust her," Clara said.

It had been two months since Peggy's desk, the Crimes Against Children Unit, had received an anonymous tip that the Cookes were trying to get something past Immigrations and Customs. She knew it couldn't be money or porn—such matters could be handled electronically. Then she made the connection.

"We want to return home. But the goddamn bureaucrats in Kiev . . ." Barry glanced nervously at the two men in leather jackets guarding the basement door. "There's people who will help us—if we give them something they need."

Peggy tried not to seem interested. Just as she feared, her pointed heels kept getting caught in the stairs' metal grating. For a moment she nearly tripped and was obliged to let Barry take her hand. Clara's eyes burned into her from behind.

"It scares me a little that you're a woman." Barry fumbled his keys into the inner door's locks. "I can't know how you'll react to . . . what you're about to see."

"Peggy." Mike's voice was broken by static now. "Yoshi's running into trouble. Before you proceed—"

Barry's hand quavered on the doorknob. "I want you to know we've been taking very good care of her."

Mike raised his voice. "Peggy, we have to abort."

Barry opened the door.

Only one of the room's twelve cages was still occupied, by someone whose face had become well known since her disappearance on Christmas morning. The victim's father had personally requested Peggy's unit for the case. All leads had dead-ended until Agent Weaver happened to notice that the child had once briefly attended Storytime Children's Academy.

The girl in the cage was five years old, wearing a ragged yellow diaper and nothing else. Her ribs showed hard against ebony skin, marked by still-darker bruises. The child's hair, raven black in family photos, was dry and frayed like scorched grass. She stared at Peggy with empty brown eyes that had moved past fear and even despair, and were on the verge of indifference.

Peggy listened for Mike's voice, heard nothing.

"So, Miss McDormand," Clara said. "Does this keep you from doing your job?"

Heavy shots rang from above: the Desert Eagle. Feet on the floor, then down the stairs. Peggy started to reach for the holster behind her back. Then the door swung open, and Adam Cooke entered breathlessly.

"He found it," the boy gasped. "That computer guy found the file. Mama, we have to get out of here. Now."

"Don't be stupid." Clara pressed a red button beside the light switch. "It's too late."

"It's not too late!" Adam looked at Peggy. "You shouldn't have come. Don't you know what they're pulling you into?"

"Adam, please—!" Fire exploded through Barry's chest as a loud report boomed in the stairwell. The shooter calmly descended, holding the smoking semiautomatic before him.

"Omigod," Adam said. "Papa."

"She's FBI. Your husband fucked us all." The gunman spat on Barry's prone body. "Bitch is carrying a piece under her jacket. Get it."

Clara was oddly calm as she took the Glock from Peggy. "Are there more of them?"

He nodded and put the muzzle to Peggy's head. "You die—the girl dies—your Jappo upstairs dies. Unless you call the man in charge. Tell him to surrender. Now."

"I can't get a signal down here." Peggy held her breath, forcing her voice to tremble.

"Upstairs, then."

Peggy stopped in front of the stairs. She could hear the girl whimpering behind her.

"I'm not walking back up in these goddamn heels." Without waiting for a response, she bent down and slipped one shoe off.

"Stop that! You stop or—!" The guard took a stiletto in the eye. As he fell, Peggy grabbed the semiautomatic. She wheeled around to see Clara aiming the Glock between her eyes.

"Mama, don't," Adam said.

Clara squeezed the trigger. Nothing happened.

"There isn't a round in the chamber," Peggy said. "Put it down, Dr. Cooke."

Clara calmly flicked the slide lock and aimed again.

*God help me.* The Desert Eagle kicked hard. Clara Cooke fell back in a spray of blood.

The boy turned to the door, breathing hard.

Peggy carefully retrieved the Glock. "Adam, step away from the door. I don't want to hurt you."

"You killed my mother." He looked at her, eyes wide. "He told me you would and I didn't believe him."

"Who did, Adam?"

"I should have seen it," he said. "You deserve everything that's coming to you, Agent Weaver." Adam ran up the stairs. Peggy was about to follow when she heard more shots from above: AK-47s against FBI submachine guns. Then another sound behind her: the child's soft breathing.

"Don't worry, honey. I'm not leaving you." As Peggy backed against the cage, the girl's fingers twined into her own.

Moments later the firing stopped, and Peggy looked up into the dark stairwell. "Mike, do you copy? What's happening?"

Agonizing seconds later, she heard her partner's voice:

"Clear up," Mike said. "We have secured the area, Peggy. What's your situation?"

She looked back. The child surveyed the dead with something like quiet satisfaction.

"Clear down," she replied. "We have the senator's daughter."


Peggy held the girl in her arms until the EMTs arrived. As she entered the computer room, Yoshi was waiting for her. His head was freshly bandaged.

"Did you get anything?" she asked.

"A concussion, maybe." He touched his temple. "I was scanning for dead spots when I noticed a hidden partition—that big lunk must have seen me trying to decrypt the data. Put a round right through the screen I was working on."

She squeezed his shoulder. "It's okay, Yoshi. What did you find?"

"You're not gonna believe this." He looked at her. "A folder with your name on it."

"What?"

"Take a look." He punched through a sequence of keys. "There's twelve photos here. I got a feeling Adam was waiting for me to find them, too. Kid was reeeall nervous."

A series of color images appeared on the computer screen. Peggy scrolled through them in silence.

"Pretty foul, aren't they?" Yoshi pointed. "Same kid in every picture—little blond girl. Even for the Storytime classic kiddie porn collection, this is some sadistic shit."

"Yoshi, that's enough."

"Sorry." He blushed. "Looks like somebody scanned them from matte prints—they're at least twenty years old."

"Twenty-five." She reached over him and shut the program down. "Has anybody else seen these?"

"Just Mike. I figured since he's our photo analyst . . . are you okay? You look kinda pale."

"I'm fine," she said. "I'll deal with Mike. Right now I need you to password-protect the files and seal the hard disk. No access without my authorization."

"You want me to restrict the files?"

"And no backups," she said. "That's an order."

He hesitated a moment. "Got it, chief."

She went outside, where a forensics team was loading Clara Cooke's remains into a meat wagon. The lot was already crowded with Philly PD and other emergency vehicles. Small knots of reporters were starting to form around the barricades.

"Holy shit," Peggy whispered as camera lights played over the open rear door of the ambulance. *Who the hell tipped the media off?*

"That was some quick work in there." Mike stood beside her, wearing an FBI flak jacket. His dark hair was damp with sweat. "How'd you get the drop on that shooter?"

"He didn't know it was my operation. He thought I was just the decoy." She looked at him. "Did you find Adam Cooke?"

He shook his head. "Either he knows a way out that we don't, or he's still in hiding."

"Adam said my name. He must have known what was coming down tonight. But he didn't warn his parents."

"Maybe he didn't think anybody'd get hurt if he kept his mouth shut."

Mike leaned in close. "Listen, what's this about you sealing those computer files?"

She touched her cheek. "How much did Yoshi show you?"

"Enough," he said. "Okay, here come the scavenger birds."

The forensics wagon had pulled away, and now the photographers were training their lenses on Peggy and Mike. She turned her back just as a strobe flash went off.

"I've got blood on my face," she said. "I'm going inside."

"Peg," he said. "Do the pictures mean something to you?"

"Yeah," she said. "I know who the girl is."

Then she walked back into the schoolhouse.

# TWO

Peggy Weaver lived in a row house in Hunting Park, a north Philadelphia neighborhood that had fallen on hard times and was struggling through
a painful recovery. Some nights she'd wake to the sound of gunfire. As far as
her neighbors knew, Peggy was just some kind of social worker—one of
those rich white chicks trying to atone for Daddy's money. The women on her
block fretted over her like a wayward child, but they didn't fear for her safety:
they'd seen what happened to the last guy who tried to grab her purse.

She was staring at the blinking red light of her answering machine when
the doorbell rang. Mike stood on the other side of the spyhole, a bag from
Kroger's under his arm.

"It's late, Yeager. What are you doing?"

"Luring you with cookies," he said. "And beer."

Peggy opened the door. At forty-three, Mike was what her landlady,
Mrs. Ramos, called a nice fixer-upper: black hair shot through with a few
early strands of silver; clear blue eyes that turned water-soft when he let his
guard down, cold as iron when he didn't; a fighter's body, plus a few extra
pounds that no hours in the gym could erase. Mike was sensitive about the
gut he'd acquired during his administrative leave. Peggy secretly thought it
made him look cuddly.

"Where's the duck pajamas?" He eyed her in her sweats and faded orange Volunteers T-shirt. Peggy's face was freshly scrubbed, her hair pulled
back. She was still having trouble removing the fake nails.

"The duck pajamas are for winter." She locked the door. "I'm only letting you see me this way because you mentioned beer."

He handed her a Yuengling. "Christ knows how you sleep with this gang-
banger shit going on. Wanna crash at my place?"

He tossed it off lightly. It had been nine months since they last shared a bed, and he still put out occasional feelers. Peggy had to admit that falling asleep next to Mike sounded fine. It was the waking-up part that made it a bad idea.

"You live in a shoebox, Yeager. What am I supposed to do, sleep in the closet?"

He smiled: can't blame a guy for trying. "You'll be pleased to know that the senator's invited you to dinner. Notice that's *you*, not *us*. I figure he wants to propose."

"I know what he wants." She pressed the beer to the back of her neck, grateful that Mike had remembered to buy it cold. "The Special Agent in Charge called while I was taking a shower. They're offering me a place on the Chief Inspector's staff. One year at HQ and I come back a unit supervisor."

"Sweet Jesus." Mike whistled. "They're really grooming you, aren't they?"

"Like Seabiscuit." She shrugged. "The senator chairs the subcommittee that pays our bills. What else were they going to do?"

"And?" He glanced at Peggy's answering machine. "You didn't take the call, did you?"

"Like I said, I was in the shower. Washing off Clara Cooke's blood." She shook her head. "Before you say anything, I fully accept that I'm stupid for dodging this. I know it's a big opportunity. I just don't feel like I got it right."

"You've got as much of a right as anybody."

"Got *it* right, Mike. I didn't get the job right." She twisted the bottle cap off. "I don't want a promotion just because the newspapers stuck my face on page one. And I sure as hell don't want it after nearly botching a recovery."

"Sometimes I think you don't want a promotion, period." He opened a Weber's root beer for himself. "It's not absolution, Peg. It's dinner. Let the man buy you a steak. You saved his daughter's life."

"I also shot a mother in front of her son." She took a long pull of her beer. "I didn't have to use deadly force. I knew the chamber was empty. Just lost control, is all."

"Maybe. We've all been there. You saw what a head case I was last year in Nevada." He reached into the bag. "The fact is, if you hadn't shot first, you'd be dead. And that little girl would be in the hands of the Ukrainian Mob." He tossed her a bag of cookies. "Here. Guilt goes better with Oreos."

"Clearly you speak from experience." She tore the package open. "Why do I get the feeling there's more than junk food in that grocery sack?"

He smiled. "You know, I always wondered why you say 'sack' instead of 'bag' like regular people. And it's always a grocery buggy, never a cart."

"That's right. And in Tennessee we don't push people's buttons, we mash them." She pried a cookie open. "You knew I was a hick the day we met."

"Yeah, but I always figured you for one of those high-toned hicks who wears Laura Ashley. And cries at Civil War reenactments."

"Never been to one." She licked the filling off. "In school, they told us to call it 'The War of the Northern Invasion.'"

"Really? We just called it 'Screw You, We Won.'" He popped half a cookie into his mouth. "I guess there's all kinds of childhood stories we never told each other."

"Yeah." She nodded. "Yoshi printed the pictures for you, didn't he?"

"He made me promise to say that I threatened to hurt him." Mike held up an evidence folder, color-coded red for Special Victims cases. "You want to tell me who she is?"

"You know, Mike, I really don't." She took the folder from him. "And if Yoshi wants to stay in the field, then maybe he ought to start taking these cases a little more seriously."

"He's a father of a newborn girl, Peg. You know he does." He sat back. "And it's not right to make him hide evidence in a child abuse investigation. Where are you going?"

"Looking for a match." She took the folder into the kitchen. "The photos aren't part of the Storytime investigation. Or any other pending case. Right now they fall under the heading of privacy." She began pulling drawers open. "Or were you about to lecture me about integrity of evidence?"

"That would be like giving Batman a lecture on capes." He followed her through the open archway. "You do realize that burning those pictures won't solve a damn thing."

"I'm not trying to solve anything." She leaned against the counter. "Do you honestly think they could be used to make an ID? After all these years?"

He raised his hands. "It wouldn't be easy. The subject's not visible in any of them. And the trail's twenty-five years cold. But it's worth a shot, yeah. It might help if you told me what happened."

"Can't do it, Yeager."

"Can't, or won't?"

"Can't," she said. "Because I don't know what happened. And even if I did . . . I don't have the right. It didn't happen to me." She shook the drawer. "Half the buildings on this street are burned out, and I can't even find one lousy match."

"Look, will you at least talk to me before you set off the fire alarm?"

She closed the drawer. "What do you want?"

"Coffee might be nice," he said. "But not girl coffee, okay? I've kind of reached my limit on nutmeg."

She gave a thin laugh. "According to you, everything's girl coffee unless you can use it to clean your carburetor."

"Damn straight." He sat down. "You were telling me earlier that you know the victim."

"We grew up together. In Avalon, Tennessee." She poured water, spooned coffee into the filter. "I always knew that . . . something happened to her. But I never imagined anything as bad as this." She shivered. "All of a sudden I'm freezing. Do you mind if I turn up the heat?"

"It's your slum."

She went to the thermostat. It read seventy-two.

"Maybe I'll just put on a sweater," she said.

"Take it slow, Peg. What's the girl's name?"

"Samantha," she said.

As she closed her eyes, Peggy saw her as she had been: a coltish preteen with dark blond hair and pale blue eyes, and wire-frames that she hated wearing. Samantha Stallworth, cruising away downhill on a yellow ten-speed. Laughing.

Peggy turned the coffee maker on. Dark liquid dripped into the carafe.

"It happened when we were ten," she said. "One day we were riding our bikes on the back roads, and . . . there was this old black Thunderbird pulled over to the side. This skinny guy, white guy, had the hood up. He said his car had stalled and nobody'd stopped by for hours. I told Sammie to stay with me, but . . ."

She waited as an ambulance siren swept past.

"She was so damn *trusting*," Peggy said. "He just grabbed her like a doll. Sammie was wearing this white jumper, and he was covered with engine grease. So when he held her, I could . . . see where his hands had been. And the whole time, you know, he was—talking to me."

"What did he say?"

"He said, 'Trade. Let's trade. You for her.'"

"You for her," Mike repeated. "I hope you got the hell out of there."

She nodded. "I knew there were trails close by, and he'd have a hard time following me into the woods. So . . ." She closed her eyes. "I left her there. I ran."

"You did what you had to, Peg. He'd have grabbed you both."

"That's what my father said." She looked away. "We went to the police station . . . and suddenly I couldn't remember anything. I mean, I remembered heat waves coming off the engine—which there shouldn't have been, if the car had really stalled out that long." She paused. "And I'll never forget the snake."

"Snake?"

"Not a real one. It was on his belt buckle. A red snake wrapped around a gold sword, with these really long fangs. He must have seen me looking at it, because he said—'If you want it, come and get it. You for her. Let's trade.' And all the while I could hear Samantha . . . screaming."

Peggy was silent for a moment. Out in the alley, glass broke. Someone laughed.

"All the local cops wanted to know was if I got the license plate number," she said. "And I couldn't tell them. And they kept asking what he looked like. And I couldn't make myself see his face."

"Sounds like you were in shock."

"I still can't remember a damn thing, Mike." She stood up to pour coffee. "The, you know, the police chief in Avalon? He said to me—'What a smart girl. If you'd only remembered a seven-digit number, your friend would be home safe.'"

"Two-bit bastard. He actually said that?"

"More than once."

"And they never caught the guy."

"No," she said. "And I never really found out what happened. Her dad told me they brought her home. He made it sound like she was okay . . . but I wasn't allowed to visit. Then Samantha went away for a long time. Almost a year. And when she came back she seemed . . . well, fine. But not fine. After that, there was always something—fragile about her. And we could never talk about that day. Like it had been cut out with a scalpel." Peggy spooned sugar into her cup. "Sometimes it's hard to make myself believe that it really happened."

"But now you've seen the pictures of her." He took the mug. "What are you going to do?"

"Finish my coffee. Maybe top it off with the rest of that six-pack." She drank. "And then you're taking me out to buy a lighter."

"Peg, you're a federal agent. That's evidence."

"Sammie's got a life now. She's teaching at Avalon College, she's got a husband and a kid. If I show her those pictures . . . it could tear her apart."

"Or it might give her a chance to heal. Maybe she deserves to make that decision for herself."

She looked at him for a long time.

"No." She shook her head. "I shouldn't have pulled you into this, Yeager. I'm sorry."

She reached for the folder.

"Peg."

The phone rang.

"That is one persistent U.S. senator." Mike looked at her. "Are you gonna get that?"

"Christ." She stared at the yellow wall phone. Another ring, then a third. One more and it would go to her machine . . .

"Damn it." She picked up the receiver. "Hello?"

"Peggy?" A woman's voice. A child was singing in the background. "I'm sorry, I know it's late."

"Hey. Don't worry about it. Give me a second." She put the phone to her chest. "I gotta take this, Mike."

He nodded and left the room.

"Samantha," she said. "What is it? Are you okay?"

"I've been better." Samantha's voice was breaking. "Something happened, and . . . I know you were probably asleep. But I thought we should talk."

"Oh no." Peggy felt her stomach drop out. "Sammie, I'm so sorry."

"My god," Samantha said. "They sent the pictures to you, too, didn't they?"

Gray light dawned over Hunting Park as Mike loaded Peggy's travel bag into the back of her old Jeep Wrangler.

"I can't believe you're packing all this shit for three days," he said. "You are coming back, right?"

She nodded. "Monday, I hope. I'm gonna make sure Sammie's okay, and . . . help her figure out what to do. After that, I don't know. But will you do something for me while I'm gone?"

"You're trusting me to water your plants again?"

"No. The plants are dead, thanks to you." She unlocked the steering wheel. "Find Adam Cooke. Whoever planted those pictures wanted me and Sammie to get them at the same time. And right now Adam's our only link."

He nodded. "What was it he said to you at the end? 'You deserve what's happening'?"

"What Adam actually said was that I'd earned everything that was coming to me. Before that, he said, 'He told me you would and I didn't believe him.' Kill his mother, that is."

"Who's 'he'?"

"It's not his father. Or the mobster with the Desert Eagle. Neither one of them knew my real name . . . and they're both dead." She looked down the street both ways. "My best guess is that whoever sent those pictures is the same man who took them twenty-five years ago."

"Maybe I should come with," Mike said. "I always wanted to meet those blueblood parents of yours. Even if I did dash your mother's hopes for a society wedding."

"The last thing I need is you talking trash about the Confederacy around my dad." She raised an eyebrow. "And I was the one who broke up with you, remember?"

"Sure. Right." He handed her the red folder. "Don't wait till things get crazy before you call me, Weaver. Snap your fingers and I'll be there."

She put her arms tightly around him.

"Just be here when I get back," she said.

# THREE

A cat-claw moon hung low over Cumberland Valley as Peggy Weaver drove south on Tennessee Highway 23. Mist clung to the skirts of the mountains; the pines were black daggers against the night sky. Every few miles, the darkness was punctured by neon invitations to buy FIRE-WORKS!!!! or SEE ROCK CITY. But it was a simple yellow diamond—25 MPH—that made Peggy's heart stop: the precise spot where, once upon a time, two young girls had crossed paths with a man in a black T-Bird.

*It's only a place in the road*, she thought. Even so, Peggy pressed a little harder on the gas as she started up the incline. From there on the highway was all steep climbs and hairpin turns, with only a battered aluminum rail between her and a death-slide down the ravine. Once in a while, some exhausted trucker or drunken college kid would take the bend just a little too fast: homemade crosses marked where their journeys ended. On maps, the road was known as Avalon Bypass. The locals called it Suicide Run.

At the crest of the hill, Highway 23 became College Avenue; then, as she crossed Sherburn Road, Peggy found herself at the center of town. She was home.

From the air, Avalon looked something like the saltire of a Confederate battle flag—not an accident, according to some local historians. Its arms reached westward from the mannered wealth of Glencoe Bluff to the rank poverty of Chillwater Cove. Residential and business districts lay to the south; the entire northern half of town belonged to the school. As she drove through Avalon's lone traffic light, a banner swayed in the night breeze: WEL-COME HOME. Friday was the start of graduation week, and by morning the quad would be alive with voices. But at that dead hour, her only company was the pale statue of General Stallworth—sword tip at shoulder, astride a marble horse, leading a ghost army into battle. Fog shrouded the clock tower of Culloden Hall, giving it what the admissions department liked to call a haunted beauty. Haunted was right. At night, Culloden seemed less like an academic building than an abandoned fortress. Or a tomb.

Then she made a right onto Sherburn, back into the fifty-five MPH zone, and Peggy Weaver—suddenly aware that she was hungry—made a beeline for the white fluorescent glow of the Piggly Wiggly. She parked beneath a flag-painted sign:

**SUPPORT OUR TROOPS**
**SAVE WITH YOUR PIGGLY WIGGLY DISCOUNT CARD**

"Civilization." She laughed, surprised to discover she'd been holding her breath.

Elevator-style country music warbled as Peggy walked through the automatic door. The store smelled the way it always had—a mingled scent of Comet cleanser, bubble gum, and frozen meat. It was empty except for the cashier, a pretty Goth girl with blue-black hair and what looked like a tiny harpoon impaled on her left ear. She crouched over her cell phone, barely acknowledging her customer.

"How come you only ever call me when you want shit?" The girl's accent was an odd mash-up of Valley Girl and Tennessee twang. "Just because I told you that one thing doesn't mean I have to keep on being your bitch. Get your own dirt."

The cashier's nametag read GRETCHEN. Her eyes were too green for anything but contacts. She'd been crying.

"I gotta go." She dragged Peggy's Diet Coke and Snickers over the scanner. "Oh, and incidentally? Find yourself another wench. Your penis is now officially no longer my concern." She closed the phone. "Why the *fuck* do I even exist?"

"You're asking me?" Peggy bagged her own groceries.

"No. I dunno. My ear hurts." She rubbed her left temple.

*Maybe it's that toothpick in your head*, Peggy thought. "Wanna do yourself a major favor, Gretchen? When he calls back, don't answer."

She looked up with confused hope. "You think he will?"

"They always do." She swiped her card. "I'm Peggy."

Interest flickered in her eyes. "Peggy Weaver."

"Yeah. How did you know that?"

"Duh." She pointed to Peggy's name on the card reader. "It's weird. 'Cause there's a family in town named Weaver. One of 'em's in the CIA or something." She smiled. "Cash back?"

There was a noise outside: trash cans falling, then running feet.

"Oh my fucking god." Gretchen's eyes swung to the door. "What was that?"

Peggy listened. A dull sound of flesh on concrete. "Sounds like fighting out back."

"Where are you going?"

"Just stay calm." Peggy moved for the swinging rubber doors near the meat department. "Lock the doors and call the police."

"I'm not calling the school cops. Those guys don't do shit." The girl froze. "Please don't leave me alone in here."

"Not campus security. The town police." She peered through the store's back window. "Ask to speak directly to the chief. Tell him I said it's a ten-thirty-two in progress." *And don't be surprised if he gives you crap about license plates*, Peggy thought as she pushed through the steel fire door.

She saw them in the alley, half-hidden in darkness: three men in dark clothes took turns pounding an olive-skinned man in a red workshirt. He fought back hard, but they were fighting dirtier. One of them swung with a tire iron, another with a black baseball bat. The tallest of them held a Taser, flashing indigo like a bug zapper. The dumpster had been overturned. Stale bread and wilted lettuce spilled across the alley.

"What the hell's going on?" Peggy didn't raise her voice, but they stopped to look at her all the same. Then she noticed the .38s on their belts. And the silver badges on their blue uniforms.

"Just go on back inside, ma'am." The cop with the Taser wiped sweat from his brow. Peggy heard a police radio crackle behind her. An Avalon PD cruiser was parked in the shadows. "This ain't no place for a lady."

At once the dark-haired young man broke past him, grabbing a fallen plastic bag as he ran hellbent down the alley.

"Holy shit, Martin. He got away." The other two cops started to follow. Then Peggy blocked their path.

"Don't move." Her FBI shield shone gold in the streetlamp. She glanced at their name plates. "Officers Martin—Ripley—Dennis. I'm dealing with this."

"Hang on." The one with the baseball bat tilted his cap back. "I've seen her before. Ain't she—"

"Shut up, Ripley. You know she is."

As she followed, Peggy noticed the young man was limping and holding his side—but he wasn't letting go of that grocery sack. He skidded, then barely recovered his balance. He was making for her Jeep.

"You sure you want to do this?" Peggy called to him, not breaking out of a walk. "Right now it's just a public disturbance. Don't make it grand theft auto."

He looked at her with eyes as blue as a Siberian husky's: pale and not entirely human. But he didn't answer. He was too busy trying to hotwire her engine.

"Son of a bitch." The car roared into life; he'd done it in five seconds flat. He threw the Jeep into reverse. Peggy realized her service pistol was still in her travel case. So were the photographs.

"I don't have time for this." She reached into her jacket, raised her keyless remote, and hit the kill switch. The motor died instantly. The young man looked at Peggy, stunned—then leapt from the car and tried to run. Just then, another Avalon police car tore into the parking lot, lights flashing. CHIEF OF POLICE was printed on the side in gold letters.

"Don't try it, son." The chief touched his revolver as he rose from his car. The young man finally dropped the bag and—with only the slightest trace of a sneer—clasped hands over his head: Peggy guessed he'd been through the routine before.

"Jesus, Mary, and Joseph." The Avalon police chief was stocky and freckled, walking with a pronounced limp. His hair was salted gray but had once been as red as Peggy's. "I got called out at midnight for this?"

By now the other policemen had caught up, out of breath. Peggy noticed they'd tossed their clubs away.

"Guess I should have known your boys were already here." She reached into the fallen bag and picked up a squashed loaf of bread. "Protecting us from garbage thieves."

The chief frowned sideways at her, a look she'd seen a thousand times over the years. "Helluva way to let us know you're comin', Peggy Jean."

"Hell of a way," she repeated. "Hello, Dad."

# FOUR

The Avalon police station consisted of three offices, a one-cell lockup, a gun safe, a unisex bathroom, and a candy machine that sold stale Zagnuts. Peggy figured she must have lost half her allowance to that machine over the years.

"Last thing I need is my own daughter tellin' me how to do my job." Police Chief Russell Weaver—"Rusty" to everyone but family—poured two cups of coffee from a Thermos on his desk. "It ain't Starbucks, but here."

"I know what I saw." She swallowed, tasting hot black acid. "What did you put on the arrest sheet, anyway?" She picked up the form before he could grab it away. "Jesus Christ, Dad. 'Looting'? He was taking day-old bread from a dumpster."

"I gotta trust my men, don't I?" He took the sheet back. "This ain't the FBI here. I'm just one old man with a bum leg, tryin' to keep law and order at Piggly Wiggly."

She folded her arms. "Are you saying you ordered your officers to do that?"

He glowered at her as he pressed the intercom button.

"Mart, will you bring Dennis and Ripley in here?"

"They're out on campus, sir. Them Sigma Nus are pissin' on their lawn again."

"Watch the language, son. My daughter's present."

"Sorry, sir. I meant to say urinatin'." He clicked off.

"This is gonna take a minute," Rusty said. "You go into the lobby, call your mama. She's up worryin' about you."

"I'm not going anywhere."

He shrugged: Suit yourself. A moment later, Officer Martin stood in the open doorway, cocky and hard-muscled. Peggy remembered babysitting him when he was six. If things got out of hand, she was ready to remind him how he used to wet the bed.

"Martin." Her father was cool but not unfriendly, a football coach who'd been forced to bench a star player. "You know the regs concerning excessive force."

"Yes, sir." He didn't blink. "Absolutely, sir."

"So you know I would not be happy to hear that you and your team assaulted that young man with a . . ." He gestured to Peggy.

"An Air Taser," she said. "Officer Dennis had a tire iron. Ripley used a baseball bat."

"What kind of bat?" Rusty sucked coffee through his teeth.

"An Old Hickory trainer. It had black electrical tape on the grip." Peggy raised her eyebrows at her father.

Martin shook his head. "Sir, he made a lunge at Ripley. We were just re-strainin' him, is all." He snapped his fingers. "Come to think, Rip had his flashlight out. That coulda been what your daughter saw."

Rusty waved him off. "Go finish bookin' the looter."

Martin shot Peggy a quick look of triumph as he left.

"Check the bruises on his back, Dad."

"Now, I'd have thought you had bigger fish to fry." He lit a Raleigh. "Weren't you just yesterday rescuin' a—what are you supposed to call 'em nowadays? Inner-city kid?"

"We usually call them children. You heard about that?"

"Read the papers," he said. "Plus I got a buddy in ATF who gave me the real low-down. Way he told it, them Russkies took your piece away from you."

"Ukrainians," she corrected. "I made it out okay."

"You had no business bein' down there in the first place. And before you start in, it ain't on account you're a girl."

"Dad . . ."

"You owe your life to one empty chamber, right? Now who taught you to do that? It sure as hell wasn't the FBI Academy."

She sighed, blowing hair from her face. "You did."

"Damn straight." He nodded. "So you know I'm not talking out of my ass here. It was your mission, Peggy Jean. You had no business walkin' point. What were your men gonna do if you'd got yourself taken hostage? Or God-forbid shot in the head?"

Peggy felt a knee-jerk defense coming on—all the contingency plans and checklists she'd prepared in advance of the raid—then realized none of it cut any ice.

"You're right," she said simply. "I should have put another agent on point. Most likely the Cookes would still be alive if I'd kept my eye on the ball."

"Listen, better them dead than you." He tapped cigarette ash into his styrofoam cup. "Wouldn't it just tear your mother's poor heart out to see that in the papers."

It was as close to *I love you* as her father ever came. Both of them broke eye contact before it could go any further.

"How is Mama doing?"

"About the same, only worse. She keeps hearin' the phone ring when nobody's there." He frowned. "Be awful nice if it did ring now and again. She gets to thinkin' you forgot all about her."

"I called her last week," Peggy said. "She says you still haven't hired a nurse. Why aren't you using the money I send?"

"Don't need a stranger to care for my wife," he said. "Anyhow, you oughta save your money for yourself. Your mama and I sacrificed too much gettin' you to college, for you to wind up livin' in some ghetto and dyin' over—well, over nothin'."

"Over what? A black girl? Or was there another word you had in mind?" She waited. "It's what I do, Dad. And for the record, I paid my own way through Avalon."

"Scholarship." He drew smoke. "Shit, I got a scholarship to Avalon. They hand those things out like candy."

"Yeah. But you never finished." She bit her lip. "Look, I'm sorry I came home unannounced. But I'm a little tired, and I really don't feel like getting called on the carpet."

He exhaled. "I just thought you promised your mama to call more often, is all."

"And I thought you promised her to quit smoking."

He glowered at her, then stubbed the cigarette out.

"You want to know why I'm here?" she asked.

"I know it ain't to keep your old man off tobacco." He reached for his jacket. "Come on, you know who's waitin' up on us. We'll finish arguin' this later."

"I need to clean up first," she said.

"Don't need my permission to go to the bathroom."

As she emerged from the washroom, she turned left instead of right—and found herself face to face with the young man in the lockup. He sat on the edge of the metal cot, palms pressed to the rail, clear-eyed and watchful: a hunter waiting for scent.

"I see your name's Elias Collins," she said.

"I know you. You're Weaver's daughter." Elias's voice was clear and heavy, like water on stone.

"That's right," she said. "You live around here?"

"Chillwater Cove," he said. "The food was for my family. I still need to get something back to them."

"I think you should work on getting yourself back to them. Kind of stinks to go to prison over a loaf of stale bread."

"Doesn't it just."

Elias smiled up at her: a cool intensity that left her feeling strangely exposed, in spite of the bars.

"I could hear you arguing with your father a moment ago," he continued. "You sounded upset."

"A little. I was trying to get you out of here."

"I guess I'm supposed to be grateful for that?" He smiled thinly. "If you're such a friend, how come I'm sitting here in your daddy's jail?"

"Just wanted to save you a beating, that's all."

"They weren't trying to beat me. They were trying to kill me." He leaned in. "Now they'll want to kill you, too."

"Christ Almighty." Rusty walked up behind Peggy. "Son, either you shut that yap or I'll give you some company you won't like." He turned to his daughter. "And I am done tellin' you, Peggy Jean. This ain't your jurisdiction."

She spoke to Elias across her father. "Don't worry about me, okay? I'm a federal agent."

"You say that like it's gonna protect you." Elias smiled faintly as he turned away from her.

The fog had settled in as Peggy and Rusty walked to the parking lot. Somewhere in the gray distance, Peggy could hear Culloden's bells: chimes at midnight.

"What'd that crazy Covite say to you back there?" Rusty blew on his hands to warm them up.

"He told me my life was in danger." She shivered against the cold. "And please don't say *Covite*. It's a redneck word."

"I may be a redneck, but I ain't dumb. Takes what, thirteen hours to drive down from Philadelphia?"

"More like sixteen for me. But then, I always obey the speed limits."

He shrugged. "So you left about eight, eight thirty this mornin'. Maybe your cell phone wasn't workin'?"

"I'm not apologizing again, Dad."

"I ain't askin'," he said. "But you did have time for at least one call before you hit the road. I know that 'cause last night, Sean Aldridge asked us to put a guard on their house, and keep a record of his wife's calls. 'Pears Samantha talked to you about three in the mornin'."

"Uh-huh. Did you get a warrant for that?"

"Like I said, we had her husband's permission." He unlocked the car door. "Then she called to say it was all a mistake, and she and her husband just had a fight, and she'd gone home to her folks and didn't need the help after all. That was right about when I tried to get you on the phone—and couldn't. Eight o'clock this morning."

She folded her arms. "So what does that prove?"

He got behind the wheel of his cruiser.

"I guess it proves you really do obey the speed limits," he said. "Stay close to me, now."

# FIVE

The Weavers' home at 265 Patton Circle was a redbrick house on the south side of town, a neighborhood that always seemed to hover somewhere between respectable and tacky. Assistant professors lived there until tenure came through. The ones who stayed were mostly third- and fourth-generation locals: the tiny caste of shopkeepers, contractors, and admins who kept Avalon College going behind the scenes.

Peggy was greeted home by the aroma of pork chops and boiled-over stringbeans. Three hand-enameled plates were set out, depicting a family of chickens. I RULE THE ROOST, read her father's plate; I RULE THE ROOSTER was written on her mother's; Peggy's read JUST PECKIN'. Chickens were a big theme in Beatrice Weaver's kitchen.

"Hey, Tigger." Peggy stopped to head-scratch their family cat, who was sitting in a fruit bowl on the kitchen counter. "Got your territory all staked out?"

Tigger meowed. Blind in one eye, his fur matted, the old ginger tom proudly stretched out his chin to accept tribute.

Rusty unceremoniously emptied the cat out of the bowl. "Bea? You awake, hon?"

"Ohh-hhh!" Peggy's mother came into the kitchen, wearing a lavender smock over her pink kitchen dress. She was shorter than either Peggy or Rusty, her hair so completely frosted that it almost counted as white. "There's my baby—girl!"

"Mama." As soon as she returned the hug, Peggy could tell her mother had been working in her craft studio. When she was little, she thought all mommies smelled like paint thinner. "Please tell me you didn't wait up just to cook supper."

"Sakes, no. I was feelin' hot in the bed, so I got myself up to do a bitty bit of work. Then I figured, as long as I'm awake and my baby's hungry . . ."

"Your cat's been up on the counter again." Rusty threw his jacket over a chair. "If he touches my food one more time, I'm havin' chicken-fried kitty."

"Nooo, Tigger's a good boy." She hung the jacket on a wall hook. "How's my handsome cop? You stop any bad men tonight?"

"Just one." He threw a look to Peggy as he embraced her.

"For that you get some sugar." She kissed him. "Peggy Jean, you come see what Mama's been makin' for you."

In her time, Beatrice had been a seamstress, a drapery maker, a modeling-clay sculptor, and a paint-by-numbers enthusiast. But her real passion was scrapbooking. Her current work in progress, laid out on the drafting table, appeared to be an account of Peggy's Bureau exploits.

"I just got the clipping on your big case!" Bea turned the cover of the scrapbook, decorated with a handmade FBI logo. "So now you get to watch me paste it in."

Rusty leaned in the door. "Are you two females comin' to the table, or am I eatin' alone again?"

"Alone," Peggy said.

Bea waved him off. "You go have your pork chops, big grumpy bear."

"Had pork for lunch." He limped away.

Peggy perched on the stool where she'd sat for endless childhood hours, winding yarn for her mother's needlepoint. She couldn't help but notice that several prescription bottles had been pressed into service as brush holders.

"Mama, please tell me you're not throwing your pills away."

"Mm? Oh, honey, you know those things just make my ulcers do hand-springs. Anyhow, they weren't working. I think they might have expired."

Peggy examined the label: Donipezil 5 Mg. The date on the side was less than a week old.

"I know the pills make you sick," Peggy said. "Maybe we can get some-thing else to help with that. But you have to promise me you'll take them. Really and truly."

"And what's the point of taking medicine that makes you sick? You and your father, I swear." She unwrapped a glue stick. "Now what shall we use for a border? Hearts, or stars?"

Peggy looked at the article her mother had cut from the *Tennessean*, an

AP account of the Storytime raid: THREE DEAD IN MAJOR KIDNAPPING BUST. The photo showed Peggy talking to Mike behind the police barricades. She hadn't realized just how shaken up she'd looked after the recovery.

"I'm always *so* relieved when these stories have a happy ending," her mother said. "What did those people want with that pretty little girl, anyhow?"

"Her father sits on the Senate Judiciary Committee. We think they were trying to blackmail him."

"A senator." She paused thoughtfully. "Stars, then."

*There will always be as many good days as bad ones*, the doctor had told Peggy when her mother's Alzheimer's was first diagnosed; *but as time goes by, your definition of "good" will start to change.* It worried Peggy that she might be seeing her mother on a good day.

"Mama." She nudged the door shut. "I need to know if I can ask you something. Just between the two of us, okay?"

"Honey, you know I don't tattle."

"Well—do you remember that time my friend Samantha disappeared, when we were kids? That guy in the car?"

"Car." Her mother turned to her. "Are you talking about that time she got sick for so long?"

"I know that's what her family said happened. But . . . we found something yesterday."

"What, dear?" Bea took off her glasses. "Found what?"

Peggy was about to reply when she heard a beer can crack open behind her, followed by her father's shuffling limp past the door.

"He'll have a few more of those before the evening's out." Bea took Peggy by the chin. "Now don't you be sad, hear? I know you don't get much time from work, and you probably just wanna relax with Sammie. That's fine, she needs you now. Only make sure I get you for Sunday dinner."

"Why does she need me now?"

"That man of hers makes her cry, bless her heart. Saw her just the other day, with her baby boy. Cute little scamp. What's his name?"

"Caden," she said. "Mama, I'm worried someone might want to hurt her."

She frowned. "You should tell your daddy about that, no?"

Peggy heard the television come on: some loudmouthed guy selling knives on a home-shopping channel.

"I can't," she said. "That's not exactly true. I don't want to. I saw how he was tonight, and—well, he's always been mean. But he's getting meaner."

"I remember when you used to love going on patrol with your daddy." Her mother shook her head sadly. "I've got the cutest picture of you in that police girl outfit I sewed. I saved it for the scrapbook I'm makin' for your fella—but now, you tell Mike if he doesn't marry you soon, no scrapbook."

"We're not getting married," she said. "We called the engagement off a year ago."

"Oh, you'll work it out, hon." Bea replaced her glasses and set back to work. "Sometime I'll tell you about the day we brought you home. I knew right then my Peggy Jean was gonna be a fighter."

"Thanks." But she'd already lost her mother to the hot glue gun. Peggy finally got up and went into the living room. Her father had cut up his pork chop and was eating the pieces with his fingers.

"You wanna watch some tube with the old man?"

"I'm gonna have my dinner and go to bed, Daddy."

"You know where your room is." He eyed her. "Don't get to thinkin' I'm done with you, kiddo. I carried that grip of yours upstairs. I can tell it's got more'n clothes in it."

"Thank you for taking my bag up," she said. "Good night."

"'Night." He drained the rest of his beer.

She went into the kitchen. A trail of gravy led from her empty plate to the floor: Tigger had claimed her pork chop. Peggy knelt down and stroked his back. "Don't worry, Tig. I won't rat you out."

She looked at the clock: it was past 1:00 A.M., too late to even think of calling Sammie at her parents' house. Instead, Peggy went up to her room, thankful that she still had the Snickers from Piggly Wiggly.

It was another two hours before her mother finally turned the TV off.

# SIX

"How d'ya say it again?" The old man blew dust off the wine bottle, then handed it over the counter to Peggy. "Shy-razz? Shee-rozz?"

"Shiraz," Peggy said. "I think it's Australian."

"Sounds Ay-rab to me. Didn't even know I had it till you asked." He rang it up. "Costs enough, don't it? Guess you got somewhere special to go today."

"Yes, Mr. Kirby." She paid in cash. Kirby's Notions was the only store in Avalon that didn't take credit cards—but it was also the only one that still offered a discount to locals. As Chief Weaver's daughter, Peggy qualified.

"Well, you sure do look pretty enough." Kirby smiled and bagged the wine. "'Preciate you shoppin' with us, Miss Weaver."

She was halfway out the door when she heard Mrs. Kirby talking to her husband. "Well, ain't *she* the fancy city gal now?"

Peggy kept walking.

There wasn't much to Avalon's business district: just a row of Depression-era storefronts along Sherburn Road, facing an abandoned spur of the East Tennessee & Western North Carolina Railroad. Most of the shops had been riding close to bankruptcy ever since the Wal-Mart opened in Sevier. The ones that catered to the college sold blue-and-crimson Avalon shirts, hand-thrown pottery, and Jägermeister. The rest of them stocked nightcrawlers, plastic lawn chairs, and Busch. Peggy liked shopping at Kirby's because it still felt like the old Avalon. The smoked ham hanging in the window was for real, and the woodstove in the back still worked. It saddened her to learn that the Kirbys were moving to Florida as soon as the semester ended.

Her Jeep was still having its steering column fixed at Dorrill's Chevron,

which left her two options for getting to the Stallworths': borrow her father's pickup, with its two-toned paint job and ashtray smell, or walk the
three miles. She'd decided it was a fine afternoon for walking. Peggy put
on her one nonregulation outfit, a light pants suit and walking shoes, and
set off for Glencoe Bluff.

As college president, Samantha's father was entitled to live in the official
residence at the center of campus. For personal reasons, he'd elected to stay
in his family's ancestral home on the bluff: a sandstone and timber cottage,
comfortably down-at-heel, whose oldest foundations had been laid in the
early days of the Jackson administration. Peggy made her way up the
gravel driveway past Mercedes sedans and Lexus SUVs, then stopped at
the door to change into low heels. As she slipped her walking shoes into
her canvas shoulder bag, she caught sight of the red folder. *Hope to God I'm
doing right by you, Sammie.* The tense feeling in her chest was both mystify-
ing and entirely new: she was genuinely afraid to see her friend.

Peggy had to ring twice before she finally realized the doorbell wasn't
working.

"Hello, *stranger!*" It was Samantha's mother, a trim-set woman in Ann
Taylor. Peggy still couldn't get used to calling her Olivia. "Now don't even
try shaking my hand. I want a hug!"

"I'm so sorry to crash the party, Mrs.—Olivia."

"Don't be silly, you're family. Now turn around for me—mm-mm. That
is the figure of a woman who's never had children. I am *boiling* with jeal-
ousy." She waved off the awful thought. "You'll excuse the doorbell. Something's funny with our new security system. Apparently it's all wired
together now."

As she closed the door, Peggy noticed something she never thought
she'd see in Avalon: an alarm keypad.

"Do you know where Samantha is?"

"Upstairs with Caden. She hates these things." Olivia lowered her voice
as she led Peggy to the library. "You haven't missed much. Harrison's still
singing for his laurels."

A dozen people in weekend casuals, well tempered and graceful, were
gathered around the room. Peggy stood in the archway—mildly alarmed
to discover that she was the only woman in slacks—and exchanged nods
with her old mentor, Dr. Harrison Stallworth.

"Graduation week has many proud traditions," he said in his easy bari-
tone. "This has to be my favorite. A chance to open our home to dear

friends . . . successful alumni . . . and favorite pupils. And the rare few who fit all three categories."

He winked at Peggy. It was only an eyeblink, too quick for anyone else to notice. But it was hers.

"And to show gratitude to the people who keep Avalon's heart beating," he continued. "So for God's sake, keep signing those checks!"

They laughed with him. If a bomb were to explode in that room, Peggy realized, there wouldn't be enough alumni money left to dedicate an aluminum park bench.

"It's also an opportunity to consider the true meaning of 'foundation' at Avalon college."

He was on a roll. Harrison Stallworth was a handsome man for his midsixties—for any age, really. Tall, a tennis player's body, serene brown eyes, blond hair fading nicely to white. It wasn't just his looks, Peggy realized: it was his courtly intelligence, his earnest way of listening, that made him so attractive.

"We stand here today on sacred ground," he said. "A forge of leaders and fountain of enlightened works for more than a century and a quarter. Our founder—my great-great-grandfather, General Lycurgus Stallworth—"

He gestured to the general's portrait over the stone fireplace: a stern man in Confederate gray, clasping a Bible. His eyes used to scare holy hell out of Peggy when she was young.

"—built this college on the very soil where so many of his soldiers had fallen in the last days of the Civil War . . . lives cut terribly short in the flower of youth." Harrison frowned. "And yet here, in this pristine desolation, he found the courage to look beyond war, and the tyranny of failed ideas."

His audience listened politely but didn't respond. Last year, Harrison had ruffled a lot of feathers by ordering the removal of the college's Rebel flags. Alumni giving had yet to fully rebound.

"Change is often painful," Harrison said. "When we integrated the school in 1968 . . . when female students arrived a few years later . . . there were many who earnestly believed that our most sacred traditions had been overturned. There are, perhaps, some who still do."

One of the men behind Peggy leaned over and whispered something to the woman beside him: Peggy only caught the words *toilet seats*. The woman blushed and playfully swatted his arm.

"This is my last year as president," Harrison said. "I hope that, in my years of service, I've made some small contribution—"

"Hear, hear." Someone tapped his glass.

"And yet I know all things must pass." Harrison politely waved off the applause. "But before I yield the floor to my successor, I want to express my sincere wish that only the best of our traditions, and none of the worst, will endure. That we carry forth our heritage like a bright torch, and leave our hatred to the ashes. Because a college is not made of buildings or books or even professors . . . as much as those things may cost."

He paused to share a laugh. Something was making noise behind Peggy. She turned to see a bright yellow ball bouncing down the stairs.

"A college is founded on trust. And shared values. And most importantly—"

"Ya ya ya yaaa." A two-year-old boy, curly-haired and blue-eyed, chased the ball down the stairs. "Ha ha!"

"Caden." Olivia tried to herd him away from the library. Some of the guests pretended to be amused, but were clearly irritated to have Dr. Stallworth's spell broken.

"Ya ha!" He bounced the ball right off Harrison's chest, then beamed. "Granpa!"

"As I was about to say." Harrison smiled as he picked up his grandson. "Our firmest foundation is built on the hope we leave to future generations."

He kissed the boy's forehead and the room broke into applause. Everyone was so intent on shaking Dr. Stallworth's hand—or tousling Caden's hair—that only Peggy noticed Samantha quietly entering the room.

She was striking; and what struck Peggy most was how Samantha never seemed to age. Her honey-blond hair hung easily over one shoulder. The white ankle socks and blue tennis shoes were an unlikely combination with her yellow sundress—but somehow she made it work. Sammie's step was graceful yet tentative, as if something in her had been caged long ago and was still waiting for release.

"Just when I thought you were gone for good." Samantha hugged her fiercely.

"Kind of spoils your whole day, doesn't it?"

They laughed. Sammie scrunched her face at Peggy.

"Samantha." Olivia hoisted Caden away from the Steinway. "I don't have to tell you what your son just did."

Samantha frowned. "Mommy, please don't hold him in the air like that. He's not a cat. He won't land on his feet."

"Huh. A cat wouldn't create half the pandemonium he has today. Right in the middle of your father's speech."

"Livy." Harrison leaned in. "It's fine. No harm done."

"Harrison, please. You may have covered well, but—" She was silenced by a dissonant pounding. Caden had squirmed free and was happily banging the piano keys. "Oh, Lord."

"Caden." Samantha pointed her index fingers toward each other, then rotated them back toward herself. The boy at once leapt into his mother's arms. "Oof. You're getting heavy, buster." She smiled at her mother. "You were saying?"

"Let's go join our guests for dinner." Harrison squeezed Peggy's arm. "Don't slip away before I get a chance to talk to you, Agent Weaver."

Samantha stroked her son's hair until the room cleared, then turned to Peggy. "You're not really hungry, are you?"

"I'm more tired than anything," she said. "My feet aren't used to these hills."

Samantha nodded sympathetically.

"Caden and I got Burger King." She glanced furtively to the garden door. "Come on, I'll share my fries."

They watched the sunset from the stone summerhouse on the mountain bluff—talking about every possible subject, it seemed, except for the one thing that had brought them together. Black women in white dresses would occasionally put their heads out, asking if Miss Samantha or Miss Weaver wanted anything from the kitchen. Samantha thanked them politely. The only other interruption was laughter and clinking silverware from the dining room. Far in the distance, the red light of a cell tower alternately burned and dimmed, growing brighter with the approach of night.

"I used to think the view was the one thing you could get for free around here." Samantha looked down into the valley: a few barns and horse trailers were just visible through the trees. "Even that's not true with all these developers moving in. Families who've lived here for generations can't afford to stay on their own land."

"I'm sure they're getting a fair price for it," Peggy said.

"That's what Sean keeps insisting—Caden?" She made another hand-sign to her son, who'd wandered within twenty yards of the bluff. He stamped back to her.

"How 'bout seeda munjuns, Mommy?"

"It's too dark now, sweetie. Maybe tomorrow."

"Seeya munjuns!" He gave Peggy a fistful of grass. "We'com!"

"Thank you." She turned to Sammie. "Munjuns?"

"It's a game of ours. The munjuns live in the forest. It's just his way of saying he wants to take a walk." She laughed. "Everything you hear about two-year-olds is true. Yesterday I caught him trying to jump down the laundry chute! Learning to communicate has mainly been a survival necessity."

"I like the sign language thing. Does it work on big boys, too?"

"Don't I wish." Sammie smiled. "My mother and Sean didn't want me teaching Caden to sign. They were worried people would think he was deaf. Which he's not. It just bugs me that they think it would be something to be ashamed of."

"What's your dad think?"

"He thinks I should have started with Homeric Greek." She furrowed her brow. "I'm sorry I couldn't talk much on the phone this morning. Not to sound paranoid . . ."

"You were worried about who might be listening," Peggy said. "I understand. The whole thing's kind of sudden, isn't it? Like lightning from a clear blue sky."

Samantha nodded, then bent down and kissed Caden. "Sweetie, will you go find Mommy a purple stone from the garden?"

"Puppaston'!" He flew away toward the house.

"It's not all that sudden. To be honest, it never really went away." Samantha looked at her. "Do you remember how it was that afternoon, Peggy? That . . . guy?"

"Some. I wish I could remember more."

"I wish I could make myself forget." She took a slow breath. "You're right about one thing, though. It is a lot like being hit by lightning."

Peggy looked around. "Think we can do this, Sam?"

She nodded. "It's time."

"Okay." Peggy took the red folder from her bag. "We found these Thursday night. In a raid on a—" She stopped herself from saying *child pornographer*. "A collector's computer. The chances of them being there by accident are—what's wrong?"

Samantha paled. "They're on the Internet?"

"No. Honey, no. As far as I know, only you and I have these."

"And whoever sent them, I suppose." Samantha held her own tan folder in her lap. "Sean doesn't know what's wrong with me. I couldn't even tell my folks. Ever since that e-mail showed up on Thursday . . ." She tilted her head back.

"Was there any note with the attachment? Or a return address?"

"I saved it for you on my office computer. The address was just a string of numbers and dots." She breathed. "The e-mail said, 'You've earned everything that's coming to you.'"

"I got the same message," Peggy said.

Samantha pursed her lip. "I know it sounds crazy. But could it be the same guy . . . ?"

"Frankly, I don't see how it could be anyone else," Peggy answered. "The bigger question is—why now? Any sudden changes in your life? New people, new things?"

Samantha shook her head. "Nothing's ever new around here. Avalon goes on being the center of the universe . . . the students keep getting younger. Meanwhile, I have my family. And my classes. There's Sean's career—and Sean's father, and his father's money, and . . . well . . ." She exhaled. "Then there's that book that nobody seems to think I'll ever finish."

"What about it?"

"Believe it or not, it's almost done. And the closer I get . . ." She laughed weakly. "You'd think history would be the one thing that never changes. But I swear, it's like wrestling a boa constrictor. Sometimes I think the damn thing's trying to kill me."

"Listen, I've had some cases that I thought were gonna swallow me whole," Peggy said. "What's it about?"

She waved absently. "Oh—local history. Ethnographic studies of early settlers. Nothing like that huge, towering narrative Daddy's always after me to write."

"You write damn well, Sammie. If I had talent like yours, I sure as hell wouldn't be putting myself down."

She smiled. "I guess I'm just not used to having people pay attention to me. It's not safe."

"You're worried you'll get hurt?"

"I'm worried other people will get hurt," she said. "About these pictures. Is there some way we could catch this guy . . . without anybody else finding out?"

"Like your family, you mean?"

"Like anybody."

Peggy put an arm around her. "I won't lie to you, honey. If we go this way, you'll be opening doors you've probably kept shut for years. And as much as you'd rather not . . . you'll have to get your family involved. There's no way you can do this without their support."

"My family." Samantha laughed weakly. "You know what my husband's biggest fear is? If I crack up, he won't get to be president. God, it really pissed him off when I asked him not to come today."

Peggy whistled. "Sean's up for president? He's got moves on him. What was he, a year behind us?"

"Two." She smiled faintly. "Remember how he angled his way into my dad's Ethics seminar as a freshman? I thought it was just so he could flirt with us."

"With you, maybe. Some of us had our eye on our books."

"Oh, I don't know. I seem to remember the two of you having a hot fling before you tossed him my way."

"And I remember him dropping me like a hot anvil the minute you finally gave him a chance." She prodded Sammie's shoulder.

"As it turns out, he wasn't that interested in either of us," Samantha said.

"Puppa stoooan!" Caden raised a pebble triumphantly.

"Thank you, honey! Now can you get one for Aunt Peggy?"

"Uh-huh." He crouched down again. "Aun' Peddy."

Peggy noticed how carefully Samantha shielded the folder from Caden whenever he turned their way.

"Maybe we don't have to use the pictures," Peggy said. "I could get you with an FBI sketch artist."

She hesitated. "I don't know how well that would work. I was out of it so much of the time. It looks like I was unconscious when the pictures were taken."

"That's . . . not completely true." Peggy struggled for the right words. "In most of them, your eyes are closed. Or you're blindfolded. In one of them, they're open. And you're staring right at the camera." She paused. "Why are you looking at me that way?"

"My eyes were always closed." Samantha pursed her lip. "I . . . think we'd better take a closer look."

Each of them had a dozen matching shots, all taken from roughly the same height: five foot ten. In the first few, Samantha still wore the dirty white jumper. Piece by piece, shot by shot, the child's clothing was taken from her, exposing her body to the harsh camera light. Black and scarlet ligature marks showed that she'd been tied with rope, not once but several times over a course of days. She'd been kept above ground: there was tinfoil on the windowpanes. The walls had exposed wooden beams, with pegboards for hanging hooks and knives. The ball gag suggested that Samantha might have been close enough to inhabited areas for someone to hear her scream.

There was only one difference: in every one of Samantha's set of pictures, she was either blindfolded or squeezing her eyes shut; and in the last of Peggy's, the child's blue eyes were wide open, calmly fixed on the man behind the camera.

"Everything else is the same," Sammie said, "except for the eyes. But they can't both be right."

"It's the same picture. One has been altered." Peggy pointed. "See? There's a moth flying around that plastic jug. Identical in both shots."

"And then there's the blood running down my legs," Samantha said plainly. "But which one's real, yours or mine?"

"There's things we can look for. Differences in grain or pixelation, evidence of retouching." She started to gather the photographs. "Ultimately, it's going to come down to what you're able to remember. And even then, we may never catch the guy. No matter how this ends—it's gonna hurt, Sammie."

"Pain, I can handle." She closed the folder. "This won't make any sense. But you know when people have out-of-body experiences? Where they kind of float above themselves? That's how it was for me. Like I wasn't in my own body anymore. And none of it was really real."

"You're not alone in that," Peggy said. "It's a coping mechanism a lot of victims use."

"Now that is a word I've always hated. Victim." She reached down and began to unlace her shoes. "You want to know the one thing I remember clearly? That never leaves me, even for a second?"

"What, Sammie?"

"Burning," she said. "You've never really seen the soles of my feet, have you?"

"I guess I must have, now and again."

"No. You haven't. Although you can't be blamed for thinking otherwise. I've gotten good at that over the years."

She removed her blue tennis shoes, then slipped off her ankle socks. And held up her feet for Peggy to see.

Once, in a grad school colloquium, Peggy had examined photographs of Chinese women whose feet had been bound: gnarled, twisted knobs of flesh, forced into inhuman shapes. Samantha's own feet were not so deformed—merely ridged and scarred, with several toes missing and skin patches the color of leather. But the placid expression in Samantha's eyes was much like those Chinese women's; a kind of practiced serenity.

"I can walk on them," Sammie was saying. "I danced at my wedding and nobody noticed. Even though Sean stepped on my toes once or twice. My doctor's seen my feet, but even she has no idea how it really feels."

"And how does it feel?"

"The same as it did the first time he burned me." She put her socks back on. "You see how I am in these pictures? Do you think I could have kept my eyes open while he was doing—that—to me?"

Peggy put a hand on her shoulder. "How do you do it now?"

"Mostly by pretending it never happened, I guess."

"Are you sure you want to go back to this, Sammie? Honestly?"

"Am I sure." She finished lacing up her shoes. "It took six operations to put me back together. Not including skin grafts. Almost a year of physical training, just to walk again. And God knows how many therapists and prescriptions and—witch doctors over the years."

Chairs and plates shifted inside: a break before dessert.

"The pain wasn't the worst of it." Samantha took a sharp breath. "The worst was having to lie. Telling friends—even best friends like you—that I'd been away to summer camp, or visiting relatives. When I was really in some hospital or . . . nuthouse. And always this feeling that I'd let everyone down. That I was never even half of what I was supposed to be. My mother. My own mother, on my wedding day, telling me—'Don't worry, honey. In the eyes of God, you're still a virgin.'"

Sunset played across Samantha's face, wet with tears.

"So yeah, I'm pretty sure I want this." She closed the folder. "Let's nail the bastard."

"I was afraid you'd say that," Peggy answered.

She raised an eyebrow. "Since when has Peggy Weaver ever been afraid of anything?"

"Gotta nudda puppaston', Mommee! Aun' Peddy!"

"Way to go, honey!" Samantha looked at Peggy. "I have to put Caden to bed. And then I guess I'd better call Sean, and . . . make him feel better about missing the donor reception."

"You want me to take the pictures?"

"I'd like to look at them some more," she said. "Can you come back in the morning? We can go to McPeake's for brunch."

"Sure. I'll buy." Peggy hugged her. "We'll get through it together, Sammie. We will."

Samantha touched her forehead to Peggy's. "Do you ever wonder why, Peg?"

"Why it happened, you mean?"

"Why he offered to trade," she said. "Was it just a trick, or—what did he want?"

"I don't know." Peggy paused. "Maybe there is no why. Maybe it's just something that guys like him do."

Samantha stood back, looking at Peggy with simple trust.

"We'll find our own answers, then." She waved Peggy on. "Here. Let me walk you out."

# SEVEN

**Peggy was dreaming.**

She was back in the basement of Storytime Academy: one of the children had been left behind, and Peggy had to return for her. The stairwell was pitch black, forcing her to feel her way down along a cold stone wall. Now and again she heard voices whispering around her. Children crying. Water lapped around Peggy's waist. Finally, she discovered the light switch and turned it on: The cages were filled with dry white bones. She was too late. All of the children were long dead and gone.

But she wasn't alone. Somebody was standing behind her, breathing hot on her neck. Peggy reached for her revolver; her holster was empty.

*Nobody rides for free, Peggy Jean.* A familiar voice laughing in her ear. *Nobody rides for free!*

Peggy knew she was asleep. She couldn't make herself wake up. All she could do was stand there, waiting for the hand on her shoulder . . .

**The downstairs phone was ringing.**

Peggy's eyes opened in darkness.

*Something's happened.*

At first she thought she was still back in Philadelphia. Then she saw the numbers on her old alarm clock: 4:17 A.M.

Someone was stomping around downstairs.

"What are you doing?" As she stumbled into the living room, Rusty was buttoning up the shirt of his police uniform.

"Go back to bed." He buckled on his gun belt. "Got business to tend to. I'll tell you about it later."

"Tell me now." She knew that iron rasp in her father's voice only ever meant bad news. "Who was on the phone just then?"

"Goddammit." He wheeled around. "What did you say to Samantha last night? Everybody saw you talking out back."

"We were . . . talking. Catching up."

"Bullshit. You don't haul gear like you brought unless you got trouble in mind. And, by God, you have opened up a boatload now."

The anger woke her up. "What does it matter what we were talking about? It's nothing to do with you."

"Well now, that ain't true by a long shot, is it?"

"Oh my god," Peggy said. And she knew.

"That's right." He turned away from her. "She's gone."

Peggy took her father by the elbow.

"I'm coming with you," she said.

# E I GHT

All the lights were on at the Stallworth home as Peggy and her father arrived. An Avalon Police car was parked beside an evidence van from Keyes County Sheriff's Department.

"Forty-five minutes from first call," she said. "They got here fast."

"Sheriff Powell owes me a couple favors." He parked at the bottom of the driveway. "We're keepin' everybody downstairs while the crew works Samantha's room. I'd appreciate it if you stayed with 'em."

"We'd have been better off taking statements at the station." She climbed out, hoisting her shoulder bag.

"Last thing I need is that wild kid climbin' on my desk." He passed her on his way up to the front door. "And for the last time, *we're* not takin' any statements. All you are to me is a material witness. If you kick up a fuss, I'll be happy to have one of my boys drive you back home."

"Since you mentioned Caden," she said, "don't you think it's strange that he wasn't abducted as well?"

"Nothin' about this bunch surprises me." He rapped on the door. "Let it drop, Peggy Jean. You are not hornin' your way into this."

"We're wasting time," she said.

Officer Dennis admitted them, holding a clipboard. At twenty-four, he was not only the youngest of Avalon's three full-time patrolmen but apparently the first to lose his hair. He seemed to be trying to compensate with a mustache.

"Who's here?" He examined Dennis's checklist. "That husband of hers ain't showed up yet?"

"No, sir. Martin went for him, but he wasn't home. I don't reckon that yellow Hummer of his'll be too hard to spot."

"We'll see." He handed the clipboard back. "Keep the exits locked. And nobody leaves the library."

"Miz Stallworth asked if she could fix breakfast."

"You heard me." Rusty glanced back at his daughter. "Mind closin' that door behind you, sweetheart?"

"The security keypad's dark." Peggy pressed the reset button twice. Nothing happened.

"I'm gettin' it looked at." He ambled down the hall. "All right. Lemme see what the butterfingers deputies found."

The alarm system appeared to be state-of-the-art. A tiny sensor was barely visible in the jamb of the massive oak door. There were more in the foyer windows—and in every window that she could see. All of the sensors appeared to be functioning: *all but the one that wasn't last night*, she reminded herself. As she entered the dining room, Peggy felt eyes on her back.

"Officer, aren't you supposed to be guarding the door?" She reached into her bag for a pair of latex gloves.

Dennis shuffled behind her. "Your daddy—'scuse me. He said everybody was to stay . . ."

She wordlessly snapped a glove on. Dennis backed away.

The dining room was a mess. Dessert plates and half-empty coffee cups littered the table. An untouched Bananas Foster sat, melted and congealed, in a large flambé pan. The chairs were pushed to the wall, napkins fallen, as if everyone had gotten out in a hurry.

"She ruined everything." Olivia stood behind Peggy, wearing a maroon housecoat. Without makeup, her face seemed to be made of marble. "I *told* Samantha what we were having for dessert. One little match and she just started—bawling."

"She probably doesn't like being close to fire." Peggy's eye wandered over a bottle of dark rum, spilled across the lace tablecloth. "What happened?"

"Oh, Samantha was an accident waiting to happen all day. I thought you might distract her from creating a scene, but . . . apparently not. So much for that fund-raiser." She hovered close to the table. "They won't even let me clean up my own house. Can't you speak to your father?" She turned to her husband, who had just entered. "Harrison?"

"Our home is a crime scene, Livy." It unnerved Peggy to see him in such disarray—hair unkempt, face unshaved, his voice hard and raw. "Come away now, and let's leave Peggy to her work."

"Do you have any idea when it might have happened?" Peggy asked.

"It would have been . . . between midnight and four?" Harrison threw a questioning glance to his wife. "I took the phone up to her around eleven thirty. Sean wanted to talk."

"She was screaming at him," Olivia said. "All he wanted was for her to come home so they could work things out. And she was saying, 'I don't want to work things out. I just want to be all right by myself. You don't know what I need.'" Olivia threw up her hands in resignation.

"Our daughter was upset." Harrison frowned, as if restraining himself. "Caden started crying around four A.M. That's when we knew she was gone."

"Where is Caden now?" Peggy asked.

"I made him a pallet in the library," Olivia said. "Any minute now, you'll hear him pulling books off the shelf."

"Livy."

"It's emotional blackmail, Harrison. Pure and simple. She knows it's your last graduation ceremony. She knows how badly the school needs money. She's just trying to sour the milk."

"You make it sound like Samantha went missing on purpose," Peggy said.

"It wouldn't be the only stunt she's ever pulled." Olivia folded her arms. "Of course, Harrison thinks she hung the moon. But I tell you, that girl is no victim."

"Actually, I think she'd agree with you on that." Peggy stood close to her. "I understand you're upset. But we have very little time to make sense of this. And you won't help your daughter by getting angry at her."

Olivia looked away. "What should we do?"

"I'd like to get a more complete timeline of the past twenty-four hours. Maybe find out why your security system conveniently decided to shut it-self down last night." She looked at Harrison. "I'll also need your authori-zation to access Samantha's e-mail accounts."

"That's Sean's area." He narrowed his gaze. "Why do you need them?"

"I'll explain later. Incidentally, have either of you seen or spoken to Sean since this happened?"

They shook their heads.

"The most important thing is to stay calm," she said. "We've got a lot of resources to put on this. And I promise you, I will make sure your daughter gets priority."

"No, you won't." Rusty had entered the room. "I already said my piece on this, Peggy Jean."

Olivia blinked. "What is he talking about?"

"He's saying that this case is currently in his sole jurisdiction, and the FBI's assistance isn't required." She took a deep breath. "And he's making a very big mistake."

"I know where my responsibility begins and ends." Rusty threw a sharp glance at Harrison. "And I think the president of Avalon College does, too. So you can all just roust yourselves back to the library, now. I've got everything well in hand."

Harrison looked up, stunned. "Peggy?"

"Dad, for God's sake. You're in over your head already." She leaned in close to him. "Don't let our family bullshit—"

"It ain't about you bein' my daughter."

"Really." She put her hands on her hips. "Are you sure it's nothing to do with the last time Samantha was kidnapped?"

He stared blood at her.

"Let's take this upstairs," he said. "Before you get into somethin' you can't talk your way out of."

"Don't worry." She looked at the Stallworths. "I'll be all right."

Peggy blushed. She'd meant to say, *I'll be right back.* She was grateful that Harrison seemed to understand.

# NINE

Rusty took the stairs deliberately, scanning each step with a flashlight. She knew it was mainly for show: Her father had to go slow because of his leg, and he didn't like anyone to see how easily he got winded.

"It's not going to wash, Dad." She followed close behind him. "In less than twenty-four hours, Lindbergh Law kicks in and this becomes a federal case."

"So wait twenty-four hours." He took a deep breath at the top of the stairs.

"You know that would be a tragic mistake," she said.

"You said it, not me." He motioned to the deputy in charge of the evidence team. "You boys finished up?"

"Near about." He handed the inventory to Rusty. "You'll see the markers where we lifted prints. Other than that, she's all yours." The deputy touched his hat—then, seemingly as an afterthought, nodded to Peggy. "Ma'am."

She followed her father down the hall. "I don't know why you want to stir things up. Is it just to punish me, or—?"

"Nope. You just don't have anything I need, is all." He took the DO NOT ENTER sign from Samantha's door. "Lemme ask you somethin'. If Samantha really was abducted, what would you expect to find?"

"Well, I'm not crazy about the way you say *if*," she answered. "But assuming it's an organized unsub with an anger excitation motive—"

"For God's sake, speak English."

"If he's sadistic and he plans well," Peggy said slowly, "then we should be looking for evidence of forced entry. Loose fibers, skin, or—" She stopped. An image of Samantha's maimed feet forced itself into her mind.

"Fluids. Maybe ladder marks or footprints, needles or sedatives, fragments of duct tape . . ."

"In other words, signs of a struggle?"

There was an odd light in Rusty's eyes as he placed his hand on the door. Peggy braced herself for the worst.

"Yes." She took a breath. "Why do you keep asking questions when you already know the answers?"

"This is why." He opened the bedroom door.

The room was in perfect condition.

It had hardly changed in the thirty years since Peggy's first sleepover: a town-and-country theme that always reflected less of Samantha's tastes than her mother's. Portraits of dressage horses and Boykin spaniels covered the walls. A new quilt lay smooth over the four-poster, matching the closed drapes. Polished silver horseshoes hung over a shelf of vintage rag-dolls. Except for the built-in hamper, all of the drawers were pulled out and empty. That and the fingerprint powder aside, it was all clean enough for *Southern Living*.

And yet something was vaguely wrong. A sense of outrage hung in the air, barely masked, like the dying echo of a scream.

"Clothes are gone." Rusty dragged his thumb across the empty drawers. "Cell phone, too . . . it's all gone, right down to contact lenses. And no sign of forced entry. All the windows and doors are locked."

Peggy reached into her shoulder bag. "And the alarms?"

"Near as I can tell, shut down from inside. Like I said, I'm gettin' it checked out." He shrugged. "Couple frat boys said they saw her gettin' dressed around three A.M. Then she closed the drapes on 'em."

"What was she supposed to do, dance on a pole for them?" She took out her PDA camera. "Let me make sure I understand this. Samantha wasn't kidnapped, she ran away. Got out of bed, packed her bags, cleaned her room, disabled the alarm, and left. Remembering her contacts, but somehow forgetting her child?"

"Simplest answer I can think of—absent any other evidence, of course." He reached for the camera. "What the hell kinda gizmo is that?"

"Federal property." Peggy started taking pictures around the room. "There's two problems with your theory. First off, Samantha didn't need to run away. She'd already done that when she left Sean to come here. Second . . . there's no way she could run anywhere by herself. Trust me."

"Talkin' about her feet, are you?"

Peggy stopped. "You knew about that?"

"I was the one who found her last time, remember?" He stood between her and the dresser she was trying to photograph. "Anyhow, I didn't say she ran off by herself. She mighta caught a ride with a friend."

"Friend." Peggy hesitated. "What are you talking about?"

"There's a lot you don't know about your old chum Samantha. And some of it is stuff you won't wanna hear." He curled his lip. "'Trust me.' That's a hot one, all right. And you sittin' on top of maybe the biggest lead we got."

"I'm tired of games." Peggy put the camera down. "If Sheriff Powell's men did their job, then they must have found the photographs. And you know the man who took those pictures was never caught."

"Photographs. Do tell." He took a sealed plastic bag from a box marked EVIDENCE. Inside was the red FBI folder. "Go ahead and look inside. It's just Samantha's prints."

She opened it up. The folder was empty.

"That's one mystery solved," he said. "Mind explainin' why you chose to sandbag that for the past forty-eight hours?"

"Samantha asked me to keep it between the two of us while I checked it out." Peggy examined the folder. "She's got a right to her privacy. That's good enough for me."

"You and I both know there's no such thing as good enough. Or privacy." He lowered his voice. "You made a personal call. A bad call. And you know damn well the FBI won't let you work this case . . . Lindbergh Law or no . . . once they see how wrapped up in it you are. And seein' as how you withheld evidence that might've stopped it from happening in the first place."

"Sure." She set her jaw. "Now remind me how I should have remembered the T-Bird driver's face."

He seemed about to answer that, then checked himself. "You been gone too long to understand. The girl's plain crazy. Just be smart and let the whole thing drop. I'll handle it. And the FBI won't ever have to find out. Nor her parents."

"Won't have to find out what? How I let it happen?"

He didn't answer her—merely shot a gimlet stare at the open door.

"Professor," he said. "Thought I asked you folks to stay downstairs."

"Sorry to intrude." Harrison stood in the doorway. "The gentleman from the security company . . ."

"Tiny. About goddamn time." Rusty checked his watch. "Doc, we're gonna need your passcode for the security system."

"My wife keeps it in the office. Center drawer of the old rolltop desk."

"Good place for it." He started for the door. "I'll trust you to put that folder back where it belongs, Peg. Then maybe you'll see fit to tell me what else it is you've been holding back from the Avalon Police."

"Chief Weaver." Harrison cleared his throat. "I would very much appreciate it if you could . . . invite your daughter's assistance."

"Ain't gonna happen, Doc. And she knows why."

Peggy closed the door after him.

"You holding up?" she asked after a silence.

"Not so well." He sat on the vanity stool. "My mind keeps running back to when I saw her last night. I should have stayed with her a little longer, I think. Something . . . felt wrong."

"I know you don't like to eavesdrop," she said. "But did you hear anything else she might have said to Sean?"

"You suspect him?"

"It's what we call victimology," Peggy said. "A portrait of Samantha at the time of her disappearance."

"Victimology, I see." He nodded. "I only heard her end of the conversation. From what I gather, it had something to do with her research."

"What about it?"

"Sean seemed to insinuate that the book is a fabrication. A cover story for . . . whatever else she's been doing with her time."

"What do you think he meant by that?"

"No idea." He tensed. "Like most untruthful men, Sean is unnaturally obsessed with the honesty of others. If Samantha says she's written a book, I choose to believe her."

"Have you seen the book? Or has she ever discussed it with you?"

He shook his head. "It's been an obsession with her for years. She seems to think her whole career is riding on it. Which isn't far from wrong. Sammie's up for tenure this year. And frankly . . . she hasn't published much lately." He passed a hand over his forehead. "She's a lovely girl, Peggy. She's just not strong like you."

"She's stronger than I gave her credit for. And if we're going to find her, we have to keep giving her credit."

He looked up. "Then you will lead the search?"

It was hard for her to meet his eyes.

"My father's wrong about a lot of things . . . but unfortunately not about this. Even under normal circumstances, it would be difficult getting me assigned to a case outside my jurisdiction. My personal connection to Samantha—not to mention my father—only makes things worse."

"But why wouldn't he want your help?"

She shrugged. "I could be glib and say it's pride. Jealous of my education. Won't take orders from his daughter. Hates the federal government. But honestly?" She took a slow breath. "I don't think he trusts me. Maybe he's right not to. The fact is, I'm not sure I trust him, either. I haven't exactly been putting my cards on the table."

He nodded. "You're referring to the photographs."

"She told you?"

"After you left. Samantha wouldn't show them to me. It was . . . a most upsetting conversation." He stood up. "Do you still want to find the person who sent them?"

"Very much so. In fact, I think it's our best hope for bringing her home."

"You know your work so well," he said. "Perhaps I could suggest that you recall the Latin you studied here. Cui bono?"

"'Who profits from the crime?' Cicero, right?"

"Cassius Longinus, actually." He smiled faintly. "But Cicero usually gets the credit for saying it."

Peggy waited until he'd left before returning to the FBI file folder in the evidence box.

*If all the subject wanted was to destroy the pictures,* Peggy reasoned, *he wouldn't have sent them in the first place. And he must have known I'd keep copies.* All except for the one photograph that was different, of course: the one that showed Samantha's eyes open. But why take them back . . . and then leave the folder behind?

*Maybe only so my father would know I had them.* The thought left Peggy feeling darkly exposed.

"Aun' Peddy seeda munjuns?"

She turned. Caden was standing right over her.

"Caden. Didn't hear you come in, sweetie." She quickly put the folder away. "What are you up to?"

He held his arms out, then brought them to his chest again. "Mommy godda puppaston'? Ennazoot?"

She stroked his hair. "That's good, Caden. I'm glad you found her a purple stone."

"Nooo! No no no. Zoooot!"

He once more gestured emphatically—and precisely: two hands crossed, as if warding off a blow. Then again. Finally Peggy took him into her arms.

"I'm sorry, baby. I don't know what you're signing to me."

"How 'bout lessee Mommy?"

"She's . . . not here, sweetie." Peggy carried him to the top of the stairs. As she looked down into the foyer, the first pale light of morning spilled through the open door—falling on the white overalls of a large, bald man kneeling beside her father.

"Whatcha got, Tiny? Power supply problem?" Rusty examined the open security panel.

"Looks more like somebody shorted out the wiring." The technician's voice was surprisingly high, considering his bulk. "See here now? All the sensors are wired into warning lights. You cross the LED wires, first time you trigger the warning—boom, whole shebang goes down."

"Who could've done it?"

"Anybody with access to the transformer. Point is, it couldna been done from outside."

"You hear that?" Rusty threw a look in Peggy's direction.

"Yeah." She came down the stairs. "The system wasn't disabled so that somebody could get in. It was so they could get out."

"Now there's a girl. Where you takin' the kid?"

"To visit the munjuns." She put Caden down. "Go run to the library and see your grandfather, honey."

"Hokay, Aun' Peddy."

"Munjuns, huh?" Rusty watched the boy tumble off. "Tiny, this here's my daughter Peggy. She's just on her way out."

"Lester Tidwell." He wiped his hand on his thigh before extending it to her. His grip was like fresh cookie dough.

"Hi." She looked at her father. "Mind if I borrow the truck? I need to run a few errands on campus."

"You know where the keys are," he said. "Watch out for that alternator, now. She stalls."

"I will. Just so you know, I'm having the FBI Crime Lab run forensics on the photographs. I'll make sure you're copied on their preliminary report." She lowered her voice. "One way or another, Dad, I will work this case."

"Hell, I'm just glad to know you made double prints." He turned back to Tidwell. "Ready to give her another go?"

"Cover your ears." Tiny pressed Reset. All at once, a piercing alarm tore through the house. He quickly shut it off.

"I guess everybody heard *that*," Rusty said. "Screams just like a woman, don't it?"

# TEN

Rusty's pickup had a police scan radio; and, as she drove to campus, Peggy listened to the search in progress. From Glencoe Bluff to the county seat at Sevier City, the voices in the air were clipped and tense:

*"We have the lady's description, but I can't make out this photograph. Please resend . . ."*

*"Won't be till Monday at least before I can scratch up the manpower for a search . . ."*

*"Powder residue, negative. Prints and fibers, negative. Bloodwork, negative."*

*"Could be anywhere by now. Ten thousand acres of godforsaken nowhere . . ."*

*"No sign of the husband. It's like the earth swallowed 'em both up."*

Her father's voice, she noticed, was not among them. Either he wasn't listening or he had nothing to say.

Peggy briefly considered joining the search on the ground. The forest trails around the bluff were a likely starting point, as well as the back roads leading in and out of town. Then she realized her presence wouldn't make a damned bit of difference. *Ten thousand acres of godforsaken nowhere.* That was Avalon in a nutshell. Ever since its founding, the college had cherished its aloofness from the modern world. Twenty miles to the nearest hospital, thirty-five to the closest shopping mall, and not a pair of golden arches in sight. The Avalon charter expressly forbade the sale, logging, mining, or exploitation of its property. Old-growth trees were as thick as they had been in Davy Crockett's boyhood, and most of the back roads were solid dirt. Even helicopters couldn't find you if you got lost out there . . . assuming, of course, that you wanted to be found.

From the center of campus, it was easy to forget that there even was a world beyond the trees. On that Sunday morning the grass was newly clipped, the dogwoods were blooming, and the churchgoers entering St. Andrew's were serene with the Holy Spirit. That was how things had always been at Avalon, how they only could be. It was, as Samantha suggested, the center of its own little universe. It was nostalgia carved in stone.

*"Gonna have to resend this picture of Samantha Aldridge,"* the voice on the police radio was saying. *"Makes her look dark enough for a goddamn minstrel show—"*

Peggy killed the radio. As she parked the truck, its engine stalled—a hard, sputtering death—forcing her to leave it askew. As she approached the library at Culloden Hall, she read the motto carved in granite above the doors. VERITAS NUMQUAM INTERIT: Truth Is Never Destroyed.

*Here's where we put that theory to the test*, Peggy thought as she went inside.

**"Hepyew, ma'am?"** The desk librarian's twang was hickory sharp.

"I'm looking for any books or periodicals on reserve to Dr. Samantha Aldridge," Peggy said. "I know she's been doing research here. But nothing's listed."

"Well now, *that's* funny. She's in here all the time." Long red fingernails clattered on her terminal keyboard. "Hm. Doesn't seem to be anything. Maybe her student assistant knows? I could find out for you."

"That's very sweet of you. Thanks."

"No trouble, ma'am."

It was starting to worry Peggy that so many people had taken to calling her "Ma'am." Even browsing the archive display, *Avalon at 130*, didn't make her feel any younger. A trio of old photos caught her eye: the college's founder, General Stallworth, flanked by his grim-faced cadets in 1877; a young and dangerously good-looking Harrison Stallworth in the class of 1962; and finally Samantha, giving her valedictory address. The picture couldn't do justice to the way the light had caught Sammie's blue eyes that morning, or how warm and elegant her simple speech had been. Only Peggy knew how hard she'd worked to make it something her father could be proud of.

*This college, this ground, does not belong to us*, Samantha had said in her clear, soft voice. *It belongs to our dreams, and our dreams have paid the price for it.* And then Peggy's about-to-be-ex-boyfriend had leaned over and whispered that maybe their dreams could pay the rent, but the college still belonged to the fucking Stallworths.

Peggy had often marveled at how their friendship had continued to grow with the years, even as others had withered away. There were always weekend visits and late-night drinking sessions—never mind the miles between them—and endless hours on the phone. Debates were frequent; genuine fights were rare. As maid of honor, Peggy had given the wedding toast for Sammie and Sean. She'd stood godmother to Caden. When she graduated from FBI Academy, it was Samantha who sat beside Peggy's mother in the gallery. And, on the night Peggy and Mike finally called it quits, it was Samantha she'd turned to for a crying shoulder. Sammie didn't even need to ask why Peggy was calling so late. She'd just known.

And yet, not once in all those years, had Sammie ever shown her scars to Peggy. And Peggy had never once dared to ask. Now her friend was gone. And Peggy didn't know why.

"Yo, booyakasha! Lady said *tu tengo una problema*? I'm friends widdat, word."

Peggy swung around. The young man standing behind her was thin, towheaded, and absolutely lily white. His clothes looked like a wealthy suburban kid's idea of gangsta cool, never mind the knee-length shorts from Urban Outfitters. Or the flip-flops held together with duct tape.

"I beg your pardon?"

"You're scopin' Docca Aldridge, innit? I'm up on it."

"You're up on . . . I'm sorry. I think you just told me you're Dr. Aldridge's assistant?"

"Check it. I am DaBiz." He held up his iced-out necklace: it read DABIZ in square-cut rhinestones.

"Well . . . DaBiz . . . my name is Special Agent Weaver of the FBI."

"Fo'shizzle?" But his smile was wearing a little tight.

"Yes. I take it you can help me." She looked around. "Or is this somebody's idea of a practical joke?"

"I'm cool," he said. "You kickin' it around here?"

"Just down from Philadelphia." She headed for the stairs. "And if you're ever up there, you might want to cool it with the fake mac-daddy routine. Or some folks in my 'hood might decide to go kill-o-matic on your Caucasian hindquarters." She threw a look back at him. "We speaking the same language now, DaBiz?"

He gulped. "Yes, ma'am."

———

"What's your real name?" She followed him down Culloden's third-floor gallery. A few students passed them in the hall, most of them stuffing late papers under their professors' doors.

"Brandon." He dropped his voice, as if afraid of being overheard. "Brandon DuBose."

"I went to school here with a Richard DuBose. Any relation?"

"Uh-huh—I mean, yes, ma'am. He's my uncle."

Peggy vividly recalled Ricky's Deadhead tie-dyes, Rasta locks, and powder blue BMW. There had been DuBoses at Avalon for as long as there had been Stallworths—almost.

"Man, it's got to be the shit workin' for the Bureau." He laughed nervously. "You into, like, antiterrorist mayhem or something?"

"Or something," she said. "About Dr. Aldridge's research. What exactly was she working on?"

He stopped. "Wazzat?"

"You're her assistant. She must have told you about her book once or twice."

"Y'know . . . regional history. I think . . ." He laughed. "Tell you the truth, I'm not too sure. Old shit."

"Okay." She stopped in front of Samantha's office. "Give me your key ring, please."

He hesitated just a moment before handing it to her. His keychain, she noted, was a Mexican Day-of-the-Dead skull. She removed the office key, then returned the ring to him.

"I'm gonna get that back, right?"

Peggy didn't answer. There was a dark spot on the tile floor: dried blood. She turned the knob carefully, handling it only by the edges. Then she looked through the office door. "Brandon, when was the last time you came in here?"

"I dunno. Friday?" He started to peek in. "How come?"

"Please sit over there by the window." She pointed. "Don't move unless I tell you to."

He craned his neck forward. "Whassup? Is it—?"

"Sit. Down."

He sat back on the stone windowsill. Peggy made sure he was unable to see around the door before going in.

The office was small but not uncomfortably so. Its shelves were filled with volumes of American history and cultural studies. A Cherokee throw rug and Arts and Crafts lamp gave the room some much-needed warmth. There were framed photos of Caden, Sean, and Sammie's parents on her desk. The phone was off the hook.

Someone had ripped Samantha's computer open. Wires and printed circuits protruded from the bent case. The monitor was a spiderweb of broken glass. Computer keys were scattered across the floor like broken teeth.

There was a woman's bloody handprint on the floor.

"Oh my god, what the fuck happened in here?" Brandon stood behind her, white faced.

"Brandon, back the hell off." She could hear her voice tighten. "I am not kidding."

He was whimpering. "What did they do to her—?"

Now there were footsteps in the hall. Other students put their heads into the room.

"Holy shit—"

"—Dr. Aldridge—"

"—happened to her?"

Peggy saw something shine in the light. Three dark blond hairs were caught in the shattered glass of the computer screen. Samantha's. She could see the root bulbs, still attached. They'd been yanked out.

The bells of Culloden Hall were ringing, loud enough to shake the windows: ten o'clock.

# ELEVEN

"—reached the Avalon Police Department," a recorded voice was saying over Peggy's cell phone. "To expedite your call, please choose one of the following options. If this is an emergency—"

"Bloody hell." She shut the phone and turned to the knot of students pressing close to Samantha's office door. "If I could please get everyone's attention—"

"What—happened—to Dr. Aldridge?" A slim girl in a Tri-Delt shirt was in Peggy's face. "Why aren't you telling us anything?"

Brandon sliced the air with his hands. "I keep tellin' you, she's dead! Somebody fucking cut her!"

"She's *dead*?" The girl tried to push her way in.

"That's far enough." Peggy held her back. "Let's stop the chatter. Please. I need your cooperation."

"Yeah?" The sorority girl curled her lip in disgust. "And who the hell are *you*?"

"Blood everywhere." Brandon put his head in his hands.

"Brandon, shut up," Peggy said. "The rest of you—"

"What's the trouble here?" Everyone went quiet as Officer Ripley strode up—a big-boned cracker with a broad, earnest face. Peggy remembered him whaling on Elias Collins with that baseball bat. At that moment, though, he seemed more worried than angry.

"Officer, you arrest that bitch." The girl jabbed a finger at Peggy. "She fucking pushed me. And she's hiding something in Dr. Aldridge's office."

"Sweetheart, take some advice," Peggy said. "Back off."

The girl sheltered herself behind her friends.

Ripley worked his jaw. "Miss Weaver, what are you doin' here? Where's your daddy?"

"That's a damned good question. There's no one on call at the station." She exhaled. "And I've got a scene here."

"Who said they saw blood?" He eyed the office door.

"I guess I did." Brandon raised his hand.

"Anybody else see anything?"

The other kids looked away.

"All right, then." He turned to Brandon. "Fella, you stay where I can keep an eye on you. Everybody else?"

He watched Peggy closely for several seconds.

"Let's back off," he said. "Give the lady some room."

The students herded themselves down the hall, whispering with dark excitement.

"Thank you," she said.

Ripley wordlessly moved past her to the office.

"Holy Christ." His mouth fell open. "I gotta call this in. You said nobody was at the station?"

"No. But I take it you somehow got my messages?"

He shook his head. "I was just on patrol. Somebody out front said there was a disturbance up here, is all."

He stared blankly, out of his depth.

"Just secure the scene. I'm getting some help." Peggy speed-dialed her cell phone. A moment later, she heard xylophone music on the far end.

"Hello?"

"Yoshi," she said. "Sorry to spoil your Sunday afternoon."

"Don't worry. The Baby Einstein's starting to melt my brain." The music muffled as a door shut. "You really think that stuff makes kids smarter?"

"Something needs to." She shot a look at Brandon. "Take a look at your PDA. I just sent you some pictures. I've got a computer emergency."

"Hang on." Yoshi took a sharp breath. "Boy, I'll say you do. Somebody didn't follow proper shutdown procedures."

"Yeager can give you the background later. Right now I need you to tell me how to pull data off the computer without disturbing any physical evidence."

"I'm not sure there's any data to pull. Looks like somebody yanked the hard drive."

She turned back to the broken metal case. "Shit."

"Of course, there's always a chance the computer may still be on. In which case—"

"Still on? Are we looking at the same pictures here?"

"Patience, boss. Just because somebody played airport baggage handler with your computer doesn't mean the power's off. Looks like it's still plugged in. Is it?"

She stood close to it. "Yes."

"Okay, then. Can you hear the little fan going?"

Peggy listened. "Go on."

"If you plug anything in to retrieve data from active memory, the CPU's going to try to access the drive—which isn't there. And then bye-bye. But if you can get the monitor working, you just might be able to see what's currently on the screen. Even browse through open windows." Silence. "Go ahead. Say it."

"You're a genius." She put him on speakerphone. "All right, Baby Einstein. Talk me through this."

"Okay. Are you standing close to the monitor?"

"Yes."

"See the reset button on the front panel?"

"Yes, I—" She blinked. "Hang on. That's it? Just turn the monitor back on?"

"First we eliminate the imbecilic, then we do the impossible." He paused. "Of course, if it doesn't work, we're probably screwed anyway. Might as well save some time."

"Thanks." There was dried blood on the control panel. Peggy felt it flake away beneath her finger as she pressed the button. A moment later there was a crackle of static, raising the hairs on the back of her hand. Blue light slowly resolved itself behind the cracked screen.

"Did it work?" Yoshi asked. "Are you getting anything?"

Peggy instantly reached for her camera. She could see it forming: Samantha's ten-year-old face, eyes closed. Writhing in terror.

"Holy fuck," Brandon said. "Is that a *kid*?"

Peggy took a picture just as the screen died. A moment later, the fan silenced. Blood-rich ozone hung in the air.

"Boss? What's happening?"

"We lost power, Yoshi." She examined her PDA. "Damn it."

"Did you get a snapshot?"

"I got—something." She exhaled. "There's an open text file. The title looks like . . . Cumbaa?"

She looked up. Ripley was standing in the doorway.

"Say again, Peggy?"

"I think it says, 'The Free City of Cumbaa.' Maybe I'm misreading it. There's a bad glare off the monitor."

"Send it to me anyway. We'll put it through image processing."

"Will do." She closed the phone.

"Agent Weaver," he said. "Evidence team's here for ya."

Peggy noticed he hadn't called her *Miss Weaver* that time.

"What *is* all that shit?" Brandon tried to look at the PDA. "Some kind of kiddie porn?"

Peggy pushed past him into the hallway. He tried to follow. Then Ripley imposed himself between them.

"What?" Brandon raised his hands. "All I did was ask a question."

"Ask her again," Ripley said, "and you'll be askin' through a mouthful of broken teeth."

Brandon instantly shrank away.

"That's cool," he said. "I'm good."

# TWELVE

It took nearly an hour for the evidence team to finish their work. Peggy noticed that Ripley seemed to be waiting for her. "Still no sign of my father?"

"He ain't even answerin' his radio. Wish to God somebody'd tell me what's goin' on."

"You and me both." She looked at him. "What's up?"

"I was just wonderin'—is that the FBI way of workin' a scene? 'Cause I never woulda thought to see if there was still anything left on a computer that bad off."

"Just lucky to have a good team, I guess." She waited. "Is that all you wanted?"

He rubbed his neck. "I don't mean to listen in. But I heard you sayin' to that guy on the phone . . . Cumbaa?"

"The 'Free City of Cumbaa.' What about it?"

"I don't know about any city. But I do know the name Cumbaa."

"Really."

"Yes, ma'am. It's a Melungeon name."

"A what?"

"It's another word for Covites—'scuse me, folks that live down in the Cove. Like that feller you saw me . . . detainin'." He cleared his throat. "He's Melungeon, too."

*How 'bout seeda Munjuns.* Samantha told her it was Caden's way of saying he wanted a walk in the forest.

"I should probably shut up now," Ripley said. "I guess I just pissed you off, huh?"

"Don't sweat it," she said.

# THIRTEEN

Ripley followed her into the main parking lot.

"How come you're not talkin' to me?" He caught up with her near her truck. "I thought I was helpin' you."

"You did. And thank-you again. But right now there are things I have to tend to. And you're on patrol."

"You're headin' down to Chillwater Cove, ain't ya?" He wiped sweat from his brow. "You can't just go there alone. Them Covites is insane."

"So I've heard."

"Lemme come with you. I don't have to do shit unless things get outa hand. Your daddy'd have my head if—" He stopped himself. "It's on account of that Collins fella, ain't it? You think I'm just some jackass cop? Be honest."

"All right, I'll be honest." She pulled out her keys. "You're no cop, Ripley. You're a plain disgrace."

"It was not my idea to lay into that boy," he said. "I'd a let him go. That shitbird Martin, him and his fuckbuddy, Dennis. They roped me in." He bit his lip. "I am a cop, dammit. I wanna be. Just give me a chance."

She opened the door of the truck. "You finished?"

"Yes'm."

"You were three on one. He was unarmed."

"You weren't there when he jumped at me." He pointed at his brow. "Look at that cut. Near about got scalped."

She just shook her head at him.

"A chance, huh?" she asked. "Go put that bat on my father's desk with a letter of resignation. Maybe then I'll believe that you really want to know what that badge means."

He seemed to sink into himself.

She climbed into the Jeep. "That word you used. 'Melungeon.' Is that something my father would know?"

"I guess. Most folks around here do."

"I didn't," she said. "And I grew up here."

"It ain't a word you generally say in front of ladies." He sighed. "Listen. Maybe I could just drive a ways behind you."

Peggy silently closed the door and started the engine. Then she drove away, watching him shrink to nothing in the rearview mirror.

**The roads around Chillwater Cove** passed through some of Avalon's most beautiful forests. They were also damned hard to navigate. Going forward was sometimes just as hard as backing up; turning around was simply not an option. The dirt trails twisted and tore their way into the mountain like living things. Peggy didn't even bother to check her map: One might as well try to map a den of snakes.

"I repeat," Peggy was saying into her cell phone. "Did Yoshi show you the image I sent?" It had been a frustrating conversation with Mike: two lost connections and lots of breakups. She'd cursed herself for leaving her satellite phone back in Philadelphia.

"—showed me," Mike answered. "Text he's decrypting. Appears to be some kind of field report." Silence. "Interviews with people in a place called the Cove."

"You mean, like oral histories?" Peggy remembered that Samantha nearly always preferred direct testimony to secondary documents. "Mike, were these Samantha's own interviews?"

"Seems like it. By the way." He was breaking up. "You know that picture?" Silence again. "Not a JPEG or bitmap."

"Say again?"

"Part of a layered file," he said. "Peg, do you copy?"

"I hear you. Do you—" She splashed through a running stream. Loose change rattled as she bounced up the far bank. "Sorry, Mike, rough ride. What do you mean, a layered file?"

"Difficult to explain." The signal was getting clearer. "You'll have my analysis on those cold-case photos tonight. I can give you something right now."

"What is it?"

"Your T-Bird driver spent a few years in the military. That, or prison. And he's a local boy."

"How do you figure that?" She waited. "Mike?"

The signal had gone dead.

"Shit." She didn't even bother redialing that time. Peggy was close to the base of the hollow, with the mountain between her and the nearest cell tower. Her father hadn't been able to answer his phone either—or, finally, his radio. And that told her something. The Cove was Avalon's one true dead zone.

The headlights dimmed as the truck ground its way up the hill. Cutting the lamps didn't help. Its engine skipped, then fluttered. She was losing the motor. Peggy downshifted. One more foot, a few more yards . . .

Peggy barely had time to step on the emergency brake before the engine coughed into silence. She was stuck on a muddy road at a bad angle. *Damned if he wasn't right about that alternator.* She climbed down and surveyed the road ahead. Fresh tracks in the dirt matched the Avalon PD's new four-wheel drive. Her father, it seemed, had been that way very recently.

Then she heard a loud snap. Peggy turned to see the truck rolling backward down the hill. She ran after it, but it was too late. The truck held for a second, its rear wheels spinning over the ravine. Then it simply went nose up. The pines quivered, shedding needles as the old Ford pickup carved a drunken path down the hillside. It was a long time before she finally heard metal crashing into stone. And then only dust and silence.

"Holy shit." Peggy walked out onto a flat base of granite, trying to see where the truck had landed. There wasn't much to look at except for trees and a sliver of robin's egg sky. But she could hear wind in the branches, and the occasional mockingbird call. And she could smell the forest.

She was quite certain she'd been there before.

Peggy shuddered a little against the afternoon chill. Then the realization struck her head on: This was the way she had come home on that long-ago afternoon, running from the black Thunderbird. A few miles down the fire road and she'd find herself at the bottom of Suicide Run.

She quickly put the thought out of mind, following the trail of fallen objects down to where the truck had wedged itself between a live oak and a ten-foot boulder. One front wheel still turned lazily, a little cockeyed from the bent axle. The dead engine was still warm.

"Nice." She was on the mountain's northern side, feeling its weight behind her. Peggy was casting about for her flashlight when she heard something move past her. Two seconds later, the Glock was in her hand.

"Who's there?" She stayed close to the truck. "Come out and show your-self."

Swift steps fell lightly on the leaves below her, hidden by a scarp of white granite. Peggy walked heel-toe, keeping the muzzle of her semiauto-matic down. She swung round a copse of trees . . . and found herself star-ing into a pair of pale blue eyes.

He was only a boy, no more than twelve years old. He resembled Elias a little, minus the ironic smile. A Savage .22 rifle was balanced against his hip.

Peggy drew back. "Put it down, son."

He stared at her plainly—then abruptly threw himself to the ground. An instant later, bark split away from the hickory he was standing in front of. Peggy heard the bone-dry snap of semiautomatic fire echoing in the hol-low. By then she was crawling, pivoting her own weapon up to the ridge above her. The boy had vanished.

"You okay?" Officer Martin showed himself on the ridge above, a bolt-action rifle across his chest. He stared down at Peggy with lurid amaze-ment.

"Better come quick, Chief," he called back over his shoulder. "I think we found your little girl."

# FOURTEEN

"I'll say this for ya, Peggy Jean. You always know when to jump ship." Her father shook the steering wheel of the pickup, then pumped the emergency brake twice. "Quit on ya, did she?"

"And the brakes," she said. "You didn't mention them."

"Wasn't nothin' wrong with 'em when I drove it last." He looked at her. "You all right? You seem a little shook up."

"I'm not crazy about getting shot at."

"We been shot at ourselves a bit today." Rusty threw a hard look at Martin. "You ever use that rifle scope, boy, or do you just fire away at anything that moves?"

"I am so sorry, Miss Weaver." Martin took off his cap, the soul of distress. "It's these shadows, and you wearin' black. All I could see was the shooter."

"Well, you sure blasted the hell out of the tree I was standing next to." She fixed her gaze on him. "But I'm fairly certain you missed the kid."

"No, he didn't." Rusty picked up a leaf, wet with blood. "This is your mess, Martin. Go track him down."

He looked cautiously at the chief. "I don't feel right leavin' you two here. Not with the gunplay we've had today."

"Oh, I'm sure my daughter can handle herself. Just because she can't drive don't mean she can't shoot." He waved Martin off. "Now, goddamnit. I don't plan on bein' here after dark."

"I'll be back directly." Martin looked back over his shoulder several times as he walked down the stream bed.

"Did I hear you right?" She looked at her father. "You were in a firefight?"

"Yeah, but it ain't nothin' to fret about now." He touched her cheek. "Looks like somethin' cut you."

"Just a hunk of bark." She turned her head away. "You do know it's a child you're shooting at, don't you?"

"I didn't think it was a mountain lion." He looked back to the ridge, as if gauging the line of fire. "Mart'll be out of earshot by now. Anything you want to say before he comes back?"

"I think I just did."

"You won't need to worry. I'll sort him out." He pointed back up the hill. "My four-wheel's parked about half a mile down the road you were on. You take the keys, lock yourself in. I won't be too much longer."

"I'm coming with you," she said. "I think we're both here to see the same people."

He raised an eyebrow. "The Munjuns, you mean?"

"Yes. The Melungeons. Do you think there's a connection to Samantha?"

"I think she's had more truck with 'em than was good for her. What do you think?"

"I think maybe somebody didn't want us knowing that she'd been talking to them."

"Told you she was nuts." He shrugged. "Gets dark a lot sooner in the Cove than it does up in town, Peggy Jean. And this is a different place at night. Right now, you and I are the ones bein' hunted."

"I'm used to finding my way out of dark places."

"Oh. Well, I guess I have nothin' to teach you, then." He looked back over Peggy's shoulder. "You see him, Martin?"

"Think he just got grazed." Martin seemed oddly disappointed. "Lit off straight for home. But there's a blood trail. We're mighty close."

"Good. You walk point. And Martin?"

"Sir?"

"Try not to waste any more rounds today," he said. "'Cause the next time my daughter accidentally winds up in your line of fire, I can guarantee you won't ever hear the one that's comin' for you."

"Yes, sir." Martin didn't meet Peggy's eyes as he walked ahead of them.

They followed a downhill path along the stream. It gradually narrowed, then disappeared entirely, forcing the three of them to wade across. *Chillwater Cove is right*, Peggy thought as she felt a stabbing cold in her legs. It put her uncomfortably in mind of her dream from the night before. Martin was focused on the way ahead, a hound pulling against his lead. Rusty kept his eye on the cliffs above them.

"Watch out you don't get your ammo wet," her father said as he joined her on the far bank. "And keep one in the pipe. You're about to need every round you got."

"You really think these are violent people?"

"I think they'd shoot a preacher just to hear him pray for death." He shook the water from his boot. "Take a look."

Two poplars flanked the path ahead of them, each of them nailed with a hand-lettered sign. JESUS IS LORD read one. The other one said, YOUR LAW ENDS HERE. Nailed beneath it—as if to underscore that last point—was a bobcat's bleached skull.

"Sheeya, don't it smell down here," Martin said.

"Quiet now." Rusty took his .38 from its holster. "Last chance, Peg. In or out?"

"We don't have a warrant, Dad."

"They wouldn't know how to read it." He paced in. After a moment's hesitation, she followed.

The stream ran down into a stagnant pool of water. Surrounding it were a few rude shacks of gray wood and plastic tarp, as well as a rusted pink trailer that looked like it might have rolled down the mountain. Patched yellow extension cords ran between the buildings, sharing out electricity from a running gas generator. There were a few wire coops and a garden of blighted melons. Peggy hated to concede the point to Martin, but the place did smell. It stank of dead chickens and pork grease, and of propane and human waste, and any number of other things that most people could afford to haul away.

As she passed a pine stump, something growled at them from the shadows. Peggy froze. It was a Doberman. He sat chewing on what appeared to be an old shoe. The dog stared at her, then slowly dragged himself up to sniff her out. As he did, she noticed that his right front leg was missing.

Peggy crouched down to the dog's eye level. The Doberman walked head down toward her, making a small grunt as he nosed the back of her hand—then dropped what he had been keeping in his mouth.

It was a woman's pale blue tennis shoe.

There was no question of who it belonged to. Cotton wadding was packed into the toe, and there was dried blood close to the heel. Peggy held it up to her father; he examined it without expression. The Doberman sat on his haunches, as if waiting for a game of fetch.

Peggy felt a wild rage seize inside her. She forced it back. Then she turned to follow her father.

She caught up with the two men behind a canebrake. Rusty gave her a questioning look: Are you with us? By way of answer, she drew her Glock. He seemed pleased. Then he made a chopping motion between him and Martin: They would go in through the front.

Peggy pointed to herself, then made a circular motion around to the back door. Her father nodded his approval. He touched his eye, then cupped a hand to his throat: Watch for hostages.

She crouch-walked around the trailer, close enough to hear noise from inside. It was hard to tell over the generator, but it sounded like someone in the living room was getting knocked around. She came up on the bedroom door, then peered through the dirty window. Shadows were moving in the next room. Just a few more seconds and her father would be ready. Then she heard the dog barking, and the noise of a chain pulling tight.

"What the hell's he found this time?" a woman asked from inside. Peggy heard a shotgun rack. She charged up the steps and kicked the door in. The bedroom was empty. She checked her danger zones—the darkened corners of the room behind her—then launched herself down the hall.

"Freeze!" she yelled. "FBI! Hands up!" Peggy came face to face with a young boy and girl in the living room, watching a martial arts film on television. Their blue eyes were riveted on the gun in her hands.

"What the hell—?" She lowered her weapon. "Where are your parents?"

They looked at each other dully. She switched the TV off.

"Listen to me," she said. "You can't be alone in here. Where's your family?"

"Right here," a woman's whiskey-roughened voice said behind her. Peggy could see the shotgun barrel reflected in the television screen. A moment later, she felt it touch the base of her skull. Peggy stood still and allowed her weapon to be taken from her. Just then, her father came in the front door, hands behind his neck. The boy from the forest stood behind him, keeping his .22 muzzle against the small of Rusty's back.

"Where's your boy Martin?" Peggy asked him.

"High-tailed it." He turned to the woman guarding Peggy. "Let her go, Zanda. She's nobody."

"Seems awful like somebody to me." The woman took the badge from Peggy's belt. "My oh my, FBI. Turn around, darlin'. Show off that pretty figger for me."

Peggy quickly sized up her situation. There were three children who would almost certainly get caught in a crossfire. Not to mention her father, favoring his game leg. Hand-to-hand, then. She turned, prepared to convert her momentum into a side-thrust kick—then caught sight of the woman behind her.

She was about Peggy's age, broad hipped and strong limbed, tall and strangely handsome. She had long dark hair, with a white streak swept back across her forehead. Her skin was dark olive, her features hawkish, her eyes bright blue. She was at least seven months pregnant. Maybe eight.

Peggy slowly raised her hands.

"Thought you was gonna kick me for a second there." Zanda smiled. "Don't you wish you might."

# FIFTEEN

As dusk fell over the Cove, the three of them—Peggy, her father, and Zanda—sat around a formica table. The twins had been sent to their room. Fletcher—the boy from the forest—stood guard with Rusty's .38, his right arm freshly bandaged. Meanwhile, Zanda amused herself by flipping through Peggy's wallet. Something was boiling on the propane stove: greens and onions, from the scent.

"Gold Amex. Platinum Visa. Dis-cover Card." Zanda tossed the cards down one by one, like a poker hand. "I swear. You could max 'em out, buy your folks a nice Winnebago. How 'bout that, Russ? Ain't it about time you retired?"

She kept the shotgun across her lap, tucked beneath her belly. The Glock rested six inches from her right hand. Peggy was pretty sure she could get to it before either Zanda or the boy would have time to fire. But then she'd have to be ready to shoot one of them, and she wasn't. Zanda seemed to know that.

"Sister, you keep starin' poison at me. You got somethin' to say, spit it out."

"Detaining an FBI agent is a federal offense," Peggy said. "Are you really prepared to take this all the way?"

"Excuse *me*." Zanda rolled her eyes. "Did I just break into your home and point a loaded gun at your kids? And shoot another one right in the arm?" She looked at Rusty. "Did I beat up on your oldest boy and throw him in jail for nothin'? Where's the federal offense that keeps you people in line?" She turned back to Peggy's wallet. "Hey, Russ, your daughter's a gold-level member of Blockbuster Video. That's free rentals from Monday to Thursday."

"Look, if you want me to talk to you, then you need to talk to me." Peggy leaned forward. "You want money, is that it?"

"Peg." Rusty didn't look at her. "For God's sake, don't waste your breath."

Zanda smiled. "I ain't a thief. I just wanted to know if you ever max out your credit cards."

"I don't like being in anyone's debt," Peggy said.

"Smart girl." Zanda pushed the wallet and cards across the table. "I guess I know enough about you." She stood up, leaning her shotgun against the refrigerator. "You folks hungry? I could eat a sow and half her brood right now. But then, I always get this way just before a baby comes."

Peggy and her father made rapid eye contact. Zanda had left the Glock on the table.

"Did I hear you right?" Peggy casually sorted out her credit cards. "Is Elias Collins really your son?"

"I think I'd know if he wasn't." She turned her back to them. "Don't even try sayin' I'm too young to have a boy his age. I broke my cherry while you were still playin' with Barbies."

Peggy started to reach across the table. The boy idly pulled back the hammer on the .38.

"I never had much time for Barbie dolls." Peggy moved her hand past her gun, retrieving a few coins instead. "My father kept me pretty busy on the rifle range—didn't you, Dad?"

He nodded. "Peggy could shoot Lincoln's head off a penny before she could read. And she was readin' pretty damn young."

Peggy put her hand back in her lap. The boy carefully eased the hammer forward.

"Now it is heartwarmin' to see a father so proud of his only child." Zanda sat down with the pot of greens and a stack of paper plates. "Apologies for settin' such a sorry table. My breadwinner's kinda gone missin'."

"Bread thief, you mean." Rusty shook his head. "Keep your slop, thanks. Ain't hungry for welfare food tonight."

"Why, you slug." She threw him a sour look. "You're lucky to get fed at all, the way you both charged in like Hell's thunder."

"We had every right to break in," Peggy said. "Your dog was chewing on a shoe belonging to my friend. Samantha Aldridge."

"I heard what happened to her." Zanda's eyes darkened. "So now you're gonna arrest my dog?"

"He's a wild animal," Rusty said.

"He ain't." Zanda frowned. "Trip was dyin' when we found him. Some rich family dumped him on their way to Nashville. All he wants now is for people to be sweet to him. He wouldn't hurt Samantha."

"Considering that he's chained up," Peggy said, "I'm guessing someone might have thrown the shoe to him."

She piled greens onto Peggy's plate. "Two things you need to know about us Collinses. One is we ain't criminals. Elias wasn't takin' a thing from Piggly Wiggly. He was protectin' his brother from gettin' beat up."

"Now even from you, that is one big, steamin' pile of hogshit." Rusty calmly reached into his jacket for his smokes.

"I'm tellin' you, Fletch was there. Now maybe he shouldn't have been into that garbage, but he's just a boy. And if Elias hadn't been close by, those peckerwoods you call policemen woulda put my baby in the county morgue."

"Can't wait to hear Fletcher testify to that in open court." He lit a cigarette. "Don't know why he's so sweet on Elias, anyhow. Ain't like they have the same daddy."

The boy put the .38 to Rusty's temple. Her father didn't move. The end of his cigarette glowed steadily.

"Dad," Peggy said.

"Fletcher." Zanda frowned. "Honey, you set that thing down. Ain't right to kill a man what ain't been fed—even if he don't have the manners God give a rattlesnake."

Fletcher stood back.

"Tell your son not to try that again." Peggy's heart was beating. "Or I swear to God, you'll have trouble."

"He won't shoot nobody 'less they hurt someone he cares about." Zanda narrowed her gaze. "You ain't eaten today, have you, girl? You got that dizzy look in your eye."

"Make him leave my father alone."

She dished out two more plates. "Fletch, you take these in to your brother and sister. Either they finish or they don't get no juice box."

He looked anxiously at his mother.

"Fletch thinks the minute he turns his back, one of you's gonna grab that pistol and shoot his mama." She looked at Peggy. "That so?"

"I don't make promises staring down a gun barrel."

She seemed to respect that. "It's all right, Fletcher. I'll handle 'em."

He left warily, leaving the bedroom door ajar.

"Is Fletcher mute?" Peggy asked, hoping she sounded calmer than she felt.

"He can talk. Just not to outsiders." She pushed the plate to Peggy. "C'mon, I just fed it to my kids. Want me to take first bite so you know it ain't cyanide?"

Peggy braced herself, then took a bite. She was pleasantly surprised by the flavor. Then she found herself breathing her father's cigarette smoke. She threw him a reproving look.

Rusty released a long stream of smoke before grinding his cigarette into the floor. "So what's the other thing we need to know about you folks? You're really natural blonds?"

"We're careful about choosin' our friends." She turned to Peggy. "Samantha's been kind to us. Her little boy plays with my children, and she eats from my table. She even paid for that generator out there so's we could run a refrigerator. What makes you think I'd harm her? Or help anybody that did?"

"You still haven't explained the shoe," Peggy said.

"Maybe somebody put it there to make us look bad. Can't defend myself against somethin' I ain't never seen."

Peggy took the shoe from her jacket. "Take a look. She was wearing it the night before she disappeared. You'll see where she stuffed the toe with cotton."

"That poor baby's feet." Zanda put a hand to her cheek. "I guess you know about the harm that's been done to her all these years."

"I know some. She kept a lot to herself."

Zanda went on guard. "Did you come here to make me tell you what Samantha said in private? You can forget about it."

"I don't know what you have to tell me. To be honest, I didn't even know you existed until you came at me with a gun."

"Likewise."

Peggy put her fork down.

"Please understand," she said. "My job . . . our job . . . is simply to bring Samantha home safe. There are things we need to know. And there's other things you have a right to keep secret. The problem is, I can't say which is which until you tell us. I can promise you that it's not my job to invade Sammie's privacy . . . or yours. And that would be true even if she wasn't my friend."

"You just want her home. Why she's gone don't matter."

"Of course it matters. But only in the line of duty."

"I don't know." Zanda softened a little. "You seem like a nice person. Even if you are federal . . . and daughter to the worst man I ever hope to meet. But I just don't see how you can put up these walls between work and personal. There's things you may not like to hear."

"Try me."

Zanda threw a look at Rusty, a whipcrack glance that immediately darted back to Peggy: as if she was trying to gauge how much difference there really was between father and daughter.

"She was about ready to leave her husband," Zanda said finally. "Maybe you should ask him what he was up to last night."

"Good advice," Rusty said. "Now tell us what you were really about to say."

She folded her arms. "Well, sir, I don't think so. You been very unpolite to me in my own home. Not at all like the nice young feller my mama always talked about."

"Did Samantha say anything about her work?" Peggy asked after a silence. "Something called *The Free City of Cumbaa*?"

Both Zanda and Rusty looked at her in surprise.

"She mighta been talkin' about Fortitude Cumbaa," Zanda said cautiously. "He was the one who brought us here, my mama says, long before the whites."

"Tell me about him." Peggy couldn't help but notice her father's extreme discomfort.

"I really don't know that much," Zanda replied. "They say he was a big man. Scars from the whips, and blue eyes like morning. Our people was slaves in Virginia, Mama says. Portuguese, maybe . . . Portuguese sailors blown off course . . ."

Rusty rolled his eyes.

"It's just a story for the kids." She seemed to blush. "Like George Washington and the cherry tree. They say Old Fort built a town up on the mountain. But if it ever was, it ain't no more."

"There never was a town," Rusty said plainly. "Just some old half-breed's dream of livin' white."

Zanda shot a hard look in Rusty's direction.

"The Cumbaas always were the big dreamers," she said. "But it ain't no matter now. They're all dead and buried." She looked at Peggy. "Sammie

just wanted to know who we are, is all. Not as Covites, or whatever ignorant people call us. She wanted to find out about Melungeons."

"And what—I should say who—are Melungeons?"

Fletcher had returned, staring anxiously at his mother.

"I wish I could tell you. 'Cause I'd like to know myself." Zanda stood up.
"I'm gonna take food up to my mama now—and I know she ain't in a
mood to see you, Russell Weaver. Anyhow, I believe your ride is here." She
took the empty plates to the garbage sack. "Fletcher? Be good, now."

Blue flashers were playing on the front windows. Fletcher held out the
.38. He seemed about to aim it—then deliberately set it down before Rusty.
Her father's fingers closed over the gun. Moments later, the front door
opened wide. Officers Martin and Dennis entered, rifles up.

"Police!" Martin strode in, firmly in command. "Chief, thank the Christ.
You okay?"

"We're fine." Rusty holstered his gun. "Nice to know you could find
your way back here."

"Hey. It's that kid who was firin' at us." Martin stood back. "Want me to
give him his rights, Chief?"

Rusty looked at Fletcher. "No harm done. He's just a slow boy, that's all.
Can't help bein' born inbred."

The men stared at him, stunned—then went back out to the cruiser.
Peggy nodded to Fletcher as she retrieved her own weapon. A moment
later, the boy returned the nod.

She met Zanda at the door.

"Thanks for the meal," she said.

"You sure cleaned your plate." Zanda put an arm around her son. "You
woulda grabbed that gun and shot us both if Fletcher had killed your
daddy. Wouldn't you?"

"Yes." There didn't seem to be much point in lying.

"I knew you would. I saw his picture in your wallet." She smiled. "See
what I mean about business and personal?"

"Point taken," she said.

"So you won't arrest us for federal detention, or whatever?"

She shook her head. "I think we need to talk some more."

"Let's leave the guns behind next time. Almost went into early labor tonight." Zanda smiled. "You keep lookin' at me like you don't think I'm
real."

"I know it's not polite to ask a lady her age," she said.

"Hell, I'm not that much older'n you and Sammie. Just seen a lot more hard road." She closed the screen door. "Had Elias when I was fourteen. Guess I met the wrong man at the wrong age, is all. It's the oldest story on earth."

"Isn't it just."

"Come on, Peggy Jean." Her father leaned on the horn. "Got a ways to go tonight."

# SIXTEEN

Rusty was strangely elated on the drive back to Avalon. He and Peggy rode together in the off-road vehicle; Dennis and Martin were in the cruiser ahead.

"I gotta say, you weren't half-bad with that Melungeon gal," he said. "Maybe that busted parkin' brake was a stroke of luck after all."

"It damn well better have been luck," Peggy said. "Those brake lines are getting a careful inspection tomorrow morning."

"Quit bein' paranoid. Take the compliment and quiet down."

"Why do you—" The words fought their way out of her. "Why is it that the only time you ever approve of me is when I'm two seconds from getting killed?"

He shrugged. "Why do you need approval so bad that it's worth gettin' killed for?"

"I don't need it that bad from you," she said.

"Then stop bending my ear." He picked up his radio mic. "Mart, ain't you got that thing workin' yet?"

"Dennis says it's up and runnin' fine," Martin answered over the speaker. "Just waitin' for something to come through."

"Roger that." He turned the microphone off. "So what'd you think of Zanda's story? She credible to you?"

"From what I could tell, yes. And from what little she said. I'd like to know what her mother's got against you."

"Thieves and moonshiners generally don't favor cops. You must know a few bad men who'd just as soon kill you as say hi."

"The point is, she didn't kill us," Peggy said. "She hasn't even trained her dog to bite strangers."

"She don't need a dog. She's got her retard."

"And about that," she said. "Did Fletcher really and truly take a shot at you today? Or was he just shooting back?"

He didn't answer. They were out of the woods now, right at the first bend of Suicide Run.

"Just because somebody looks helpless don't mean they're safe," he finally replied. "And just 'cause somebody feeds you don't make 'em your friend. Speaking of which—there's gonna be supper on the table when we get home. And unless you plan to make your mama cry, you better at least pretend to have an appetite. Thought you was gonna choke on them greens."

"They were good. You should have had some." She looked at the 25 MPH sign as it flew past. "You always taught me not to get close to strangers, didn't you?"

"That I did." He stepped on the gas. "It's why you never wound up like your friend."

"I know." She paused. "That other officer of yours—the big guy, Ripley? He watched me handle Sammie's computer today. And he asked if that was the FBI way of working a scene."

"Rip's young, so what? He still thinks the FBI's shit don't stink."

"I was actually going to tell him that the FBI didn't show me how to work a scene," she said. "You did."

Rusty took a breath. "Why didn't you tell him?"

"Because somewhere along the line, you stopped giving the right lessons," she said. "And you started giving the wrong ones."

"I ain't the one who went off and changed, Peggy."

"Then I guess I'm just seeing you differently now," she said.

The radio crackled. "Chief, we got it."

Rusty switched the mic on. "Pipe it through."

"What is this?" she asked.

"Shh." He cranked the volume.

At first all Peggy could hear was a lot of yelling and breaking wood. Then she recognized it as the tail end of the martial arts film Zanda's kids had been watching.

"Holy shit, Dad. Please tell me you didn't plant a wire."

"Bet your ass I did. Why d'you think I let you girls carry on with that hen party for so long?"

The next sound was a knock at the door. A chair moved, and a second later Peggy heard the screen door open.

"Thought those po-lice'd never leave." It was a man's voice, weathered with age. "You all right, Zandy? I been worried."

"Oh, Abe, you're sweet," Zanda said. "I'm fine. They were tryin' to pin somethin' bad on me, but they couldn't."

"You best be careful of Weaver, now. He's got a loooong memory. Was that his girl I saw you talkin' to?"

"Trust me. She's nothin' to worry about."

Rusty smiled at Peggy: Told you so.

"Dad," Peggy said. "I don't know how you rigged this. But it's illegal for us even to be listening."

He put his flashers on. "Best plug your ears, then."

"I come to bring you a message," Abe was saying over the radio. "I ain't sayin' how I heard. But your Elias wants you to know he's got himself free."

Her father sat up like he'd been stuck with a needle.

Zanda gasped. "They let him go?"

"Now, he didn't say *that*," Abe replied. "I kinda got the feelin' he mighta paroled himself somehow."

Rusty slammed on the brakes. The cruiser barely stopped in time to avoid rear-ending them.

"Jesus, Dad."

He grabbed the mic. "Martin, what the hell."

"News to me, Chief."

"I told that goddamn Martin not to leave the station empty," Rusty said. "He swore up and down that his relief had come—"

"Dad." Peggy let go of the passenger bar. "I think you might actually need to hear this part."

"—God's sake, Abe, he shouldn't have done it," Zanda was saying. "He's got to go back and tell 'em it was all a mistake. And maybe I can get them to go easy."

"You know he ain't gonna do it," Abe replied. "It's not safe, he says. Somethin' wicked bad is about to happen, and he wants to be here to protect his fambly."

"You mean what happened to Sammie?"

"Worse than that even," Abe said. "Krypteia is coming."

The old man said it in three long syllables: Krip-*tie*-yuh. Peggy realized that her father was no longer angry. He was scared shitless.

"Chief." Martin was on the radio. "We gotta move one way or the other. Can't just sit here on the hill waitin' for some eighteen-wheeler to pick us off."

Rusty pressed the mic button. "Is Dennis recording this?"

"Yessir. You want us to go back down and round 'em up?"

"Can't," Rusty said. "They'll know it was a transmitter. I'll call Sherburn Police, ask 'em to set up a watch at their end of the bypass. Let's just . . . head back. We're almost at the station, anyhow."

"Ten-four."

"And you can cut the signal to me. I've heard all I need to for now." Rusty drove on, hands sweating.

"Did you mean to leave your flashers on?" she asked.

He wordlessly turned them off.

"Dad." She looked at him. "What is Krypteia?"

"Sorry," he said. "Didn't catch that part, myself."

The only person on duty at the station was the dispatch clerk, Matilda—a formidable black woman who had seemed ancient when Peggy was young, and now appeared to be made of iron.

"You boys done playin' Robin Hood in the forest?" she asked in her leather-lung croak. "'Cause you got messages on that machine to choke a pig, Chief. And I ain't wadin' through 'em."

Rusty walked straight past her to the lock-up. The cell door was wide open.

"Where's the prisoner?"

"*Prisoner?*" Matilda snorted. "You tell me, hon. I been askin' myself since I got here, where's the Avalon *Po*-lice?"

Martin and Dennis caught up with him—standing well out of the arc of her father's fist, it seemed.

"We-ell." Matilda yawned as she stood up. "You're here now. And I am goin' home to coax some love outa my man before he craps out."

Rusty touched his cap. "You take care, Miss Matilda."

He waited until she was gone before turning on his men.

"Who was officer on patrol?" His voice was low, a coiled spring.

"Ripley," Martin said.

He turned to Peggy. "And he was with you at the college?"

"Yes," she said. "He wanted to come with me, but I said no."

He cocked a thumb at Martin. "Bring him here. And for God's sake, get on findin' the Collins boy."

He walked back down the hall to his office. Peggy was about to follow when she noticed a look pass between Martin and Dennis. They were smiling.

"Martin." She crossed the room. "I have to admit, you did a good job of planting that bug. Must be a high-wattage transmitter to bring a signal that clear out of the Cove."

"It was. And thank you. Just doin' my duty."

"You even had me convinced you'd run away like a coward. In fact." She got in his face, five foot seven to his six foot two. "I was this close to believing you didn't see me standing next to that boy, Fletcher."

Dennis looked worried. "Mart."

"I said I was sorry for that. And I am." Martin put his hands on his hips. "But just to put your mind at ease. I only ever hit what I aim for . . . Peggy."

"Martin, for chrissakes. She's the chief's daughter."

"No, she isn't," Peggy said. "She's FBI. And she's had your number since you were pissing in your Hulk Hogan pajamas. So watch your ass next time." She folded her arms. "Marty."

Martin's smile faded dead away.

"Peg," Rusty said behind her. "Stop teasin' the boy and get in here."

She turned away. Her father's wrath had burned away to an ashen fury. "What is it?"

"You tell me." He led her into his office. "What the hell is this supposed to mean?"

The Old Hickory bat lay across his desk. Beside it was a memorandum to Chief Weaver, signed by Officer Ripley. The subject was a single word: *Confession*.

"Looks like someone just made me eat my words," she said.

# SEVENTEEN

Hours later, Peggy was jolted from deep concentration by her cell phone: Mike's ringtone.

"What time is it?" she asked.

"Just before midnight on your end. Were you asleep?"

"I can't sleep. I'm still trying to figure out these crime scene photos of Samantha's office."

"Hey, that's my racket. Go get your own."

"Don't worry, your job's secure." She yawned. "Sorry I couldn't talk when you called the station. My dad's batteries took longer to run down than I expected."

"He's still mad about that cop, right? What's his name?"

"Ripley. And no, he's merely pissed off about the resignation." She stretched. "Honestly? I think my dad knows this case is getting beyond his control. And that sends him freaking ballistic."

"Sure—but that's why he's got his brilliant daughter."

"Or not so brilliant." She paused. "I'm sorry I never told you that my father was the police chief here. Seems like a dumb thing to hide."

"I'm guessing you didn't want me knowing he was the same guy who guilted you out over T-Bird Man's description."

"Yeah. I still should have told you. All this time you probably thought I was some kind of . . . debutante."

"So what? I'm as white trash as they come." He laughed. "Don't sweat it, hillbilly. You've had a hard day. You've been shot at, yelled at, and forced to eat . . . what?"

"Mustard greens. For the record, they were delicious."

"No doubt." He yawned. "Meanwhile, all Yoshi and I have been doing is fielding the thousand bits of physical evidence you keep tossing at us like popcorn at a movie screen."

She reached for her PDA. "Yeah? What did you get?"

"Your friend had a couple of open documents on the screen. I'm guessing her abductor took her straight from her parents' house to her office?"

"And forced her to unlock her PC," Peggy said. "They didn't have to hurt Samantha to get her out of the house. But when they tried to smash her computer, she fought back."

"Because of what?"

"My guess is that her book was on that hard disk. Whatever she's been writing has some people scared."

"You might be right about that. We were only able to decode a few fragments from that picture you took. I'm no scholar, but they do look a bit like a researcher's field notes. Or a diary, maybe. I've sent them to your handheld."

"Got 'em," she said. "What about that photograph of Samantha that you said was a layered file?"

"The interface looks like photo editing software," he corrected. "When you modify a picture, it can create hidden layers of information. Obviously, we can't know what's on those layers without seeing the original. But I can tell you this. Samantha's eyes have definitely been altered to make them appear closed. Your version—the one where her eyes are open—that's the original. Whoever changed it did a very good job."

Peggy examined the photograph on her PDA. Now that she was seeing it in extreme close-up, there did appear to be a subtle discrepancy around the eyes.

"These aren't Samantha's eyelids, are they? It's like somebody pasted them in from another photograph." She stared. "Whose *are* these?"

"You really don't know? Go check a mirror. I'm pretty sure they're yours."

"My god, you're right." She pulled back for a better look. "But why make the change?"

"I'll tell you that when I see the complete file. Yoshi says the university's e-mail server should have backups. Who's ultimately responsible for that?"

"Harrison says it's Sean. Samantha's husband."

"And he's gone missing."

"Right about the same time she did. The only difference is, nobody's been looking for him."

"I'll take this opportunity to remind you of Peggy Weaver's first rule of criminal investigation."

"Never chase crooks on an empty stomach?"

"Sort of. I was going to say, everybody has to eat."

"Follow the money, right. I'll get on Sean's bank transactions."

"Good call. Speaking of food, I've got a Philly cheese steak sandwich awaiting my gullet."

"For the last time, Yeager. Cheez Whiz is not cheese. That's why the law requires them to spell it with a *z*." She paused. "And God damn you for making me hungry again."

"Just trying to remind you of the pleasures of home."

"Thanks." She closed the PDA. "While you're eating your Frankencheese sandwich, try to remember that profile you owe me. What were you saying when we got cut off before?"

"It's pretty clear our subject had neighbors," Mike said. "Otherwise he wouldn't have needed the tinfoil and ball gag. But he couldn't be close to town, or people would have seen him coming and going. A lot of these guys like to hang out right on the county line. They think it'll save their asses if they can hop between jurisdictions. The ruse he employed— pretending to be stalled out—suggests a planned abduction. He knew when to expect you coming down that hill."

"You don't think there's any chance we were just victims of opportunity?"

"Disorganized molesters go for the easy targets—they don't plan. And they're rarely sadists. Let's also not ignore the fact that both you and your friend are the children of community leaders—the college president and the chief of police. That says revenge motive to me."

"You see who got abducted both times." She breathed. "What about the other feature you mentioned?"

"Military or prison? It's mainly a guess. But you notice how he's got her restrained?"

"Hog-tied," she said. "Prone position, hands and feet bound behind her back."

"Very popular with military police and prison guards. Probably he would have been about the right age to serve in Vietnam. Which would put him in his midfifties to early sixties today." He paused. "You okay?"

"I'm a little faint. I think my blood sugar's low."

"So eat."

"I will," she said. "Mike, have you ever heard of someone—or something—called Krypteia?"

"Isn't that the name of Superman's dog?"

"I'm serious. Will you see if it checks against any known hate groups?" She listened at the door. "I have to hang up. Can I ask you something personal?"

"Is it a pants-on or pants-off kind of question?"

"On. On." She rolled her eyes. "What do you do when both of your parents start cracking up at exactly the same time, but in completely opposite ways?"

He was silent for a while. "I'm sorry, kid. I can't help you there."

"It's all right anyway. Mike?"

"Yeah, babe."

"If he's local . . . why don't I know him?"

"Chances are you did. You just don't remember him."

"I love you." She closed the phone before he could answer. Someone was standing right outside her door.

"Ma?"

She opened the door. Her mother held the kitchen phone receiver. She was fully dressed.

"Why didn't you answer me when I called up?" Bea asked. "I think Mike's waiting to talk to you."

"Sorry, I didn't hear it ring. He wound up calling my cell phone."

Her mother looked irritated. "But I've just now been chatting with him."

"Mama—" Peggy took the receiver: dial tone.

"Did he hang up?"

"It's okay," Peggy said. "Don't worry about it."

"Wait, now. I did talk to a friend of yours just a minute ago." She furrowed her brow. "You don't believe me, do you?"

"I believe you. What was his name?"

"It was—well, he didn't say. I just assumed it was your friend Mike. He was *very* nice. He wanted to know if you liked the pictures he sent you."

"Well, Mike did—" Peggy stopped. "Pictures."

"Of Sammie. He said he's been saving them for you for the longest time. And he's got more if you'd like to have them. Something about . . . ?" She brightened. "*That's* it. He'll be happy to give you a ride to his house any time you want one!"

Peggy held the receiver button down, making sure there was no one holding on the other end.

"Where's Dad?"

"Oh, your father went back to the station as soon as he dropped you off. He's got a bee in his bonnet."

Peggy was already dialing the phone as she led her mother to the stairs.

"Federal Bureau of Investigation," answered a neutral voice. "Chatanooga Resident Agency. How may I direct your call?"

"This is Special Agent Weaver," she said. "Authorization Juliet Foxtrot King, Three-One-Three. Requesting ID on incoming calls to this number within the past thirty minutes."

"Hold, please." There was a static silence.

"Peggy Jean Weaver, what has gotten *into* you?" She shook her head. "Are you just upset about Samantha? Or is it about missing your friend's call?"

They had reached the bottom of the stairs. Peggy looked through the open curtains of the front window. Darkness only.

"Or is it only that you skipped dinner?" Bea mused. "You do look hungry to me. Are you?"

She looked back. "Ma, I'm starving."

"Well, that settles *that*. I'm going to heat up some chicken and biscuit for you."

She went into the kitchen.

"Agent Weaver?" A male voice on the phone, clear and correct. "This is Special Agent Blaine Randall. There's been no activity on your number in the past three hours. Except for a call two hours ago from the Avalon Police . . . ?"

"No, that's . . . nothing. Thank you."

"I've been meaning to look you up anyway," he said. "This missing person . . . Samantha Aldridge? Her file was flagged to my desk this morning. Anything I can do to help?"

"Possibly," she said. "Can we talk tomorrow?"

"Absolutely. Take care." He hung up.

She came into the kitchen. Her mother was cheerfully peeling waxed paper from a tray of frozen biscuits.

"Mama, are you absolutely sure you just now spoke to him? Because I didn't hear the phone ring."

"Well, you know how you are when you're into your work." She looked back. "He said he'd left a package for you."

"Where?"

"Out front." She set the biscuits onto a cookie sheet. "I didn't check, myself. I'm scared to open the door at night."

Peggy went to the door. She unlocked it with her left hand, unholstering her weapon with her right.

"Peggy, *please*. You know how I feel about guns in the house—!"

"Stay in the kitchen. Please." Peggy threw the door open, aiming into nothing. Then she looked down.

A piece of cloth lay on the welcome mat. It might have been white once, but was stained a mottled copper-brown: dried blood. Something was coiled up inside. At first Peggy thought it might be a leather belt. Then, as she reached down, it fell out, an unwinding streak of yellow and black.

"Snake." She leapt back. "Oh, Jesus."

It had been neatly decapitated. And, as the initial shock began to recede, Peggy realized just what it was that the snake had been wrapped inside.

Underwear. About the right size for a ten-year-old girl. The initials S.P.S. were neatly embroidered on the waistband.

Samantha Patrice Stallworth.

"What is it, Peggy?" Bea called from the kitchen. "Was the package there?"

"Yes," she answered. "It's there."

"Well, if you're willing to let me make copies of those photographs, I'd *love* to put them in that scrapbook I'm making for Mike." She turned back to her cooking. "But don't tell him about it just yet. It's a surprise for your wedding."

# EIGHTEEN

Peggy woke with a start around three o'clock in the morning, thinking she'd heard Samantha's voice. She had the strangest feeling she wasn't alone.

"Hello?" No answer. "Who is it?"

She turned on the bedside lamp. The dark shape in the corner turned out to be nothing more than her FBI shell jacket, thrown across an enormous stuffed tiger from childhood. It was only a toy her father had won for her at the county fair. So why was her heart still beating so quickly?

*Prison*. The word presented itself like a title on a movie screen, white against black. Was that what she'd been dreaming about?

The television was on downstairs again: an old cop show from the 1970s. Peggy's late dinner kicked back a little as she tiptoed downstairs. Six dented Pabst cans stood guard over the empty sofa. Her father snored from the open door of the master bedroom. Somewhere in the room was the dead snake, and Samantha's underwear, bagged for evidence. Pale light flickered against the paneled wall of the living room, reflecting off glass frames.

Something about prison.

Most of the pictures on the wall were from family vacations. There were a few plaques and citations from her father's years of service with the Avalon police, but not many. Rusty didn't like to brag on himself. He wouldn't even hang his high school diploma. But there was one certificate, from the first job he ever held:

THIS IS TO CERTIFY
That Russell K. Weaver, Jr.
Having Successfully Completed a Six-Week Program of Instruction
Is Hereby Approved and Accepted for Employment
Within the Tennessee Correctional System
This Day of April the Twenty-Third, 1970, A.D.

He'd never talked much about it—and she'd never really thought to ask—but her father must have had few options after flunking out of Avalon College. Even the army wouldn't take him because of his bad leg. But it seemed that the Tennessee prison system would.

*What does it mean?* She struggled with her fear like a weak stomach she was trying to quell. *Probably nothing. Go to bed.*

Peggy realized she'd left fingerprints in the dust on the frame. For reasons she didn't entirely understand, she found herself trying to rub them away. Then she turned off the television set and went back to bed. Her sleep after that was fitful and torn, and one thought never left her head:

*Why didn't he ever talk about it?*

It followed her all the way to the first light of dawn.

# NINETEEN

Monday morning began with the 5:00 A.M. screech of the garbage truck. As Peggy emerged from the shower, her father was already on his way out the door. He'd taken the dead snake into evidence—but his response to it was prefunctory, as if he had darker matters to consider than a threat to his home and family. "We'll deal with it later," he'd told her—familiar Rusty-speak for, *I'm not going to discuss this with you, ever.* Then he'd driven off alone.

And so Peggy walked again—this time to the student center, where she could take advantage of the school's wireless network. Using her handheld computer, she submitted Samantha's photo and description to the FBI Registry of Missing Persons, and cross-checked addresses of sexual predators. She refiled a request for assignment to the Aldridge investigation. Then she began to pore over the text fragments that Image Analysis had painstakingly reconstructed from Samantha's computer screen:

```
Abraham Bunch [BRANCH?] . . .
in [ILLEGIBLE] mid-eighties . . .
served moonshine . . .
U.S. Army in WWII.
Today he demonstrated water-witching skills . . .
made a believer of me.
The spring looked cool and clear but Abe said
the waters of Stiller's Cave are poisoned now.
```

It was, as Yoshi warned, like trying to rebuild a Scrabble game from scattered pieces. Peggy gathered that a man named Bunch or Branch, who either served in World War II—or served whiskey to soldiers in World War II—had shown Samantha the art of divining, or water-witching, to locate a poisoned spring. It appeared to mean nothing: and yet it was information that Samantha's kidnapper seemed desperate to hide.

At least it gave Peggy a lead on the "Abe" she'd heard talking to Zanda. The second fragment, on the other hand, was a migraine-maker:

```
1870 Keyes Co. census 5K Melungeons.
1970 75.
Collins/Goines, Bunch/Branch, Crow/Coffey . . .
Identity pending: mitochonDNA project Key Co. Hosp
```

It seemed to suggest that the number of Melungeons living in the region had dwindled from five thousand to seventy-five over the course of a century. The third line might be a list of common surnames. But what was the reference to mitochondrial DNA at Keyes County Hospital?

The third—and final—fragment had been taken from a text message, possibly an e-mail, partly hidden behind Samantha's photograph:

```
BLUEYES
LETHAL WHITE
YOU D
```

"You deserve everything that's coming to you," Peggy whispered—certain now that she was staring at the words of Samantha's kidnapper.

Her cell phone rang: The caller ID read UNKNOWN.

"Special Agent Weaver?"

She recognized the voice. "Agent Randall."

"Call me Blaine." There was chatter on his end—people milling around, metal gates opening. "Have I caught you at a bad time?"

"Yes and no. You're out in the field today?"

"You could say I'm in *a* field." He laughed. "Listen, Knoxville SAC's asked me to follow up on your request for financial search warrants on . . . Sean Aldridge?"

"That's correct. So you're the case agent for this investigation."

"On paper, maybe. I was hoping we could meet in person and sort things out. I'm sure you've got plenty to contribute."

"Give me a second." As she reached for the newspaper beside her, she heard a clear amplified voice on his end:

*"Pick 'em up, move 'em out,"* the announcer said. *"This buckskin will do a nice running walk with a brisk twelve-inch stride—"*

"Agent Weaver?" Blaine Randall asked.

"Sorry. Driving to Chattanooga's going to be a little tough. It's an hour away and I still don't have a car."

"Actually, I'm in your neck of the woods. I just need an hour for an information dump. Maybe we could . . ."

"Why don't we just meet where you're calling from? Logan Farms, right?"

"Goddamn." He was briefly silent. "How did you figure that out?"

"I could hear the auctioneer. From the description, those had to be Tennessee Walking Horses. And according to the paper, Logan Farms is the only place holding a horse auction this morning." She paused. "How's one thirty?"

"You're as good as advertised," he said. "Do you need directions?"

"Not to find Logan Farms," she said. "No offense to protocol, Agent Randall. But is there some reason we're not doing the data download via e-mail, or over the phone? I've got my hands pretty full here on the ground."

"I think it's in your interest to make the drive." He paused. "But now, I'd better get back to business."

"What about those warrants?"

"It's all been approved. See you soon."

As Peggy hung up the phone, she noticed a voice mail waiting from Dorrill's Garage. He was off towing Rusty's truck from the Cove . . . but he'd be back by ten and badly wanted to speak to her. She checked her watch: nine o'clock. That would leave her just enough time to eat.

Tom Fool's Diner—"The Fool," as it was known locally—had proudly served breakfast to hungover Avalon students since the late sixties. The building itself was a creaking survivor from an age before construction codes. Each summer, it listed just a bit more off plumb; each winter, the owner had to plane a little off the front door to make it close. Like every other storefront in downtown Avalon, Tom Fool's was something between a hallowed institution and an accident waiting to happen.

As Peggy came in, the room was packed with graduating seniors, enjoying a breather between finals and the impending arrival of their parents.

"Milf," a buzz-topped student whispered as Peggy walked by with her coffee. His smile evaporated when she sat down.

"Todd Simcha?" She showed her badge. "Special Agent Weaver. I'm told you were one of a group of students who saw Dr. Aldridge just before her disappearance on Sunday morning."

His grin was halfway between embarrassment and sly pride. "Well, I guess that's . . . one way of putting it."

"What would be the correct way?"

He scratched the back of his head. "I mean, I *saw* her, Ma'am, but I was—shit, somebody help me out." Two of his friends stifled laughter. "Cut it out, guys. How do I say this without sounding like a total dick?"

"He means he touched himself like a scummy perv while poor Dr. Aldridge was standing there naked." It was Gretchen, this time in a green Tom Fool's apron. She carried plates on each arm. "Who gets the deep-fried pork fat?"

"That would be me." Todd grabbed his plate. "How the hell would you know, Crotch-en? Were you watching me?"

"Stuff it, Scumcha. You know I was."

"She was watching his belly button," Todd's friend said. "With her nose in his pubes."

Gretchen just kept setting plates down.

"Seems like you boys are a little too distracted," Peggy said. "Why not let's take this down to the county lockup? I think some of those meth dealers might like to meet a rich-boy Peeping Tom."

That shut them up. Gretchen's green eyes lit on her.

"I can't go to jail." Todd blinked. "My parents are flying me to South Padre next week."

Peggy sipped her coffee.

"Eat your bacon," she said. "This could take a while."

**Forty-five minutes later, Peggy sat** in the back of the room checking her notes. Gretchen slung her apron over a chair.

Peggy reached for her wallet. "Sorry. You're closing out your register, aren't you?"

"The entire waitstaff just paid your bill." She sat down. "Congrats on decapitating Avalon's reigning dickhead."

"Just getting his attention," Peggy said.

"Todd's evil and clueless. He swallows date-rape pills and complains that they don't work."

Peggy looked up. "What did he call me? 'Milf?'"

"Trust me, you do not want to know." She rolled her eyes. "It stands for 'Mom I'd Like to . . .'" She mouthed the final word.

"Right. So you were also there at three A.M., huh?"

She nodded. "It wasn't just Todd and his Masturbatory Mafia. It was a whole bunch of us coming home from the Armageddon Ball at the AT-Zero house." She took out a cigarette. "You mind if I smoke? Don't worry, it's all-natural, cruelty-free carcinogens."

"I'll let you smoke if you let me put this on tape. My writing hand's cramped up." She took out her voice recorder. "If memory serves, the Armageddon usually doesn't break up until the paramedics arrive."

"It was lame this year. Anyhow, I had to get up for early shift at the Pig."

"You ever find time for studying between all these jobs?"

Gretchen looked down. "I don't go to the college. I got accepted, but I had to drop out. My folks died."

"Oh. Well, there's no shame in . . ."

"That was stupid. God. I am a student here. I just fucking lied to the FBI on tape." She stared at the recorder's red light. "Can you erase that last part?"

Peggy didn't move. "Look, if you're not going to be any help, I don't have time for you. I'm trying to find my friend."

"I want to help! I was the one who called out Todd's name so Dr. Aldridge would know to close the curtains." She paused. "I didn't mean to lie. I just get nervous."

"Why did you lie, Gretchen?"

"I'm embarrassed about being a townie. I know these rich kids from Mountain Brook and Gwinnett County all think we're *Deliverance* people playing banjos. And you look so nice . . ."

"You thought I was one of them?" Peggy asked. "You didn't make the connection to all the other Weavers around here?"

Gretchen smiled, astonished. "Holy shit, that's right! Chief Weaver's your dad? God, I loved the way you handled that guy who tried to steal your Jeep. You know what was so great? You didn't hurt him."

"I try not to if I can help it," she said. "Gretchen, I'm going to level with you. As far as I can tell, you and Todd Simcha were the only witnesses who weren't too bombed to know what they were seeing that night. And frankly, I'd rather not pin my hopes on Todd."

"And you want to know if you can trust me." She cupped her elbows. "I just get scared, that's all. And the weirdest crap comes flying out. Like this time in drama class? We were all supposed to tell our worst memory. And everybody's going on about getting STDs and grandparents dying—and I'm thinking, *fuck*, I do not have anything. Never even had a puppy get hit by a car. Pathetic."

She took a drag off her cigarette.

"I stood up and announced how my brother raped me when I was twelve," she said. "I thought, no way is anybody gonna buy this. But the more I talked, the more I could see everybody was getting into it. Even *I* was starting to believe it. By the end they were all applauding, and hugging me and crying . . . and the whole time I just felt like whale vomit."

"Because your brother really didn't rape you."

"Not even," she said. "All he did was make me jerk him off one time."

Peggy shut off her recorder.

"You know what I think, Gretchen?"

"I know. You think I'm full of it."

"I think you want me to believe you're a liar so I'll stop asking you questions. But I also think you went out of your way to sit down and talk to me." She leaned forward. "Just tell me what you saw. Don't expect any applause."

"I got a D in that class anyway." She stubbed her cigarette out. "Dr. Aldridge is the only professor on this whole sorry campus who didn't automatically assume I was insane. I want you to find the asshole who kidnapped her. I wouldn't lie about that."

"What makes you think she was kidnapped?"

She looked around. "I hung around that night after everybody took off. And I saw who was waiting outside." She lowered her voice. "This guy opens the door and goes in. And a while later, he drags her out by both hands—like they're tied together—and shoves her into a black SUV."

Peggy looked closely at her. "How did Dr. Aldridge appear to you? Was she fighting back? Scared?"

"She looked scared. But she wasn't fighting."

"What was she wearing?"

Gretchen breathed. "Pink shirt, purple sweater, blue jeans. And deck shoes."

"Anything else? Suitcase, shoulder bag?"

She shook her head. "He had her by the wrists, duh. How was she gonna carry a bag?"

"Gretchen, do you know who abducted Samantha Aldridge?"

She raised her eyebrow. "Is this a lie detector thing?"

"Just answer the question."

"No." She paused. "I've never seen him before. And I hope to never again. He scared the holy shit out of me."

"Describe him for me."

"Old guy—like my dad's age, I mean. His face was all leathery and he had curly gray hair. He looked real mean."

"What was he wearing?"

"Black. All black. Like some survivalist dickwad." She tried to look at Peggy's notes. "Who do you think he was?"

"It's a pretty thin description." Peggy held the pad closer. "You don't recall any distinctive marks? Something that might set him apart from every other gray-haired man with bad skin in Tennessee?"

"I can't think of anything," she said. "I was drunk."

"And the license number of the SUV?"

"Like I said."

Peggy put her hand on the recorder.

"If I was to turn this back on," she asked, "would you be able to repeat everything exactly as before? Or is this another drama class exercise?"

"I didn't make it up." Her glass-green eyes flashed cold. "Jesus God. Freak out, will you?"

"You didn't tell this to the police. Can you explain how you just happened to be hiding near Glencoe Bluff at the precise moment Samantha Aldridge was forced into a black SUV?"

The girl looked away.

"What were you doing there, Gretchen?"

"Oh my Christ." She mumbled something to the ashtray.

"What?" Peggy asked.

"I said I was giving Todd Simcha a blow job!"

The room instantly fell silent. Gretchen pressed both palms into her eyes.

"We waited until everyone went away. And then I took off his pants. And he passed out. That's when the SUV pulled up." She exhaled. "Todd was wearing bright red sports briefs. Go ask him."

Peggy watched carefully as Gretchen moved her hands away. She wasn't crying. But the look of desperate anger in her eyes was absolutely real.

"I did it to get back at my loser boyfriend," she said. "And the reason I didn't go to the cops is because they wouldn't believe me. They never fucking do. Just like you're not believing me right now."

"Um, Gretch?" Another server, a young man, cautiously approached the table.

"Go. Away." She slumped down onto the table.

He coughed anxiously. "I kinda need your register key? I have to start my shift."

"In my apron."

"Thanks." He reached into the pocket for her key ring.

It was a Mexican Day-of-the-Dead skull. The same one Brandon had been using on Sunday.

"Sorry to bother you guys." He slunk away.

"Gretchen," Peggy said. "Is your boyfriend by any chance named Brandon DuBose?"

"Oh, my God. He is gonna find out, isn't he?"

"I think it's fair to say that cat's out of the bag. I know this is a touchy subject for you, but . . ." It took all of her strength not to ask, *Why him?* "Brandon introduced himself to me yesterday as Dr. Aldridge's student assistant."

"That is total weapons-grade bullshit." She looked up. "He's not. I am."

"Why would he lie about that?"

"Probably just wanted to screw with you. He gets off on that shit."

"Can you tell me about the book?"

"Yes." She looked up. "In fact . . . crap, I hope she doesn't mind. Do you want to read it? It's in my room."

"Which dorm are you in?"

"Varnado. I'm in six-one-six. I've got to punch out first. Do you want to come by in like maybe an hour?"

"I'll drive you there in ten minutes," she said. "First I have to pick up my car. If your statement checks out, I'm going to want you to talk to a sketch artist about this guy you saw." She stood up. "Assuming there really was a guy, of course."

She didn't speak until Peggy reached the screen door.

"He had a snake," she said.

"A what?"

"On his belt. A red snake on a sword."

Peggy turned. "You're certain of that."

She nodded. "It wasn't there when he left the house. Only when he went in."

"What color was the sword?"

"Silver," she said. "I think."

Peggy stood for a moment with her hand on the door.

"I'll see you in a few minutes," she said. "Don't burn me by not being here when I get back, okay?"

"Don't worry." Gretchen smiled timidly. "I won't burn you."

# TWENTY

"How's tricks, Mr. Dorrill? Still selling cracked engine blocks to the snowbirds from Michigan?"

Hank Dorrill, a squat bullfrog of a man, laughed through broken teeth as he wiped motor grease from his hands. "Naw, even Yankees is too smart for that nowadays. But I'm happy to charge 'em twice for organic motor oil."

She smiled, following him into the garage. The Ford pickup was already on the hydraulic lift. "What do you make of it?"

"That old brake just give out." He shook his head. "I been beggin' Rusty to lemme fix it. He's a fine man, but he is dad-gum stubborn about his proppity." Dorrill inspected the broken axle. "Thank the Lord you knew when to jump out."

Her father had said almost the same thing. Coming from Mr. Dorrill, it didn't sting. "Did you have a hard time towing it out of the hollow?"

"Yeah, but I tell you. It's fortunate she got wedged in that tree. Another few yards and she'd have tumbled right down into the cave. And then bye-bye, truck."

"Cave?"

"Yes, ma'am. Whole side of the mountain's caves. That's why the moon-shiners used to like to hide out in the Cove—that, and the underground springs."

"Did you ever hear of a place called Stiller's Cave? Something about its waters being poisoned?"

He scratched his head. "Well, I never heard *that*. But . . . well, seems I do recollect a cave-in there, long time ago. If it's the same place I'm thinkin' of."

"When would this have happened?"

"You'd have been a baby then. And, oh, it was a shame. I do miss that liquor." He shook his head sadly. "But now listen. That ain't why I axed you to come by. It's that Jeep of yours."

"Please don't worry if it's not ready. I know it's awfully short notice."

"It's fixed. I just don't think you should be drivin' it."

Her Jeep waited in the yard. He'd even washed it down.

"I kinda thought the electrics was actin' funny," he continued. "So I checked under the hood. And we found some sorta box. My son-in-law says it's a . . . GPS device?"

He raised the hood and pointed to a black transceiver, carefully concealed inside the body.

"That's the antitheft system, Mr. Dorrill. It's supposed to be there."

He frowned at her. "I know what it is. But there's somethin' else hooked into it."

She bent closer. A white box the size of a cigarette pack was fixed beneath the main unit.

"My son-in-law used to drive a tractor-trailer. And he says the comp'ny uses 'em to check up on drivers. How long they stop for, which way they go, how much gas . . ." He stood back. "I didn't want to take it out. 'Cause if we do cut them wires . . ."

*Whoever planted it will know.* "I'm sure it's no matter, Mr. Dorrill."

"Yeah?"

Peggy nodded. "The Bureau recently upgraded security on all field vehicles. It's probably just part of the new system." She reached into her purse. "How much do I owe you?"

He waved her off. "It's fine. Your daddy already paid the bill."

"Mr. Dorrill, I couldn't."

"You know how daddies are about their little girls." He smiled. "Come back, now."

"Thanks. I will."

Peggy kept her Jeep under the speed limit all the way back to the diner.

## "Yeah? Who is it?"

Gretchen had been a no-show at the diner; Peggy cursed herself all the way to Varnado Hall. She'd been knocking at Room 616 for close to a minute before someone finally appeared. The fact that it was a boy didn't shock her. But it blew her mind to see just who opened the door.

"Brandon." She tried to look around him into the darkened room. "Where's Gretchen? She was supposed to wait for me."

"She's chillin'." He was naked except for a pair of green briefs. It took her a moment to notice a cartoon Tinkerbell on the crotch. Peggy immediately looked away.

"Sorry, G. Hadda borrow somethin' fast. Couldn't find my own tighty whiteys." He laughed, embarrassed. "You like?"

"Keep it," she said. The darkened room smelled heavily of marijuana and sex. "Gretchen? It's Agent Weaver. You okay in there?"

Peggy could just make out the girl's white skin, hidden beneath a still-whiter sheet.

"Yeah. I'm fine." Her eyes flashed pale green, like a cat's. "Sorry about ditching you. Can you come back?"

"I'm afraid not. You mind coming out, please?"

"Oh my fucking god. No."

"Hang on a second." Brandon smiled and shut the door. Peggy heard him whispering. ". . . bringing her here for?"

She couldn't make out Gretchen's reply—but the tone in the girl's voice was halfway between pleading and rage.

"So just give it to her," Brandon said. "What's the fucking problem?"

The door opened again. Gretchen stood with the sheet wrapped around her like a toga. She handed Peggy a CD-ROM.

"Here," she said. "You took longer than you said. I kinda got bored waiting."

"I guess you did. Is this the book?"

She nodded. "It's not really a book. More like . . ." She compressed the air with her hands. "A bunch of stuff she was trying to put together. You'll see."

"Well, I'm going to need some help figuring it out. Want to come take a look at it with me?"

She struggled to keep the sheet on. "Maybe. I . . ."

"I say Goddamn!" Brandon called out. "Hurry up and get back on it! I'm losing my wood!"

Gretchen looked up with a look of desperate embarrassment.

"Maybe later?" she asked.

"Now look—"

Gretchen closed the door.

"Wassamatta, you didn't invite her in for a little girl-on-girl?" Brandon chuckled. "Me love you loooooong tiiime!"

"Shut up! I hate your stupid cock face!" But Gretchen was already giggling. And now they were really going at it: squeaking, pounding, doorknob-rattling sex. Peggy made it to the stairwell in three quick strides.

# TWENTY-ONE

The driveway was empty when Peggy arrived at the Stallworth home. As she walked around the side, she found Harrison sitting precisely where Samantha had been on Saturday evening—in the stone summerhouse, staring intently at a notepad. He barely noticed her until she was a few feet away. Then he smiled.

"Didn't mean to surprise you," she said. "Nobody was answering the door."

"Olivia's taking Caden to day care." He rose to his feet. "Sorry, I must have completely disappeared into the graduation speech I was working on."

She looked at the pad. Apart from a few scattered notes, the page was completely blank.

"Or rather not working on." He smiled apologetically. "It's been frenetic today. Olivia is . . . how do I say this?"

"Driving you insane?"

He half-smiled, not denying it. "My manners. Can I get you something?"

"Please don't wait on me. I'm just on my way to meet a colleague. At Logan Farms, no less."

"Logan Farms?" Harrison raised an eyebrow. "Why would an FBI agent be meeting you at the home of Sean's father?"

"Good question. Want to share the ride and find out?"

He seemed to consider it. "It's a tempting offer. But I spend enough time with Logan Aldridge as it is. And to be honest . . . I don't seem to be much good to anyone today."

A shadow of exhaustion passed across his face. Peggy had a sudden impulse to put her arm around him. Instead, she placed the CD-ROM in his hand.

"We'll see about that," she said. "Come on, I'm putting you to work."

They sat in the study—Harrison in his oxblood leather armchair, Peggy on the sofa, pages spread out between them.

"As far as I can tell from a quick read," she said, "Samantha's book concerns a local tribe known as Melungeons. Are you familiar with them?"

"Vaguely," he said. "I believe there's a small community of them nearby?"

"That's correct. I was down there yesterday. Apparently Samantha's been doing field research with them over the past year. They're what's referred to as 'triracial isolates'—a blend of Caucasian, African, and Native American ancestry. There are other theories. Some people think they're Turkish; others, Portuguese . . . all anyone can agree on is that they've been in this part of Tennessee for a very long time."

"Was that the entire scope of her research?"

"Hard to say," she said. "The documents from her assistant—who is not Brandon DuBose—are a complete mess. You'll see the same chapters rewritten from ten different angles. It's like Samantha's a blade of grass trying to find her way up through concrete."

"Take a good look at the roads around here," Harrison said, "and you'll see that the grass often does find a way through. Show me what you mean."

"Take a look." She pointed to a circled passage:

In the early 1600s, the English explorer Stanton Keyes encountered a vibrant settlement on the plateau now known as Avalon Mountain. The inhabitants were described as dark-haired and blue-eyed, living "in thee stile of savage fowlke," as Keyes noted in his journal.

"It seems fairly clear," Harrison said. "Though I'm not sure what her sources are."

"Here's another piece of the puzzle," Peggy said.

General Stallworth's purchase of Avalon Mountain in 1870 was complicated by the arrival of approximately 5,000 "mixed-race squatters" (as described by contemporary press), who claimed ancestral rights to the land as descendants of the "lost" Melungeon colony reportedly discovered by Stanton Keyes. According to records in the Avalon College archives, a quit-claim deed was negotiated in exchange for a grant of sharecropping rights in the area now known as Chillwater Cove . . .

"So now it's 'reportedly discovered,'" Harrison said. "As Samantha suggests, the dispute was resolved amicably. This is the first time I've heard the Melungeon angle, however."

"What do you think happened to all the Melungeons? Five thousand to seventy-five is a pretty significant drop."

"Not considering the length of time involved." He held out his hands. "There could have been intermarriage, migration to the North . . . possibly they simply abandoned their old identities for new ones. 'Passing for white' was a common practice in those days . . . probably still is. The one-drop rule—otherwise known as, 'If you ain't all white, you ain't all right'—is very much in force around here."

Peggy didn't answer right away. She'd heard those very words on her father's lips any number of times.

"So you think they just blended in," she said finally.

"Unless you can produce mass graves—which I dearly hope you won't. I'll check it against the school archives."

She smiled. "Thank you. I know it's a lot of work."

"In a way, it's a chance to share something with my daughter that we never could before." He leaned forward. "But first we have to allow ourselves some refreshment."

"You think?"

"A small sherry? It's practically afternoon."

"You go ahead. I'm driving." She waited. "There's something else I was wondering if you could help me with."

He poured himself a glass from a decanter. "What is it?"

"Do you know anything about the word 'Krypteia'?"

He took a sip. "I think you'll find it's pronounced 'Kryp-tay-uh.' They were the secret police of ancient Sparta."

"Really."

He nodded. "More than any other Greek tribe, the Spartans sought perfection through military discipline. They were also, in a real sense, pioneers of ethnic cleansing. Each year, the Spartan kings ritually declared war on their own slaves—sending their young men out in the dead of night to kill any who seemed capable of leading a rebellion. That was the Krypteia. The name translates as 'Hidden Matters.'"

"And that's all it is? Something ancient?"

"Ancient things have power," he said. "Is there a connection to my daughter?"

"The word seems to frighten the Melungeons. And Samantha was concerned with their welfare." She paused. "Maybe I'm just chasing down shadows. I don't really know."

He leaned back. "To say 'I don't know' is the beginning of all wisdom. But only a beginning. If you want to find answers . . . what is it?"

She couldn't help smiling. "Sorry. I guess I'm waiting for you to pound the table and say, 'Think, Weaver, think.'"

"Well, then—think, Weaver, think. Don't let an old man's ramblings slow you down." He smiled back. "Let me see that fierce young debater who never once failed to pin her opponent to the mat."

"All right. I believe that Samantha's disappearance was carefully planned. Possibly as part of a larger strategy."

"How so?"

"I have an eyewitness," she said. "Not very reliable. But she claims to have seen your daughter leave the house around three A.M . . . in the company of a man in black paramilitary gear. Assuming it's the same man who kidnapped her before . . . he'd be about the right age, as described."

"Described how?"

"Curly gray hair, leathery skin. Mean looking. As I said, I don't know if the witness is reliable. But she did mention a snake on his belt buckle. I don't know how else she could have known about that . . . unless Samantha mentioned it to her."

"Seems unlikely," he said.

"The description was pretty messed up. One minute he was wearing the snake, and the next it was gone. She said it was a silver sword . . . but I distinctly remember it being gold."

"Does it . . . please forgive me for asking . . ."

"It doesn't jog my memory. I've been trying to force myself to picture him. But I still can't see his face."

"Don't worry about it," he said. "Go on."

"Did you ever receive any communication from the kidnapper the first time she was abducted?"

He shook his head slowly. "None."

"I have," she said. "Last night he left me a dead snake, wrapped in her . . ." She stopped.

"Wrapped in what?"

"Underclothes. Very likely the ones she'd been wearing when she was taken as a child." It took all of Peggy's strength to say it.

He looked at her in stunned silence.

"I've been trying not to think about that." She took a breath. "We also found physical evidence on Sammie's computer."

"I'm afraid that's already made its way through the student grapevine." He looked down. "In several gruesome variations."

"I'm sorry. You deserved to hear that from me directly." She exhaled. "It all seems to confirm a connection between the two kidnappings—so I think it's fair to start looking for common patterns. When Samantha was recovered years ago, where did you find her? Was it anywhere close to town?"

"Yes. The town dump." Harrison pinched the bridge of his nose. "You know, I still can't force myself to go there."

"Somewhere on the edge of the community," Peggy said. "But also somewhere she was likely to be found quickly."

"I suppose so. Why?"

"He wanted her to suffer," Peggy said. "But he didn't want her to die. That's significant. In all these years, she's never identified him, so he can't be worried about that. Maybe she has some intrinsic value to him."

"What value?"

"It's either based on what she knows . . . or who she is. If it's the former, then the answer may lie in the pages of her book. But it also can't be ignored that Samantha is the daughter of the outgoing president . . . and the wife of the heir apparent. And she was taken from your house. If you haven't had a message yet, expect one soon."

"An offer to negotiate?"

"That . . . or simply an attempt to torment you." She stood up. "Before I go, do you think I could take a quick look at Samantha's room?"

Harrison nodded thoughtfully. Then the doorbell rang.

"That must be the man from the security company," he said.

"The what?"

He stood up. "Your father seems to think that none of this would have happened if the alarms had worked properly. So he convinced the company to put in a new one for free."

"That was—nice of him."

"For what it's worth. We might as well have had nothing, for all the good it's done." He sighed. "Take as long as you like upstairs."

Peggy went up to Samantha's room, moving the yellow crime-scene tape aside to enter. It was just as she'd seen it the day before—clean and simple and perfect. And yet she had the same nagging feeling that something was out of place. Then Peggy noticed the bed: a corner of the quilt had been tucked underneath the mattress. On an impulse, she pulled it up.

There were no sheets underneath. Just the bare mattress.

Peggy looked at the empty drawers. Her father surmised—as anyone would—that Samantha had taken everything, even her contact lenses. But what had Gretchen said before? *He had her by the wrists, duh. How was she gonna carry a bag?*

She bent down to the three-sided hatch of the laundry chute and stared into darkness.

"Peggy." Harrison stood in the doorway. "The security company's here to install a new system. Will you be all right while I tend to this?"

She nodded. "Harrison, have you or Olivia done any laundry this weekend?"

"No." Then he seemed to understand what she was saying.

"So you haven't been down to the basement?"

He didn't answer.

When they were children, Peggy and Samantha used to dare each other to jump down the laundry chute, but never quite got up the nerve. Only two days before, Sammie told her that Caden had tried to do the very same thing. Something about bottomless hampers, it seemed, was simply too much for children to resist.

As they entered the basement, the first thing Peggy saw was a large bundle of sheets lying at the bottom of the chute.

It wouldn't have seemed out of place to anyone who casually looked down the basement stairs. But as she stepped closer, Peggy noticed that the ends of the sheets had been tied together. Inside were Samantha's clothes, her makeup . . . even a single tennis shoe and ankle sock. And as Peggy took hold of the pile, something clattered down against the washing machine.

A belt buckle.

It was in the shape of a red snake, curled around a sword. Gold paint had long since flaked away from the blade, leaving it a naked silver.

*Mommy godda puppaston'? Ennazoot?*

"In the chute," Peggy whispered.

She looked at Harrison.

"Somehow Caden knew," she said. "He saw."

# TWENTY-TWO

"For chrissakes slow down," Peggy's father was saying into her cell phone. "You're tellin' me my crew didn't do their job?"

"You're not listening." She paced around Harrison's study. "The subject put everything down the chute because he wanted it all to be found. Just not right away. There's a blue tennis shoe, matching the one we found. That's not a coincidence."

"Shoes, socks, panties. What's next? Her brassiere?"

"Dad, Jesus Christ!" She breathed. "I found his belt buckle, okay? Red snake with a silver sword. I think that pretty well decides who it is we're looking for."

"Always thought you said it was gold."

"Well, I guess we both get to be wrong today."

He exhaled. "Look, I promise I'll check it out. But now you just gotta try and stay calm till I get back over that way."

"I can't stay. I'm meeting somebody." She looked at her watch. "In fact, I'm gonna be late."

"Do what you gotta do, I guess."

Something was different in her father's voice. He wasn't exactly being conciliatory. But his back-the-hell-off snarl was definitely in check.

"Dad, it's been twenty-four hours," she said. "You need to know that the case is now officially under FBI jurisdiction. The person I'm on my way to meet . . ."

"Peg. Hang on one second." He paused. "Ain't no point arguin' that we said some hard things to each other lately. Maybe you shouldn't have held those pictures back. And maybe I did miss findin' that belt buckle. But now we gotta leave that aside. You start draggin' other folks in, federals and suchlike, it's gonna be a royal foul-up. They're not gonna care two shits about your friend Samantha. And if you think they're gonna let you run this show—"

"Dad?" She took a breath. "You're right. There's no point arguing. You burned a whole day on this investigation. And you blocked me. And if, God forbid, Samantha dies . . ."

She stopped herself. He didn't speak.

"I'm going to meet with my FBI case agent," she said. "We'll talk about this when I get back."

"Oh, will we?" He paused. "You have fun with your new boss, now. Be sure he knows what a fine memory you got for details."

He hung up before she could answer him.

*Well, you just go to hell, then.* She was a hairbreadth from throwing her cell phone at the fireplace when Harrison walked in.

"Peggy, the man from—are you all right?"

"I'm fine," she said. "What's the matter?"

"The gentleman from the security firm. He's getting a little impatient. You'd asked him to wait . . ."

"I'm so sorry. I'll talk to him now." She stopped at the door. "It is the same belt buckle, isn't it?"

He stared at it. "Unquestionably."

"All those years ago—he said that if I wanted it, I should come and get it." She took it back. "I don't want it."

"Just because he left something behind doesn't mean you've agreed to a bargain." He stopped. "I don't mean to pry. Was that Rusty on the phone just now?"

"Yes. He . . ." She bit her lip. "Sorry. I'm a little stressed."

"You'd need a heart of stone to stay calm right now." He put a hand on her shoulder. "Your father rides you pretty hard, doesn't he?"

"I think he prefers the whip to the bridle. But yeah." She exhaled. "Now I'm wishing I'd had that sherry."

"Have it when you come back," he said. "From the depth of my heart, Peggy. There's no one on earth I'd rather have searching for my daughter right now."

She wanted to thank him. But she couldn't quite bring the words to her lips. Instead, she simply smiled and nodded.

"I'd better see to the security guy." She went into the foyer. "Mr. Tidwell . . . ?"

It wasn't the same person she'd met the day before. That one was fat and pink, as hairless as any baby. And he'd been wearing white. The man in the green SecurTrek coveralls was reed thin, a forelock of dark hair hanging down over his eyebrow.

"Look, I ain't got all day," he said. "You folks positive you need a replacement? 'Cause I can't find a thing wrong."

"Not a thing wrong?" She approached him cautiously. "Did your boss explain what happened here yesterday?"

"Lady, I am the boss, the chief technician, and accounts payable. You got a beef, it ain't goin' to anyone but me."

"Harrison?" She turned to him.

"Another man was here from your company yesterday," Harrison said. "He told me that someone had shorted out the wiring."

"Do what?" He laughed. "Did it say SecurTrek on his uniform?"

Peggy shook her head. "His name is Lester Tidwell."

"Christ. That ole boy's slick as a shithouse mouse." The man rolled his eyes. "I fired Tiny Tidwell two weeks back. Like as not, he's just tryin' to steal my customers."

"But you did talk to Chief Weaver," Harrison said.

He shrugged. "Rusty throws work my way. Figured I owed him a favor by comin' here." He cocked a thumb at the door. "You folks want a new system, or don't you?"

"Let's take a look at the old one first," Peggy said.

# TWENTY-THREE

When Peggy was a child, the country surrounding Logan Farms had all been corn acreage and dairy meadow. At some point, the cattle and John Deeres had given way to McMansions and gated communities. One of the largest and most obnoxious looking insisted on calling itself Mill Creek: even though there was no mill, and—at least as far as Peggy could see—no creek.

"Peg, I've got Yoshi with me on speaker," Mike said on her cell phone. "He's made a partial ID on that GPS tracker."

"What is it?"

"I'd have an easier time telling you what it isn't," Yoshi said. "It's not commercial, it's not military—at least not our military—and it didn't come out of a box of Cracker Jack. If I had to take a guess, I'd say it looks home-made."

"Really."

"A source in the hacker community confirmed it to me on a promise of anonymity. He says it's designed to clone all the data coming in or out of your car's GPS device, and pipe it somewhere else. Where it's going, I can't say—unless you're willing to let me break it open."

"Not just yet. How strong a signal is it putting out?"

"Weak. In fact, that's our best lead. It's not satellite—more likely it's routing data through local cell phone providers. Which means that whoever's tracking you is likely to turn up inside a fifty-mile radius."

"That could be any one of two thousand households in the area," she said. "Can you block the signal without tipping off whoever's listening?"

"Listen, buy me a plane ticket to wherever you are and I'll reroute it through the pope's Yahoo! account."

"Good idea. Mike, can you pick up?"

"Yeah, Peg." He'd taken her off speaker.

"I dunno. What do you think?"

"Awful lot of trouble to go to just to find out where Peggy Weaver buys gas," he said. "But then, Yoshi's rarely wrong about this stuff."

"Think you could spare him to me for a couple of days?"

"That's gonna be a little hairy." He lowered his voice. "The ASAC's start-ing to take an unhealthy interest in our activity logs. Technically we're not supposed to be working this case . . . especially since you're now officially AWOL. Frankly, I think we ought to pull Yoshi back before he hurts his chances for promotion. Kid's got a family to support now."

"What about you? Are you pulling back?"

"I've got nothing to lose. I'm so politically dead around here, my checks get sent to the county morgue." He paused. "Anyway, you're my family. You and that Asian sci-fi geek in the next cubicle."

She smiled. "Thanks, Yeager. I'd say you're like family, too—but the way things are, that might not be a compliment."

"Parents still cracking up?"

"Actually, I think I'm the one who's starting to crack," she said. "The ice princess finally melts."

"Goddamn global warming," he said. "What's your dad's take on all of this?"

"He's not talking to me," she said. "Next time you invest in home secu-rity, make sure you get references. This guy Tidwell is a cipher. He worked for SecurTrek for a few months—but nobody except my father seems to know anything about him."

"And the security system?"

"There's no way the alarm could have been disabled the way Tidwell says. Apparently there's redundant wiring that would automatically pre-vent a power failure. However . . . the owner's pretty sure the front door sensor doesn't belong to the original system. Looks like a patch job."

"So when Tiwdell showed up Sunday morning . . ."

"He could have easily swapped something out to cover his tracks." She exhaled. "My dad was standing there watching him. But now he's sending my calls straight to voice mail."

"You don't think he's covering for this guy, do you?"

"If you'd asked me forty-eight hours ago, I'd have said no way in hell. But from what I've seen lately . . . I just don't know."

They said their good-byes as Peggy turned into the main gate at Logan Farms. Half a mile away, trailers and tents were set up around the stable. She could just make out a few horses being led around the ring.

"Help you?" A dark-suited security officer held up his clipboard, formally polite.

"FBI Special Agent Weaver." She showed her creds. "I'm meeting a colleague."

He nodded and checked a name off. "Go on up to the main house. One of us will park your car for you."

"Thanks." She drove on.

As she reached the house, another dark-suited man—a handsome African American in his twenties—was waiting.

"How do you do?" He held out his hand.

"Fine, thanks." She gave him her car keys. "I'm looking for someone named Randall. Could you please see if he's here?"

"Certainly." He passed the keys to a valet. "Follow me, please."

The young man led her through the vast entrance hall, crowded with Chardonnay-sipping men and women in pastels and seersucker. "Is this your first visit to Logan Farms?"

"I've been here a few times." She didn't feel like telling a security guard that she'd once dated the owner's son. "Is Mr. Aldridge receiving his guests today?"

"As a matter of fact, he's asked to speak to you." He pressed the elevator button. "Will that be acceptable?"

"Certainly. But first . . ." She stopped cold. "Oh, boy. Now I recognize that voice. Special Agent Randall?"

"Guilty as charged." A boyish grin broke across his face. "Sorry, I was going to say something. But when you handed me your keys, I just couldn't resist."

"Guess I'm busted." She could feel her cheeks burning. "You're a lot younger than you sounded on the phone."

"I'm precocious, what can I say." His smile tempered a bit. "In a way, we've already met. The senator's a family friend of ours. He hasn't stopped raving about you since you brought his daughter home."

The brass elevator doors opened. He held them for her.

"How's she doing?"

"I suppose I could quote the official statement and say that she's recovering with her family." He paused while the doors closed. "The truth is, she won't let anyone close to her. The way her mother described it to me, it's as if one child was taken away, and an entirely different one came home."

"It's still the same girl," Peggy said. "Give her time."

The doors opened on the third-floor suite. A duty nurse glanced up at Peggy and Randall as they approached. Logan Aldridge, third richest man in Tennessee, lay on a hospital bed with an oxygen mask over his face and a tube running from beneath his white bathrobe.

"I'll catch up with you in the horse ring," Blaine whispered. "We have a lot to talk over."

The old man watched Peggy with owlish gray eyes. As she approached, a smell of sterile bandages and urine met her nostrils, sharpened by ozone from the respirator.

"Hello, Mr. Aldridge." She smiled, a well-bred Southern girl, and took the hand that was offered to her. He suddenly seized it in an iron grip.

"Gotcha." And Logan Aldridge grinned.

# TWENTY-FOUR

"So nice to have refreshing company for a change," Logan Aldridge said in his dry, rolling voice. "I'm so tired of being picked at by money-lusting relatives and—bedpan artisans."

"You do have a large family, Mr. Aldridge." Peggy looked through the window: a swarm of red-vested car valets zipped in and out of the car barn. "And a lot of room to keep them in."

"Half the folks here today are mine, one way or another," he mused. "As my daddy used to say, 'There ain't enough tits for the piglets.'"

She noticed a stack of papers at his bedside: stock transactions from Morgan Stanley. "So what's the occasion for the auction? Surely you don't need the money?"

"Certain traditions must be honored," he said. "I'll tell you a secret if you promise not to blab." Logan drew himself up in the bed, a scarecrow of the six foot seven giant she'd known since childhood. "I don't intend to leave a penny to any of those leeches. I'm going to bury 'em all. Want to know how?"

"How, Mr. Aldridge?" She rubbed her hand, trying to restore the warmth he'd stolen from it.

"Discipline," he said. "The way it was when I was an Avalon boy. Three-mile runs before daybreak, rain or shine. Then showers, then chapel—*then* morning drills and formation. And then you got a little oatmeal and coffee. That was all *before* eight A.M. classes, you understand. Iron-hard discipline. They used to teach it at Avalon, before you girls came along and softened things up."

"Sorry we had to spoil the party," she said.

"Understand, I'm not talking about you *specifically*." Logan winked.

"You, my dear, are of sterner stock—pure Tennessee yeomanry, hundred proof. Why, I had half a mind to marry you myself when Sean didn't propose."

Peggy earned a sympathetic smile from the nurse.

"Now don't jerk your chin at me, child. Sean's mother was far younger than you are now when first I bedded her. And I put seven babies into that fertile belly. Daresay I could do it now if somebody gave me a chance."

"Mister A.," the duty nurse said. "That's mighty rude of you. Mrs. A.'s gonna be sad up there in Heaven."

"Traditional theology assures us that sorrow is an impossibility in Heaven. Anyhow, I don't plan on joining her there, so what the hell."

"For what it's worth, I think Sean married well," Peggy said. "Have you spoken to him since Samantha disappeared?"

A cold glint stole into his eyes. "What makes you say so?"

"He hasn't used any of his credit cards since Sunday. So either he's dead . . . or he moved back into his old room." She pointed through the window. "Considering that his yellow Hummer's parked in that aircraft hangar you call a garage, I'll vote for not dead."

"I have seen no such vehicle." He looked away, indignant. "Nor, may I say with perfect candor, have I spoken to the boy."

The nurse frowned. "Mister A."

"I damn well *shouted* at him a few times," he said. "Never did see a boy so shit-all dumb as to run off when his wife gets taken. Might as well have 'guilty' tattooed on your behind."

Peggy looked back over her shoulder. "I guess that explains who's been shuffling back and forth behind me for the past two minutes."

"Aw, foot." Logan gestured impatiently. "Boy, cease playing pocket pool with yourself back there. Come up and show some manners to the girl."

Peggy turned as Sean Aldridge stepped from the shadows.

She never told anyone—not Samantha, and definitely not Mike—but Sean had been her first lover. She often considered that he might ultimately be her best. Sometimes she had to work very hard to remind herself what a rat he was.

"Hello, Peg." Sean wasn't as tall as his father . . . but he was damned good looking, naturally athletic without having to work at it. The dealer's gleam in his gray eyes absolutely marked him as an Aldridge. "Papa told me that—"

His sentence was cut short as Peggy slapped him hard across the face.

"Where the hell have you been?" She was as surprised as he was by the rage in her voice.

"Christ Almighty, Peg." He took a step back.

"Your wife's gone. Your two-year-old son's scared out of his mind . . . probably wondering where his father is. And the whole time you're *here*?"

Out of the corner of her eye, Peggy saw Logan smile.

"I know my wife's been abducted, dammit." Sean rubbed his jaw. "I've been trying to do something about it. You don't have to slap me."

"Slap you? I should break you in half." She shook her head. "What's your idea of doing something? Calling a lawyer? Mixing martinis?"

"Told you not to expect a kiss." Logan cackled. "Peggy Jean, it is good to know all that soft city life hasn't leached the spitfire from your blood."

She flexed her hand. "Sean Parker Aldridge, you've got ten seconds to convince me you're not a total slimeball. Then I Mirandize you for unlawful flight to avoid prosecution."

"Peggy, that's not fair," he whimpered. "This happened to me as much as—"

"Nine. Eight. Seven." She waited. "You were saying?"

He slumped down into a chair. "All right. When I got the news, I panicked. I flat-fuck ran. But the first thing I did when I got here was have someone call to make sure Caden was all right. I couldn't do more than that without jeopardizing Samantha's safety." He turned to his father. "Is she listening to me, or is she still counting down?"

"You 'had' someone call?" she asked quietly.

"Let me back up. I'd been worried about Samantha for weeks. She'd been . . . not her old self lately."

She nodded. "Is that why you asked my father to put a trap-and-trace on her calls?"

"I got suspicious. Sammie's been spending time with strange characters. She gives them money—she's way too close to that woman and her son . . ."

"Just tell her the truth," Logan said. "Sammie's been rutting that young Covite buck, Elias Collins."

Sean winced. For several seconds, the only sound was the beep of Logan Aldridge's heart monitor. It never rose above sixty-five.

Peggy finally broke the silence. "Sean?"

"She'd promised me it was over," he said. "Then Papa convinced me to hire a private detective. So we have pictures." He looked away. "Harrison and Olivia don't know."

"Did you tell my father?"

"What do I say to her?" he asked Logan.

"Son, you're the pride of my loins, and before God I love you. But you're nutless." Logan looked at Peggy. "We told Rusty straight out. He's chief of police, isn't he?"

"Thank you," Peggy said. "I'll try this again, Sean. Where were you at the time of your wife's disappearance?"

"Getting drunk." He exhaled. "And yes, before you ask, I do blame myself. If I'd tried just a little harder to get her to come home . . . instead of slamming beers and eye-balling barmaids when my wife needed me most . . ."

"Where did you go drinking?"

He hesitated slightly. "The Double-D."

"Well, I don't know about the barmaids. But the Double-D closes at two A.M. And Samantha was abducted just after three." She paused. "So?"

Sean looked away. "I wasn't alone."

"Uh-huh. Is the other party willing to corroborate that?"

His head hung down. "She already has."

"We've been through all of this with your compatriot from the FBI," Logan said. "I got him involved the instant Sean came to me. So just you leave off from arresting my son. And let's put our heads onto bringing Samantha home."

She looked at Logan. "When did you first speak to Agent Randall?"

"Five thirty A.M. Sunday morning." Blaine had entered the room and took his place at Logan's bedside. "I advised Sean to lie low. And I can promise you that no laws were broken."

"No kidding," Peggy said. "Didn't you just promise me that you'd wait down at the horse ring?"

Blaine gave a thin smile.

"Sounds like a plan," he said. "Let's go."

The auction was nearly over by the time Peggy and Blaine reached the stable. But it seemed that they'd saved the best horses for last. A gorgeous perlino mare snapped her amber mane with quiet grace as she flat-walked around the ring, led by a chain-smoking trainer in mottled leathers.

"Are you familiar with Tennessee Walking Horses?" Blaine folded his hands across the rail. "I guess you must be. I can't get enough of them. Those babies don't just walk. They damn well strut."

"I know enough about Tennessee Walkers," she said. "What I'd like to know was why I had to drive all the way here just to find out that you're covering for Sean Aldridge."

"Some things need to be discussed in person," he said. "Logan warned me that you weren't much for small talk, so I'll be frank. I spoke to your boss in Philadelphia. You can work the case as an adviser to the Chattanooga resident agency—under my direct supervision."

"And if that's not acceptable?"

"Oh, I think it is. For one thing, it'll spare you the embarrassment of having to explain why members of your team are working on those Storytime Academy pictures—photographs that, for whatever reason, you chose to withhold from the proper authorities."

Peggy drew back. When she first met him, Blaine had seemed like a lightweight—the kind of agent who inevitably settled into Administration or PR. Now that she could hear the well-honed edge in his voice, she found him mildly unsettling.

"You're smiling," Blaine said. "Did I accidentally say something funny?"

"Not really. It's just that my father warned me something like this might happen."

"It's my party, Agent Weaver. Chattanooga is office of origin for this investigation. And the Aldridges are important people. I don't intend to let it all go south because you had an argument with your father." He shrugged. "Call the senator if think you can get a better deal without me. Maybe it's not too late for that job at the Inspector General's office."

He reached out to stroke the horse's flanks as it was led past him. The mare reared her head and continued on, taking each step in a brisk, sweeping arc. The horse was perfect, all right—except for the dark hairs on her pasterns, she was as close to pure white as a young perlino could get.

"That one won't go today for less than ten thousand." He smiled wistfully. "If I only had a couple more zeroes on my paycheck . . . maybe next year."

"Blaine, I grew up around these people. The money doesn't impress me. Nor do you—if I may also be frank?"

"Something tells me I don't have a choice."

"Protecting the Aldridges and protecting Samantha are not the same thing," Peggy said. "What have you got?"

"Hm?"

"They wouldn't call you in without asking you to hide something. You put what you have on the table, and then we'll see about your 'information dump.'"

"Considering that I'm the case agent," he said, "I think it's appropriate that you go first."

"Fine. At this point I have the photographs. I've got a witness to the kidnapping. I have a partial profile on the unsub. And I'm accumulating evidence that suggests the alarm system at the Stallworth home may have been selectively tampered with. What have you got?"

He didn't answer.

"Shall I go on?" she asked. "I got a little suspicious when you were so quick to green-light warrants on Sean without even bothering to ask why I needed them. So I figured I'd see what kind of money his father's been moving around."

Blaine's eyes widened slightly.

"Don't worry, it all came through public channels," she said. "I just wonder why Tennessee's most notorious tightwad decided to liquidate close to two million dollars' worth of assets right after this morning's opening bell. Why the sudden need for cash?"

"I can't answer that," Blaine said. "Not without the family's permission."

"I guess I'll have to keep digging, then. Maybe I'll even find out why Sean decided to call you directly, instead of the local FBI office at Winchester." She pointed to the stable. "Somebody just bought your horse."

For the first time since she laid eyes on him, Agent Randall's practiced calm seemed to waver.

"We've received a communication," he said.

# TWENTY-FIVE

As she and Blaine returned to the third floor, Logan Aldridge was in the process of receiving a pint of blood. Sean sat at the foot of his father's bed.

"Pried it out of you, didn't she?" The old man gave a dry laugh. "Peggy, my Peggy, where have you been all these years? We could have had *fun* on this bed if I wasn't dying in it."

"I'm going to show her the message." Blaine picked up the BlackBerry and held it to Peggy. She looked it over in silence. There was no salutation or subject line to the e-mail, and the return address was only a meaningless string of symbols.

```
HERE ARE THE PROTCOLS
$1,6M BY WIRE TRANSFER BEFORE 0900 WED
GET IT FROM HER RICH DADDY
DETAILS TO FOLLOW
DO NOT INVOLVE AUTHORIES OR "FEDS"
DO NOT ATTEMPT TO TRACE THIS OR ANY OTHER COMM
DONT CATCH A CASE OF THE DUMBASS
OR YOU GET HER BACK IN A BOX
AND YOURE STUCK RAISING A REAL MANS BABY
AMF
```

"We've been running matches on that signature line," Blaine said. "There's approximately nine thousand organizations and individuals in the region with the initials AMF."

"There's another message here." Peggy tabbed down. It read, simply,

KRYPTEIA IS COMING

"We don't know what that means, either," Blaine said. "But maybe now you can see why I had to be so discreet."

Peggy looked at Sean. "I noticed you received these at . . . four forty-five A.M. Sunday morning."

He nodded. "And that's how I found out my wife was kidnapped."

"I guess I can take it for granted," she said, "that no one outside this room knows about this? Not my dad, or . . . Samantha's parents?"

"I didn't get this old by being stupid," Logan said. "Harrison doesn't have a million and a half. What's he going do except cry and quote Socrates at us?"

"And my father?"

"I advised them not to," Blaine said. "Based on the warning in the note . . ."

"You know as well as I do that your daddy would only screw the pooch," Logan said. "I'm willing to bet he already has."

She took out her cell phone and started dialing.

"What are you—" Blaine reached for the BlackBerry.

"Shh." She waited. "Miss Matilda, it's Peggy. Can you please send a patrol car to Logan Farms? We need to book Sean Aldridge on a charge of withholding evidence, and—hang on a second." She looked up from the phone. "Sean, are you planning to resist arrest?"

He didn't answer.

"He seems harmless," she said. "With all the security problems at the Avalon lockup, I'd recommend booking him at the sheriff's department. But it's your call."

She closed the phone. Sean and Blaine stood horrified.

"Peggy Jean Weaver. What kind of stunt—?" The blood in Logan's bag seemed ready to boil.

"Your son is going to jail, Mr. Aldridge. And if he makes any further attempt to evade arrest, he'll be in violation of federal law. Regardless of whatever promises Agent Randall's made, I assure you that charge will be prosecuted."

"That's an empty gesture," Blaine said.

"Actually, it's the law." She handed the BlackBerry to him. "As you say, my father's the Avalon police chief. And I think he needs to know what's been happening in his own backyard."

She didn't wait to be shown out.

# TWENTY-SIX

Peggy stood out front until the police cruiser left with Sean in the back. As she waited for her Jeep, she couldn't help noticing that one of the black-suited security guards was watching her.

"Officer Ripley," she said. "You've had a lot of people looking for you."

"Just plain Ripley now, I guess." He tugged at his collar. "Mr. Aldridge always said to call if I needed work. And I do."

"How do you like the new job?"

"Supervisor's kind of a dick." He shifted nervously. "Did you see the . . . y'know, what I left for the chief?"

"Yeah. I saw it."

"And?"

"You did the right thing," she said. "If you want to know the truth, I think you called my bluff."

"Well, you kinda called mine first." He smiled. "They're payin' me more'n the town did."

"That's the private sector for you." Peggy handed a tip to the valet. "Ripley, have you ever heard my father mention a guy named Tidwell? Used to work for a home security company?"

He shook his head. "Tiny, you mean? He's a caution, ain't he? I guess I won't get in trouble talkin' about him now."

"Trouble for what?"

"The boys call him your dad's White Shadow. 'Cause he always wears white. And we've been warned to keep quiet about him." He opened the driver's-side door for her. "Tiny does favors for us sometimes. Like, whenever we need surveillance . . ."

"Really."

He nodded. "He's got some shit in that garage, I tell ya. Thought all the electronics was gonna make me sterile. I figure that's how come Tidwell's bald as a cueball."

She'd been resting her hand on the steering wheel, but now she took it away. "You know, I really don't think this Jeep's going to make it to town. Think you could help me find a cab?"

"Well, there ain't no taxi to speak of since Joad Washburn wrapped his Oldsmobile 'round a tree." He thought a moment. "But if you can wait, I'm about to go on lunch. I could run you into town myself."

Peggy considered her options. She could try to reach her father. She could ask Harrison to come get her. But she wasn't getting any help from the Aldridges. And she wasn't getting back into that Jeep.

"I'll figure something out," she said. "I don't want you landing in trouble on your first day."

"Agent Weaver." He set his hands on his hips. "Last night I had to tell my mama about what I did to the Collins boy. It was hard. And she wasn't too happy. But she reckons you gave me a chance to save my soul. And I wouldn't be much of a Christian if I didn't at least offer you a ride."

She handed the keys back to the valet.

"Then I guess I'd better say yes." She smiled. "For your mother's sake."

"I'll go clock out." He walked back to the gatehouse.

As the valet took her Jeep away, Peggy noticed two men trying to lead the perlino up into a horse trailer. But the mare didn't seem to want to go in. She was favoring her front legs—possibly because of the uneven surface. The men were gentle with her but clearly perplexed.

"She's a wild young thing," one of them said.

"Skittish," answered his companion. "Where's that trainer of hers?"

The trainer showed up a moment later. He silently took off his gloves to stroke her with two liver-spotted hands, then leaned in and whispered into her ear. The mare instantly calmed down and allowed herself to be guided in.

"Gonna have to show us how you did that!" The perlino's new owner slapped him on the back. "Man's a goddamn magician."

"Wish my wife was that easy to manage," the other said.

The trainer smiled shyly at Peggy as he replaced his gloves—then jumped, startled, as the doors of the trailer were slammed shut. Peggy almost jumped herself as she felt fingers tapping her shoulder.

"Where to, ma'am?" Ripley was back.

"I'll tell you on the way." As she followed Ripley to the staff garage, Peggy looked back at the old trainer. He stood alone, watching his mare disappear down the long driveway. Peggy thought he looked very lost indeed.

# TWENTY-SEVEN

"Damn." Peggy shut her cell phone.

"Still can't get through to your friend?" Ripley asked from the driver's seat of his Dodge Ram.

She shook her head. It was one thing for Mike not to answer his desk phone—he hated to sit still—and something else entirely for him to ignore his cell, especially if her name was on the display. Yoshi wasn't picking up either. She wondered if Agent Randall might have placed a few calls after her departure.

"I guess they're in meetings." She checked the map on her handheld. "Okay, make the next right."

"I think that computer's lyin' to ya," he said. "This ain't the right way to Tiny's."

"We're not going that way," she said.

"You don't mean..." He brightened. "Goddamn. We're chargin' in hard, ain't we? Shit, where's my pump gun?"

"Listen to me," she said. "You want to learn about investigation?"

"Yes, ma'am. Very much so."

"Stop here." She waited for him to pull over. "First rule of hostage recovery is that you never just 'charge in.' Not unless you know exactly what's waiting for you inside. And not without plenty of backup. Otherwise you could get people killed ... and maybe yourself in the bargain. Got it?"

He nodded. "Yes'm."

"Ninety percent of the job is about getting information. And that's all we're here for. Information."

"If that's so ..." He pointed to the rise of ground ahead. "How come we're approachin' Tidwell's property from the woods?"

She checked her ammunition. "Why do you think?"

"You don't have a warrant," he said.

"Yeah. And?"

"And you don't want Tiny keepin' you at the gate." He gave a conspiratorial smile. "But if we come this way . . . over county land . . . we might get close enough to overhear a crime in progress? Maybe go in on reasonable suspicion?"

"Stranger things have been known to happen." She climbed down. "But this is where you and I part company. You don't want to be late from lunch on your first day."

"Uh-uh. Ain't fallin' for that one again." He took the key from the ignition. "If you're willin' to hump half a mile through weeds just to avoid bein' seen, then you're gonna need a wingman. So either I come with you, or you don't go."

"That's the way it is, huh?"

"Yes, ma'am." He smiled. "And I'll tell you something else. You're a federal agent. You gotta worry about standin' before a judge. But me?" He tapped his chest. "I'm just some shitkicker who used to work for the Avalon Police. And I've been known to kick up reasonable suspicion now and again."

"In that case, lose the coat and tie." She set off around the base of the hill. "And for God's sake start calling me Agent Weaver. Or Peggy. And save 'Ma'am' for the queen of England."

Tidwell's log cabin faced the creek. It looked like he'd spent a lot of money trying to make it look down home and traditional. His glassed-in porch and heat pump tended to spoil the effect. Three flagpoles stood high in his front yard: The Confederate battle flag in the center waved just a few feet higher than the U.S. and POW/MIA flags to either side. A white van was parked alone near a corrugated metal workshop. The barbed wire surrounding Tidwell's property didn't concern her. The wireless sensor network did.

"It'll be better if we can get him to come out," Peggy whispered. "Wait for my signal—then, on a slow count of three, trigger one of those sensor nodes." She pointed to the line of thin green tubes, nearly hidden in the tall grass. "Throw something big."

"Sure, but—can I ask why we're goin' to this much trouble? I mean, Tiny's weird but he ain't scary."

Peggy looked at the workshop. The windows were covered with tinfoil.

"I've got my reasons," she said. "Let's go."

She high-crawled to the fence line, working her way to the side of the cabin: There were no windows on that end, making it a safer approach. She noticed how, even though it was a dry seventy degrees outside, the heat pump's fan was working full blast. As Peggy slipped off her shell jacket, she suddenly thought of a way to bring Tidwell out.

The sensors were definitely a problem. They appeared to be infrared, both proximity and motion sensitive. They'd almost certainly pick up anything bigger than a falling leaf. Her best bet was to time her movements to whatever distraction Ripley created—hoping that her own signal would be lost in the resulting sensor spike.

She spat on the barbed wire fence. It didn't smoke, so at least she wouldn't electrocute herself. Then she looked down at the creek, using her watch face to reflect sunlight in Ripley's direction. *Three, two, one . . .*

A poplar branch came flying out of the brush, landing on the far side of the fence. At that same instant, Peggy threw her jacket on top of the barbed wire and leaped across. She landed, rolled, and hot-footed it to the side of the house. A video surveillance camera, hidden in the rain gutter, turned its red eye to the tree branch. It held for only a moment before angling itself back to a wide view of the yard. As it did, Peggy pulled up an iron garden stake and wedged it through the grating of the heat pump's fan. It jammed against the blade. The motor strained for a moment, then cut out. Peggy pressed her ear against the logs, hearing footsteps inside the cabin.

"Somethin's goin' on here." It was Tiny's high-pitched rasp. The back door opened, but her view of him was blocked. "Hope to God nobody followed you—"

Tidwell came round the corner, nose-to-muzzle with Peggy's Glock. He froze.

She put a finger to her lips.

"Looks like we're fine!" Tidwell called out. "Just threw a breaker, that's all."

A second pair of steps was approaching on the wooden deck: a long, off-rhythm shuffle that she recognized at once.

"Ah, bullshit." Her father's voice. "Tiny?"

"Oh, boy." She put the weapon down. "Dad, it's me."

It was Ripley who came round the corner first—hands raised—followed by her father, holding his .38 muzzle-down.

"Mexican standoff," Rusty said to her. "You and I just can't stay on the same side of the law, can we?"

# TWENTY-EIGHT

The strain of removing the iron garden stake seemed to exhaust all of Tidwell's strength, and sweat beaded his bald head as he reset the circuit breaker.

"Your boy here was makin' enough noise to wake Nicodemus." Rusty idly nodded in Ripley's direction. "If I was hostile, I coulda taken you both out before you got off a round."

She glanced up. "Lucky for me you're not hostile, then."

Rusty laughed. Tiny breathed a sigh of relief as the fan kicked back into action.

"I think we're gonna be okay." A loose smile broke across Tidwell's face, as if the air conditioner was everybody's first concern. "We can go back inside now."

"We ain't goin' back in just yet." Rusty leaned on the wall. "I was freezin' my butt off in there. And I think my daughter and her little friend were just fixin' to leave." He glowered at Peggy. "Why the hell are you here, anyhow?"

"I was about to ask you the same question," she said.

"You mean, why didn't I take the bait and go flyin' off to the Aldridge place when I heard how you booked Sean?" He shared a grin with Tidwell. "And kids think we don't understand them."

"You coulda rung the bell." Tidwell mopped his forehead. "I like visitors."

"We need to talk," she said to her father.

"We might." Rusty looked to his side. "You still here, Rip? Thought you had a new boss to answer to."

"I'm not leavin' her alone here." He paused. "Sir."

She waved him off. "Ripley, it's okay."

"You know, Peg, I think he might be sweet on you." Her father faced him, cool and quiet. "Glad I got the chance to reply to your resignation in person, Rip."

"Yeah? What did you want to say?"

"Nothin'." Quick as wildfire, her father reared back and struck Ripley hard in the solar plexus. The boy dropped like a load of cordwood.

"Dad!"

"Your resignation's accepted." Rusty rubbed his hand. "Now stay the hell away from me, hear? And my family."

Ripley crawled away, scarcely breathing.

"Well, I guess I better go in." Tidwell tried to smile. "I'm burnin' up out here."

Tidwell went inside. Peggy tried to help Ripley up, but he pushed her away.

"Don't give him—satisfaction." Ripley stood up and staggered back down to the creek path. A chill light shone in Rusty's eyes as Peggy stared her father down.

"What the hell did you do that for?"

"He got off cheap," Rusty said. "That boy's responsible for a lot of mischief. Shoulda broke his jaw for him."

"He could have kicked the crap out of you. He's half your age and twice your size."

"He's a coward." Rusty looked at her. "I guess I can thank you for showing me that."

"You never pay attention to things I actually want you to hear," she said. "Now I'm starting to wonder why I fucking bother."

"Takes more to be smart than a smart mouth." He stretched. "So this ransom note. What'd it say?"

She took a breath. "It's what it didn't say that matters. Sean told me it was how he found out his wife had been kidnapped . . . but the note doesn't mention that. It doesn't even say she's missing. It's not like any first communication I've ever seen."

"You think Aldridge made it up?"

"Well, he's hiding something—but considering how embarrassing that note is to him, probably not. It seems to imply that Sean isn't Caden's natural father."

"Oh, right. That." Rusty nodded. "I guess Old Man Aldridge musta got 'round to tellin' you who your friend's been spreadin' her legs for."

She stared at him. He smiled back.

"It also mentions Krypteia," she said. "'Krypteia is coming.'"

He turned away. "So is Jesus. So what?"

"You know what? I'm done talking to you." She passed him on the way to the door. "Your friend Tiny's about to be arrested for tampering with the Stallworths' alarm system. So you'd better back off—"

He yanked her arm away before it could reach the doorknob. His grip was tight, desperate.

"Dad," she said. "Daddy, you're hurting me."

He quickly released her. "Sorry."

"Don't ever do that again," she said simply.

He looked away. "You . . . really think he tampered with it?"

"You know he did. Or else you wouldn't be here right now."

"Maybe." He waved, crestfallen. "All right. Let's—go in and talk to him."

"You go first," she said.

"I'm so sorry, honey." He opened the door. She didn't answer. Peggy waited for the door to close behind him. Then her hand sought the place where he'd grabbed her.

It was fifty-four degrees inside by the thermostat, cold enough to raise condensation on the storm windows. Old magazines were stacked in Tidwell's bookcases like prized heirlooms. A series of computer monitors showed video readouts of the house and property. The walls were covered with paint-by-numbers reproductions of famous Civil War battles—all of them Rebel victories, Peggy noted.

"—how she spiked that infra-red," Tiny was saying from the great room. "Oh, Miss Weaver. I was just tellin' your daddy how impressed I was by the way you spiked the readout on my wireless sensors. I gotta make sure to refine the output so that don't happen again."

"You all right?" Rusty looked up at her from the sofa.

"Don't mind me." Her eyes lit on a portrait of Lycurgus Stallworth, CSA. It appeared to be a copy of the oil painting in Harrison's library. In the original, she recalled, the general held a Bible in his lap. In Tidwell's version, he cradled a bronze sword.

"You like that?" Tiny asked. "Took me near about a month just to get his eyes right. You know, his men always said one look into General Stallworth's eyes was enough to banish all fear—except of the Old Wolf himself." He laughed. " 'Course, his greatest hour was right around here, near Shagbark Ravine—one thousand Tennessee boys against ten times that many Yankees. But the general knew his history, so he kind of re-created the ancient battle of Thermopylae, when the Spartans—"

"The who?" Peggy asked.

"The Spartans. In the, um. Persian war."

"This ain't a Sons of Confederate Veterans meetin', Tiny." Rusty cleared his throat. "Explain to my daughter about that business at the Stallworth house."

"Well, of course I'm sorry about the whole misunderstanding." He looked at Peggy. "I never meant to give anybody the idea I was workin' for SecurTrek when I wasn't. But when I installed the system a few weeks ago, I was short a couple parts. So I guess I might've—cut a few corners, as you'd say. I thought I'd come by in a day or two and finish. But then Jimmy Stokes up and fired me."

She held his gaze. "You are aware, Mr. Tidwell, that what you told me and my father on Sunday is not possible, given the capabilities of the system. You can't crash the transformer by shorting out the warning lights."

Tiny frowned. "All due respect, miss. If Stokes told you that, he's wrong. The redundant wiring—" Something buzzed in his pocket. "That's my pager. I'm supposed to be at a job at Cliffside Condos right now. Mind if I return this?"

"Call 'em back," Rusty said.

"I'll put it on silent." He pushed a button, then slipped it back into his vest pocket. "What was I sayin'?"

"Some of the parts in the Stallworths' system appear to be homemade," Peggy said. "Was that your doing, Mr. Tidwell?"

"I'd prefer you said 'custom built.'" He sniffed. "I do fashion my own parts sometimes."

"Really? Like surveillance equipment, possibly?"

"You'd need to ask your daddy about that." Tiny's eyes darted away. "Rusty, how many years have I been doin' work for you? And not askin' a penny for it?"

"A long time," her father answered.

"And in all those years, have I ever once lied to you or cheated you? Or in any small way let you down?"

He thought a moment. "Not that I know, Tiny."

"Well, then, I think I'm entitled to a little trust now. I'm sorry about what happened at the Stallworths'. Maybe I did miss somethin' on that front door sensor, but that's just not a criminal act."

Rusty looked up at his daughter. "You satisfied?"

Her eyes were fixed on Tidwell's forehead. Fifty-four degrees and the guy was sweating bullets.

"Why do you have tinfoil on your workshop windows?" she asked.

"Hah?"

"You don't have any neighbors. And your property's fenced in. What are you afraid people will see?"

He blushed. "Now listen. I don't have to explain that to you. No laws that I know of against blackin' out windows."

"Well, then, I guess you won't mind if we take a peek."

"You women make me insane." Tidwell looked to her father. "Rusty, for God's sake. Can you please make her shut up?"

"Maybe the best way to shut my daughter up," he said, "is to show her that you got nothin' to hide."

"But you don't have a search warrant."

Rusty raised his eyebrows. "Didn't you just now get done tellin' me how much we *trust* each other, Tiny?"

Tiny pursed his lip. "All right, then. A *quick* look. But then I gotta run or I'm gonna get fired again."

He led them outside. Peggy shivered as she came back into warm air. Her arm—her firing arm—still ached a little.

Tidwell looked nervously over his shoulder. "I have to tell you, Russ, I take this a mite personal. All the good work I done for you—and not a penny asked, nor a penny paid. Didn't I just come out on a Sunday mornin' and help you with that transmitter, so you could spy on them Covites? Did I say, 'Sorry, Rusty, Lord's Day'? No sir, I did not."

"Well, I know that is a big deal for you, Tiny. Seein' how much you love Jesus and all."

Tidwell stopped in front of the workshop door. "I'll unlock this door on one condition. You gotta promise not to tell anybody. I mean it. It's kinda embarrassing to me."

Rusty breathed. "Open the goddamn door."

He unlocked the door. "It's just that I been so lonely out here."

The proportions of the darkened workshop didn't seem much like the room in the cold-case photos. But power tools were hanging from the walls, and electronic parts were scattered around the room. And the form of a naked woman, pale and dark haired, was lying supine on a work-table.

Peggy's hand touched her weapon. Then the lights came on.

"Her name's Suki," Tiny said in a voice filled with tender shame. "She came to me a week ago. Cost me ten grand, not counting overseas shipping."

The figure on the table wasn't moving or breathing—and with good reason, Peggy realized as she prodded the doll's synthetic skin. What she touched gave like flesh, but wasn't: more like the soft, slippery texture of a gummi bear. Its features were big-eyed Japanese animé, its lips gaping in an open-mouthed smile. The breasts were cartoonishly huge. Peggy tried not to blush as she realized the doll was anatomically accurate in every respect . . . right down to the last hair.

"I know she ain't as good as real," Tiny said. "But a fella in my place ain't got much choice. Hookers is too filthy, and regular gals—"

"Jesus Fucking Christ, Tidwell. Thought I'd seen everything." Rusty shook his head. "Peg?"

"He's not lying." She picked up an invoice. "He really did pay ten thousand dollars for this hunk of plastic."

"Her name. Is. Suki." Tidwell brooded. "Okay, now you know. And you've both had your laugh. And I think you better leave. I got stuff to do."

"I just bet you do," Rusty said. "Tell me one thing, Tiny. How'd you know it was the front door sensor that went out at the Stallworth place?"

Tidwell blinked. "Your, ah, daughter. She said."

"No, I didn't," Peggy answered. "Not to you."

"On Sunday you told me the whole system crashed," Rusty said. "And now it's only the front door?"

"Your girl just now talked about custom sensors. Right?" Tiny's voice pitched higher. "Well, I put one of 'em in the front. And the rest was on the upstairs windows. So by process of elimination, I just kinda figured—"

Rusty held up his hands. "Okay, Tiny. I was just askin'. That sounds logical to me."

"Yeah?" Tiny still looked nervous.

"Dad?"

"Let's head on back to town, and let the lady get her beauty sleep." Rusty chuckled. "Lord knows she's got a hard night ahead of her."

Rusty turned to the door, briefly leaving his back to Tidwell. As he did, Tiny reached into a drawer and pulled out a Walther 9 mm.

"Dad, he's armed!"

She'd already drawn. Before she could aim, Rusty had swung around, grappling for the weapon. The Walther went off with a loud report. Tiny screamed.

"Omigod, no! Please, no!"

He fired again, a wild shot. Peggy felt the round whistle past her head. Tiny threw his weight against her father, driving his knee straight into Rusty's bad leg. Rusty fell to the ground like a sack of cement.

"He's getting away." She crawled to him. "Can you move?"

Rusty's face was blotched white, turning to red. He shook his head quickly. "You'll have to—take him." He gasped, clutching his leg. "For chrissakes, be careful."

Tiny had run through the open door. Her first instinct was to give chase—but he could easily be waiting in ambush. Instead she took off for the loading doors at the far end of the workshop. As she passed the table, she saw what made Tiny scream. Suki's head had been blown off.

She pushed the rolling metal doors up, hearing the engine of Tidwell's van roar into life. Peggy stepped into its path. Tiny gunned the engine, a look of insane panic in his eyes.

She calmly fired two shots at his tires. The van skidded in the dirt, then began to pitch. It bounced end over end, throwing off metal shards. She jumped out of its path. Finally it came to a stop, clouds of dust settling around it.

"Tidwell?" Peggy circled the vehicle, aiming her weapon two-handed. "Put your weapon down slowly. I'm giving you one warning—"

The windshield shattered as Tidwell fired. Peggy ducked and returned fire. Then he leapt from the vehicle—a pale, bald man in blood-streaked white coveralls, screaming like an animal. He knocked her to the ground before she could pivot away.

Tidwell stood over her. A drop of his sweat landed on her cheek.

"Don't do it." She aimed between his eyes.

The gun wavered in his hand. A moment later, it jerked away as blood burst through his right forearm. He fell to the ground beside Peggy, writhing like a fat snake.

Peggy looked up to see her father leaning against the open door of the workshop, breathing heavily. The .38 was smoking in his right hand.

"My arm." Droplets of Tidwell's blood merged with the dirt. Tiny was whimpering, his breath quick and shallow. Peggy checked herself for wounds. Then she stood up.

"Dammit, Dad," she said. "He was about to drop the gun. I had him."

Rusty simply stared at her, dazed.

"I woulda let her go." Tiny's white face was caked with dirt. "My fuck-ing *arm.*"

"Shut up, Tiny. It coulda been lower." Rusty hobbled over to them. His face tightened as he bent down to retrieve the pager from Tidwell's pocket. "Ah, Christ."

She took it from him. The text message read, simply,

```
THEYRE ONTO YOU
SHUT THE FUCK UP OR DIE
```

"Guess that's not from Cliffside Condos," Peggy said.

"Guess not," her father answered.

# TWENTY-NINE

"Now I gotta give this girl a hug."

Peggy remembered Sheriff Corey Powell as a good-natured, slightly goofy presence at family barbecues. He had a white beard and light brown hair: once, when she was very young, Peggy embarrassed herself by confusing him with Kenny Rogers. Thirty years later, he still boomed with laughter whenever anyone—usually the sheriff himself—mentioned the incident.

"We are all so proud of you." Powell put an arm around Peggy as she came through the metal detector at Keyes County Sheriff's Department. "It's gotta feel like Old Home Week for you, bein' back here."

"It's been a week, all right." Peggy smiled wearily. "I really appreciate your hosting the meeting. With everyone getting involved, it just wasn't going to happen anywhere else."

"No problem." He nodded soberly. "And don't you worry about Miss Samantha, now. We'll have her home for supper."

"Thanks, Sheriff. You don't know—"

"Hold that thought, darlin'." He whistled to the desk deputy. "Now who let this psych-io maniac through security?"

Powell strode over and slapped Rusty on the back. Her father, who had been silent and sour faced all the way to the station, at once broke into a wide grin.

"Shit on a brick, Powell. Ain't they caught you for bribery and corruption yet?"

"Rusty, you know it ain't bribery if the check bounces." They shared a laugh.

"Dad." Peggy retrieved her bag from the X-ray machine. "Can you hurry through, please? Everyone's waiting."

"Guess I been told." Rusty removed his gun belt, then dropped his keys and loose change into the basket. As he stepped through, the metal detector let out an electronic squeal. "Dammit, Corey, when's this thing gonna learn not to go batshit every time I put my messed-up leg through it?"

"Now, Rusty, you can't blame it for thinkin' you're a deadly weapon." He smiled. "But you listen to Peggy, now. We gotta move. Team Aldridge came out in force today."

Rusty gathered his belongings. "That old fart's here? Didn't see no hearse parked out front."

"It's the young fart, actually. That lawyer of his was waitin' on Sean with a bail bond the moment Dennis brought him in." He chuckled. "Even gave the boy a change of clothes."

"We gotta get our ducks in a row," he said. "Peg."

"Yeah?"

"Go let 'em know Powell and I'll be there directly."

"Actually, I think I'll check on Tidwell," she said. "With your permission, Sheriff?"

Powell pointed down the hall. "He's in the infirmary."

Rusty didn't say another word until she was around the corner.


**Peggy signed in at the** infirmary. A plain yellow folder marked TIDWELL sat in the hanging tray beside the door.

"Is this the entire file?" she asked the deputy on guard, a stout young woman. "Looks pretty slim. Where'd you pull it from?"

"We didn't pull that file," she answered. "We had to make a new one. Just now today."

Peggy studied its single page in silence. "Yikes."

"Kinda sorry, ain't it?" the deputy asked. "I'll need to check your weapon in, ma'am."

She handed it over and went inside.

Lester Tidwell had exchanged his trademark white coveralls for county orange. The right sleeve of his jumpsuit had been cut away to make room for a brace. Tiny sat back on his narrow bed, watching the saline drip into his arm.

"I need painkillers." Tidwell didn't look at her. "All I get is Motrin. Make 'em give me something."

"I think you're better off hearing this wide awake," she said. "You're under arrest for attempted homicide of a federal agent and assault of a police officer. By the end of the day, I predict we'll be adding accessory to kidnapping to the list. And that's capital. I wouldn't expect too much from the air conditioners on death row."

"My heat sensitivity is a medical condition." He looked at her dimly. "Anyhow, I ain't scared of prison. I've been there before."

"You served your time at the DeBerry Special Needs Facility, Tidwell. You got free therapy and drugs at taxpayer's expense. I somehow don't think you'll be going back."

"You know about me?"

"I know you had a good attorney last time. He got you a sweet deal on that charge of soliciting a minor. How old was she, anyhow? Thirteen? Fourteen?" Peggy waited. "Twelve?"

"She was hitchhiking," he said. "I asked an honest question and the girl jumped to conclusions."

"You're lucky she jumped from the car. You were two seconds away from attempted rape." She paused. "You know what they do to child molesters at Riverbend Max, Tiny?"

"You don't got my permission to call me Tiny."

"Well, I'm sure as hell not going to call you 'White Shadow.'" She waited. "Who are you, really?"

"You're a fooler. You mean you really don't know?" He squinted at her. "You don't even know how old the girl was, do you? They struck that as prejudicial to my defense. You're just fishin'."

"I know you went away for two years," she said. "And released on good behavior. So you had to be a snitch, right?"

"What else you got?" he asked. "Come on. What's my birthday? Where'd I go to school?" He smiled. "What'd my mommy get me for Christmas when I was ten?"

Peggy didn't answer.

"Now you know why they call me White Shadow." He grinned. "Go 'way. I don't like you. Wanna talk to Rusty."

"My father's busy," she said. "How'd a guy like you make friends with him, anyway?"

He didn't reply. After a few moments of silence, she signaled to the guard deputy. The door opened.

"We'll have the background on you soon enough," she said. "In the meantime, Tidwell . . . we've got you."

He looked up. "You were a cute little girl."

"I beg your pardon?"

"When your daddy was a guard at DeBerry—oh, long ago—he used to show me pictures of you." Tidwell smiled. He was looking at the cleft in her blouse. "You were so *pretty*. And *sweet*. Now whatever happened to that sweet, pretty girl?"

Sheriff Powell was at her side before she could move.

"There you are." Powell took her by the arm. "Come on, honey. We're all waitin' on you!"

The sheriff wasn't kidding about the Aldridge contingent, Peggy thought as she entered the conference room. Between Blaine Randall and Sean—newly attired in Armani, as befitting a future college president—sat an attorney taking notes. The lean, hard-bitten man in the corner was introduced to her as a private detective on retainer to the Aldridge family. She wondered if it was the same one Logan had hired to spy on Samantha.

Except for Peggy, everyone on her side of the table was in uniform: the sheriff, Rusty, and the Sherburn police chief, Lem Singleton. Nobody expected a peep out of Lem. Sherburn PD consisted of two Crown Victorias and an office next door to a tanning salon.

"I guess most everybody's here," Powell said. "And I hope we're all here for the same reason. Which is to bring Samantha Aldridge home safe to her husband and baby boy. If anybody's got a different agenda—" He glanced at Sean's attorney. "I trust they'll do us the favor of clearin' the room so the rest of us can get a little more air."

"Sheriff Powell." Blaine stood up, an emissary of a higher power. "First of all, thank you for hosting this meeting. Since the Aldridge case is now under federal jurisdiction, I'd like to start by asking—"

"Is it?" Rusty asked. "We sure about that?"

"Yes," Blaine said, polite but unequivocal. "With all respect, I'd like to ask that we abide by two policies. One is that nothing leaves this room. The kidnapper demanded that no attempt be made to enlist help from the authorities. Since we've now violated that condition, any leaks will almost certainly prove harmful to Mrs. Aldridge."

"Dr. Aldridge," Peggy said.

"Dr. Aldridge, of course. Second—as Sheriff Powell put it so well—we must have one agenda. We can't allow Samantha to suffer while we bicker over areas of responsibility."

"I think he wants us to know he's in charge," Rusty said to Powell in an exaggerated whisper.

"This is only about what's practical," Blaine continued. "Our communication loop must begin and end with the Bureau. Do you agree, Peggy?"

She didn't answer right away. More than a few times in her career, Peggy had been stuck with the thankless job of ego-herding a roomful of cops. It pained her all the more to see Agent Randall playing the FBI card so soon.

"Why not let's take a look at the ransom demand," she suggested, "and leave procedures to the end."

"Fair enough." Blaine tapped a few keys on his laptop. "Lights, please?"

Nobody got up to turn off the lights; he finally had to do it himself. Everyone turned to look at the screen.

"We're attempting to trace the ransom note," Blaine said. "Unfortunately it's been routed through so many servers and dummy accounts, it's almost impossible to say where. They could have been sent from next door . . . or from Timbuktu."

"So we've checked the e-mail servers?" Peggy asked.

"That's happening." Sean didn't meet her eyes. "We'll have it all for you tonight."

"When tonight?" she asked. "Nine, ten?"

"Ten." He looked at Blaine. "Just to be safe."

"That will be fine," Blaine said before Peggy could answer. The door opened, spilling light in. Harrison Stallworth entered cautiously.

"My apologies." Harrison sat in the last empty chair, between Peggy and her father.

"It's good to see you," Sean said. "You allright?"

"I've been better. You seem to be thriving." He looked back to Sheriff Powell. "Please don't let me interrupt."

"Your timing's perfect," Blaine said. "I was about to remark on the kidnapper's demand that Sean obtain one-point-six million dollars from you, Dr. Stallworth. Do either of you have any idea what that number might represent?"

Harrison began running figures on a scratch pad. Sean whispered back and forth with his attorney.

"Gentlemen?" Blaine asked.

The attorney leaned in. "Mr. Aldridge does not deem it necessary to amplify his previous statement on this matter."

"Sweet Jesus," Rusty said. "Does he know, or don't he?"

"I can speak for myself," Sean said. "The answer's no."

"I believe I can clear this up." Harrison put on his reading glasses. "The figure is roughly equivalent to my total accumulated salary from the college over the past thirty years."

"Not bad," Rusty mused. "But that's a bit of a stretch, ain't it? I mean, where would you get that kinda money from?"

"I think Harrison's point," Peggy said, "is that the precise demand is meant to injure him in some way."

"In other words, to cancel out everything I've ever received from the college for my services," Harrison said. "Which could support Peggy's theory that the kidnapper has a personal grudge against me."

Sean bristled. "He sent the note to me, Harrison. She's my wife."

"I've never disputed that," Harrison answered.

"Sounds like this guy's tryin' to rattle both your cages," Rusty said lightly. "Maybe that's why the kidnapper put that part in about, 'You're stuck raising a real man's baby.'"

"Possibly," Blaine said. "On a technical note—"

"Excuse me." Sean stared at Rusty. "Why is my wife's sexual history up for discussion? I realize she's had her failings. But really, Chief Weaver."

"Sean, if it's all the same," Harrison said. "I wouldn't start giving sermons on the virtues of marital fidelity."

"That's—neither here nor there, fellas." Powell raised his hands. "I realize you're both family. But you're also here as a courtesy. Understood?"

They both relented. Now Peggy was starting to perceive her father's strategy. Rusty would pick fights so Powell could step in and play Solomon. And all the while, Blaine's hold on the meeting would get progressively weaker.

Powell waved. "You go on, son—Agent Randall, I mean."

"Thank you," Blaine said uncertainly. "I was about to observe that there's missing letters in the note, but no misspelled words. Could mean he was typing on a cell phone keypad or handheld computer. He's keeping his language terse to avoid giving any clues to his personality. However, the likelihood is high that our subject's background is . . ." He stopped to check his notes.

"Military," Peggy said. "All that business about 'comm' and 'protocols.'"

"And 'zero-nine-hundred hours,' yes. There's two major mysteries here. One is the 'Krypteia is coming' line. Dr. Stallworth, Agent Weaver tells me you believe it's strictly a classical reference? Academic?"

"That's all I have for now," Harrison said. "Unless someone can add to it?"

No one answered. But Rusty was staring at Peggy.

"The other obscure reference is the signature, AMF," Blaine said. "Unfortunately, our efforts so far . . . I'm sorry, Chief Weaver. Does this mean something to you?"

"I guess you never served in the armed forces." Rusty turned to Powell. "You did, didn't you, Corey?"

"As did I," Harrison said. "Alpha Mike Foxtrot."

"Beg pardon?"

"The professor's right." Powell looked at Peggy. "That's military phonetic code for—'scuse me, darlin'—it's somethin' you say right before you blast your enemy to Kingdom Come."

"Adios, Mother Fucker," Rusty added.

Blaine made a note on his pad.

"So he is military," Blaine said. "Now the question is, how to proceed? I'd like to hear opinions on that. Sheriff?"

"No opinion. I'll stand wherever you boys tell me to."

"Chief Weaver?"

"Hm." Rusty set his jaw. "I'd like to hear what *you* advise, Agent Randall. You are the man in charge, correct?"

Blaine frowned, his patience thin. "I say we keep this low-key. Proceed as if the ransom's going to happen. Let the kidnapper think his strategy's working. Peggy will handle victimology and forensics, I'll coordinate communications . . . and Chief Weaver, you go on with—well, with whatever it is you've been doing."

"Thanks. I will." Rusty drummed the table. "So basically your big plan is to sit on our hands and wait."

"What I *said* was that we should keep this low-key. My background's in undercover work. We'll maintain the facade of separate investigations, meanwhile . . ."

"Under*cover*?" Rusty no longer bothered to cover his amusement. "No offense, son. But you don't exactly blend in."

Blaine simply folded his arms. Sean looked away. The lawyer's pencil stopped moving. From the corner of her eye, Peggy saw the private detective rest his thumb on his chin.

"I can't believe I just heard that," she said in a low voice. "Even from you."

"Why? 'Cause he's black and he talks like some—Harvard boy? We're in for-chrissakes Tennessee. Why do I always gotta be the one to point this shit out?"

"Dad, you are so goddamn wrong, it's not even funny."

"No," Blaine said. "He's right. I never expected to walk point on this investigation. I'd assumed that we'd develop our own local network of informants. Which I would mainly look to you for, Chief Weaver."

"To me?"

"You were the one who brought in Lester Tidwell. And I understand you have some—personal connection with him?" A daring light rose in Blaine's eye. "Am I mistaken?"

Rusty smiled. "I helped him get parole, yeah. He's a smart fella. Good with electronics. Thought he deserved a break. And he's helped me quite a lot over the years."

"No doubt. Seems to have helped himself in the process, hasn't he?"

Now it was Rusty's turn to fold his arms. "Why don't you just come out and say what's on your mind?"

"I assumed you'd be the one to turn him," Blaine said evenly. "Since he's your friend."

"I'm done," Rusty said. "Corey, I thank you for the room. But it's a mite small for us and the FBI. And Peggy, if your friend here intends to go on making insinuations—" He pushed his chair back. "He's gonna need to ask pretty please if he wants me 'turning' Tidwell. Now 'scuse me, I got work to do."

Peggy had seen it happen before: Her father was staging a walkout. He had the only link to Tidwell, and everybody knew they couldn't move without him. By the time Sheriff Powell was done brokering a truce, the case would almost surely be back in Rusty's jurisdiction. And God only knew how much time would have been lost by then. Peggy had to stop her father before his hand touched the door.

"Chief Singleton." She turned to the Sherburn police chief. "I understand you've been leading the search for Elias Collins. Any luck?"

Singleton looked about as surprised as everyone else to hear his name mentioned.

"Well, I, um—" He cleared his throat. "We put a squad car on our end of the Run, like Rusty said to—"

"No sign, then?"

He shook his head. Her father didn't sit down . . . but he was no longer moving for the exit.

"In your opinion," Peggy used her most respectful tone, the one usually reserved for FBI superiors. "How should we be allocating our ground resources?"

"Well—"

"Excuse me," Rusty said. "What resources? Lem's got two prowlers, and one of 'em's up on cinder blocks."

It was a false move, and he seemed to know it almost instantly. Singleton bristled: a mouse turning to defend his nest from a cat.

"If it was up to me," Lem said, "I think we oughta deprioritize the Collins boy. Whatever he's done, he ain't the man who wrote this ransom note. Maybe Agent Randall's right. Maybe Russ oughta get on makin' Tidwell talk to us."

Several of the men murmured assent; all at once, the room seemed to snap into focus. Rusty gave Peggy a thin smile—then darted a look to Corey Powell.

"Okay, then," Powell said. "Good meeting, everybody."

# THIRTY

Rusty was already getting into his cruiser by the time Peggy finally caught up with him in the parking lot.

"Dad?"

"That was a nice little maneuver you pulled with Lem Singleton," he said. "Put the slowest guy in the room on top, so the rest of us jump in line tryin' to outshine him. I gotta say, that's one trick I never taught you."

"You never had to babysit," she said. "Just tell me this. Was that tantrum of yours only because of Blaine? Or is it about your connection to Tidwell?" She paused. "Or is it me?"

"It's all of you." He took a breath. "I warned you about bringin' these warm bodies in. You think you're in charge now, just because you opened up a can of whup-ass?" He shook his head. "They'll use you as long as you're useful. Then they'll flush you like toilet paper. Trust me, I been there."

"What would you do?" She waited. "I'm genuinely listening. How would you run this case any differently?"

"It's what I *am* doin' that counts. While you talk philosophy with Harrison Stallworth, I got men goin' door to door. While you drink sherry with the Aldridges, I'm checkin' hotels and gas stations. It ain't fancy FBI tapdancin'—but it's my job, the only way I know how."

"I know you haven't been sitting around," she said. "But then, neither have I. And we have to start sharing information. Because if we somehow miss something important, all your cop work . . . and all my 'tap-dancing' . . . might not be enough."

"It might not be." He thought a moment. "What did Tiny say to you?"

Peggy didn't answer.

"Lemme guess. Diddly squat, right?" Rusty nodded. "That's right. And he'll go on that way until somebody who knows him can make him change his mind."

"That somebody being you, of course." She watched him. "Please don't tell me you're holding this investigation hostage."

"Just protectin' it from the royal foul-up," he said. "Tell me something. Is it more important to find out why Samantha got kidnapped . . . or to save her life?"

"I don't accept the question. Before I can do the second, I have to accomplish the first."

"Well—suppose you could bring her home with no questions asked." He waited. "Could you live without the explanation?"

"That's pretty much what happened the first time. And it didn't work." She looked down at him. "What would be the explanation I'd be living without?"

"I wouldn't even get to find that out myself," he said. "This is what I'm sayin'. We've got Tidwell. Tidwell will give us what we need . . . but maybe we don't ask how he gets it for us. Maybe it's better we don't know."

She looked around, suddenly aware that it was getting late.

"You're really starting to scare me lately," she said.

"Welcome to my world," he answered. "That's my whole plan, Peggy Jean. It's all I got. But believe me, it will work."

"And if I say no?"

"You can try cuttin' a deal. But I'm the one he talks to."

"He did pull a gun on you, Dad."

"It was just you bein' there. Women make Tiny panic."

"And if I hadn't been there? You'd have let him go, wouldn't you? You very nearly did."

"Only in a good cause," he said. "Did I ever tell you about my time as a prison guard?"

"Hardly anything," she said.

"You couldn't have been more'n two," he said. "Most people think a prison runs on guards and lockdowns. But that ain't so. What it runs on . . . is information. You always gotta know who's about to do what to who. Problem is, nobody gives up the good shit for free. That's where fellas like Tiny come in. He's like the pilot fish that the sharks don't eat. You let him swim away . . . he'll take us to where the big fish is."

"Or lead the shark to us," she said. "Why is there nothing in Tidwell's file? His prison record is pretty much the only thing that proves he even exists."

"Wasn't my doin'." He stared flat at her.

"Dad . . . do you know who Lester Tidwell's really working for?"

"Even Tiny don't always know whose side he's on." He laughed. "But then again, neither do you."

He shut the door and drove away.

# THIRTY-ONE

Neither Mike nor Yoshi were responding to their work or cell numbers. Mike didn't even have an answering machine at home . . . which left Peggy one last number to call.

"Hiraka Baby Motel," answered a bright young female voice.

"Shoreh, it's Peggy Weaver. Yoshi's squad—"

"*Peggy*! Omi*god*!" Shoreh Hiraka's voice bounced between octaves. "Are you *okay*? We've been so worried!"

"I'm—fine. Sorry to bother you. I'm trying to find your husband."

"You and me both. The man hasn't even called me since he landed in Virginia. And Rina made the *cutest* face today."

"What's he doing in Virginia?"

"Him and Mike both. They're at some kind of . . . inquest?"

"An inquest," she said. "At Quantico, you mean?"

"Maybe I'm using the wrong word. Grown-up isn't my first language anymore, since Her Majesty arrived. Anyway, I'm surprised he didn't tell *you* about it. That's kind of dumb."

She looked back across the parking lot. Blaine was saying good-bye to Sean and his entourage.

"Not so dumb," she said. "Please tell him I called."

"I will," she said. "And you come *visit*, okay? You and Mike. Yoshi's always working . . . and it seems like forever since I've had a conversation with somebody who can actually answer questions in plain English."

Now Blaine was idling his way toward her.

"I know the feeling, Shoreh," she said. "I surely do."

As they said good-bye, Agent Randall stood a few yards away—his back turned, but still with an ear in her direction.

"Are you ready for me?" he asked as she hung up.

"In a minute," she said, already dialing her field office.

Chip's Café—"Home of the Big Bad Burger"—was far enough from town to avoid the usual college crowd. Or any crowd. The menu was literally so awful that only old die-hard regulars ever ate there . . . and even they were dying off. It was widely rumored that the food had killed them. As Peggy and Blaine pretended to eat, the only thing moving—besides the flies— was the elderly janitor, slapping a sour mop against the gray linoleum.

"You've met this Elias Collins character," Blaine said. "Were you just throwing out chaff, or do you really think he's worth bringing in?"

"I suppose we'd be negligent not to. He's apparently the father of Samantha's child. He was alluded to in the ransom note. And he's a fugitive from justice. But is he a prime suspect?" She shrugged. "He's not at the top of my list."

"He's on mine." Blaine picked at his iceberg wedge. "Does it change your opinion of Samantha, knowing she never told you about him?"

"Not in the slightest." She hoped she sounded convincing.

"No offense. I hope you understand why I'm asking."

"I believe so, yes."

Peggy took a bite of her alleged tuna melt. Blaine cautiously speared a cherry tomato. The janitor kept mopping.

"And how is your special agent in charge?" he asked. "That is who you were calling, right?"

"I had to settle for the ASAC," she answered baldly. "You'll be happy to know he's confirmed that you're running the show. Against my strong objection."

"So you and your dad agree on something after all." He smiled without much humor.

"For different reasons," she said. "I'll be honest, Blaine. You seem like a smart guy—but you're inexperienced. And you nearly made a train wreck of that meeting." She watched him. "It's your prerogative to disagree, of course."

"I never argue with members of my team in public," he said. "Let's get to work."

She took out a notepad. "Here's my recommendation for a ground team. In my opinion, we need to be operational within twenty-four hours—if not sooner."

He read through it. "This looks a lot like hostage rescue to me. I thought we agreed to go ahead with the ransom negotiations."

"We agreed to behave as if they were proceeding. Samantha's not going to live till the deadline. It's like the ransom amount—strictly symbolic."

"Symbolic of what?"

"Wednesday is Avalon's hundred and twenty-fifth commencement ceremony," she said. "It's also Harrison Stallworth's final day as president. At nine o'clock that morning, the Avalon College trustees are meeting to confirm Sean's appointment as president. Supposedly he's got some big dog-and-pony show planned for them. Any idea what it might be?"

"None whatsoever." He scanned the list. "It's not a bad duty roster, Weaver . . . but it's a little ambitious on short notice. I can tell you that two of these names are definitely not available." He pointed.

"Mike Yeager and Yoshi Hiraka? That's my core team. For God's sake, why?"

"I can get my own people to fill these slots. Just as good and twice as fast." He paused. "If this were Philadelphia, I'm sure you'd view my attempts to pack the squad with equal suspicion. This isn't Philadelphia."

"And I'm not that suspicious," she said. "I heard about their trip to headquarters. Mike and Yoshi should not be punished just because I got their help without authorization."

"They're not being punished," he said. "You are."

"Really." She put her fork down. "For what?"

"I really don't know how to put this politely. You didn't piss off Logan Aldridge today. You pissed *on* him. And frankly, it's taking way too much of my time and energy keeping a heat shield on this investigation."

"Who brought the heat down in the first place? You?"

"I'm the one who's keeping you on the team." He examined the notepad. "Maybe I can get you Hiraka. But Yeager's too much of a liability where you're concerned."

"Meaning what?"

"Chill out, okay?" He held up his hands. "I'm not talking about whatever relationship you've got with him off the clock. As far as I'm concerned, that's a nonissue."

"Glad to hear it," she said.

"But last November—so I'm told—he was this close to getting an administrative discharge for falsifying evidence in a major kidnapping case, back in Philadelphia."

"He was cleared."

"He was guilty as sin. That's how I heard it."

"Last November, Mike Yeager saved the lives of two children in Nevada. That's why he's still on my team. Period."

"Your loyalty is admirable—"

"Thank you."

"But if you'll forgive me for saying, it's misplaced. And there's no room for it on my investigation."

"Because you've got a job to do," she said.

He exhaled. "Thank you for understanding."

"Believe me, I do. And I'm sure you don't plan on staying a resident agent forever. Not with friends like the senator on your side. Or Logan Aldridge."

He looked her right in the eye. "Would you?"

"Talk about ambitious," she said. "Can we get back to work, please?"

"Fine," he said. "What about Tidwell? What are we going to do with him?"

"Hard to say without background. We didn't find anything at his cabin. Tidwell's business operates on a cash basis . . . he's apparently self-educated and self-employed. All the Bureau has on him is what we saw on his rap sheet . . . plus a couple of passport stamps for vacations to Thailand in the nineteen-eighties. Sex tourism, most likely. He's not even on the Tennessee Registry of Sex Offenders. Which is pretty strange, considering that he was convicted under a child predator law."

"You think your dad pulled some strings?"

"My father doesn't have that kind of power," she said.

"Maybe, maybe not. Will he help us?"

She exhaled. "My father's only willing to approach Tidwell with a no-questions-asked deal. We'll get the information we need to bring Samantha back—he says—and Tiny's free to go home to his love doll. How does that suit you?"

"He wants to let an informant control the investigation? Forget it." He paused thoughtfully. "Does Tidwell trust him?"

"He seems to. For what that's worth."

"So let your father approach him," he said. "Let them talk."

"Believe me, it would be much easier if my dad was cooperating. But there's no way."

"Who said anything about asking for his cooperation?"

"Well, how else—"

Peggy fell silent. The janitor muttered something about dirty water as he shuffled past.

"You're talking surveillance?" she whispered. "What good would that do?"

"For starters, we'll know exactly what Tidwell's saying—instead of what little your father chooses to relate. And very likely we'll get the background we need to break this case."

"Maybe. But I'd like to meet the judge who'll go along with wiretapping a police officer."

"Already got it covered," he said. "I understand your scruples. All due respect, I'm sure your father's a fine man."

She frowned. "You don't think he's a fine man. You think he's a bitter old racist. And he was out of bounds today. But that was personal, not professional. Rise above it."

"Personal?" He nearly laughed. "I have sources around here. Your father buried a racially motivated police brutality incident. He approved illegal surveillance on Samantha Aldridge. He planted a bug at the Collins trailer. And, for all we know, he got Tidwell to hide that GPS tracker on your Jeep. Not to mince words. Russell Weaver's a bad cop."

"So give him a taste of his own medicine, is that it?" She put her napkin down. "Even if you can get past the legal hurdles . . . I can't. It's plain wrong. I'm sorry."

"None of the items I just mentioned are on your daily reports or 302s," he said. "I think you've been covering for him. How right is that?"

She looked down. "I haven't filed all my reports yet."

"Hey, I get it. He's family. Forget the whole thing." He shrugged. "Maybe we'll get lucky and find all the information we need through normal channels before Samantha Aldridge dies."

She stopped. The waitress was standing over them.

He reached for his wallet. "Don't worry, I've got this."

"That's all right. I have to pay for something on this trip." Peggy took out her credit card.

"Cash only," the waitress said.

"Keep the change." Blaine held up a twenty. The waitress examined it throroughly—and with no small distaste—before finally accepting it from him.

"She should work for the Treasury Department," Blaine said after she'd walked away. "Guess your father was right about my not blending in."

Peggy put her credit card away. "You really are a cold one, aren't you, Agent Randall?"

"And I thought we were just being honest with each other." He stood up. "I'll see what I can do about your list."

"Do I at least get Agent Hiraka?"

"You're okay with losing Yeager?"

"Of course I'm not okay. I think it's a huge mistake." She practically had to chew the words out. "But you're the case agent. It's your call."

He gave an approving nod. "And that other matter we discussed?"

She stared through the window for several seconds, seeing her half-reflection against the cobalt sky. Another day gone.

"Do it," she said.

"It's done," he answered.

As she stood to go, she found herself looking at the janitor. His eyes were filled with cataracts, milky white.

"Dirty water," he said to the empty air. "Just can't get a floor clean with dirty water."

She followed Blaine into the parking lot.

# THIRTY-TWO

The men of the kitchen staff were taking a smoke break as Peggy joined Blaine outside. They smiled as she walked by, watching her with slow and sullen eyes.

"I have to give you credit." Blaine fished for his keys. "You're cooler about this than I'd be if it was my father."

"Do us both a huge favor," she said. "Stop talking to me until we're back on the road."

One of the kitchen boys leaned in to his companion: Peggy didn't have to read lips to know what he was whispering. She stared back and the men shrank away. But as Peggy walked on, she could still feel their eyes burning on her.

Blaine placed calls as they drove down a mist-streaked Highway 23: most of his responses were clipped, a kind of half-code that Peggy was only too familiar with.

"Affirmative," he said. "Yup. Everybody's on board." He pocketed his phone. "Agent Hiraka's on a plane to Chattanooga. We're set for a situation conference at eight A.M. tomorrow."

"Sounds like you've got things well in hand," she said. "So what's the story on the wiretap?"

"It's handled," he said. "All that's left is your part."

"My part?" She looked at him. "What's my part?"

"You need to tell your father we've discussed it, and everything's cool. He's empowered to negotiate with Tidwell."

"And that's all," she said.

"Well." He took a careful pause. "There is the matter of the transmitter itself."

"You want me to plant the damn thing? Jesus, why didn't I see that one coming?" She looked into her side-view mirror. "I'm not sure I can pull this off."

"You'll have to find a way. You think he's going to let me get close to him?" He adjusted his rearview mirror. "Goddamn tailgaters. Look, other people are getting involved. If you can't hack it, I need to know right now." He paused. "Well?"

"We're not being tailgated," she said. "We're being followed."

She looked over her shoulder. An old Chevy pickup had been closing in over the past few miles, and was now riding their bumper. It took Peggy a moment to notice the canvas sacks covering the faces of the men inside.

"I guess Chip's closed down early tonight," she said.

"Jesus," he said. "Okay, let's see what eight cylinders can do."

He floored it. The Chevy instantly took off in pursuit.

"How well do you know these roads?" she asked.

He pointed. "I've got a GPS display."

"That's not gonna do it. We'll have to slow way down when we hit the Run. And that gives them two miles of empty highway to play with."

"What the hell is 'the Run'?" His eyes darted nervously.

"Suicide Run," she said. "That's where we're going."

He reached for his phone. "I'm calling for backup. Who's closer, county or t—?"

"Blaine, watch the road!"

He slammed hard on the brakes, nearly spinning out of control. A second truck was parked broadside across the highway. Two more hooded men were inside, plus three in the bed. The other truck was closing in fast from behind.

"We're pinned both ways. What do I do?"

"Hard left," she said. "Off the highway. Now."

"That's gonna take us into the woods—"

"Do it!"

The men were jumping down, carrying rifles and tire irons. As Blaine peeled out, one of them smashed a crowbar down: Peggy's side-view mirror sheared away.

"They're on us," he said. "This is not where I think we should be right now."

The car rattled and bumped as it found the deep ruts of the fire road, heading into the treeline. The pursuing vehicles gradually fell back.

"We need to throw them off," she said. "Turn right."

"Turn where? I can't see anything—"

"Here!" She pointed. "Blaine, damn it!"

He sped past the turn up the hill. They were heading into the deep woods, away from town.

"It went by too fast." He picked up his cell phone, dialed. "Oh, come on. Don't do this to me."

"Cell phones don't work in the Cove," she said. "There's another turnout about a quarter mile from here. It's not as good, but it'll rejoin the main road close to town. And then we can call for backup." She pointed. "Slow down."

He braked to forty just in time to make the turn.

"Who *are* these guys? Those crackers from the diner?"

"Not sure," she said. "Dim your lamps. We can see well enough by moonlight."

He switched them off. "You sure you know where you're going? Because I'm lost."

"I've gone home this way before," she said. "You ever been in a pursuit situation before?"

"I'm usually flying a desk," he said. "I do not want to wind up in some cold-case file that takes the Justice Department forty years to solve. I just want to see my children tonight." He looked at her. "Do you have kids?"

"No."

"And you're not afraid."

She thought about it. "I'm saving it for later, I guess. Easy, now. We're almost there."

They'd reached a clearing. Blue moonlight shone faintly down on the boulders and trees. A tiny red tongue of flame burned up from a campfire, throwing sparks to heaven.

"What's this?" he asked. "Are we getting close to town?"

"We really should have taken that first turn," she said.

Now she could see the truck, idling in the shadows. And a group of armed men in hoods, cutting off their escape.

# THIRTY-THREE

Peggy's Glock had fifteen rounds in the magazine, plus the spare clip on her belt. It would have to be enough.

"Still no signal?" she asked.

Blaine closed his cell phone. "No."

"Are you armed?"

He nodded.

Yellow light spilled across their backs as the second truck pulled in behind them. There looked to be ten attackers, only half of them armed with rifles or handguns. Peggy knew that a sharpened tire iron would kill her fast enough. The hooded men took their time getting close, coyotes on a cornered prey.

"What the hell are you doing, Peggy?"

"We're going to have to bring some of them down." She carefully unlocked her door. "Whatever happens, don't let them pull you from the car."

"You can't—"

She reached over and threw on the lights. Several of them fell back, disoriented. At that same moment, she kicked her door open, knocking another one to the ground.

"FBI!" She yelled as she stood forth, a steel-sharp voice of command. "Put your weapons down now!"

"You put yours down." The leader's voice was winter ice, muffled by canvas. His twelve-gauge was aimed at her heart.

"Stop!" she called. One of them was charging at her: she squeezed the trigger and took him down by the leg. There was a dull cry, and the sound of bolts and hammers drawing back.

"We're federal agents." Blaine rose from the car, a tremor in his voice. "You discharge these weapons and you're dead."

*I'm dead*, Peggy thought with a perplexing lack of emotion. She could hear the wounded man moaning. Then she saw a dog pace out of the shadows: a three-legged Doberman.

"Trip." She looked up at the leader. "Am I speaking to the infamous Elias Collins?"

"Just so. I'm told you mean to arrest me." He pulled off his hood: Blue-black hair fell to his shoulders. "Here I am."

"Bullshit," another said. "Come on and let's waste 'em."

"She saved my life," Elias answered. "She gets a chance to save hers."

"She shot Coffey."

"Coffey jumped when he shouldn't have. He'll live." He nodded to her. "Go on, Weaver's daughter. Flat on the ground."

"You first." She pivoted the Glock's muzzle down.

He smiled and lowered his shotgun. Peggy waited till it was fully down before setting hers on the grass.

"Now throw down the cars keys," he said to Blaine.

"Like hell." Blaine didn't budge. "Damned white trash."

"Agent Randall," Peggy said. "Please put your keys down."

Blaine frowned as he dropped his ring a foot in front of him. "Just make sure it comes back with a full tank."

"Douse the lights," Elias said.

Someone switched off the BMW's headlamps, leaving only moonlight and fire.

"Now that we're all being civilized." Elias stepped down from the rock. "Maybe you can tell me why you saw fit to harass my poor mama yesterday."

"Zanda's a brave woman," Peggy said. "Think she'd approve of your chasing people in the dark?"

"I don't need my mother's permission to protect the ones I love," Elias said. "You have no license to threaten me or my people. Your law ends here."

"It's because of Samantha that I came to Chillwater Cove," Peggy said. "How much do you love *her*?"

The others seemed to tense as Peggy spoke.

"More than you'll understand," he said. "Have you seen Caden? How well is he being looked after?"

"Caden's fine, as far as I know. He's with his people."

"No, he's not. Any more than you are." He went cold. "We ain't white, sir, no more than you. Nor trash." He swept his hand across the horizon. "All this here is Cumbaa territory, from the Cove to the eastern bluff. Has been since the day Old Fortitude brought us here out of slavery in Virginia. Changing the history books won't make it yours—any more than a river is yours, just because you've pissed into it."

"I keep hearing that name," Peggy said. "Cumbaa."

"It was a great name once," Elias answered. "To hear Samantha tell, it could be again."

"There's a lot of things I'd like to hear from Samantha. Do you think you could help me talk to her?"

"If I could, do you think I'd be wasting time on you?" He narrowed his eyes. "She's like the land to you folks—only good while you're using her. You call yourself your friend?"

"Yes," she said.

"Prove it," he said.

"I'm not going to open my heart just to amuse you," she said. "And I couldn't give a rat's butt about your claims. But I know Samantha cares about you. So I guess I'm going to have to care about you, too. One of you is named . . . Abraham Branch?"

Elias's eyes registered faint interest. "What about him?"

"He showed Samantha how to witch water. A long time ago, he used to be a moonshiner."

"My name's Bunch." He pulled off his mask: she was only mildly surprised to recognize him as the janitor from Chip's. "I never was a moonshiner. Drunk enough of it in my day, though."

There was scattered laughter, but it didn't seem to dissipate the anger. Their weapons could be raised in an eyeblink. And Peggy's escape was still cut off.

"You told her the waters of Stiller's Cave are poisoned," she said. "There used to be thousands of you, and now there's only a few. And four hundred years ago, you believe . . . you *were* . . . living up on the plateau." She looked at Elias. "That's all I have."

"What about Krypteia?" Elias asked. "Do you know that?"

"I don't," she said. "Please. I'm just trying to find Samantha. I want her to be safe. I need to . . . talk to her again."

"And what would you say to her, if you could?"

"I'd tell her I was sorry for running away, all those years ago. And leaving her with that man who . . . cut and burned her."

Elias stepped into the firelight.

"Your cheeks are wet, Weaver's daughter." His voice was quieter. "I thought you weren't going to open your heart."

She didn't wipe her tears away. "I'll help you, if you'll help me. That's all I can promise."

"Considering that you shot my cousin Joe Coffey," he said. "One question, one answer. That's all you've earned."

"Fair enough," she said. "What is Krypteia?"

"Being who you are," he asked, "you really need me to say?"

He held his hand over the flame.

"Krypteia killed nearly all of my people more than a century ago," he continued. "Only because they were bold enough to live on the land God gave them. It's a sad, sorry tale. Your beloved General Stallworth showed up one day . . . graciously offered us a chance to give him our land and be his servants. We just as politely said no. So he ordered his young men to put on white hoods—and burn us out."

"You've got proof of this?"

"The only proof would be if we were all dead." He smiled archly. "Oh, the general covered his tracks good enough. But Sammie thought she might've found proof that we owned this land by right . . . and will again, by God's help."

He bent down and took up two handfuls of earth.

"You're surrounded by men made of lies, Weaver's daughter. You might think you have the truth about them . . . but they *know* the truth about you. And until you know your own secrets as well as they do . . . you're walking naked in the dark."

He threw down the dirt. The flames died in a swirl of red ash. Then there was only darkness.

"Well, that was helpful," Blaine said from behind her.

"Elias?" Peggy's eyes slowly adjusted to the dim light. "Blaine, where are you?"

"Right here," he said. "I think we're alone now."

He opened the car door: Light spilled over the ground. The clearing was empty. Even the trucks were gone.

"How the hell did they do *that*?" Peggy asked.

"Never mind that." Blaine aimed a flashlight around. "Where the hell are my *keys*?"

"Wait. Stop." She pointed to the rock. "Aim over there."

He shone the beam onto the rock Elias had stood upon. A black bound notebook, its pages yellowed and water warped, lay flat on the boulder. The word *Journal* was written across the cover in a woman's handwriting.

Peggy picked it up. She could smell Samantha's perfume.

"It's hers," she said.

# THIRTY-FOUR

Olivia was ready with hot tea as Peggy came through the front door. Harrison and Blaine were close behind.

"Sweetie, you look like you've been through *Purgatory*." Olivia set down the tray and put her arms around Peggy. "Harrison, you didn't tell me they were so—tempest tossed."

"I didn't know what to expect." He took a mug. "It's not every night that an old college professor gets called out to rescue two hitchhiking federal agents."

"So *awful*." She extended her hand to Blaine. "You must be the one helping out at the Aldridges'. Special Agent . . . ?"

"Just plain Blaine," he said. "I'll admit I've become something of a fixture at Logan Farms. I keep waiting for someone to toss me a pitchfork and set me to throwing hay."

"Plain Blaine! That's terribly funny." Olivia laughed brightly. "I've got soup and sandwich in the works. Come give me a hand in the kitchen and tell me how poor Logan's doing."

She didn't wait for a response, but merely led Blaine away. Peggy exchanged a weary smile with Harrison.

"We must have wasted half an hour looking for those damn keys." She set her bag down. "Thanks for not asking why I didn't call my father."

"No problem." He waved her over. "Come into the study."

"I'd like to see Caden first," she said. "Is he asleep?"

"Finally, I think. But you can look in on him."

"Come with me," she said.

They tiptoed in quietly. Caden lay sprawled in his crib. His blue eyes moved rapidly behind closed lids: REM sleep, dream sleep. *Hope to God they're good ones*. Peggy doubted they were. The child clutched something tightly in his right hand.

"What's that he's got?" she whispered.

"Just a rock from the garden. He wouldn't accept any of his sleep toys. And he cried when Olivia tried to take it away from him . . . so now he sleeps with a pebble."

"Puppaston'."

Peggy went to make sure the window was locked. As she looked through, a white minivan was pulling up the drive.

"Must be Agent Randall's ride," she said.

As they came downstairs, Blaine was standing in the open doorway. Another agent was behind the wheel of the minivan.

"I'll come back in the morning for my BMW—assuming it hasn't been stripped for parts." Blaine waved her through the open door. "Walk out with me, okay?"

As she joined him on the front step, Agent Randall took a small plastic box from his jacket.

"My driver brought this for you." He opened it. Inside was a dime-size graphite disk. "Recognize the model?"

"I've used them before," she said. "I'm assuming the surveillance warrants are all in order?"

"Definitely. Now this is self-activating—"

"Let me see the warrants," she said. "Show me the magistrate's signature."

"It was all done over the phone. Relax. We'll get paperwork in the morning." He closed the box. "I figured this was the right tool for the job. It's audio only, but it's got unbelievable range and clarity for its size. It automatically filters out background noise and optimizes human voices. And it's damn near indestructible. The only problem is the titanium alloy in the inner casing."

"I know. It'll set off the metal detector at Keyes County Sheriff's Department."

"But you know how to get around that, right?"

"Yes." She took the box. "Have you ever visited a real farm? The kind where you might actually have to pitch hay?"

"My father invests in pork futures. Does that count?"

"My dad's people raised livestock," she said. "On Grampa's farm, there was this one old wether goat they used to lead the cattle between pens. The animals always trusted him to, you know . . . look after their interests?

Until one day each year, that goat would lead them all right onto the truck for the slaughterhouse. Know what we called him?"

"No offense, Agent Weaver. But I'd like to save *Charlotte's Web* for my kids' bedtime story."

"We called him the Judas Goat," she said. "And here I am, spying on my own father."

"As I understand it, you gunned down Clara Cooke in full view of her son," Blaine said. "I think you'll manage."

She stared cold at him.

"I hope to God you're in this for more than a free horse from the Aldridges," she said. "You damn well better be."

**"Blaine didn't want to stay** for supper?" Olivia set the sandwich tray down between Peggy and Harrison.

"He had to get home to his family." Peggy sat across from Harrison in the study. "He'll be back in the morning."

"I *like* him." She turned in the archway. "I think it's wonderful that, as a society, we've progressed to where blacks can be members of the upper class. Don't you think?"

"Absolutely." Harrison barely looked at her. "Tremendous progress."

"I just feel so secure, knowing men like him are around."

As she left, Harrison looked at Peggy. "Ready for that sherry?"

"I can't," Peggy said.

"Something to steady your nerves," he said. "Good strong Tennessee bourbon, perhaps?"

"A *small* one," she said. "What do you think of Agent Randall?"

"He definitely won Livy over with his Aldridge connections." He poured out two glasses. "Personally, I think he'd have made a fine member of the Nixon administration."

She started to laugh—then stifled tears as the whiskey scalded her throat.

"Maybe even the Krypteia?" she said.

"That might be a bit unkind. Would you like some water on that?" He took the glass from her. "Did he at least let you keep the notebook?"

"Only the photocopy we made at your office." She took the sheaf of papers from her bag. "He's going to run handwriting tests. But I already know it's Samantha's. It *smells* like her, Harrison. For a minute I could almost feel her next to me."

He poured water. "Show me what we've got."

"There's a few discrepancies between this and the document I showed you earlier," she said. "Particularly with regard to General Stallworth's purchase of Avalon Mountain."

She pointed to a tabbed passage:

> Whether or not there ever was a "Free City" or "Lost Colony" is, for my purpose, irrelevant—what matters is what I've suspected all along: The Cumbaas' names do not appear on the deed.

"Elias called the mountain 'Cumbaa territory,'" she said. "Has that name ever come up in your own research?"

"Well, no one ever hears the dog that didn't bark." Harrison handed the glass back. "The name Cumbaa doesn't appear on the quit-claim deed . . . but that could just as easily prove that there weren't any Cumbaas here to begin with. Does she offer any positive evidence?"

"Doesn't say." Peggy took another sip; the watered bourbon went down a little easier. "A lot of what's in here is . . . very personal, Harrison."

He reflected a moment. "Would you rather I didn't see?"

"Just be prepared." She turned the page around for him.

> Today began like any other Thursday morning. I struggled through my final lecture on Reconstruction, while my students sent text messages and stole glances out the window. I was actually feeling a bit spring-ish myself, in spite of a bad night and a queasy morning.
>
> Then I found the pictures waiting for me on my computer.
>
> I went to Elias, wanting to tell him everything. But, in the end, I just couldn't. He'd want to hide me here. Or try to save me. And I know what they'd do to him for trying.
>
> He loved me on the same mattress where Caden began—softly, because he knew that he'd be a father again come winter. I feel it's a girl inside me this time. We made the same love for different reasons. Elias was joyful and wanted to celebrate. I only wanted him close to me, because the discovery is so terrifying.

They warned me what would happen if I let a child come from my body. I've doomed my daughter to die before she can ever be born.

I would run, but my feet won't carry me far enough. And Sean will never let me have Caden. He's been asking too many questions about the land, and the names of dead children. I am quite certain he's had me followed.

I just want my baby to be safe.

And Lord, I'm alone.

Peggy took the page back.

"And that's all?" Harrison said quietly.

"There's one final entry." She tried not to notice his tears. "So many of the pages are out of order. I'm not sure where it belongs."

Can you protect people by keeping secrets from them?

For twenty-five years I played the Comedy of Innocence, hiding the truth about what they did to me, hoping only to protect the ones I love. Now I know there's no such thing as safe. I've held back so many words that I feel as if I'm almost completely made of silence. Is that what Heraklitus meant by 'φυσιζδε καθ Ηρακλειτον κρυπτεσκαι πιλει3?'

"Can you translate the Greek?" she asked.

"It's from the ancient philosopher Heraklitus," Harrison said. "The one who taught us that no one ever steps in the same river twice. It means, 'Nature loves to hide itself.'"

"Hide? As in, 'Hidden Matters'?"

"The root word is the same. Kryptos, cryptic, crypt . . ."

"Krypteia." Peggy set her glass down. "Elias said that his people were burned from their homes . . . forced to sell their land by a Klan-style organization calling itself Krypteia. Led by General Stallworth."

Harrison stared at her. "My god."

"Elias doesn't claim to have any proof of this. But he thinks Samantha did. Have you ever heard this rumor before?"

"Never," he said. "Do you think it's true?"

"I don't know. But Sammie writes that 'they' will do things to Elias. And 'they' warned her not to have children. I was with her at Suicide Run. There was only one guy standing next to that black Thunderbird."

"What does that tell you?"

"Whoever he is, he can't be working alone. Maybe Krypteia isn't coming after all. Maybe they never went away."

He seemed about to speak—then Olivia called from the next room. "Harrison, do you still want your soup?"

"Thank you, Livy." He exhaled.

"I have to get myself home," Peggy said. "There's something I need to take care of."

"Not to worry. I'll drive you."

"I don't mean to upset you by saying this." She gathered the pages. "But you've had a drink, and . . . my father's not going to be happy to see your car in his driveway."

"Surely you're not planning to walk?"

"Don't worry. I can handle myself."

He looked at her cautiously. "I'll come with you."

"All right." Peggy smiled.

They passed Olivia on the way to the door.

"You didn't even eat your sandwiches," she said. "Isn't *anybody* hungry for my cooking tonight?"

# THIRTY-FIVE

A few weeknight parties were still underway as they walked down College Avenue; rap music blasted from the Lambda Chi house. Students and alumni stopped to wave or chat with Dr. Stallworth, while Peggy's presence was less frequently acknowledged. They all seemed to be wondering what she might be doing at the president's side.

"The 'Comedy of Innocence,'" Peggy said. "What do you think Samantha meant by that? That she was just tired of pretending everything was okay?"

"It's a religious custom," Harrison said. "The ancient Greeks believed that, before you could slaughter a wild animal, you had to ritually obtain its permission to be killed—usually by luring the victim into the place of sacrifice. Strange idea, isn't it?"

"Not to me," Peggy said. "Talk to any rapist or pedophile, and they'll tell you the same thing. 'She asked for it.' Families will say, 'She made it up.'" Peggy looked at him carefully. "Or even, 'She's just trying to sour the milk.'"

Harrison winced.

"You'll have to forgive Olivia's judgments," he said. "She's convinced that the only way to solve a problem is to pretend it never happened."

"Do *you* forgive it?" Peggy asked.

"I've made my peace with it," he said. "She was much the same after the last time Samantha went missing."

"How so?"

He hesitated before telling her.

"It was a pointless argument," he said. "Livy wanted Samantha to resume her ballet lessons. Even when the child was still . . . barely hobbling." His brow furrowed. "My wife even argued the doctors into submission."

"She does tend to get her way," Peggy said.

"She always did when it came to Sammie. Witness the poor girl's untoward marriage to Sean. He's a fine administrator—well, a capable one. But he's not much of a person."

Peggy knew that Harrison was chary with insults. *Not much of a person* weighed as much from him as any string of four-letter words did from her father.

"Why are you backing him for president, then?"

Harrison looked around briefly. "I don't have a choice. The endowment's been hit hard—far worse than most people know. In the past, I would have been able to turn directly to the alumni for support . . ."

"I guess they're not crazy about you tearing down those Confederate flags."

"That's only the latest battle in an ongoing war," he said. "I keep thinking of Samantha's question—'Can you protect people by keeping secrets?' This place has . . . so many secrets to keep. When I was a student here, I firmly believed that the Civil War had nothing to do with slavery. I accepted that the Klan was—if excessive in its tactics—at least sincerely motivated by the desire to safeguard home and family. And I was absolutely convinced that my great-great-grandfather was a noble human being. I clung to these beliefs like a weed on a mausoleum. And still I knew it was every inch a lie."

They had reached the south end of campus and were standing beneath the statue of General Lycurgus Stallworth. Dark streaks of soot fell from his marble eyes like tears.

"If this modern-day Krypteia does exist, perhaps these are its principles." Harrison pointed to the granite base. "Can you read the inscription?"

"*Exitus Acta Probat*," she said. "That's a hell of a motto. 'The End Justifies the Means'?"

"That's how it was always translated for me. Later, of course, I learned that the phrase actually means, 'the end *tests* the act'—it forces you to consider whether any cause is good enough to purify foul deeds."

He shrugged and led her away from the statue, as if refusing to hear any defense the general might offer.

"There are only two things in my life that I can look to with complete joy," he said. "One is my daughter Samantha. The other is . . . well, being the president of Avalon. Both of them were born of the same resolve: to ensure that the lies of my childhood would not survive to harm future generations."

"You succeeded," she said.

"Did I?" he asked. "Avalon is bankrupt. Logan Aldridge has promised sufficient funds to ensure our survival . . . but God knows what he plans to do once his son's hand is on the till. We can certainly say good-bye to need-based scholarships." He lowered his voice. "To lose my post is a small thing. To lose my daughter . . ."

"Samantha is still alive, Harrison. I know she is."

He smiled but didn't answer. They were beyond the campus now, heading into town. Harrison cast a final glance back, as if saying farewell.

"My father got one of those scholarships," Peggy said at last.

"Yes," he said. "He was a freshman during my first year teaching. Rusty was a bright fellow . . . I always thought he ran with a bad crowd, though. Those fellows on the boxing team prided themselves on Neanderthal behavior."

"Is that how he hurt his leg?"

"I don't know how it happened," he said. "I don't think it was in a boxing match."

They stopped at the traffic light, flashing yellow. Peggy put her hand into her pocket, touching the radio transmitter.

"Do you . . . believe it's forgivable to do the wrong thing for the right reason?" she asked. "Or that good can come from bad?"

He seemed to consider carefully before answering.

"You're asking me to solve a very old philosophical dilemma," he said. "Do I believe that might makes right? I hope not. But there is such a thing as the greater good. I suppose . . . there are moments when you have to make sacrifices for that greater good."

A car drove past, leaving the street empty.

"As for what good can come of bad . . ." He looked at her. "We learn by making mistakes. Don't you think?"

He held her in his soft brown eyes for a very long time, and Peggy wasn't sure if he wanted more than a simple answer. Finally she put her hand on his arm.

"I hope so," she said. "I think this is as far as you need to come with me. I'll be all right by myself from here."

He moved toward her awkwardly, as if debating whether to hug her or take her hand. Finally they both laughed.

"Will *you* be all right by yourself?" she asked.

He smiled uncertainly. Then an Avalon police car slowed down at the light.

"Officer." Harrison shielded his eyes, squinting.

"Evenin'." Officer Dennis shone his sidelight at Peggy. "Got your daddy real worried about you, Miss Weaver. Might wanna give him a call."

She frowned. "I'll leave that to you, thanks."

He nodded and drove away, eyeing Harrison with bald curiosity.

"Now I'd *really* better go," she said. "Before my dad comes out looking for us both."

"Thanks for the talk," he said. "It's been difficult keeping this all to myself."

"Thank you for trusting me." She watched him walk away. "Harrison?"

He turned back.

"Do you believe that General Stallworth ordered the deaths of Elias's people?"

"Given what I know of the man," Harrison said, "I'm very much afraid he did."

He nodded and waved. As he retreated into the mist, Peggy found herself staring at the traffic light. Its caution lights brightened and dimmed, one after the other, like a pair of yellow eyes winking down on her.

# THIRTY-SIX

Peggy followed the trail of her father's gear from the kitchen to the living room—hat on the counter, gunbelt over a chair, jacket and badge on the doorknob. Rusty was on the phone as she came in: he sat with an open file in his lap, propping his left leg on the sofa arm for comfort. His black boots were thrown against the coffee table.

"I don't think the house calls are doin' a bit of good, Corey." Rusty barely looked up as she sat across from him. "Hell's bells. *You* think he'd tell us if they got another message? Hang on. Our insider just arrived." He set the receiver on his neck. "You know if there's been another ransom communication to Aldridge? Like where they're supposed to wire the money to, anything like that?"

"Not to my knowledge. I can find out from Agent Randall."

"They got her in the dark, too." He rolled his eyes. "How's ole Tiny? Don't like the mint on his pillow? I dunno, turn a fire hose on him . . . see if that cools him off." He stretched. "Thanks for the call. Glad to know somebody's still keepin' me up to date."

He hung up—then continued to leaf through the file, as if Peggy wasn't even in the room.

"Tidwell?" she asked finally.

"Yeah. Seems like he's takin' that 'shut the fuck up or die' message pretty literal. You're the last one he actually said anything to. How's the professor?"

"Harrison's fine. Well, not fine. But he's okay."

"Harrison . . . is . . . okay. Good to know." He nodded. "I talked to your FBI buddy. Figured it'd get you off my case if I said I was sorry about callin' him black. He told me not to worry."

"Really."

"Yeah, I thought that was just too goddamn easy. So I reckoned he was settin' me up to argue about givin' my prisoner over to him." He raised his hand. "But whattya know? He said he it was all right by him if I wanted to negotiate with Tidwell. And maybe the two of us—meanin' you and me—should work out the details."

He eyed her like an old slow cat waiting on a bird.

"So it started me thinkin' about what you said today. About sharing information. Makes me wonder what my only girl's been up to these past few hours."

"Tap-dancing."

He laughed. "Young Master Blaine thinks I should offer Tidwell immunity. Plus a relocation to the Federal Witness Protection Program. Or even money."

"You think he'll go for it?"

"Tiny?" He shook his head. "Minute we put all that on the table, he'll know he's dead meat. Only thing that boy wants is someone to unlock his cell door and turn the other way. And maybe leave some keys in an unlocked car for him."

"And then we get what we want."

"Then we do," Rusty said. "What do you say?"

"Don't you care about breaking the law?"

He smiled and shook his head. "About as much as you and Agent Randall do, it appears."

She looked down at his boots. "How do you want to handle it?"

"Oh—I go into a room with him. We make sure the windows and doors are shut. And all the cameras are off, et cetera. Five minutes later I come out . . . and we've got us a deal."

In the silence that followed, she could hear easy-listening music from her mother's studio.

"Guess you don't think that's too much of a plan, huh?"

"It's great," she said. "Dad, how did you hurt your leg?"

He frowned. "What's that got to do with anything?"

"Skip it." She rubbed her temple. "Wait, no. Don't skip it. What happened? Why did you flunk out of school?"

"What the hell gives you a big enough lip to ask me that?"

"Because I want to know. I want to know who you are."

"I'm your goddamn father, that's who."

"I mean really. You got a scholarship to Avalon College that wasn't easy to get . . . and you pissed it away. You smashed up your leg—I don't know how or why—and then you became a guard at DeBerry and made friends with Uncle-Fester, Lester-the-Molester Tidwell. And you showed him my *baby pictures.*" She stopped, breathless. "And I want you to tell me who you really are, before I have to find out on my own."

He looked at her blankly. "How did you know?"

"How did I know what?"

"How did you know . . . they called Tidwell that?"

"I don't know," she said, stunned. "I just do."

"This was a bad idea." His shock went to sullen anger. "Agent Randall's wrong. I don't think you and I should be workin' this out together." He looked away. "Bea?"

"Dad, please tell me."

"Hold your water." He closed the file. "Bea, honey? You awake in there?"

"Is everything okay?" Peggy asked.

"I just smell somethin' burnin', is all." He set his leg down painfully. "Sometimes she falls asleep over the damn wood-burner, and it's like to set the whole house on fire."

"Let me go in with you."

"She's fine." He struggled up. "You tell Randall his offer's accepted. I'll put your mother to bed . . . and then I guess I'll drive over and have my say with Tiny. Should be over and done with inside two hours." He finally got his weight under him. "Tell him I only got one thing to ask in return."

"What's that?"

"You don't come within twenty yards of me on this investigation," he said. "Nor within a mile of Lester Tidwell."

She didn't answer him. He tucked the folder under his arm and went into the studio.

Peggy took the box from her jacket and opened it.

"Bea?" her father said. "Wake up, darlin'. You're havin' a bad dream."

"Where's—my baby girl?" Her mother's voice was slurred.

"Peggy's in the living room. We're just talkin', is all. You wanna go to bed? Let's get you to bed."

"I want to make sure my baby's all right. We had so much trouble getting her home. I want her to be safe."

Peggy looked into the sole of her father's left boot. The insole was loose and lifted up easily. She peeled the white sticker off the back of the transmitter—then placed the disk against the arch, where she knew Rusty would be least likely to feel it. She rubbed it for several seconds to make sure the adhesive took. Then she ran her finger slowly along the pad, making sure there was no noticeable bulge.

"What are you doin', Peggy Jean?"

Her father stared at her. Peggy's mother leaned in his arms—half-walking, half-carried.

"Hi, Mama."

She squinted hard at Peggy. "I want my *baby*."

"Bea, please," Rusty said. "Peg, I just asked you a question. What are you doin' with my boots?"

"Cleaning up after you." Peggy picked up the boots, then went for his jacket. "I'm tired of your mess."

# THIRTY-SEVEN

Peggy listened as the sound of her father's engine disappeared down the driveway. He'd grabbed his gear and gone: hat, jacket, gun. And boots. She started to phone Blaine—then thought better of it. *This was my call. I have to be the one to deal with it.*

She went upstairs to her room.

Peggy practically had to turn her field kit inside out before she finally located her wide-band surveillance radio. She switched it on and plugged in her earbuds, piping the signal through to a digital recorder. Getting the encryption properly keyed took a little longer. She could only hope that Blaine hadn't decided to change the code on her.

Peggy slowly tuned up through frequencies, dipping in and out of transmissions: a DEA meth lab stakeout near Manchester, an ATF wiretap of illegal gun dealers in Shelbyville. Then the static suddenly dropped out, replaced by clear silence.

*I am spying on my father.* Then, riding the wave of that stark knowledge: *And if Blaine doesn't come through with that warrant, I am breaking the law.* She wasn't sure which transgression was more shameful in the eyes of God—but she knew which would weigh heavier with the Office of Professional Responsibility.

Peggy was about to yank out the earphone jack when she heard it—the sound of a car engine, and four underinflated tires rolling over bad road. Blaine was right: That transmitter put out damned good audio.

*He'll be close to the train tracks by now,* she thought. Sure enough, she heard metal rails hit the tires a few seconds later. He always took those tracks too fast. It might be Rusty . . . or it might not. But there was one way to make sure. She picked up her cell phone and speed-dialed.

She heard it ringing at both ends.

"Yeah, go ahead." Her father's voice over the earbuds.

"Hello, Dad—?" Peggy turned the volume down to avoid a feedback loop. Then she realized that her own cell phone was still ringing; the voice that finally answered her was recorded. She'd gotten Rusty's voice mail.

Peggy quietly closed her phone.

"Yeah, hang on a second." He was talking to someone on his own cell . . . but not to her. "Thought I was gettin' another call. Sounds like they hung up. What do you want?"

Silence. Peggy made a note of the time: 11:59 P.M.

"I'm on my way to see him," Rusty said. "You want my opinion, whole thing feels set up. If it ain't, it's the first time in recorded history that the FBI ever kicked a prime suspect downstairs to a small-town cop."

Peggy heard rap music, slightly muffled, on his end. He was passing the Lambda house, as Peggy and Harrison had before.

"They ain't found dick on Tidwell," Rusty said. "He's safe. Why do we have to do this?"

The music faded. He was heading out of town. She'd have maybe another sixty seconds before the signal was gone. Peggy maxed out the gain. If there was a sudden noise, it would blow her eardrums out—but she had to get the other half of that conversation.

". . . terms of our arrangement." The new voice was faint, thinned out, broken by background noise and the nervous tapping of her father's foot. "You will proceed as directed and complete your mission. Or the little cunt dies."

"*Watch your mouth.*" She was unprepared for the boom in her father's voice. "Don't need to hear you talkin' that way."

Peggy had to stop to rub her ear.

". . . who's in command here, Rusty." It took her a second to adjust to hearing the quiet voice again. "You've done a fair enough job so far. But you screwed the pooch . . ." A wave of static swept through. ". . . daughter too close to the truth."

"Peggy don't know shit." Now that she had the rhythm of conversation down, it was easier to anticipate the volume changes. "I got the file right next to me in the car—and without that, she's nowhere."

"File or no file, we don't underestimate her. And something tells me you don't, either."

The only person her father trusted enough for that kind of frank conversation was Sheriff Powell. But Powell's voice was loose and drawling, like a bassett hound's. The voice she heard was more like the snarl of a wolf—hungry, patient, and keen. And there was no way Powell would ever use language like that.

"Just tell me what I gotta do," Rusty said. "How far does this thing have to go before it's finally over?"

"It ends when we say, not you. Be a good little boy, and I promise I won't shoot the bitch. Try to be a hero, and—hold on." There was a brief silence. And then she heard the stranger yelling:

"SHUT YOUR HOLE OR I'LL GUT YOU LIKE A FISH."

And then another human voice: a woman, softly weeping.

Samantha.

"Christ, what are you doin'?" Rusty asked, his voice tight. "Look, I'm tryin' like hell to cooperate. But if I pull a trigger, they're gonna land on me. And you'll lose your man inside this investigation."

"Don't be a broke-dick, Weaver. Finish the job."

The signal vanished in a foam of static.

For a brief instant, Peggy froze. She didn't know who her father was talking to . . . and yet she did. She'd heard that voice years before. *You know you want it, come and get it. Let's trade. You for her.*

And Samantha was alive . . . but for how long?

"Daddy," she said. "Oh, God."

Peggy grabbed for her cell phone. Agonizing seconds later:

"Blaine Randall." His name ended in a yawn.

"It's Weaver. The signal is working. My father—"

"Huh." A note of suspicion. "How do you know it's working?"

"I just do. Shut up and listen. You need to begin monitoring my father's frequency now. Find out if any other agency's accidentally landed on it during the past few minutes. And you'd better send somebody over to Keyes County Sheriff's Department. We've got less than half an hour before he arrives."

"Is Rusty still planning to let Tidwell go?"

"I don't think so. Not anymore."

Peggy was already strapping her weapon back on. And she knew she had no choice but to tell Blaine everything.

"I think he's going there to kill him," she said.

# THIRTY-EIGHT

Blaine said he could be there within the hour; Peggy knew they didn't have that long. She made a call of her own, then waited at her mother's bedside. Less than five minutes later, a truck's headlights flashed through the curtains.

"Mama," Peggy said. "I have to go now. Will you be okay?"

"Mm? Think so." Beatrice smiled. "That medicine makes my head funny. I hate it."

"Just go back to sleep," she said. "I'm locking the deadbolt behind me. If you get scared—or if anything happens—call my cell. Daddy may not be able to pick up."

"That Rusty, I swear." Bea opened her eyes. "How long are you staying home this time, dear?"

Someone was coming up the front walk. The doorbell rang.

"Only until we find Samantha." She started to stand up. But her mother wouldn't let go of her hand.

"All we ever wanted was for you to be safe," she said. "You will be, won't you? Safe?"

"Sure, Ma." The doorbell rang again. "Look, I also wrote down the number of the local FBI office. They'll know how to reach me ... if ... you know, I can't answer my phone."

"Of course. The FBI." She brightened. "Why, you must know my daughter. She's in the FBI, too."

Peggy started to talk ... and suddenly found she couldn't. Instead she simply bent down and kissed her mother good-bye.

---

Ripley was waiting for her next to his Dodge Ram. He'd thrown a leather jacket over his Logan Farms dress shirt.

"Sorry it took me so long," he said. "Hadda fill up."

"I owe you gas money." She climbed in. "Don't worry about the speed limits. Just don't get us killed." She took out her cell phone. "Be advised that you're going to hear me making some very confidential phone calls in the next twenty minutes."

He threw the truck into gear and backed out. "That's fine. I'm silent as the grave."

"Wish you'd put that differently. But thanks." She dialed. "Blaine, I'm on my way. What's the latest?"

"Sounds like he's almost to the station." There was highway noise on Agent Randall's end. "He hasn't made any other calls. Are you absolutely sure about what you heard?"

"I've got a record of the entire conversation." She took a breath. "We've got proof-of-life on Samantha. But she's being badly mistreated. I don't think we can expect the subject to honor his end of a ransom agreement."

"So noted. I was actually asking about your father."

"For the record, my father was not explicitly ordered to kill him. But I did hear him say that if he pulled the trigger on Tidwell, we'd know. He also referred to himself as the 'inside man.'"

"Exactly how did the other party respond?"

She cast a quick glance in Ripley's direction. "He said, 'Don't be a broke-dick, Weaver. Finish the job.'"

Ripley kept his eyes on the road.

"Well, it doesn't look good for your father," Blaine said. "I know this must be hard on y—"

"Please." Her voice was cool, even. "Do not offer me sympathy right now. I am not kidding."

"Suit yourself," he said. "As I see it, we have several options. We can detain your father as soon as he comes through the door. Or we can try and have Tidwell moved. Either of those could be difficult if Powell's men don't cooperate."

"So what's the alternative? Let the meeting happen?"

"Couldn't have said it better myself."

She blinked. "Blaine, are you out of your freaking mind?"

"Hear me out. Suppose that your father really is working with Samantha's kidnapper. That's a valuable link. If he's arrested . . . if he even suspects a trap . . . that connection is broken."

"I've heard that line of reasoning before, and it's never washed. We have a duty to protect our witness—even scumbags like Lester Tidwell. I say we move Tiny . . . I don't know, tell my father that we changed our minds."

"And if he doesn't buy it?"

"Then we detain him." She pinched her forehead. "And we trace the cell node from that phone call—which I hope to God is happening anyway."

"For what it's worth, yeah. But if the subject's smart, that phone's already been ditched. I still say we've been given a golden opportunity . . . and I think we'd be idiots to throw it away. Let's at least find out what Tidwell's got."

"It's not worth the risk." She took a breath. "I'm taking this to my SAC. It should be his call."

"You do that and you'll be sending your father to the lethal injection chamber," he said. "You do know that, right?"

"Yes." Peggy swayed a little, suddenly dizzy as Ripley took the turns down Suicide Run. For some reason, the words *working with Samantha's kidnapper* had yet to completely sink in.

"It doesn't have to be this way," Blaine said. "The risk is manageable. He'll have to surrender his weapon at the security checkpoint. We'll clear the room before he arrives. He'll have guards on him all the way . . . and you'll be there."

"I know you think my father's just a dumb hick," she said. "But he knows more about tactics than I learned at FBI Academy. If we're thinking a step ahead, then he's thought two."

"Look, I'm still—" Blaine paused. "Forty minutes away. He's probably less than ten. If you think you can stop him—without showing your hand—go ahead. I'll call Powell and see if I can buy you a few minutes. But that meeting will happen. Otherwise, all our sacrifices will have been for nothing."

"Pardon me, Blaine. 'Our' sacrifices?"

"I know you don't want to hear this," he said. "But it's time for you to stop thinking of this as a tragedy, and see it for what it is. A break. And you broke it."

"That's right. I broke it." She hung up.

She listened to the highway roll by. They were passing the 25 MPH sign, headed into open country.

"How much of that conversation did you hear, Ripley?"

"Not a word, Agent Weaver."

"So you don't have an opinion as to whether my father should be allowed to get close to Tidwell?"

"Oh, that. Yeah." He whistled. "You're right about the chief. He does think two steps ahead."

"He taught me everything I know," she said. "Why would he do it? Why would my father help the man who . . . did these things?"

"Beats me. When I first went to work for your daddy, I thought he was the best man in the world. And then today, when he knocked me down . . ."

It was no use. She'd used up all her strength arguing with Blaine, and she was fresh out. The tears tore through her, in spite of her, hot and angry.

*Why would he help the people who hurt Samantha?*

She wanted Mike. But Mike was gone, and she didn't know how to find him. It would have to be enough that Ripley was there, his hand on the wheel, showing the simple respect of not looking her way as she bawled her eyes out. And so the two of them passed the empty silence of Highway 23.

# THIRTY-NINE

Ten minutes later, they parked beside her father's cruiser in front of the Keyes County Sheriff's Station. The e-mail Peggy had been waiting for was on her handheld:

```
FROM:     Ass't Deputy Director, Investigations
TO:       SAC Knoxville
CC:       Knoxville; Philadelphia; Weaver; Randall
TITLE:    Unsub
          Samantha Aldridge-Victim
          Kidnapping Matter
          00-Chattanooga RA
SUBJECT:  Special Weaver's request for override of Special
          Agent Randall's operational authority in ALDRIDGE
          investigation has been duly considered and is
          deemed inadvisable. Proceed per his directives.
```

Like so many memos from headquarters, its language was at once unequivocal and totally vague. Nothing about her father or Tidwell—or the wiretap—had been committed to writing: She'd asked for judgment and they'd tossed her a fig leaf.

"You need me to come in with you?" Ripley asked.

Peggy shook her head. Her eyes were dry.

As she pushed open the wire-glass doors, Sheriff Powell was waiting for her, worn out and plainly frustrated.

"Maybe now I can get some answers," he said. "Where does Agent Randall get off 'instructing' me to restrict access to Tidwell? I gotta say, I do not like his tone."

"It's my fault," she said. "There's a couple of minor protocols I forgot to review with my father. Mostly concerning the immunity from prosecution we're authorized to grant Tidwell in exchange for his assistance."

He frowned. "Come on, girl. You know I deserve better than that line of BS."

She lowered her voice. "Did Randall say anything else?"

"No." But something in his eyes made her think that wasn't entirely true.

"It's something I really need to discuss with my father," she said. "Can you tell me where he is?"

"Right here," her father said as he emerged from the men's room.

"I'll wait for you at the barrier, Rusty." Powell backed off to the checkpoint. "Lemme know when you're ready to go in."

"I'm ready now." He waited till Powell was out of earshot. "Thought I made myself pretty damn clear, Peg."

"Well, I'm not standing twenty yards away," she said. "I think we need to finish the conversation we started before."

"Yeah? Is that why you called me in the car? And hung up two seconds later?" He snorted. "Or did you just want to hear my voice?"

"Dad, I want you to resign from the investigation."

He walked away from her. "Why? You think I'm a bad cop?"

She followed him. "You're a good cop. That's the trouble. Maybe you never finished college—" She watched him wince. "And I was wrong to hold that over you. But you're too good to be thrown off the trail so easily. And too smart to put so much blind faith in Tidwell."

He unbuckled his gun belt and handed it to the security deputy. "If you think so highly of me, why do you want me off the case? Is it because I haven't found your friend?"

"No," she said. "But I'm starting to think you don't want to."

She'd expected her father to blow a gasket, and she was strangely unnerved when he didn't. All he did was smile, as if to say "Nice try."

"Sorry I haven't been actin' up to your high standards," he said. "But I ain't gonna let you question my intentions."

"Right," she said. "*Exitus acta probat.*"

"You been hangin' around that Harrison too damn much." He finished emptying his pockets into the basket—then, as a final gesture, removed his silver badge and handed it to the deputy. Then Rusty put his left boot through the metal detector.

Peggy took a breath. The machine whined . . . and fell silent again as he passed through.

"Corey," he said. "What's that you say every time that leg of mine fires off the machine?"

"Can't blame it for thinkin' you're a deadly weapon," Powell answered without smiling.

Peggy watched her father's belongings pass through the X-ray scanner: all clear.

"Funny thing about that," Rusty said. "I never had to kill anybody in my entire life." He glanced back at Peggy. "My daughter, though—she knows how it feels to take someone out. She's got those hunter's eyes."

He retrieved his wallet and keys, leaving his weapon—and his badge— on the belt of the X-ray machine.

"Let's see how Tidwell's faring the heat," Rusty said. "Good night, Peggy Jean."

He walked away. As he disappeared around the corner, Peggy's eyes met Powell's.

"I'd like to watch them move Tidwell," she said.

"Sure." Powell waved her along.


He brought her into the darkened security room. Black-and-white monitors covered the hallways leading to the lockup, as well as the individual cells. Lester Tidwell stood in one of them, a deputy on each arm. He wore handcuffs and leg irons, and seemed desperately worried.

"They're gonna move Tiny first. Into there." Powell pointed to another screen. "That's the room for attorney-client meetings. It's the only one with no cameras or microphones. Your daddy will have to stay behind the inner security gate until he gets the all-clear. Then he'll be escorted every step of the way."

"How much did Blaine tell you?" she asked.

Powell turned to the surveillance technician. "Hoke, give us the room, please."

The deputy nodded and left.

"Agent Randall said a lot of things," he said after the door closed. "You think your daddy's capable of gunning down a suspect?"

"Yes." It was the hardest single word she'd ever spoken.

"I just don't see it. Maybe they forced him, or—hell, let's talk to the man. Probably it's all a big mistake."

Peggy didn't answer. On screen, the guards uncuffed Tidwell, leaving him alone in the interview room. The deputies locked the door, then took their posts to either side.

"Sheriff, this is Checkpoint Two," a voice said over Powell's walkie-talkie. "Prisoner's in place. Request authorization to admit Chief Weaver to secure area."

Powell looked at Peggy. "What do I tell them?"

"Give me a minute." She watched her father stop at the barred automatic gate to the cell block. He submitted grimly to another pat-down for weapons. Finally he got the thumbs-up.

"Why are we letting this happen?" The sheriff was beginning to look terrified.

"Agent Randall thinks we need to hear what Tidwell has to say to my father. Any small clue that could lead us to Samantha's kidnappers. And my superiors are backing him up."

"And what do you think?"

"I think it's a bad idea." She swallowed; her mouth had gone dry. "Send him through, please."

Peggy felt her stomach tighten as Powell gave the order.

"Are your men ready to move in on your signal?" she asked.

"Yeah. But how would I know when to give it?"

She looked at him. "We've got my father bugged."

Powell's eyes opened wide—then he simply nodded.

The barred door of the security gate was sliding open. Her father walked through, a few feet ahead of his escort. As he passed the camera, he looked straight up—almost as if he could see Peggy watching him. And there was no mistaking the hard certainty in his eyes.

"Something's not right," she said. "We're not doing this. Get Tidwell back to his cell. Now."

"Peggy, what—"

She was already moving for the door.

As she ran for the metal detector, the deputy tried to block her way. "Can't go through—"

Peggy knocked him aside. The alarm went off as she ran through.

The hallway seemed endlessly huge, and she nearly slipped as she rounded the corner. Her father was slower than her—but he had the advantage of a head start. And even as the amber lockdown beacons began to flash, the gate was sliding shut between them . . . trapping Peggy and the deputies on the wrong side.

"Open the gate! Open it up!"

"We got a lockdown," the deputy said. "Sheriff says—"

"It's okay." Powell caught up, out of breath. "They'll . . . stop him at the door. Your daddy won't get in."

"I don't care," she said. "Open the gate!"

Powell signalled. It slid open with agonizing slowness, and she had to squeeze herself through. As Peggy ran, she could hear her father's footsteps of her.

*"Daddy, stop!"*

Her father's hand was on the handle of the interview room door. He looked at her—angered, but not surprised.

"Has he gone in?" she asked the deputies. "Answer me. Has he opened that door yet?"

The two men numbly shook their heads.

"What are you doing here?" Rusty's voice was oddly calm.

"It's over, Dad. Whatever you're carrying, put it down." She waited. "Please take your hand from the door."

"I'm not carrying anything." He set his jaw. "Y'all search me again if you want."

"Put your hands up," she commanded. "Slowly."

He raised his palms to her. And then she saw.

His right hand was red and blistered from where it had touched the handle. And now smoke was pouring from beneath the door. A smell of burning fat.

"Oh my god," she said. "Get a medical team. Now."

"Child, don't go in there." Her father was suddenly fearful as the deputies took hold of his elbows. "Peggy!"

By then she could hear screaming from inside the interview room. Peggy moved for the door.

"Honey, get back!" Rusty threw himself on her.

They struck the ground—and the door exploded outward. Black smoke poured into the hallway. And fire.

Lester Tidwell was burning.

# FORTY

Peggy looked at the clock as Blaine came into the morgue: almost 2:00 A.M.

"My father said it'd all be over and done with in two hours. He was right." She turned, but only slightly: her forehead and the back of her right hand were freshly bandaged.

Blaine flinched, holding his nose against the smell of charred flesh. Lester Tidwell's remains lay under a plastic sheet, still dusted with the white foam of the fire extinguishers. His right foot and most of his left arm were still intact; Peggy could count the hairs on his forearm. Near the elbow was a scrap of orange cloth . . . and above that, only blackened bone. There wasn't enough left of him to fill a grocery bag.

"You've made positive ID?" Blaine asked.

Peggy nodded. "And we still don't know how my father did it." She looked at him. "It was a bad call, Blaine."

He frowned. "Let's go talk to the sheriff."

She stood with some difficulty: The painkillers were making her dizzy, and that was only half as much as the EMTs had wanted to give her. The skin on her gun hand throbbed dully.

"The deputies got away with superficial burns," she told him as they walked to the surveillance room. "My dad was shielding me with his body, so he took more of the heat. They've got him sedated at Keyes County Hospital."

"We should bring him around," he said. "Find out who sent him."

She didn't answer—just froze him with her eyes.

"My father will be awake soon enough," she said. "And when he does . . . I promise you, I'll be the one talking to him."

They went into the darkened video room. Sheriff Powell looked at her with muted sorrow.

"Hey, girl," he said to her. "Agent Randall. Y'all come and see this."

On the monitor was a ten-second video loop from the camera outside the interview room. It showed Rusty approaching the door, followed by his escort. A moment later, the guards turned away and moved off-camera. Rusty stood perfectly still.

Peggy leaned in for a closer view. Her father simply stepped up to the door of the interview room and took hold of the steel handle. Then the loop began again.

"Who else had access to that room?" she asked.

"We made a sweep as soon as your daddy showed up," Powell said. "It was clean."

"Maybe one of your deputies planted a device," Blaine said.

Powell seemed at the end of his tether. "I checked the room myself, Agent Randall."

"This isn't getting us anywhere," Peggy said. "The fact is, Tidwell's dead. And my father's the only remaining link we have. So we better make damn well sure he's protected."

"Understood," Powell said. "Now about Rusty's personal effects—"

"The phone, right." She turned to Blaine. "The incoming call didn't show up on my father's account. So let's get on finding the phone itself. The number's probably encoded in the SIM card."

"I'm pretty sure he pitched it out the window," Blaine said. "How many miles between here and Avalon, Sheriff?"

"Thirty-five." Powell exhaled. "I don't wanna tell you how long it'll take to work that entire stretch."

"We won't have to," she said. "We've got the audio surveillance on tape. Let's just play it back until we hear a window opening. Estimate the distance from Avalon at—let's say, sixty-five miles per hour. That should narrow it down."

"Good idea," Blaine said. "Now we've got a briefing in less than six hours. So I suggest we grab as much sleep as we can. Sheriff, you know any decent hotels in the area?"

"I don't think we'll be sleeping tonight." Peggy looked at her watch. "Given Samantha's condition, we have to move now. Have there been any more communications to the Aldridges?"

"Not that I know of," Blaine said.

"Maybe we should find out for sure?" She shook her head. "And where's that file of Samantha's e-mails that Sean was supposed to give us by ten o'clock?"

"Understood. I'll speak to him."

"Sean doesn't deserve another warning," she said. "You and I are going over there. Sheriff, I may need you to join us in a while."

"You got it," he said.

"Hold on." Blaine held up his hands. "If we're going there to impound anything, we'll need search warrants."

"Send them along with the one you promised me for my father," she said. "Come on. I'll provide the wheels this time."

She let him get through the door ahead of her. Then she took Sheriff Powell by the arm.

"When my father was on the phone," she said, "he talked about a file. Did you find anything . . . ?"

"I was about to mention it before. I figured you must've had a good reason for cutting me off." Powell handed her a brown folder—the same one she'd seen Rusty looking through before. "Can't say what good it's gonna do ya, though. Don't make much sense, does it?"

She opened the file, studied it in silence.

"Not much," she said finally. "I need you to take care of something else while I'm gone."

# FORTY-ONE

The three of them somehow managed to crowd into the seat of the Dodge Ram—Ripley at the wheel, Peggy on the right, Blaine uncomfortably in the middle.

"I know you haven't been working for the Aldridges very long," Peggy said to Ripley, "but did you happen to overhear any conversations about Sean's appointment as president? Maybe some financial plan they've got in the works?"

"Not really." Of the three of them, Ripley was the closest to cheerful. "The only time Mr. Logan mentioned business was to ask me how I felt about all them big luxury houses they're puttin' up over to Mill Creek. I told him that my idea of luxury is bein' able to afford a washer *and* dryer on the front yard. He thought that was pretty funny."

"Glad to know we're traveling with a man of taste," Blaine said evenly.

Peggy shot a look at him. But Ripley didn't seem ruffled.

"I've been running scenarios on my handheld," she said to Blaine. "We'll have to cut our operational deadline in half. Any chance of getting your just-as-good, twice-as-fast hostage rescue team in place before dawn?"

He shifted uncomfortably. "In place where? We don't even have a general location for Samantha Aldridge."

"That's correct. But if she's anywhere inside a hundred-mile radius, we'd better be prepared to move."

"I can patch something together in a few hours," he said. "We'll have to beg a squad from ATF in Chattanooga . . . possibly bring in a few warm bodies from Knoxville. . . ."

"We'd better do more than just 'patch it together,' or those guys are gonna be tripping over each other's boots. What's the recovery plan?"

"Nice to know you're still asking my opinion," he fumed. "I'm only the case agent here."

"That's an accident of geography," she said. "No offense to the great state of Tennessee."

"None taken." It was Ripley who answered. "Looks like they left the lights on for us at Logan Farms."

Half a dozen security trucks and black GMC four-wheels were parked close to the mansion. Guards in flak vests and dark baseball caps were checking equipment . . . and weapons. There looked to be enough force to guard a federal reserve bank, Peggy decided—or to rob one, for that matter.

"Who are these knuckleheads?" she asked.

"You're gonna have to believe me when I say I don't know." Blaine squinted as the gatehouse guard shone a flashlight into his eyes.

"What are you people doing here?" It wasn't one of the regular security, but a man in gray fatigues, with the bricklike appearance of a retired gunnery sergeant. He openly wore a .45 sidearm on his hip.

Blaine held up his badge. "My name is Special Agent Randall, FBI. This is Special Agent Weaver. We're here on official business." He waited. "So we'd like you to open up the gate."

"And move the damn flashlight," Ripley muttered.

"Those are not my instructions." The guard didn't budge. "This is private property. You'll have to turn around."

"Or what?" Peggy asked.

"Believe me, you don't wanna know," he said baldly.

"I believe we've just been threatened, Agent Randall."

"Enough of this." Blaine speed-dialed his phone. "Yeah. Sean, it's me. We're at the gate and . . . we'd like to come in, okay?"

He closed the phone, looking strangely unrelieved.

"Well?" Peggy asked.

"Voice mail," he said.

"Keeping in mind that we're federal agents," Peggy said to the guard, "what exactly are you prepared to do?"

"Ma'am, I am done talking to you." He tensed. "Now you and your two boyfriends clear the goddamn area."

She raised her hands, a timid woman put in her place. "Okay, okay. We're just gonna back up, and . . . turn around? Is that all right?"

He didn't answer. Peggy motioned Ripley to put it in reverse.

"Roll up the window," she said. "Blaine, are we going home, or what?"

"Sean sent my call to voice mail," he said. "You can see the lights on in his room. Doesn't he know it's me out here?"

"Oh, I think he does." She watched the guard bearing down on them. "Crash the gate, Ripley."

Ripley sighed. "Don't suppose you got another job lined up for me? 'Cause I'm pretty sure I'm about to get fired."

"Don't worry," she said. "I'll keep you covered."

"Damn collar kept itchin' my neck anyhow." He floored it.

The guard barely had time to move before they punched through the barrier. The armed men in front of the house were beginning to fan out.

"Do not get into a moving vehicle with Peggy Weaver," Blaine said to her. "That's my lesson for the day."

She looked over her shoulder. "Blaine, get down!"

She pushed him down as cordite flashed around the guard's .45. A split-second later, the truck's rear windshield burst.

"Motherfuckers!" Ripley tore off across the lawn. "I ain't even got this thing paid off yet!"

"Steady," she said. "We're right where we need to be."

He skidded to a halt in front of the house. The red dots of half a dozen laser scopes fell on them as the security team closed in. Peggy looked up as the front door to the house opened. The Aldridge family's private detective looked down, hands on hips. As soon as they saw him, the guards silently raised their rifles.

"At least we know who's giving orders," Peggy said. "Looks like Sean's brought in a few warm bodies of his own."

Sean was waiting for them in the main gallery, dressed in Abercrombie & Fitch hiking clothes.

"Hey, what's with the stormy eyes?" he said. "You okay?"

"We're fine," Peggy said. "Better change into something a little more functional. You're about to pay another visit to County. Your man at the gate took a shot at us."

"*And* trashed my windshield," Ripley said.

"Well, now, that's your understanding of things," Sean said. "My understanding is that the guard was under orders to protect this property, and you people failed to show a proper search warrant. And then you just barreled on through." He turned to Blaine. "What's *your* understanding, Agent Randall?"

Blaine was impassive. "He fired at us, Sean."

"Okay, that was excessive. And contrary to my instructions. He'll be ter-minated for that. And then you can arrest him if it suits you. We'll be happy to . . . make a generous severance offer to Ripley." He looked to Peggy. "Satisfied?"

"Oh, you'd know if I was." She pointed at his guards. "What's with the private army?"

"Just looking after my family. After what happened to Lester Tidwell, my father's been forced to conclude that neither the FBI nor local authori-ties are up to the job of finding my wife. So we're taking out a little insur-ance. Incidentally, all these men are licensed to carry heavy firearms. Just so you don't jump to the wrong conclusions again."

"How'd you hear about Tidwell?" Peggy said.

"Turn on your police radio," he answered. "Now if you're interested to know what we're planning . . ."

"Where's Logan?" she said. "I want to hear this directly from him."

"My father's asleep," Sean answered evenly. "As I understand yours is, too?"

She cooled, letting him know he hadn't earned a reply.

"Let me guess," he said. "You want to hit me in the face again."

She folded her arms. "Actually, I had a different part of your anatomy in mind."

He started to turn pale—then just as suddenly laughed.

"Same old Peggy," he said. "Now, girl, don't be so pissed off. It's not like anybody got hurt."

# FORTY-TWO

There was a gas log in the fireplace of the billiards room, and Peggy decided to switch it on while she tried again to reach Mike. Whether it was from the the burns, the painkillers, or sheer exhaustion, she just couldn't stay warm.

The gas flames glowed yellow. *The color of his eyes,* she thought irrationally. She still couldn't make herself see him. But she was beginning to hear his voice: *Complete your mission. Or the little cunt dies.* That was enough to make her skin crawl.

Peggy cautiously opened the creased brown folder Powell had given her. It still smelled like her father's leather jacket. Inside was a single sheet of yellow construction paper.

It was a child's drawing of a man standing in front of a black automobile.

There was very little finesse to it. The young artist seemed to be trying very hard to get the details right: the sharklike curves of the T-Bird's hood, its chromium trim colored silver; the flame yellow eyes of the man in black. The red snake on his belt buckle. The thin, terrified blond girl in his arms, writhing as she stared with helpless blue eyes. And the car's bumper sticker, childishly lettered in orange-red:

**ASS, GAS, OR GRASS**
**NOBODY RIDES FOR FREE!**

It was just as she'd heard it in her dream. The drawing was signed: *Peggy Jean Weaver, Age Ten.* And Peggy had absolutely no recollection of making it. Ever.

As she heard several pairs of footsteps approaching, Peggy sent a text message to Mike Yeager:

things are officially crazy
can you hear me snapping my fingers?

Sean was the first to enter, carrying a computer hard disk. The private detective was immediately behind him, followed by his attorney. Agent Randall entered last.

"Here's those server files we promised you." Sean set the disk in the center of the red baize pool table. "It includes the daily backups of Samantha's network disk over the past week, as well as all of her e-mails. The one she received on Thursday is literally an eye-opener."

"Have we traced the source of the e-mail yet?"

No one answered.

"There have been at least four communications from the unsub," she said. "A text message to Sean, another to Tidwell, an e-mail to Samantha, and a phone call to my father. We ought to be capable of triangulating a source from one of them."

"We've had our people working on this for two days," Sean said. "If you think you can get better results, by all means."

"You know, that's a very good idea." She placed a call on her cell phone. "Hey, it's me. We're ready for you."

She hung up.

"Who did you just speak to?" Blaine asked.

"You'll find out," she said. "Sean, have you received any follow-up instructions from the kidnapper?"

"Negative," he said.

"No destination for a wire transfer or cash dropoff—or any communication of any kind?"

"Have we?" He glanced to the detective. "It appears not."

"Don't you think that's strange?" she asked. "Or are you still waiting for the Wednesday morning deadline?"

"We're not waiting," he said. "As a matter of fact—"

A moment later, the night butler entered the room and whispered something to Sean. He nodded and turned to the room.

"Sheriff Powell is here," he said. "And he's brought . . . some Chinese guy with him?"

"My God, civilization!" Yoshi Hiraka entered wearing a blue FBI windbreaker, a travel kit over his arm. The bruise on his forehead—souvenir of the Storytime raid—was partly concealed by a Phillies baseball cap. "Boss, I thought I was gonna starve to death before I found you. This place is like *Gone With the Wind* on creatine."

She smiled in spite of herself. "I'm glad you got my message. Did Shoreh tell you I called?"

"Yeah, and watch out. She's got some idea that you and Mike are doubledating with us next week, and—holy *crap*, is that one of the new hot-swap server boxes?" He lifted the disk, inspecting it like a dog show judge. "This must be the famous hard disk of Dr. Aldridge. I guess you pulled it directly from the network array?"

"Absolutely," Sean said. "Peggy, who is this guy?"

"Well, to start with, 'this guy' isn't Chinese," Peggy said. "This is Special Agent Hiraka. For the record, I believe he's from—where are you from, Yoshi?"

"South Bend, Indiana." He sat down. "Mind if I plug in? I'm still riding a buzz from all that airline coffee."

"Knock yourself out," Peggy said.

As he set up his laptop, she went to meet Sheriff Powell, standing in the doorway with a plastic evidence bag.

"Here's all we could find of your daddy's cell phone," the sheriff whispered. "Agent Hiraka's already looked it over. Hope you don't mind."

"That's why I wanted you to bring him," she said.

Powell leaned in. "I've been runnin' tag numbers on those GMC offroads out front. They're all registered to a company called Kadmos Security. Whoever the hell they are."

"Good to know," she said. "You mind sticking around?"

"Listen, you say the word, I'll run the lot of 'em in for loitering. I don't like the looks of those guys."

"Me neither," she said. "I do have one more favor to ask. Ripley could get in a lot of trouble for crashing that gate on my command. I know my father probably blackballed him . . ."

"Rip and me had a talk earlier on. He's a fine boy. I'll deputize him for ya."

"Thanks, Sheriff." She rejoined the room. Yoshi was in high gear, scanning files from the hard disk. "Got anything?"

"I've got *something*," he said. "Agent Randall, can you or Mr. Aldridge tell me what you used to trace this e-mail?"

"Standard tracking software," Sean said. "We checked host names in the Internet headers against IP addresses. They all dead-ended at nonfunctioning servers."

"Well, there's your trouble. Never trust a computer to tell you its true name." He pointed to a highlighted section of text on the screen. "The domain server shown as the e-mail's point of origin is fake. The *real* IP address is ten lines back, surrounded by a bunch of false ones. Classic misdirection."

"Hidden in plain sight, huh?" Sean nodded. "They do look a lot alike."

"I guess that's how so many Japanese-Americans get mistaken for Chinese," Yoshi said with no detectable rancor. "Anyhow, it's not just *where* the message was sent from that's important, but *how* they sent it. And right there, you can see the software program is one used by handheld computers."

"So they're using cell phone telephony to send messages," Peggy said. "How would they be operating?"

"Verrry carefully," Yoshi said. "My guess is they've commandeered a cell tower node, and the phone company doesn't know about it."

"Could that explain the untraceable calls my mother's been receiving?"

"Sure. But if they're gonna do that, they're also going to need a direct input signal. Which means they're probably based within . . . oh, ten miles of the tower?"

"That's still three hundred square miles," Blaine said. "And we don't even know which base station they'd be using."

"There's a tower two miles east of Glencoe Bluff," Peggy said. "You can see it from the Stallworths' house."

The men all fell silent. Yoshi shared a smile with her.

"I'll get started on surveillance," Blaine said. "We should be able to pull some recent satellite images."

"Let me know if you need any help." Yoshi cracked his knuckles. "So that's done. What's next?"

"Show me the e-mail to Samantha," Peggy said.

He opened it for her:

HELLO BLUEYES
REMEMBER WHAT I SAID ABOUT CROSSBREEDING
YOU GET LETHAL WHITE
SO QUIT CRYING AND KEEP QUIET
YOU'VE EARNED EVERYTHING THAT'S COMING

"You've seen that last photograph?" Sean asked.

Peggy nodded. "Yoshi, you said it was a layered file?"

"Yup." He pressed a few buttons. "At first it looks like the eyes are shut. But if you hide that layer, you can see that they're really open. And maybe . . . just maybe if you turn the background off . . ."

He clicked a button, and the photograph of Samantha disappeared. All that was left were Peggy's closed eyelids, against white—and three words:

**YOU FOR HER**

"We don't know what that means," Sean said. "Do you?"

"Not a clue," Peggy answered.

# FORTY-THREE

"How could it be directed at you?" Yoshi asked.

Peggy looked over her shoulder before answering. The two of them had retreated to an alcove near the front door.

"It's what the subject said to me the first time Samantha was kidnapped," she replied finally. "Based on that—and considering that he used a picture of my eyes—I believe the photograph was intended as a message to me."

"If that's the case . . . aren't you in danger?"

"Maybe." She looked at him. "You can't tell anybody, Yoshi. I know I'm putting you in a hell of a position. But you've got to trust me on this."

"Okay." Yoshi looked at her, deeply troubled. "So what's 'Lethal White'? Some kind of skinhead band?"

"It's a horse-breeding term," Peggy said. "Most so-called white horses are actually pale gray or cream. True whites are very rare . . . usually the result of bad interbreeding . . . and they don't live very long. So, 'lethal white syndrome.'"

"I'm guessing this guy Aldridge would know that, too?" He looked around. "So . . . maybe we shouldn't be talking here?"

She nodded. "Good point."

"There's a couple of things I didn't want to say in front of everybody." He lowered his voice. "We identified that GPS device on your Jeep. It's Ukrainian."

"What?"

"The components are all of a type developed by the KGB. Very popular with mobsters like the ones the Cookes hired. I'll know for sure when I send it back to the lab . . . but my guy doesn't think it was planted around here. Chances are that little white box hitched a ride with you all the way from Philadelphia."

Peggy whistled. "What's the other thing?"

"I'm pretty sure Aldridge is lying to you about that hard drive. There's no way it could be the original server disk. If it was, there'd be overwritten data, and you'd see fragments of other people's accounts. And it's just way too clean and pretty for that."

"You mean it's a copy?"

"Big time. It's even got that new-server-disk smell." He stood up. "Food for thought, huh?"

"Let's get that damn thing off my Jeep," she said.

Fifteen minutes later, the GPS device was safely deactivated. Peggy and Yoshi rode east on Highway 23 with the top down. Glencoe Bluff, Avalon Mountain's eastern face, was behind them. The cell phone tower's red beacon glowed in the distance ahead.

"Can we use the tracker to triangulate a point of origin?" She had to raise her voice to be heard over the wind.

"Yes and no." He checked the box, now wired into his laptop. "Once every cycle, the tracking device pings back to its source. Sort of like sonar. We can get an approximate range by measuring the time it takes to echo back. But if they're moving around, it's gonna be hard to lock down."

"Trouble is, even if we have the distance, we won't know which direction to go." She shivered. "We'll get one shot at this. And if we're wrong . . ."

She fell silent as they passed the cell tower.

"You took a big risk helping me these past couple of days," Peggy said finally. "I hope they went easy on you at Quantico."

"Like an enema," he said. "Actually, Mike took most of the heat. They threw everything at him."

"You're talking about those charges from last year? The evidence-tampering thing?"

"That was just for openers. I'm talking mean stuff, Peggy. They read his psych report out loud, right in front of me. Stuff I never even suspected. Like how his father used to kick him around, and his mother's killing herself . . ."

"What?"

"Mike's mother committed suicide when he was—nine, I think they said. He never told you?"

"No."

"Shoreh said I should keep my mouth shut." Yoshi shrank. "I just figured, as close as you guys are . . ."

"Maybe not so close," she said. "Seems like you can know someone your whole life, and . . . not know them at all."

"Sorry, boss. I had no idea."

"I've been trying to get ahold of Mike all day. I sent him a text message an hour ago, and he still hasn't returned it."

Yoshi was silent for a moment. "I know I'm really digging my grave now. But when I got my orders to Tennessee—and Mike didn't—the guy from OPR sort of suggested it was because you were only allowed to choose one of us."

"And I chose you," Peggy said. "My problems are mainly tech related. And you're my tech guy. Mike knows that."

"He does. But . . . well, you know Yeager. It hurt him a little. He swore a sacred oath to protect you."

"I know." Peggy sighed. "I can't do anything about hurt feelings, Yoshi."

"No prob," he said. "But can I ask you one question?"

She nodded.

He looked around. "Where are we going?"

"To the hospital," she said. "I have to see my father."

# FORTY-FOUR

She found him sitting up in bed. The sharp, greasy smell of medicated cream hung in the air. Rusty's neck was bandaged, and some of his hair had scorched away. But he still looked ready to go another fifteen rounds with the whole damn world.

"He gave me my rights." Her father's voice was slow from heavy painkillers. "Corey Powell . . . who I've known since kiddygarten . . . read me my fuckin' Mirandas." He took a slow breath. "I guess your old man's a criminal now."

"Did you do it?" she asked. "Did you murder Tidwell?"

He hesitated. "Yeah. I did it. Burned him."

"Why?"

He looked at her. "Don't you wanna know *how*?"

"Sure, Dad. Tell me how."

"Soon as you figure it out, let me know," he said. "Can't seem to work it out."

He laughed weakly—but there wasn't a trace of sarcasm in his voice. He seemed to be genuinely mystified.

"Dad, did you go in there with intent to kill . . . or not?"

"Maybe you should check that bug you planted in my boot. The audio might give you a clue."

"Maybe I should just ask you about this." She held out the drawing. "Was this me? Did I draw this?"

"Yeah." He didn't look at it.

"When I was ten. Right after it all happened."

He nodded. "Yeah."

"Why don't I remember?"

"Maybe you're smarter not to," he said.

She stared at the floor. "Look, we're going to try to save Samantha tonight. It's a long shot. But you heard how she sounded on the phone. What that guy said. If you could . . ."

"I don't know where they're keepin' her," he said.

"You know who he is. The same man who took her all those years ago." She nodded. "And I guess you must have known who he was, even then. Didn't you? Because you saw this drawing. And all these years, you hid the truth from me."

He seemed about to speak—then looked away.

"I am so tired of hating you," she said. "Not just for getting on my case over the license plate, or his description. And you've got to admit that was pretty goddamn cruel."

Finally he nodded.

"And you still won't tell me his name," she said.

"I can't," he said. "I don't expect you to understand."

"Believe me, I don't." She put the drawing away. "You know what I hated you for the most? Training me to run away at the first sign of danger. To be the one who got away clean. And never got hurt."

She took a deep breath.

"Well, I'm hurting now, Daddy. I really am."

"I'm sorry, kiddo. I am. But that's as good as I got."

"He sent me a message," she said. "Through Samantha. 'You for her.' What does he want with me?"

Rusty looked at her, surprised. "That's what it said?"

"Yes. What does it mean?"

"Go back to Philadelphia." He closed his eyes. "For your mama's sake, just . . . go away. And don't ever come back."

"Krypteia," she said. "Is that who kidnapped Samantha?"

"Yes." He spoke as if making a confession.

"Are you part of Krypteia?"

"No," he said.

"Will you tell me who's behind this?"

"I don't know who's behind it," he said. "And there's no way in hell I'll tell you who's in front of it. You just gotta know that everything was to protect you. If your hating me is the price for that . . . then I guess it's a price I have to pay."

"Samantha said it best. You can't protect people by hiding the truth from them." She stood to leave.

"I never lied to you about anything that mattered," he said. "I know you think your old man's a broke-leg redneck, with no grace or pity in his heart. Well, guess what? He is. And that's just a truth you're gonna have to live with. You can get all the college degrees you want, but it's still my blood in your veins. These fine Avalon people you been courtin' all these years . . . they're not our kind. They'll let us warm their beds and die in their wars . . . they'll never let us inside. Not unless it's to carry their garbage out."

"So you've been telling me all my life."

"I know I was mean to you. But it's a mean old world. I had to stay rough . . . push you hard as you'd go . . . so you'd keep your guard up, and your wits about you. And not let people use you. I never thought you'd love me for it. All I ever wanted was to make you strong. And you are, Peggy. Stronger than me."

She didn't answer him.

"Reckon I've taught you all I know, over the years," he said. "Haven't I?"

She nodded.

"But I didn't teach you all *you* know. There's one thing you can do that I can't. And that's to cut out the things that hurt you—like love, and fear, and . . . bad memories. Like some button you can push that turns your heart off, when you have to. You proved it tonight when you planted that wire on me."

"I can't apologize for who I am," she said.

"You shouldn't." He shook his head. "But if people know that about you . . . they can use that knowledge to kill you."

"It goes with the job." She reached for the door. "If I have to die to save Samantha, I will."

"Baby." Her father's voice was achingly soft. "In spite of everything . . . are you still my little girl?"

He was looking at her in a way she'd never seen from him before: a pinched sadness in the mouth, a growing terror in his eyes. Absolute heartbreak.

She couldn't make herself say what he wanted to hear. And the words she wanted to say could never be taken back. In the end, she simply stood silent, watching her father's expression turn to stone.

"Fair enough." He nodded grimly. "Go on, then."

# FORTY-FIVE

"Is your dad okay?" Yoshi asked as she returned to the Jeep.

"He won't help us," she said.

They drove in silence for a while.

"Yoshi, what would Mike do if he was here?"

He looked up. "You mean, apart from making us drive around all night looking for a convenience store that sells his particular brand of nauseating root beer?"

"Apart from that, yeah. How would Mike be reading the evidence?"

"Hm." Yoshi pursed his lips. "You know how you're always telling us to ask ourselves, 'Who profits from the crime?'"

"You're the second person who's reminded me of that lately. The problem is, I just can't see who stands to gain from Samantha's suffering. Unless it really is about the ransom."

"Maybe. But see, that's your question. Mike doesn't ask himself, 'Who gets helped?' He asks, 'Who gets hurt?' You know that's all he ever talks about. Who's suffering?"

"Well, that's obvious. Samantha."

"And who else?"

"Lots of people. Her son . . . her father . . . Elias . . ." Peggy concentrated for a moment. "That's as far as I can think."

"You don't include yourself?"

"I do," she said. "But that's been my problem from the beginning. If I can't shut my feelings down, I can't be objective. And if I can't be objective . . . do you see what I mean?"

"Not really. You're only flesh and blood. Somebody cuts you, you're gonna feel it."

"Says you. I've seen you work death scenes with a mouth full of french fries. I don't know how you avoid nightmares."

"Mostly I think about my family," he said. "During the Storytime raid, when that mobster had a gun to my head? All I could think was, 'Tomorrow's the first night of Passover. And Shoreh is gonna *kill* me if I don't come home.'"

"Passover, my butt. You're . . . what? Methodist? Baptist?"

"Presbyterian. And Shoreh's Muslim. So when we had Rina, we sort of . . . improvised."

"Please don't start making me laugh," she said. "Whatever happened to 'Who suffers'?"

"That's Mike's question. My question is, 'What's for lunch?' Speaking of which . . ."

"I'm sure they'll feed you back at Logan Farms."

"Super. What do they grow there, anyway? Loganberries?"

"It's not that kind of farm," she said. "It's horses, mostly. Tennessee Walkers."

"Big money in that, huh?"

"You wouldn't believe what they were going for at the auction yesterday. The thing is, nobody seemed to care about the horses themselves. Except for this . . . old trainer." She shook her head. "Talk about suffering. He had this beautiful perlino—kind of a pale cream horse—and he was just heartbroken when her new owners took her away. And she was scared to leave him, too. So the trainer leaned up and . . ." Her voice trailed off.

"And?"

"You know what? He wasn't hurting at all. It was the horse who was in pain." Peggy shook her head. "She was favoring her front legs, like she was afraid to put weight on them, and . . . holy fucking shit."

Peggy could picture the old trainer as she saw him—turning his lost, ancient eyes to her. His amber-colored eyes.

"Lethal White," she whispered.

"Oh boy," he said. "We're not going for root beer, are we?"

"No." She stepped on the gas. "Grab onto something."

As she returned to the house, Sean and Blaine were busy running through hostage rescue procedures with the assault team. Peggy counted a number of FBI and ATF jackets in the billiard parlor. And a few too many from Kadmos Security to suit her.

"You're late," Blaine said. "We had to start without you."

"I've got him," she said. "I don't know his name, but I can tell you where to look."

Blaine's mouth fell open. Sean seemed to shrink away.

"Put the satellite photos onto the projector," she said.

It took Blaine a moment to comply. The resulting image took up an entire wall: an overhead shot of Keyes County, showing countryside and tiny buildings in low relief. Peggy stood over the laptop, drawing white lines with a stylus pad.

"Here's the cell tower." Peggy made an X over the center of the image, then drew a wide ring around it. "That's about the effective range of its signal."

She zoomed in closer.

"Yoshi, what's the approximate distance to whoever's been tracking that GPS device?"

"At last ping? About twenty miles from here."

Peggy drew another X over Logan Farms—then a second ring, intersecting with the first one at two points.

"That leaves us a pretty small search area," she said. "Zoom in, please."

Blaine complied. Only three large buildings remained within the selected area.

"If memory serves," she said, "one of these is a private home, and the other two are farms. Let's leave the house aside for now. Both of the farms have outbuildings that could be used for holding a kidnap victim. They're far enough from town . . . and from each other . . . to make it possible to move in and out undetected. Do we have names for these two addresses?"

"One of 'em is Dudley Feaster," Powell said. "The other one belongs to the Whitelaws—Martha and Jonas."

"Tell me about them," Peggy said.

"Oh—Dudley used to fly a crop duster till he went blind," Powell said. "The Whitelaws are both in their eighties . . . nice enough people. Not exactly the killer types. Church of God folk. I believe they're fixin' to sell their property."

"Did either one of these families ever breed horses?" she asked. "Specifically Tennessee Walkers? Because that looks an awful lot like a stable on the Whitelaws' property."

Blaine gave her a curious look. "Why are you asking?"

"Didn't you notice the discolored pasterns on that mare you were admiring? Sean, I know you recognize those symptoms."

"I sure as hell do," Powell said. "Soring."

Sean blinked. "What?"

"You heard him. Soring." Peggy turned to the room. "Some trainers will intentionally maim a horse's hooves. Cut them, burn them with acid—so they step higher, like a walking horse should. Needless to say, it's illegal in Tennessee."

"And it's not practiced on any of the horses we deal in," Sean added quickly.

"It was practiced on that perlino," she said. "But she was obviously well stewarded—trained, or rather tortured, to behave as if she wasn't feeling any pain." Peggy began to punch up keys on the laptop. "All the trainer had to do was touch her, and say something into her ear—and she obeyed him."

"That doesn't prove he was the one who tortured her."

"He had skin cancers on both hands," she said. "The chemicals used in soring are known carcinogens."

"Guys, please." Sean appealed to the room for support. "If he sored that horse, he'll go to jail—whoever he is. Why are we wasting time on a trainer?"

"Here's why." Peggy tapped a computer key. Several men in the room gasped. Sean just looked worried.

They were looking at a photograph of Samantha at ten years old—hogtied, her maimed feet exposed and lifted up, her blue eyes staring helplessly into the camera lens. Peggy pointed to a plastic jug in the background.

"I believe that jug contains dimethyl sulfoxide," she said. "It's used as an absorption enhancer with kerosene and mustard oil to 'cook' horses' hooves. Or in this case . . . human feet." She looked directly at Sean. "That's your wife. Now tell me who brought that perlino to the auction yesterday?"

His mouth fell open. Then another voice spoke behind her:

"Stop playing games, girl. You know who it was."

Everybody turned. Logan Aldridge was in the doorway, scarcely standing on two withered legs, supported only by a mahogany cane.

"Dad—"

"Shut up, boy. She's right. It was the Goddamn Whitelaws." He smiled. "Stop holding your dicks and let's ride."

# FORTY-SIX

Ten minutes later, the front gallery at Logan Farms was a hornet's nest: armed security teams swarmed around Peggy as she fought to keep up with Agent Randall.

"Blaine," she said. "Two seconds, for God's sake."

"Weaver, I'm done arguing this. We have to move."

"Not this way," she said. "I've seen your duty roster. You're letting Sean's people get too close to the action. Maybe they could work perimeter, but not prime position. If they—" She watched an agent pass with a black crate. "Jesus, Blaine, those are fragmentation grenades. This is supposed to be a recovery, not an invasion."

He wheeled around. "You said it yourself. We don't have time to bring in a full complement. All we've got are you, me, two squads from Knoxville field office and ATF, some sheriff's deputies—and your father's second-in-command, whoever he is."

He nodded back in the direction of Officer Martin, who watched Peggy sullenly from the front colonnade.

"We could have gotten the right team in place," she said, "if you hadn't tossed my personnel request aside."

"That's Monday morning quarterbacking. You saw the ops plan. It's all standard. Can you find any mistakes?"

"Yes," she said. "Insufficient reconnaissance. We don't know enough about the interior layout of those buildings. We haven't been watching the property, so we don't know who's been moving in or out. We aren't even set up to monitor phone calls. And my fear . . . my *concern* . . . is that if we make the wrong assault, we won't have time to adjust tactics before Samantha's dead."

"You want to call this off? Wait another day?"

"We can't wait," she said.

"I'll put Sean's people on perimeter," he said. "I think they can handle that much. They've provided security for civilian contractors in Afghanistan and Saudi Arabia. And they've got the only surveillance helicopter within easy reach." He exhaled. "Let me remind you, all of this is happening on your recommendation. Now are you absolutely sure it's the Whitelaws?"

"As sure as I can be."

"Not good enough." He reached into his ops folder. "We just got this picture sent over from the Tennessee Walkers Association. That's Martha and Jonas Whitelaw. Do they look anything like your horse trainer?"

Peggy examined the photograph: an elderly couple, sweet faced and genial, posing with a speckled gray colt.

"No."

"Does either one of them match the description your witness gave you? Or what you remember from childhood?"

Peggy hesitated. "I only have a drawing. I don't really remember anything."

"We've got a thirty-minute satellite window, and a whole bunch of guys standing around. So either you tell me to abort this recovery . . . or we're going in with the resources we have."

Peggy looked through the open front door. Men were piling into the GMC wagons. Engines fired into life.

"There's another option," she said. "If I approach the house alone . . . I can provide some direct reconaissance. And it might distract the kidnappers long enough for our team to stage a stealth entry or dynamic assault."

The idea seemed to interest him. "How would you do it?"

"You hide a micro camera on me," she said. "I walk up to the front door and knock. They'll probably recognize me, so I can't pretend to be lost. But my father's been making door-to-door calls in the area since Sunday. I'll just tell them I'm following up. Believe me, I can play helpless if I have to."

"You might not be playing." Blaine raised an eyebrow. "We wouldn't be able to armor you. And we'd have to hold back at the treeline. You'd be a sitting duck if the shit goes down."

"I realize that," she said. "Well?"

"Let's have a quick huddle with tactical. It might work."

As Blaine waved his team leader over, Peggy looked to where Martin had been standing a moment ago. At some point during her conversation with Blaine, Officer Martin had disappeared.

Peggy drove her Jeep down the dark highway, Yoshi beside her. Ripley sat in the back, wearing a Keyes County deputy's badge on his civilian clothes.

"Let's synchronize," she said. "I've got two minutes shy of zero-five-hundred."

"Check." Yoshi adjusted his watch a fraction. "We're less than two clicks from primary target."

She looked into her rearview mirror—satisfied, at least, that the other strike-team vehicles were keeping out of sight. "What's the latest satellite imagery?"

"No activity at the Whitelaw place. No phone traffic, either." Yoshi examined his laptop. "Nobody named Whitelaw was listed as attending the auction on Monday. And, according to Social Security and Voter Registration, it's only those two nice old people living on that farm."

"At least that the government knows about," she said.

She got the feeling Yoshi was debating whether to say more.

"So we wake the Whitelaws up for nothing," she continued. "They're farmers. They'll be up early, anyhow." She tapped her ear. "Blaine, are you reading all this?"

"Affirmative," his voice spoke into her hidden earpiece.

"What's the disposition of our team?"

"Powell's men are controlling highway access. Sean's people are providing second-wave security and recon. The Nashville SWAT team is in position, ready to move on whatever target you identify. ATF will handle backup."

"And where will you be?"

"I'm still at Logan Farms," he said. "We're coordinating surveillance and tactical from here."

She rolled her eyes. "Didn't completely copy that. Sounds like we're getting radio interference on this channel."

"I don't hear it," Blaine said. "But just to be safe, let's switch to frequency . . ."

"Sorry, losing you. I'll have Agent Hiraka recalibrate. See if that clears up the static."

She removed the earpiece and switched it off.

"That buys us sixty seconds without Big Brother," she said. "Tell me what you really think, Yoshi. Are we heading for the right target?"

"I didn't want to look stupid," he said. "Totally random data. Probably doesn't mean a damn thing."

"But?" She waited.

"The Whitelaws' tax returns report income from U.S. Army death benefit checks for every year since nineteen-seventy. And only immediate family of the deceased are eligible for those."

"And only for soldiers who die in the line of duty," she said. "The trainer would be about the right age for a son or nephew. Know what he did when somebody slammed the door to that horse trailer? He flinched."

"My uncle Ray was in Vietnam," Ripley said from the back. "He used to hit the dirt any time a truck backfired. Or if somebody set a firecracker off."

"So we definitely don't want to go in shooting," she said. "What's the name on those death benefits?"

"Can't get it. Looks like we're out of wireless range." Yoshi tapped a few keys. "I'll keep working on it."

"Have the VA work on it. You just keep an eye out for me. Okay, I'm going back on live comm."

"Agent Weaver?" Ripley said. "Before you do . . ."

She turned to him.

"I'd like to come in with you," he said. "Just in case . . . well, in case."

"We have to stick to our plan," she said. "If things go the way I think they will . . . you won't be able to protect me regardless."

"I know. But I . . ." He nodded grimly. "Privilege serving with you, Agent Weaver."

"Stop looking at me like that. I'll be fine." She pulled over to the side of the road. The farmhouse was just ahead. Peggy switched her earpiece back on. "Blaine, is that better?"

"Affirmative," he said through the receiver. "Video looks good. You're coming in clear."

"I'm leaving Agent Hiraka at zero-point-six kilometers south of target zone. Have an unmarked transport bring him back to forward ops position. And make sure he's cleared to monitor all data, video, and vox transmissions."

"Roger. What about your boy Ripley?"

She looked back at Ripley. He nodded to her.

"He's got his own ride," she said. "Okay, I'm going in."

# FORTY–SEVEN

Peggy drove the remaining distance alone. If Mike had been running tactical, he'd almost certainly have insisted on maintaining a closed comm channel to her—if only so that she wouldn't have to listen to the confused back-chatter that was flooding her earpiece:

"Sniper rifle in position . . ."

"Issue shock-lock rounds to go-team . . ."

"Confirm EMTs wagons in transit, plasma and O-neg units standing by."

"Final decision on approach pattern? Are we going with airborne insertion, or wall-flood, or . . ."

"Decoy is approaching the target."

So that's who she was: the decoy. Peggy had heard herself called worse. During her first FBI assignment—posing as an underage teenager on an Internet sex chatroom—she was known to her squad members as Special Agent Jailbait. She still remembered the old-timers who casually referred to female agents as Betty Bureaus. Or split-tails. And now she was the decoy.

"I am within visual range of the site." She wasn't entirely sure if anyone was listening to her. As she turned into the narrow dirt driveway, Peggy stopped to examine the mailbox. There was no mail. But she did see several rolls of colored newsprint lying in the dirt: coupon fliers, some of them weeks old. And a neglected FOR SALE BY OWNER sign hanging loosely from the three-barred fence.

The farmhouse and its outlying buildings were completely dark. The only vehicle in sight was an old John Deere tractor, scaled with rust and red earth. The cell tower stood above, less than a mile away. Peggy realized with a mild shock that she must have driven past that very building at least three or four times since her arrival in Tennesssee.

"Place looks empty," Peggy said. "I'm driving in for a closer look. Advise you bring assault team to second position." She adjusted the microscopic camera, neatly hidden in her neck pendant. "Agent Randall, do you copy video?"

"Yeah—hang on," he said. "Sorry, it looks like go-team's moved to a secondary vox channel. I'm trying to find out why."

"Don't ask why. Just get them back on our damn channel."

Peggy drew her shoulders up a little as she approached the house. Anyone watching from inside would be able to see her, and she wanted to make herself seem just a little bit lost—a sheep strayed from the flock. Peggy parked under the yellow streetlamp, then reflexively checked her Glock. Normally that was her cue to pray that she wouldn't have to use it . . . but something told her that would be a useless appeal.

She realized with cold certainty that someone was watching her from the shadows.

Peggy stepped down from the Jeep and looked around. The manure pile was unusually high, and the stock of hay seemed feeble. The posts and hurdles were overturned and weather beaten, the grass calf high. On the whole, the place seemed not merely empty but forsaken.

Then she caught movement along the treeline. Peggy could see at least two or three dark shapes, trying to stay hidden. Her heart froze. If she could make out the assault team that easily, so could anyone else.

"Peggy." It was Blaine talking to her. "We don't see a damn thing. You wanna call it a night?"

"Let me check the house and stables first." She whispered without moving her lips, a skill acquired through countless operations. "If nobody's there, we'll do a site search and pull back. In the meantime, tell your men to stop moving around. They're giving away their position."

The place was still and quiet, and she was surrounded by friendlies. So why was her heart beating a mile a minute?

*I have been here.* The knowledge had started to gather as soon as she saw the mailbox; now it struck her like a dull hammer. Even as she rounded the building, she knew there would be a dilapidated brick barbecue behind the back porch, and a rusted green pumphouse beside it. And so there was. She was strangely aware that the kitchen would have blue wallpaper, patterned with bunches of grapes. The floor would be alternating black-and-white tiles. And the whole house would smell of hickory and old linens. And gun oil.

"Anybody home?" She rapped on the screen door, then again. No answer. Peggy craned her neck to look in. A pair of feet rested against the living room sofa . . . or maybe it was just a pair of slippers.

"House seems empty," she whispered. "But I—"

*Check the far side of the house.* The words presented themselves in her mind, a silent command.

"I'm going around the building now," she said.

"Peggy." Blaine's voice on comm. "The team wants a go-no-go. Sean thinks—"

"I don't give a crap what Sean thinks." She sidled toward the rain spout. "Just tell me what's waiting around the corner."

"Satellite image is a little fuzzy," he said. "Some kind of canvas tarp . . . maybe a woodpile, or . . ."

"Dear God."

The fitted car cover had been bleached white by years of sun and bird droppings. Still, the canvas clung tight enough to give some idea as to what lay beneath. It would be wiser to keep walking. But she had to know.

The cover yielded stubbornly as she pulled it aside. And there it was: corroded, wheel-less on cinderblocks, hood up, sourgrass growing through its engine block. A cracked windshield.

The black Thunderbird.

Peggy circled around it. The license plate had long since been pried off. But the bumper sticker was still pasted to the front bumper.

"Ass, gas, or grass," she read off the sticker. "Nobody rides for free."

Then a flash of light reflected off the hood.

"Whoa," she said. "Where did that come from?"

"What?" Blaine asked.

Peggy turned to see a flashlight aimed at her from between the boarded window slats of the closed stable.

"I've been made," she said. "Agent Randall, please confirm that none of your team is placed in the stable."

"So confirmed," he said.

"That's our entry point. Please advise if satellite reveals any getaway vehicles—or armed enemy targets."

"We're good. I'm authorizing assault team to primary."

"Wait for my signal." She walked toward the stable, a gable-style pole barn with two wings of stalls and a pair of large doors. "Let's not go changing an active operation plan, Blaine. Let me get close enough to assess—"

As she approached the twin barn doors, she saw dark-uniformed men pacing toward her from half a mile away.

"Blaine, order your men back."

"I did," he said. "Peggy, we've lost satellite."

As her hand sought the door latch, she thought she heard something like footsteps inside. She touched her weapon. *Here I go . . .*

Then she heard the helicopter blades on approach.

She turned as it fixed her in its searchlight, bearing down in an assault pattern. Dust and grass whipped up around her.

"Pull the copter back, Blaine! Pull it—"

A moment later, the barn doors flew open. A black SUV broke out, nearly striking Peggy down as it took off for the gate. Automatic fire bounced off the vehicle's smoked windows. The assault team was charging in.

"Blaine, who gave the order to open fire?" she asked. "Agent Randall!"

Flames burst from inside the barn. As she looked in, she saw white plastic jugs, already melting in the heat. Sharp tools hanging from a pegboard. Windows covered with tinfoil. Glass aquarium tanks. And piles of bloody white feathers on the clean straw.

"Get out!" One of the ATF men was shouting at her. "Right now! You've got a chemical fire—!"

Peggy ran for her Jeep, parked near the house. At least half a dozen voices yelled into her earpiece.

"Switching to Channel Two." She tapped her wrist control and the noise dropped out. "Yoshi, do you have satellite?"

"Affirmative," Yoshi said. "Somebody killed the signal, but I managed to hop onto a backup transponder. Your forward team is chasing their tails. A lot of blue-on-blue fire. Advise that you get the hell out."

Armed men were all around her, kicking in doors and shouting. Flames licked the sides of the barn. Peggy revved her engine and took off. A truck from Kadmos Security was blocking the gate.

*What are these idiots doing here?* She tapped her earpiece. "Blaine, where's the black SUV?"

"Already off the property," he said. "Heading west on the main highway."

She accelerated to seventy-five and crashed the fence, bouncing hard as she jumped over the drainage ditch.

"Inform Agent Randall and Sheriff Powell. And tell Ripley that's his cue to move. I am in pursuit."

"Copy," he said. "I'm piping the live satellite feed to your PDA. Overlaying road and traffic information."

"Got it." She floored the engine. The red brake lights of the SUV were just visible, about a mile ahead. On her handheld computer's display, the vehicle showed as a single red dot.

"Sheriff Powell, do you read me?"

"Affirmative, Peggy. Sounds like a hell of a lot of angry fellas on Channel One."

"Never mind them," she said. "The target is less than one mile from your western roadblock. Do not use deadly force. Enemy vehicle has bulletproof windows. And the hostage may be inside."

"Roger. I see him."

There were only two logical escape routes from the Whitelaw farm: eastbound Highway 23 was the more obvious choice, since it led to the Interstate. But it was also a more densely populated area, likely to be haunted by speed traps. The westbound lane would lead into the mountains, into forest and fire trails. It would be harder to drive through at speed . . . but much easier to disappear into. And that was where Peggy had told Sheriff Powell to concentrate his strength.

"Roadblock is set up and secure," Powell said.

"All right," she said. "Let's drive him into the gauntlet."

The SUV had speed, Peggy realized, and a lot of power. It almost certainly had off-road capability . . . perfect for angling around rough dirt roads. As she closed in, she could see the flashers of the sheriff's barricade in the far distance. The subject would either have to crash through those vehicles, or make the only turn available to him. Just as Peggy hoped, he took the bait—scattering pebbles and burning rubber as his vehicle swung a hard left down a dirt road into the woods.

"Ripley, are you hearing me?"

"Yes, ma'am."

"He's coming your way," she said. "It's up to you, now."

Peggy turned onto the dirt road. The pale shapes of trees whipped past her as she floored the accelerator. She could already see the SUV ahead of her. And the headlights of Ripley's off-road vehicle, racing back at him in a full-throttle game of chicken.

If the subject had found a way to listen in, Peggy reasoned, then he'd know about the trap set for him—the assault team, the barricade, even the helicopter. But only she and Yoshi had known that Ripley would be waiting on the other end of that dirt road. A searchlight fell on them: the helicopter was back on the approach. *Damned if this isn't going to work . . .*

Then she saw the driver's side window of the SUV roll down. A long, black tube emerged, held in a jacketed arm.

"RPG," she said. "Ripley, he's got a gren—"

A streak of smoke burst from the rocket-propelled grenade. White flame burst from Ripley's cruiser. The ground shook, nearly throwing Peggy from her Jeep. The helicopter swung crazily overhead, fighting to regain attitude. Shards of hot metal were falling all around. Several of them struck the hood of the SUV.

Something screamed into Peggy's earpiece.

The SUV downshifted hard, slinging dirt behind it—then drove around the flaming mass of metal, as if it were nothing more than an animal carcass in the road.

Peggy threw on the brakes, watching the SUV disappear.

"We have a man down!" she said. "Agent Randall, are you on this channel?"

"Affirmative," Blaine said. "We have your visual. What do you want to do?"

Then she saw Ripley, lying in the dirt.

"Agent Weaver," Blaine said. "Peggy?"

Ripley had been thrown clear. He was caked with blood and dirt. But he was still alive. His one remaining arm lay across his chest. He was breathing rapidly, going into shock.

Peggy watched the beam of the helicopter's searchlight shining down as it coursed the road ahead.

"Blaine, can the pilot disable the vehicle without harming anyone inside?" She waited. "Is anyone else in position?"

"Negative," he said. "Too much tree cover. The helicopter pilot advises you pursue. It's up to you, Weaver."

Ripley's head began to turn in her direction. His eyes were opening.

"Please forgive me," she whispered.

"Didn't copy that," Blaine said.

"I said—I'm in pursuit." She put the Jeep in gear and drove around the burning shell of the cruiser. As she floored the accelerator, Peggy tried very hard to convince herself that she hadn't heard Ripley calling her name.

# FORTY-EIGHT

She knew where she was going. There was a clearing less than a mile ahead, and beyond that a fork in the road. Past that, there was no telling which way the SUV would take. The forest was too dense for even the helicopter to spot them. And the other vehicles were at least two miles back.

"Agent Randall, do you read me?" She waited. "Anyone on this channel?" She switched channels. "Anyone at all?"

Silence.

The SUV's brake lights bounced in the road ahead, a hundred yards away. Smoke was pouring from its engine. *Must have damaged itself in that RPG attack.* She had only one chance—and, knowing she might be taking it with Samantha's life, Peggy rolled the window down and aimed at the SUV's tires.

For some reason, it was her father's voice she heard in the back of her head—a command from countless target practices: *You have to be as good with the left as you are with the right. One hand for the wheel, one for your piece.*

Her hand on the wheel was shaking badly. Peggy took a breath to steady herself, then aimed low. The first shot struck sparks off the rear bumper. The second round missed.

*Don't screw around, Peggy Jean. Make it count.*

Then, as the third shot blew out the left rear tire, Peggy saw—or thought she saw—a pale face in the smoked glass of the SUV's rear window. The vehicle skidded . . . then simply rolled onto its left side and slid into the clearing, clouding itself with dust.

The helicopter found them within moments, pinning the SUV in its lights. Peggy cut her motor and leapt down.

"Come out with your hands up! Weapons down!" She had to scream to make herself heard over the copter blades. Then the driver's side door opened. And he lifted himself up.

"Damn you to hell," she heard herself say.

He was just as she'd seen him at Logan Farms the day before: a man in his fifties, dressed in tattered gray, with dark patched skin and curly gray hair. But where he had stooped before, he now stood upright on top of the vehicle, lean and confident. Yellow snake-eyes glowed in the light shining down on him from above. And as she saw him, she knew him.

"Down to the ground," she commanded. "Lock hands behind your neck. It's over, you sick bastard."

Peggy couldn't be sure if he was even hearing her over the noise. But he didn't seem much concerned. He simply tilted his head at her, as a dog might observe his master. And kissed the air in her direction.

"Lie down," she said. "Or I will shoot you."

Sirens were approaching now, and the lights of the sheriff's squad cars. He was trapped . . . and he had to know how easily she could kill him. But still he wouldn't move. And he wouldn't wipe that damned smile off his face.

Peggy felt her finger tighten on the trigger.

He looked up with bland interest as a rope ladder fell from the helicopter above him. Then the man with yellow eyes simply placed his foot on the bottom rung, took hold with his left hand, and allowed himself to be carried away.

Peggy fired twice. But her wounded hand was freshly bleeding, a mass of raw nerve endings. And the helicopter spun harmlessly away into the first light of dawn. Only when it was completely silent again did she realize how she was trembling from head to toe.

Then she heard a soft sound from inside the vehicle.

The SUV's rear door was dented. Peggy pulled hard at it, ripping it away. As she did, she saw blue eyes watching at her.

"Samantha?" she said. "Honey?"

Samantha Aldridge stared at her, splayed and unmoving, a marionette tangled in its own strings. A white bedsheet, spotted with blood, was wrapped around her bare flesh.

"Sammie—?" Peggy crawled to her friend.

"Peggy." Samantha spoke to the empty air, her voice thin and wandering. "Why did you do it? You shouldn't have—not to come looking for me . . ."

"It's all right, honey. Don't move. You're okay now."

But Samantha merely shook her head.

"You've killed yourself," she said. "Me for you. Don't you see?"

Peggy could hear the sound of approaching vehicles.

"Me for you," Samantha said. "Now you're his."

# FORTY-NINE

The ride to the hospital was a dark blur—Peggy holding Samantha's cold hand in the ambulance, begging her friend to breathe. Then chaos at the emergency room: a mask pressed to Sammie's face, a green vinyl bag zipped around Officer Ripley's ravaged flesh. Only later, as Peggy waited under stark hospital lights, did exhaustion finally begin to take the upper hand.

"What time is it?" She jolted upright as Harrison sat down beside her on the Naugahyde couch.

"Eight o'clock Tuesday morning." He smelled of harsh soap. She could tell at a glance that he hadn't slept.

"You should take a nap, dear." Olivia wore a dark blue dress that, in Peggy's addled state, looked for a moment like funeral black. "Poor angel. We owe you everything."

"Can't sleep," Peggy said. "I should . . . find out what the doctors are saying."

"They won't tell us anything," Harrison said. "Except that Sammie hasn't regained consciousness."

Peggy rubbed her face to wake up. Her hand came away with traces of black powder.

"I'll see what I can do," she said.

Everyone seemed to back out of Peggy's way as she walked down the hall to intensive care: she guessed it had less to do with her FBI badge than the blood and cordite on her blouse.

". . . pressure immobilization," the doctor—a petite Latina in green scrubs—was head-to-head with her chief attendant. "I'm chiefly worried about . . ."

"Dr. Santos," Peggy said, reading the woman's name tag.

". . . peripheral edema." The doctor looked at Peggy. "Speak quickly, please. We're in a critical situation."

"I'm aware of that," Peggy said. "I just need your diagnosis."

"Why?" Dr. Santos raised an eyebrow. "Why do you need to know?"

"I'm an FBI agent assigned to his investigation, and . . ."

"Ah. More police. Out of my way, thank you." The doctor brushed past her to the swinging doors—then turned as Peggy put a hand on her shoulder.

"My name's Peggy Weaver," she said. "She's my friend."

"She's—spoken of you." The doctor seemed to relent. "Sammie's in very bad shape. There's neurotoxin in her muscle tissue. We're trying to keep it out of her major organs, but . . . frankly, we're losing that battle."

"She's been poisoned?"

"Lower your voice," she said. "We don't know the precise cause. She's experiencing severe paralysis, so there's likely a myotoxin as well. Now you must excuse me—"

"I'd like to see her," Peggy said.

Dr. Santos looked at her soberly.

"Put on a mask," she said. "And brace yourself."

Samantha was, of necessity, covered only by a light hospital gown, an oxygen mask pressed to her face. Her left arm had swollen badly. Heavy straps immobilized her limbs. There was an awful rigidity to Sammie's frame, like rigor mortis—except that, once every few seconds, she twitched. Her skin was covered with bruises and ligature marks, some of them partly healed. Samantha's feet were entirely exposed to view.

"Her eyes are open," Peggy said. "Can't you give her something for the pain?"

"She's not conscious," Dr. Santos said. "And pain medication will most likely kill her. She's on the verge of cardiac arrest."

Peggy noticed the cloth packed between Samantha's legs.

"Doctor . . . she's pregnant," Peggy said.

"Agent Weaver, she lost the baby," the doctor said quietly. "Now I think you'd better go have one of the nurses tend to your burns. We're doing what we can for her."

Peggy didn't answer. Both women seemed to know just how little those words meant at that particular moment.

Peggy found Sheriff Powell, Agent Randall, and Yoshi Hiraka gathered in an empty examination room.

"You all right?" Powell asked.

"He's still out there," Peggy answered. "Why did he give her back to us . . . like this?" She turned on Blaine. "And who the *hell* was flying that helicopter?"

"We don't know." Blaine's eyes went to the floor. "The registered pilot's dead. They found him garrotted in a tack room near the helipad. Which means that whoever was flying it . . ."

". . . had to be monitoring our comm traffic. And probably had the visual from my pendant camera as well." The knowledge left Peggy feeling strangely violated.

"I'm pretty sure the bad guys were the ones who screwed up our communications," Yoshi said. "Which means they also had access to our command-and-control network. It wasn't Kadmos's fault, strictly speaking. Everybody got the same coded signal to charge in. It just didn't come from us, that's all."

"Somebody on our end sure as hell leaked the encryption codes," Peggy said. "Any ideas, Blaine?"

His eyes darted away. "May I speak to you in private?"

She looked at Yoshi and Powell. "Don't get up."

They went into the hallway.

"You were right not to trust Sean's people," Blaine said. "Some of his guys . . . there's recent transfers, incomplete background checks. It could easily have been one of them who cloned the data stream."

"Or you."

He bit his lip hard. "This whole fiasco makes me look like shit. Why would I burn myself to protect Kadmos Security?"

"Fine. So let's start interrogating Kadmos."

"First you and I need to get our story straight," he said. "My SAC's leaning on me for a mission report . . . but I needed to talk to you beforehand. I know we haven't been friendly . . ."

"Where's the warrant, Blaine?"

"The what?"

"The electronic surveillance warrant on my father. You said I'd have paperwork in the morning." She pointed to the window. "Well?"

"Why are you still harping on that? We've got much bigger problems right now."

"We most definitely do." She shook her head. "This didn't work out at all the way you planned, did it? You thought you'd buddy up to the Aldridges, catch the crooks, make early transfer to your office of preference . . . and somehow get home in time to tuck in your kids. What I can't figure out is how you expected to get away without securing a simple bench warrant."

"A friend of mine at Justice was supposed to come through with an emergency warrant. It would have provided blanket coverage for all surveillance related to this case." Blaine exhaled. "Jerk flaked on me at the last minute."

"Tough break," she said. "That transmitter you gave me. It wasn't even federal issue. Was it?"

"It was a loaner from Sean," he said. "I screwed up, I know. But you knew the urgency of the situation. If we'd waited . . ."

"Go wait in Chattanooga, okay? I'm getting back to work."

"You're in this too, Weaver." A desperate whine broke into his voice. "You planted that wire on your father. If you let me burn for this, you'll burn, too."

She fixed her eyes on him.

"Make no mistake, I am not proud of myself," she said. "On the other hand . . . I do have a memo from the deputy director, instructing me to obey your directives. So right or wrong . . . it does appear I'm covered in the Bureau's eyes."

He looked at her, stunned.

"And by the way," she said. "Considering what happened to Samantha and Ripley . . . *and* Tidwell . . . the next time you decide to throw that word 'burn' in my face, you'd better be ready to get your ass kicked for it. Understood?"

"Yeah." He didn't even try to meet her eyes.

# FIFTY

"Where's Agent Randall?" Yoshi said as Peggy closed the examination room door.

"On his way back to Chattanooga," she said. "I've just spoken with his superiors at the Chattanooga Resident Agency. Blaine will stay on purely as a matter of record . . . but I've been assigned to coordinate operations here."

"Finally." Powell nodded. "Maybe now we can get somewhere, with you in charge."

"I wish that were true," she said. "But it seems like the subject's the one who's been calling the shots."

"There's some good news on that score, at least." Yoshi pulled out his laptop. "I've got a name for you."

"Okay."

"Kevin Whitelaw Slayton," he said. "Master Sergeant, U.S. Army. Served in COMSEC Intelligence during the Vietnam War—that's the section responsible for the physical security of classified documents."

"Missing and feared dead." She read the file from Yoshi's computer screen. "What was his exact assignment?"

"That's the problem with people who handle classified information— he's classified, too. However, Slayton's service record clearly stipulates that he went MIA during combat. Which is not likely to happen to a clerk licking envelopes at HQ. And if you notice his medals and commendations . . ."

"They're all for front-line operations." She looked at the sheriff. "You know anything about this guy?"

"I remember when they said he wasn't comin' home." Powell scratched his neck. "Seems like he was a . . . nephew? Cousin? I'm pretty sure Jonas and Martha didn't have any kids of their own."

"He was their nephew," Yoshi said. "His VA insurance names the Whitelaws as beneficiaries. And his enlistment papers register them both as legal guardians."

"How did his natural parents die?" Peggy asked.

"Beats me," Yoshi said. "Why are we chasing a dead guy?"

"I don't see anything that says he died," she said. "Sheriff, what else do you remember about Kevin Slayton?"

"Smiled a lot," he said. "Didn't talk much. Any time I was out there—which wasn't too often—he just stayed with the horses."

"Do you know anyone who can talk to us about him?"

"Not too many. I always got the feeling people made him nervous." Powell glanced over at Yoshi.

"You can speak freely in front of Agent Hiraka," she said.

"Well, you know, when they were teenagers . . ."

The door opened. A deputy put his head in.

"Evidence technician's on the phone, Sheriff."

"Probably wants to tell me what all they found at the Whitelaw farm," he said. "You mind?"

"What were you about to say a moment ago?"

"I never could get Rusty to explain why." Powell lowered his voice. "But before your daddy dropped out of college—and Kevin went into the army—those two were thick as thieves."

# FIFTY-ONE

As she returned to the waiting room, Dr. Santos was deep in conversation with Harrison and Olivia. Caden had been left on the floor to play with an old copy of *Field and Stream*.

"We're keeping her hydrated," the doctor was saying. "And we have her on dialysis. It's enough to slow the progress . . . but it's not going to save her. And without knowing the exact toxin, any antidote we try carries a grave risk."

"Any theories on that?" Peggy asked.

Dr. Santos frowned. "Blood analysis shows an abnormally high white cell count . . . tissue samples indicate something organic."

"Organic," Peggy said. "You mean like plants, herbs?"

"Not with the elevated myoglobin levels, no. If it weren't for the absence of fang marks, I'd have no trouble saying . . ."

"Snake venom." Olivia raised her palm. "I *told* Harrison that would be it. Why won't anyone ever listen to me?"

"Mrs. Stallworth." The doctor spoke with unbending precision. "As I said, snake antivenoms must be precisely administered. Use the wrong one and you've killed the patient."

"Oh, come now. How many different kinds of poisonous snakes can there be around here? Harrison, you'd know."

"As do I," Dr. Santos said. "I've seen my share of coral and rattlesnake bites. I repeat, there's no fang marks to go by. Envenomation appears to have been achieved through hypodermic injection. So it could be almost anything."

"Spare me." Olivia reddened. "I have endured *twenty-five* years of physicians and specialists playing could-be-might-be. And if I'd listened to you people all these years—"

"Olivia," Harrison said.

"—my daughter would have grown up in a *wheelchair*, getting her meals through a tube in her nose, and communicating by—*eyeblinks*. And if I were you—"

"Gammy," Caden said to her.

"Not *now*, Caden." She breathed hoarsely. "I don't know, Doctor, just *pick* an antivenom. Choose the one that's the least dangerous. At least make a *decision*."

"Mrs. Stallworth, I'm trying to tell you that your daughter might not have very long to live."

Harrison put his face in his hands. Olivia folded her arms. "You'll excuse me, dear, if I refuse to accept that."

"I certainly do," she said. "But given our options—"

"*Gammy*," Caden said. "Hung'y, Gammy."

"Oh, for *God's sake*, child!"

Caden's eyes widened.

"Olivia," Harrison said. "Please take care of Caden."

"Oh, and leave *you* to manage this? I don't think so."

He tensed. "Take him outside . . . calmly . . . and get him fed. And then let's try to compose ourselves before we go in to see our daughter."

Olivia seemed ready to fire back . . . then met Peggy's eyes. Finally she looked away. As she left, Olivia picked Caden up, tucking him under her arm like a piglet. Harrison winced.

"She's not entirely wrong, you know," Peggy said as the door closed. "Even with no bite radius to measure, you should be able to identify the venom fairly simply."

"We've narrowed the list down." Santos reached into her pocket. "An ophiologist in Atlanta sent pictures."

Santos handed her several color printouts. One of them showed a winding snake in a blue sea: black Rorschach patterns against luminous gold, wide and flat as a man's belt.

"That one." Peggy touched it. "It's bigger than the one Slayton left on my doorstep. But the color and markings are the same."

"Our expert agrees with you—unfortunately." Dr. Santos frowned. "It's a species of hydrophiidae . . . sometimes known as the yellow-bellied or pelagic sea snake. Its venom is arguably the deadliest known to science."

Harrison looked up. "We're five hundred miles from the ocean. How is that possible?"

"I don't know. They're tropical animals . . . mostly from the western Pacific and Indian Ocean. They wouldn't survive freshwater conditions. Possibly the snakes were raised locally under aquarium conditions and culled for their venom. Or maybe samples were stolen from a lab."

"Does 'western Pacific' include Vietnam?" Peggy asked.

She thought a moment. "I believe so, yes. The problem is that there are no stocks of the antivenom in North America . . . it simply never happens here."

"Where is the nearest supply?" Peggy asked.

"Melbourne, Australia," she answered. "Anywhere from twenty-four to thirty-six hours away by air."

Peggy took a breath. "And how long does Sammie have?"

"Dialysis buys us time," the doctor said. "But it's not a cure. And at the current rate of degeneration . . ."

"Doctor, how long?"

"No more than a day," she answered. "And unless the serum is administered within the next few hours . . . even that won't make a difference."

For a moment the only sound was hospital traffic.

"Is there anything you can do for her?" Harrison asked.

"We can keep her comfortable," the doctor said.

"Keep her alive," Peggy said. "That's the priority."

"Agent Weaver . . ."

"She's got twenty-four hours to live. Make sure she gets every second." Peggy checked her watch. "Harrison, it's almost exactly nine A.M. What happens this time tomorrow?"

"The trustees' meeting."

"Slayton said she'd die unless the ransom was paid before Wednesday at nine. If he's given her back to us alive . . . then he must also have the cure. And he'll bargain for it."

Harrison paled. "What name did you just say?"

"Kevin Slayton," she answered. "A local man. Former Avalon student. Apparently, a friend of my father's."

"I know who he is," Harrison said. "Dr. Santos, we must keep Samantha alive for as long as possible."

"I have every intention of it . . . within humane limits. But I hope you're not asking me to prolong your daughter's agony, just to gain a few hours."

He took a breath before answering. "I'm afraid that's precisely what I'm asking."

"You do realize it may not be your decision," she said.

"Whose, then?"

"Her husband's—regrettably." Dr. Santos turned to the door. "I must see to my patient. Regardless of which course we take, we'd better make up our minds quickly. By sunset . . . all this may well be academic."

The doctor nodded—a fleeting look of empathy—and went back into ICU. Peggy turned to see the sheriff behind her.

"We've got our work cut out for us," she said. "Sheriff, we need to round up everyone who was detailed to the rescue operation. That includes Sean's private detective . . . and I think it's time for another talk with Sean himself."

"Supposedly he's on his way here," Powell said. "But now, I just got done talkin' to my evidence crew. They found a body at the house."

"The Whitelaws?" Peggy recalled the feet on the sofa.

"Just Jonas," he said. "I heard what the doctor told ya. ME's pretty sure the old man was poisoned, too."

"That's it," she said. "Tell your crew to look for ampoules, needles . . . reptile tanks . . . anything associated with snake venom. That's how they're killing Samantha."

He exhaled. "We're gonna need some extra manpower."

"You'll get it," she said. "Harrison, who is Kevin Slayton? A former student of yours?"

"Briefly, yes. He was expelled the same year your father dropped out. It's a long story. The records are in the attic of Culloden Hall."

"Let's go take a look." She turned to Powell. "What's the latest on my father's condition?"

"Out of treatment, last I checked. They're getting ready to put him back under sedation."

"Make sure I'm notified when he wakes up." She started for the door. "I'll be on my cell."

As she went to the door, Peggy's eyes fell on the magazine Caden had been tearing to pieces. FIRST KILL! was the headline: the accompanying photograph showed a ten-year-old boy, cheeks painted with blood, holding his rifle proudly over the carcass of a white-tailed deer.

# FIFTY-TWO

Like all attics, the top floor of Culloden Hall was a place for lost and forgotten things—boxes of documents, shelves full of decaying Latin grammars, racks of never-worn cadet uniforms. Even the air Peggy breathed seemed to belong to another time: a smell of damp stone and ancient timber.

"Student records from the late sixties were moved here two years ago." Harrison turned on a bare yellow lightbulb. "It shouldn't take more than a minute to find them."

As he searched the files, Peggy scanned a stack of Avalon College yearbooks. She found a picture of the 1968–69 boxing team: a small group of college boys in trunks and gloves, standing in mock-fighting poses around a ring—eyes narrow, nostrils flaring. Most of them had unfashionable crewcuts or sideburns worthy of George Jones. Peggy instantly recognized Russell Weaver—a smiling young tough, weight planted firmly on his left leg.

The young man at the center was Kevin Slayton.

"Peggy?" Harrison was standing beside her, a dust-covered folder in his hand. "What's the matter?"

"Slayton seems—more familiar now." She found herself transfixed by his smile: the same, curious tilt that she'd seen early that morning. "What did you find?"

"His academic record." He opened it for her. "I'd forgotten what a good student young Kevin was . . . considering what he was expelled for."

"'Threatening and inflammatory correspondence,'" she read. "Who did he threaten?"

"Me," Harrison said. "He wrote this essay for my freshman composition class . . . it was so revolting, it practically demanded expulsion. You'll find it attached to the back of the report."

Peggy read the title aloud. "'A Modern Thermopylae: Pure Brothers Against the Mongrel Hordes.'"

"You may recall the original battle of Thermopylae," he said. "Three hundred Spartan warriors died fighting a thousand times that many Persian invaders."

"Tidwell mentioned that General Stallworth used Spartan tactics at Shagbark Ravine," she said. "What happened?"

"It was one of the Civil War's most useless sacrifices," he said. "My great-great-grandfather had somehow convinced himself that his nine hundred and fifty men were capable of turning back an entire Union division. He entrenched in a narrow pass . . . held out for three days until his troops ran out of ammunition. Finally they were reduced to fighting with rocks and their bare hands."

Peggy scanned the document. "Slayton seems to consider Shagbark Ravine the Confederacy's finest hour."

Harrison frowned. "The Lost-Cause buffs generally forget two important facts about that engagement. One is that nearly every one of the general's men died. The other is that the general didn't die with them."

"I take it Slayton's essay didn't get an A."

"Hardly. It's a call for a return to the supposed 'Golden Age' of Avalon . . . when blacks were subservient, women were silent breeders, et cetera. Remember, this was written at the height of the Civil Rights era. I and a number of other junior faculty had just signed a petition to integrate the campus . . . as a Stallworth, I was obviously considered an arch-turncoat. I believe this was young Mr. Slayton's way of issuing a warning."

"I'll say." She read aloud. "'Our sovereign duty is to our race. Those whites who seek to gain temporary favor by allying themselves to "Sambo Washington" and "Isidor Mandelbaum"—be their names and bloodlines ever so lofty—will be the first to bleed when their corrupt cause is finally overturned. The unalterable truth of history is that traitors die . . . but their children always die before them.'"

"I'd forgotten the threat against my children," he said. "Samantha hadn't even been born yet."

"Harrison." Peggy read further. "You do realize he uses the word 'Krypteia,' don't you?"

She held the passage for him to read:

> As the ancient Spartans ensured the purity and dominion of their blood—and as the Ku Klux Klan protected Southern home and womanhood by manly force of arms—so shall our new Krypteia strike down, serpent-like and remorseless, both half-breeds and scalawags alike.

"You don't remember this?" she asked.

He shook his head, confused. "It's been decades since I saw it last. I thought the matter was ended when the dean of men sent him packing . . . next I knew, Slayton had lost his deferment and was drafted into the army." He paused. "I'd always assumed he was dead."

"Tell me something," she said. "How does some local kid with no connections . . . no college degree . . . and an attitude like *that* . . . get a choice assignment like Army Intelligence?"

"Perhaps he wasn't entirely without connections," he said. "After all, he wasn't a scholarship student like your father. *Somebody* had to pay for his tuition . . . and it wasn't his family."

"Let's see whose names are on the checks." She dialed her cell phone. "Yoshi?"

"Boss, thank God," he answered. "This hospital's going crazy."

"I don't doubt it," she said. "Listen, in a minute I'm going to have you talk to Dr. Stallworth about pulling financial records on Kevin Slayton. In the meantime, I need contact information for Slayton's commanding officer in Vietnam."

"Are you coming back here?"

"Soon as I can," she said. "Why? What's going on?"

"Right after you left, that Aldridge guy showed up with his goon squad. It almost came to blows between them and the sheriff's people. Nobody would let me into the ICU . . . but, well, I listened in anyhow. And it doesn't look at all good for your friend."

"Has Samantha taken a turn for the worse?"

"Not that I know," he said. "But it sounds like her husband's decided to pull the plug on her anyway."

# FIFTY-THREE

Harrison's hands were white on the steering wheel of his Mercedes on the drive back.

"It's confirmed." Peggy closed her phone. "Sean's requested immediate termination of Samantha's life support. Apparently it's what she would have wanted."

"Why would he even conceive of doing such a thing?"

"If we were talking about anybody else, I'd probably say it's the compassionate move. Samantha's dying. And she's in extraordinary pain." Peggy took a breath. "But I honestly don't think Sean has a compassionate bone in his body."

Harrison looked at her. "Do you think—"

Peggy's eyes swung to the road. "Harrison!"

He braked just in time to avoid barreling through a pedestrian crossing in front of the elementary school. The crossing guard grimly tapped her Stop sign. Seconds later, a line of children walked toward a waiting school bus.

"Maybe you'd better let me take the wheel," Peggy said.

"You can't be in much better shape than I am."

"I'm not," she said. "But I'll manage."

He nodded silently as she opened the door.

"Nothing's likely to happen before we get there," she said as they changed places. "Claims like Sean's are very easy to contest. And Dr. Santos has promised to keep him and his crew at arm's length until we arrive." She buckled in. "I guess the real question is how compassionate we'd be to stop him."

"You don't think Samantha wants to die, do you?"

"I don't know what she wants," she said. "Ever since she vanished, I've been trying to second-guess her—what she'd gone through in childhood, what her research was about . . . all the secrets she's been keeping, all her life. I never stopped to consider what she might want for herself."

"And what do you think that is?"

Peggy waited for the children to finish crossing.

"Samantha said it in her journal. She wants her child to be safe."

"If that's so," he said, "and if Samantha dies—do you really think Caden's likely to be safe in his father's custody?"

"In his father's, maybe. But not in Sean's."

The doors of the school bus closed. As it drove away, children waved at her; one of them stuck his tongue out. Peggy smiled—then saw the sign that had been concealed behind the yellow bus:

MILL CREEK, PHASE II
Gated Community
*Choice Lots and Heritage Homes Available this Autumn*

"Phase Two." She shook her head. "Seems like everybody in the valley's selling out to these people. Next thing you know, they'll be making an offer on Culloden Hall."

"Not bloody likely," Harrison said. "My ancestors were wise in that regard, at least. The college charter expressly forbids selling school property to outside parties."

"Really?"

He nodded. "Practically the entire mountain belongs to the Avalon corporation. Which has to be galling to whoever's behind this Mill Creek operation. The land's probably worth millions."

"Sure. But . . ." She thought a moment. "What would it take to amend the charter?"

"A motion by the president." He looked at her with sudden awareness. "And a two-thirds vote of the trustees and regents."

"And now that you're retiring," she said, "who's in the best position to accomplish that?"

"Good Lord," he said.

The crossing guard turned her sign from STOP to SLOW.

"*Cui bono*," Peggy said. "Always follow the God-damned money."

---

As they neared the hospital, Peggy's cell phone rang.

"Special Agent Weaver."

"Yes." It was an older man's voice, cautiously matter-of-fact. "Someone paged me from this number?"

She checked her PDA display. "Am I speaking to Lieutenant Colonel Marcus L. Hankins?"

"That's what it says on my army retirement. How can I be of service, Agent . . . ?"

"Weaver, sir. FBI. I'm looking for information on a former soldier under your command in Vietnam—Master Sergeant Kevin W. Slayton."

"Ah." A guarded note crept into his voice. "Agent Weaver, can I please ask how you got this number?"

"Through legal channels, Colonel. Please contact the Bureau if you have any concerns." She waited. "Would you at least confirm that I'm speaking to the right person?"

Silence.

"What did he say?" Harrison asked from the passenger seat.

"Hung up on me." She shut her phone. "I gather Slayton's something of a hot potato. At least now we know—"

The phone rang again.

"Weaver," she said.

"I can speak to you on background only." It was the colonel's voice. "I will not give any on-the-record statements. If you make any attempt to record or transcribe my words, I'll know. And that will be the end of this or any future conversation. Understood?"

"Yes, sir, I do."

"All right," he said. "Fire away."

"I'm told that Slayton was posted to U.S. Army COMSEC Intelligence," she said. "And that he disappeared in action on February twenty-eighth, nineteen seventy-one, near the Ben Het region of Vietnam. Is this correct?"

There was a brief silence. Peggy got the feeling she'd been put on mute.

"Your information is not completely accurate," Hankins said finally. "Slayton wasn't assigned to COMSEC at the time of his disappearance. And he wasn't in Vietnam. He was in Laos."

"What was he doing in Laos?"

"Bringing down Armageddon," he said. "Slayton was ordered to provide intelligence support to a classified unit known as Military Assistance Command, Vietnam—MACVSOG for short. His team—my team—was trained to coordinate partisan activities behind enemy lines. Legally, we weren't supposed to be in Laos . . . so, naturally, secrecy was a prime concern. By nineteen seventy, we were mainly assisting in the 'Vietnamization' of the war as a prelude to U.S. withdrawal. Slayton, it turned out, had plans of his own."

"He went rogue?"

"That's putting it mildly. Some of his squad refused to participate . . . Slayton had them disemboweled. The rest of his command joined with South Vietnamese elements to attack a school on the Laotian side."

"What kind of school?"

"A kindergarten," he said. "When the Laotian Army arrived . . . they found the children hanging in the trees, or half-buried . . . as if animals had torn them to pieces. The youngest victim was three years old." He paused. "This was not an isolated incident. By the turn of the new year, Slayton had earned himself a reputation as a butcher—and that reputation was threatening to drag America back into a war that we were trying very desperately to end."

"Which I suppose was a factor in his disappearance?"

He hesitated. "Officially, it was the NVA and Pathet Lao who took him out. They'd dispatched special cadres into his mountain stronghold . . . but, despite their best information, they were never able to force him into a standoff."

"Who told them how to find him, then?"

"Surely I don't need to explain that to an FBI agent." His voice went cold. "They found him. And, in the end, everyone was satisfied. The Communists got their man . . . Slayton got his heroic last stand . . . and our servicemen got to come home." He paused. "You could say that a kind of justice was served."

"How well did you know Slayton?"

"Hardly at all," Hankins answered. "I saw what he did to those children. That's all I ever needed to know."

"Thank you, Colonel. You've been extraordinarily helpful."

"May I ask a question? Slayton's been MIA for more than thirty-five years. Why the sudden interest?"

"He's come home, sir. I saw him with my own eyes early this morning." She glanced briefly at Harrison. "Twenty-five years ago, he kidnapped and mutilated my best friend. And now he's here in Tennessee . . . trying to finish the job."

"My god," Hankins said. "But we'd received confirmation . . ."

"Perhaps it would have been best not to 'Vietnamize' that particular operation," she said. "Good day, Colonel."

She hung up the phone. As they pulled into the hospital parking lot, an array of official vehicles—some of them Bureau cars—were lined up alongside local law enforcement.

"Who are these people?" Harrison asked.

"Looks like our reinforcements have arrived," she said. "I don't know how much of that conversation you picked up . . ."

"Enough, I think."

"I'm going to assign some of these men to take you and your family home," she answered. "Slayton's a washer."

"A what?"

"Sorry, that's FBI slang," she said. "He's a government-trained assassin."

# FIFTY-FOUR

The recent arrival of FBI agents from Memphis and Knoxville had transformed the lobby of Keyes County Hospital into an ad hoc field headquarters. Peggy didn't see a single familiar face until Dr. Santos met her at the entrance to ICU.

"There was some real chaos when Sean arrived," the doctor told her. "I don't suppose you could clear these men out of here? The guns aren't too healthy for my patients."

"Most of them will be relocating to the sheriff's department." Peggy followed her back down the hall. "But I'm going to have to leave a few teams here to provide security . . . and complete forensic analysis."

"Forensic analysis of what? This isn't a crime scene."

"I'm talking about physical evidence on Samantha." Peggy breathed. "How is she doing?"

"She's losing ground," the doctor said. "But she's fighting for every inch."

"That's my girl." Then Peggy caught sight of Sean's attorney—and some half-dozen of his security guards—surrounding the door to ICU. Dr. Santos was on them before Peggy could speak.

"I thought I told you men to stay the *hell* away." The fierceness in the doctor's voice set everyone on their toes, Peggy included. "I turn my back for five seconds . . ."

"Mr. Aldridge has the right to visit his wife alone," the attorney said. "That's all he's doing."

"We'll see." Peggy stepped forward. "In any case, this entire group is to report directly to Keyes County Sheriff's Department for debrief. Either they comply immediately . . . or I'm placing them all under arrest."

The men stood stock still, as if daring her to try.

"I'm not alone here," Peggy said to the lawyer. "And I really don't think you want to take me on."

After a moment he nodded, relenting. Peggy watched them go.

"Her vitals are weak." Santos checked a display. "We'd better go in."

"Let me clear him out of there first." She opened the door. "Sean, I don't know what game this is, but—"

The lights were dim as the door closed behind her. Light puffs of mist formed in Samantha's oxygen mask, then cleared as the respirator forced more into her chest. Sean crouched close beside his wife's head, as if kneeling in prayer.

"Back away from her, Sean."

He turned. Tears were streaming down his face.

"Peggy . . . ?"

Something in his expression took her off guard; her voice softened in spite of herself. "Please, Sean. Sammie doesn't need us here right now."

"She's . . . my wife." The words were plain, desperately confused. "I'm just trying to say good-bye."

"There's a room next door." Peggy nodded over her shoulder. "Let's step back and let the doctors help her."

She led him into a side room. Peggy could still hear Samantha's respirator through the wall.

"You shouldn't talk that way in front of her," Peggy said. "There's a chance she can still hear you."

"I wanted her to hear me." White butcher paper creased as Sean sat on an examination table. "I wanted her to know I'm sorry for . . . treating her the way I did. No wonder she threw herself in with those scumbags. It was all my fault."

Peggy rubbed her temple. "Look, if we could do the confessional another time . . ."

"You're tired, aren't you?" He looked at her closely. "Two days without sleep or food . . . I'll bet you're ready to collapse."

"Don't worry about me," she said. "Why do you want to pull her life support?"

"It's the only thing I could think to do for her." His faced wrenched, aching. "I know people think I'm a shitty husband. Just like I'm a shitty son, and a shitty father . . . but I have to do *something* for her. I can't leave her like this."

"One of your men may be working with Slayton," Peggy said. "If you want to do something for her, help us find the mole."

"One of *my* men." He looked at her in stunned anger. "Are you suggesting I'm somehow responsible for this?"

She narrowed her eyes. "Are you?"

"If I . . ." He looked around. "What happened to my attorney?"

"Oh, boy." She folded her arms. "You know, you almost had me convinced with those puppy-dog eyes. And then the minute I pose a direct question, you start asking for your lawyer."

"Maybe you should read me my rights." His voice was steady and cool. "But you won't, will you? You wasted your shot at me with that bullshit arrest for withholding evidence. You won't get another one."

"You weren't cleared of that charge, Sean. You're just walking around on bail." She shrugged. "Just once, try telling the truth without a subpoena in your hand. You know—for your wife's sake?"

"We put up a million and a half for my wife's sake." Sean reddened. "She was worth twice that much. Then you and Blaine went and screwed the whole thing to hell. Now you're trying to stick me with the blame?"

"Listen to me," she said. "Soon—very soon—one of your crack security team is going to cut a deal to save himself. And then you'll really be stuck. That's what happens when you try to buy people's loyalty the same way you buy horses. Or land."

"Land." His eyes shone cold. "What land?"

"Mill Creek Properties," she said. "Otherwise known as Logan D. Aldridge the Third. It took a little digging, but we found a way through all the holding accounts and dummy corporations you set up. Your dad's going to make a fortune carving Avalon up for weekend homes, isn't he?"

Sean didn't answer.

"I've seen him pull some pretty smooth moves," she said. "But paying off the Avalon trustees to amend the charter, and put you in Harrison's job—that's a masterpiece."

"We didn't have to bribe them all." He half-smiled. "Believe me, a lot of people are done waiting for Harrison Stallworth to retire. No offense, I know you're a disciple of his. But the man's a financial idiot. He practically bankrupted Avalon with all his half-assed dreams."

"It's your father's dreams I'm more concerned about," she said. "And why Samantha should have to die for them."

"It wasn't my father's dream. It was mine." He glowered at her. "Nobody thinks I can do jack shit without the old man. But this one was *mine*. And it's a total win-win, Peggy. Avalon College's finances are back in the black . . . some classy houses get built on the bluff . . . no laws are broken . . . and nobody gets hurt."

"You know who got hurt," she said. "Don't be stupid."

"My dad was right about you." He laughed. "You really are the one I should have married. Christ, can you imagine the insanely smart kids we would have had?"

"Don't flatter yourself."

"I still remember how you were that first time," he said. "All those nights in the pool house . . . or your bedroom on the white-trash side of town? You ever think about that shit?"

"This conversation is over." She turned back to the door. "I wouldn't get too used to the idea of president. I don't think the trustees are going to risk the job on somebody under federal investigation."

"You screamed like a cat." He stood up. "And, damn, you sure cried like one when I dumped you for Samantha. That's why you hate me, isn't it? You blame me for marrying a woman I didn't love . . . and driving a wedge between you and Samantha. I am so sorry, Peggy. Really. I was insensitive to your feelings."

"You go to hell," she said.

Sean struck her hard in the solar plexus.

On a good day, Peggy would have broken his collarbone before he could move. But he'd taken her off guard, and her reflexes were shot. She hit the tile floor like a broken doll.

In the next room she could hear the broken, rhythmless pulse of Samantha's heart monitor.

Sean was locking the doors.

# FIFTY-FIVE

"Shh. It's okay." Sean knelt beside her. "Christ, I didn't want to hurt you. But you weren't *listening* to me, honey. Understand?"

Peggy had involuntarily drawn up fetal; her limbs were bloodless and cold.

"So listen to me now." He caressed her back softly, as if comforting a child. "Because everything we've been saying has been monitored. And I think you know who's on the other end."

She gasped—a sharp hiccup, a tiny fistful of air.

"Don't try to talk," he said. "If you open your mouth, it won't just be Samantha who dies. It'll be my father, and Caden . . . and chances are, your folks as well. Trust me, the guy's that fucking crazy."

Dark flowers swam across her field of vision; she was starting to black out.

"Slayton's promised us the antivenom," he said. "If we do *exactly* as he says. But if you screw around one little bit . . . he'll make you wish you'd let me pull the plug on her."

Peggy didn't stir. She had maybe one move left in her, and she needed him just a little closer.

"I'll let you up if you promise not to tell anyone." He was suddenly anxious. "This never happened, okay?"

He bent over her, putting his mouth close to her cheek.

"Peggy . . . ?"

She drove her elbow sharply into his Adam's apple. Sean fell away, choking—but he was just as quickly on top of her again. He flung her against the cabinets; aluminum pans rattled and fell. Peggy tried to stand and as quickly collapsed.

"That's *it*." He crawled to her, gray eyes smoking.

There was a knock on the door. Feet shuffled outside.

"Make one sound and you've killed her." He placed a hand to her throat. "Not joking."

Another knock. The door handle jiggled. Sean seemed to make a rapid calculation.

"For her sake, you'd better make this look real." Then he bent down and kissed her full on the mouth. His hand slid along her left breast.

The door broke open.

"Peggy." A man's voice.

Sean lifted himself up—squinting, as if the lights had been out for a while. Peggy turned to see who was silhouetted in the doorway.

"Mike . . . ?"

"Sorry I missed the party," he said.

Mike Yeager's blue eyes shone clear as he switched on the light. He wore a brown leather jacket and held a carry-on bag. "Or maybe I should just head back to the airport?"

"Shit, this is embarrassing." Sean smiled ruefully, a frat boy caught cheating. "It's cool, okay? Don't get the lady in trouble. It's not her fault. She was just . . . comforting me."

"Really." He looked around the room, then back at her. "Can you stand up, Peg?"

Peggy sat up to adjust her blouse. Her breath was coming back, but just barely.

"We're old friends." Sean stood up. "Old flames, really. Your girl was—"

"I wasn't talking to you, asshole." Mike held his hand out. "Come along, Peggy Jean. Everybody's looking for you."

"I'm . . . okay." She looked at Sean; his eyes registered caution. "Nothing happened, Mike. We're good."

"Swell." Mike set his bag down. "Maybe we should all take a moment to get acquainted, huh? I've always wanted to meet an old flame of Peggy's."

Sean drew himself to his full height. "Look, whoever you are, this is a private time, and—"

Mike turned around and pressed the muzzle of his Sig P226 to Sean Aldridge's forehead.

"Finish your sentence," Mike said. "Tell me about your poor sick wife in the next room."

Sean froze.

"Mike." Peggy pulled herself to her feet.

"Dead or alive, Peg?"

"We'll need him conscious," she said. "He claims to know where we can find the antidote for Samantha. Or was that just more bullshit, Sean?"

Sean seemed to be trying to speak, but no words came.

"Agent Weaver's ordered me not to blow your brains out," Mike said coolly. "She didn't say anything about the rest of you. So stop spitting on me and answer her question."

"We . . ." He looked at Peggy. "I *told* you what would happen . . ."

Mike pivoted the gun around and poised himself to swing the butt down.

"Stop it!" He fell back into a chair. "I don't know where the antidote is. All I know is that Slayton said it was for real. And if we pay his price, he'll give it to us."

"What's the price?" she asked.

He looked at her. "You."

"What?"

"Last night's raid was supposed to be the handoff," Sean said. "Just a big diversion to get you alone in the open. Samantha would have been released as soon as you were in Slayton's custody. But you surprised the hell out of him with that kid, Ripley . . . forced him to fire his RPG at close range and blew out his own engine manifold."

Peggy bore down on him. "You spoke to Slayton?"

"Mostly I listened." He threw her a sullen glance.

"And you would have given me to him," she said.

He didn't answer.

"Correct me if I'm wrong," she said to Mike. "I believe that's accessory after the fact."

"Don't forget assault of a federal agent," Mike said.

"Good point," she said. "Blow off his kneecap."

Mike aimed the pistol.

"You can't do this!" Sean drew back. "You're FBI agents."

"Don't worry," Mike said. "You're in a hospital. They'll fix you up."

His voice shook. "I'll tell you what you want to know. Just for chrissakes put the gun down."

Peggy shut the door. "Exactly how much 'listening' have you been doing, Sean?"

"You saw the first communication," he said. "There've been a few since then. Text messages, mostly—including Slayton's instruction to file for life-support termination on Sammie."

"Weren't you just now telling me you wanted her alive?"

"I was playing for time," he said. "To be honest, I don't know what he even wants with her at this point."

"Of course not. He wants me."

"*And* the one-point-six million," he said. "He's a very good negotiator."

"And what do you want with her, Sean? Don't waste my time talking about love."

"I'm not saying another word without some kind of immunity." He bristled. "You should know that I'm the only one Slayton talks to. Without me, there's no deal. Think about that before you screw around with me."

"In case you hadn't noticed, you're already screwed." She looked at Mike. "You see the nerve on this jerk?"

"I just can't believe you used to go out with him."

"Me neither." She reached into Sean's jacket pocket and pulled out a transmitter the size of a lipstick tube. "I take it this is how he's been listening to us?"

"He's listening now. Anything you say to me, you're saying to him." He held up his palms. "Let me fix this, Peggy. I promise you won't get caught in the middle again."

She turned to Mike. "Give me your piece, Yeager."

"No kneecap, huh?"

"No." She took it with her left hand, holding the microphone in her right. "Sorry, Sean. Time to cut out the middleman."

"He won't deal with you," Sean said.

"Yes, he will," she said. "Sean Parker Aldridge, you have the right to remain silent. Anything you say can and will be used against you in a court of law. You have the right to speak to an attorney, and to have an attorney present during any questioning. If you cannot afford a lawyer, one will be provided for you at government expense."

Sean looked at her with cold amusement.

"Do you understand the rights I have just read to you?" she asked. "With these rights in mind, do you wish to speak to me?"

"No need," he said. "Good luck, Peggy. We'll all miss you."

# FIFTY-SIX

"Peggy." Mike turned back as the deputies escorted Sean through the hospital doors. "You mind telling me what happened back there?"

"In a second." She waved Yoshi over to her. "What's the story on that transmitter?"

"For one thing, it's got a seventy-two-hour battery." Yoshi held it out for her inspection. "There's slightly less than one-third power remaining—so I'll guess Aldridge has been holding onto it since early Sunday morning."

"Right around the time Samantha went missing," she said. "And the battery's set to run out just as she's scheduled to die."

"Let me see that." Mike took it from Yoshi. "It is deactivated, right?"

"I *think* so," Yoshi said. "To be honest, it's a little out of my league. For all we know, it's doing brain scans on us right now."

"So Slayton's got money and connections," Mike said. "Have you found anything new on him?"

"Not as such. But I'm getting some interesting collateral data on Tidwell. We still don't know much about who he was—but at least now we know *where* he was. And when."

"How so?"

"Those military magazines all over his house," Yoshi said. "Apparently, Tidwell was some kind of armed forces groupie. The address labels go back to nineteen sixty-eight."

"Anything unusual?"

"Mm-hmm." Yoshi nodded. "Guess where he was getting his mail the year Samantha Aldridge was first kidnapped?"

"Here in Avalon?"

"The Whitelaw Farm," he said. "Seems like Tidwell moved there right after his release from prison—then cut out for Mexico about the same time Samantha disappeared."

"He did call himself 'White Shadow,'" she mused. "Maybe it wasn't my father he was shadowing all those years."

"Take a look." Yoshi handed her an old newsletter. "This comes from a POW/MIA group that used to make regular trips to Southeast Asia during the nineteen eighties."

The issue was from 1981. The caption read, "3rd Annual Recovery Quest." Tidwell stood in the back. He was the only one smiling.

Peggy read through. "Says here that their first expedition was to . . . Vientiane province. That's in Laos, isn't it?"

Yoshi nodded. "Most of the people in the group are relatives," he said. "Quite a few of the missing servicemen belonged to the same unit."

"MACVSOG," she said. "Slayton's group."

"And there's Slayton's name on the list." He pointed. "The article says no POW remains were found that year. But you already know about the trips Tidwell took on his own, right?"

"To Thailand, you mean. The sex tours."

"Possibly that was all just a cover. He could easily have landed in Bangkok with the rest of the horny businessmen, then bribed his way across the Lao border."

"And found Slayton on one of those trips." She handed the newsletter back. "Good work, Yoshi."

"Thanks." He smiled. "I've gotta grab some sleep, boss. I'm toasty."

She nodded. "Just make sure your cell's on. I'm heading back to the sheriff's department to monitor interviews on Sean and his security team. We may need you to run background."

"Hold on." Mike held up his hand. "Am I right in understanding that your father befriended Tidwell in nineteen seventy-one—the same year Slayton went missing in Laos?"

Peggy nodded.

"And Slayton's a college friend of your father's," he said.

"What's your point, Mike?"

"Why are you going all the way back to the sheriff's station for a debrief," he said, "when your father's right upstairs?"

Peggy couldn't help but notice that Mike was still holding onto the transmitter.

"My father has second-degree burns," she said. "I don't want to put him under the hot lights unless it's critical."

"Seems pretty critical to me," he said. "Look, if you're reluctant to interrogate your own dad, I'll talk to him. I know how tired you are—"

"I'm fine."

"No, you're not." Mike looked at Yoshi. "Call the sheriff's department and tell them Agent Weaver's going to be a little late. We need to talk about this, Peg."

Yoshi started to speak. Peggy stilled him with a warning glance.

"I'm gonna go put myself to sleep with some of Tidwell's military journals." Yoshi eagerly waved himself away. "Great to see the team together, huh? Please don't kill each other."

She waited until Agent Hiraka was out of sight before turning back to Mike.

"I know," Mike said. "I shouldn't give orders over your head. Sorry."

"Just give me the transmitter," she said evenly.

"What do you need it for?"

"Maybe because it's my investigation?" she asked. "I've had two solid days of people questioning my judgment, my authority, and my integrity. I'm not taking it from you."

"I'm not questioning anything," he said. "But I'd like to know what you meant by 'cutting out the middleman.'"

"Stop holding that damn thing like it's a grenade you're ready to throw yourself on," she said. "I know what I'm doing. And if I choose to negotiate directly with Slayton, it will be at my discretion. Not yours."

"Negotiate with what? Your flesh?"

"Mike!"

He handed it over.

She took a breath. "I'm glad you're here, Yeager. Believe me, I am. But you can't just charge in and start kicking butts. A lot's been happening since you dropped out of sight."

"'Dropped out'?" He tensed. "I haven't exactly been at a spa these past twenty-four hours."

"You weren't in a dungeon, either. Yoshi called his wife, for chrissakes. You could have called me."

"So now you're my wife?"

"That's not what I meant," she said. "I know the OPR was rubbing your nose in a lot of shit. And I'm sorry. But it's getting to be a pattern with you. Every time somebody shames you in public, you run and hide. It was the same last year, when the Madrigal case blew up in your face. Next thing I knew, you were in fucking Nevada. Never mind how badly you were needed at home."

"You needed me. Right." He took her by the arm. "That's why you requested Yoshi for this case instead of me?"

"I didn't have a choice. Let go."

"Well, I'm not running away now," he said. "Last night, people were trying to kill you—or worse—and I wasn't here. How do you think that makes me feel?"

"I don't give a shit how you feel. Do your job." She pulled away. "You can't always protect me, Mike. Sometimes we get killed. It goes with the badge. Who the Christ cares?"

He didn't answer. Peggy was keenly aware that the lobby was full of people not looking her way. She gradually turned to see who'd come into the room.

The woman was much smaller than her son, wearing the pink uniform of a truck-stop waitress. A pretty girl in her late teens or early twenties— red-eyed and plainly furious—held Mrs. Ripley's arthritic hand.

"Mrs. Ripley," Peggy said.

Peggy badly wanted to say more. She was ready to tell the woman that her son had died a hero, that his death had a purpose. Then she noticed the girl's hand resting on her smock: a slight bulge in her stomach, a quarter-carat engagement ring on her finger. And Peggy knew that nothing she had to say mattered in the least.

Finally the women passed on. And as the lobby staff cautiously set about their business again, Peggy felt Mike's hand on her shoulder.

"What were we arguing about just now?" she asked.

"Beats the holy hell out of me," he answered.

She reached up and placed her hand on his. "You think we should go talk to my dad?"

"If you're ready to, yeah."

"I'm not," she said. "It doesn't bother me to die, Mike. But I'm scared shitless to find out what my father's been keeping from me all these years."

"Like I said, I'll handle it."

"No, you won't." She smiled at him. "But thanks for trying."

# FIFTY-SEVEN

Spots of blood—many of them smeared across the floor by bare footprints—trailed from Rusty's empty bed to the open door of his private room. As she inspected the hanging IV needle, Peggy saw hairs from her father's hand still clinging to the white surgical tape.

"We thought your daddy was asleep." The deputy shuffled nervously in front of her. "So when Aldridge showed up, we ran out to help that doctor back 'em off. We were gone maybe . . . sixty seconds? And when we came back, the door was still locked. Didn't think any sick man could move that fast."

"Mike?" Peggy turned to him as he entered the room.

"The front desk says your father got an outside call directly to his room at nine oh-three A.M.," Mike said. "Maybe two minutes before Sean and his people barged in."

"And less than five minutes after I left the building." She slumped into a chair, noticing a black gym bag shoved under the bed. "Guys, can we have this room, please?"

The deputies nodded and left.

"My father's part of this whole thing," she said. "I'm still trying to make myself believe it."

"You don't know that for a fact, Peg. From what you told me, he might have been coerced."

"See this?" She reached for the gym bag. "About the right size for a full suit of clothes, wouldn't you say?"

"Or an abduction kit." He turned the bag out: empty.

"My dad was out of here as soon as he got that call. Right under the noses of doctors, nurses, deputies, and federal agents. Even if Sean's arrival was meant as a diversion . . . how could anyone have gotten my father out of the hospital without his cooperation?"

"People cooperate with kidnappers for a lot of reasons," he said. "Seems like you're forgetting how he wound up in the hospital in the first place."

"Because he planted an incendiary device on Tidwell. And because . . ." She pressed a hand to her forehead. "Because he was shielding me from the explosion with his body."

"And when you asked him why he murdered Tidwell?"

She exhaled. "He said it was to protect me."

"Maybe he's still protecting you," Mike said. "Yoshi told me about that message on Samantha's picture. 'You for her.' That's the deal the Aldridges made, right? It would have been you and Slayton alone."

"And Samantha would have gotten the cure." Peggy nodded. "So where's Slayton getting the cure? I doubt he's been flying back and forth to Melbourne."

"Well—what's he got close at hand?"

Something flashed through Peggy's mind from the night before: an image of glass tanks . . . and bloody white feathers in the burning barn.

"Chickens and horses," she said. "Most serums are processed through livestock blood, aren't they?"

"Horses, yeah. I don't know about chickens." He tossed the bag down. "But they'd both make pretty good test subjects if you're trying to calibrate a dosage for humans."

She stood up.

"So where to now?" he asked.

"I want to see what else Slayton had close at hand," she said.

The evidence response team had finished at the Whitelaw Farm by the time Peggy and Mike arrived. All the doors were freshly padlocked and sealed with police tape.

"Think we should wait for somebody to bring us the key?" She took the tire iron from the back of her Jeep. "Me neither."

She shoved the iron through the hasp of the lock, breaking it off in a single hard twist. As they entered the living room, the corpse-stink was palpable. Mike coughed.

"It's enough to kill the cockroaches." He lifted the plastic sheeting covering the sofa. There was a dark wet stain on the cushions, matching indentations left after Jonas Whitelaw's body was removed. "Looks like the old man was leaking a lot of fluid. I'm guessing he's been dead . . . a week, maybe?"

Peggy noticed a framed photo beside the sofa: Jonas Whitelaw, proudly smiling next to Slayton in front of a Greyhound bus. Young Kevin wore a crisp new army uniform with PFC stripes; he seemed almost shy of the camera.

"His uncle died first," she said. "And he died fast. Slayton pumped enough venom into him to kill an elephant."

"And his wife?"

"Crime scene crew couldn't find her," she said.

"They weren't looking hard enough," Mike said. "She's here."

She nodded. "Slayton had to shut her up, didn't he?"

"Well, she's not gonna keep cooking and cleaning for her nephew with her husband dead on the couch," he said. "Where do you want to look?"

Peggy went into the kitchen.

"They already checked the bedrooms," she said. "And there's no remains in the barn—unless you count the chickens." She thought. "And then there's the fruit cellar."

He looked around. "I don't see it."

Without saying a word, she opened the kitchen pantry—then pushed aside a small knotted mat, revealing the trap door.

"Don't even ask me how I knew that," she said.

As she preceded Mike down the stairs, Peggy saw her breath form in the air. She was strangely relieved to know that—for once, at least—the chill she felt wasn't in her imagination. Then she switched on the light.

"That son of a bitch," she said.

The first thing she saw was a pale foot, still wearing a fuzzy pink slipper. Between the racks of mason jars, close to a folding metal chair, a thin shape lay curled up beneath a knitted blanket: Martha Whitelaw. Still, and quiet, and cold.

"Check out the little piles of cigarette butts." Mike pointed to several places on the floor. "Beer cans . . . bag of corn chips . . . Slayton was down here a lot over the past few days."

She didn't answer immediately. Something about the old woman's contorted expression reminded Peggy of the way Sammie had looked in the emergency room. Naked terror behind half-closed lids.

"Slayton was keeping her clean." Mike knelt down. "Wash basin, antibacterial wipes . . . I guess he liked Auntie best, huh?"

"No, he didn't," she said. "He put his uncle right out of his misery. All he wanted from Martha was to watch her suffer." She shivered. "Let's call the crime scene crew back. Tell them to finish their goddamn job."

Mike took out his cell phone. "No signal down here. We'll have to—Peg, what is it?"

"Something bad happened here," she said.

"Yeah. Two nice old people got murdered by their nephew."

"Something else," she said. "I don't remember ever coming to this house until today, Mike. But I'm starting to feel like I know my way around too damn well." Peggy looked up at the low ceiling. "What was that?"

Mike listened. "I didn't hear anything."

"Sounded like a door closing upstairs," she said. "I don't want to be down here anymore."

"So we'll leave."

"Okay." She waited. "Maybe I'm just imagining things, huh?"

But both of them were already unholstering their weapons.

As they returned to the front parlor, the screen door was swaying loosely on its broken spring.

"There's no other vehicles around." Mike scanned the yard. "Somebody must have followed us in."

Peggy reflexively checked over her shoulder. Swirls of dust were turning rapidly down the long stairwell.

"More like somebody was waiting for a chance to get out." She pointed to a fresh indentation in the carpet runner: a small footprint, angled toward the front door. "The sheriff's team didn't check upstairs as well as they should have."

"There's some high grass that wasn't trampled a moment ago." Mike traced a path to the burned-out shell of the pole barn. "Somebody's hauling ass across the yard."

They approached the barn over scorched earth, strewn with heavy bootprints and spent shells. Tendrils of smoke spun away from blackened timbers, still warm from several feet away. Part of the roof had fallen in— but the aluminum stairs to the loft were still mostly intact.

Mike looked up into darkness. "Not the world's smartest place to hide, is it?"

"She's not the world's smartest person," Peggy said.

"'She'?"

Peggy pointed to what had fallen on the bottom rung: a harpoonlike earring.

"Gretchen?" She called up the stairs. "This isn't good, kid. The building's about to collapse under you."

There was a long silence. Then:

"So?"

"So either come down, or chances are we're gonna get killed trying to save you. What were you doing inside the house, anyhow?"

"None of your damn business," Gretchen said from the darkness above. "Tell that guy to go away. He's scary."

Peggy waved Mike off. He frowned as he stepped away.

"He's at a safe distance. Now come down, please. One step at a time."

"Screw you. I like it up here."

But Peggy could hear the terror in the girl's voice.

"All right," Peggy said. "I'm coming up."

"You won't shoot me or anything?"

"I won't shoot you." Peggy holstered her Glock, then gingerly tested her weight on the stairs. "But if you make me break my leg, Gretchen, I promise I will slap you sideways."

As she pulled herself up into the loft, Peggy could feel the timbers shift beneath her. Gretchen huddled in the shadows, quivering in a pair of men's boxers and T-shirt.

"Look at my hands." Peggy held them up. "No gun."

"I don't care. Stay back."

"I just want some answers. How'd you get locked in the house?"

"I don't know how I got here. They knocked me out and I woke up in a fucking closet."

"Who did?"

"Some guys I was partying with, okay? I drank an open beer and it tasted like shit. Then I was out. Jerks didn't even put my clothes back on after they finished."

"Why didn't you call the police as soon as you woke up?"

Gretchen looked at her, stunned.

"Peg, are you coming down?" Mike called up from below. "Is the kid okay?"

For whatever reason, the mere sound of Mike's voice was enough to make Gretchen seize up like a cornered mouse.

"I wasn't lying about the drugs," Gretchen said. "These clothes were all I could find to wear. And they stink."

"Uh-huh. So who gave you the beer?"

She hesitated. "I don't know. Somebody said they were down from Vanderbilt. I don't even know where the fuck I am."

"Yes, you do. You grew up here, just like I did." Peggy inched closer. "This is a murder scene, Gretchen. It also happens to be where the kidnapper was holding Dr. Aldridge. Now why do you think—out of all the places in the world—this is where you just happened to wake up today?"

"Leave me alone." Gretchen took a breath. "I told you I don't remember anything about him."

"'Guys'," Peggy said.

"Huh?"

"You told me it was 'some guys' you were partying with." She waited. "Who was it, really? Brandon?"

Her face collapsed. "Please don't be angry at me."

"I'm not even started getting angry." Peggy turned to the open hatch. "Mike?"

"Yeah."

"Let's switch places. I think she'd rather talk to you."

"I'm too heavy for those stairs," he said. "Just kick her down here, okay?"

"Wait." Gretchen pulled back. "Just wait, okay?"

"I can't wait anymore. Samantha's dying. You may not care about that, but I do."

"I care. She's my friend, too." She steeled herself. "It was Brandon, okay? He swore up and down that Dr. Aldridge wouldn't get hurt. All they wanted was to keep you from finding the bones. And I made them promise . . ."

"What bones?" Peggy waited. "Gretchen, what bones?"

Gretchen rolled her eyes. "The ones in her goddamn *book*, idiot. Some dead woman named Mara Cumbaa, and her baby, and a bunch of other people. Jesus, didn't you even *read* the damn thing?" Her voice rose several pitches. "I don't believe this. I went to all that fucking trouble to get that shit to you . . ."

"There's nothing about bones on that CD-ROM you gave me. Or anyone named Mara Cumbaa. Or any baby."

"But I . . ." She blinked. "I made the disk for you."

"It's not there," Peggy said. "Maybe you should ask Brandon."

"Boys are such lying *assholes*." Gretchen snarled. "I never should have told Brandon about Dr. Aldridge's book. She *said* it was a secret. And then that *pigfucker* went and started *blabbing* . . ."

Gretchen slammed her fist down, scattering ashes from the loose ceiling joists.

"That's it," Peggy said. "You're coming with me."

"No! Stay back! He'll kill me for talking to you. He said he'd kill any-body who tries to help you."

"Who are you talking about? Brandon?"

"No, no, no. *Him*."

"Slayton," she said.

"Yeah." For once she didn't look away. "He was there, too. Freaked the hell out of me."

"And you knew what they were going to do to Samantha . . . didn't you? You knew it all along." Peggy shook her head. "And you call yourself her friend."

"They said she'd be left alone." Gretchen gasped. "Don't you know how I *hurt* bottling all this up? I never wanted to be anybody's fuckdoll. I only wanted to be nice, and smart, like Dr. Aldridge . . . and now I'm all *screwed*. Like those bones she wrote about. That's all I'm gonna be soon. Old dead bones."

"Calm down," she said. "You're going into custody. I'll make sure you're protected."

"No, you *won't*. You couldn't protect Tidwell. You can't even protect yourself." Gretchen's face contorted; she was beginning to hyperventilate. "They told me what happened to Tidwell. Know how they made you do it? Fucking radio waves. And they can make you do it to me just as easy."

Peggy held up her hands. "I'm not carrying a radio."

"And you think *I'm* stupid?" She burst into giggles. "I guess you never figured out how cell phones work?"

And then Peggy felt it vibrate in her pocket. And before she could hurl it away, it was ringing.

"Mike, get back—!"

The last thing she heard before the explosion was Gretchen's terrified laughter.

# FIFTY-EIGHT

Peggy's next clear thought was that Mike was pulling her from the building. When they were about twenty-five yards away, she looked back to see that the barn had collapsed. A knot of flame had broken through the fallen timbers and licked the air. Peggy had a hard time keeping her feet under her.

"We have to go back." She could hear herself slurring. "Gretchen's . . . still alive."

"No, she's not." He was pushing her into the Jeep.

It took her a moment to realize that Mike had turned right instead of left onto the main highway: they were heading away from the mountain, into the valley.

"Where are we going?"

"Back to the hospital," he said. "You're bleeding, Peg. It's a miracle you survived."

She touched her forehead. The blood had the consistency of hot grease. "How did I get out?"

"You don't remember?" He looked over. "You were moving even before the charge went off. Best damn reflexes in the business."

"Yeah. Great reflexes." She opened the glove box, casting about for her first-aid kit. "Turn around, Yeager."

"We're not going back to that farm."

"Not to the farm. Home." She pulled out a sterile bandage and an antiseptic pack. "Gretchen said Slayton was a threat to anybody who tried to help me. And Sean mentioned my family. My mother's been alone since last night."

"You can call her from my phone," he said. "We'll get a car to your house. But right now—"

"*Mike.*"

He stared at her for a moment—then slammed on the brakes.

"God damn me for ever coming back to work for you," he said.

The house on Patton Circle was deathly still as they pulled into the driveway. The curtains were closed in her parents' bedroom, just as they had been the night before.

The front door was open.

She pushed past Mike into the living room. "Mama . . . ?"

Peggy smelled burning wax. Sickly music played on the AM radio. As she ran into the kitchen, Tigger brushed around her legs: His food bowl was empty. The refrigerator door was open, leaking freezer water onto the floor.

"Mama!" Peggy nearly fell over herself on her way to the studio. Nobody there. Beatrice's hot glue gun lay in a pool of yellowish liquid, smoking a hole into the table beneath.

"Oh my god." She went into the master bedroom: The bed was unmade on her mother's side. "I was supposed to call her last night, and I didn't. I just left her here by herself."

"Peggy, calm down. Maybe she just went out."

"How? There's no car here. And she doesn't even drive." Peggy paced back through the living room. "In case you hadn't noticed, my mother's halfway out of her mind. If we're *lucky*, all she did was wander off. But after what happened to my dad today—"

She came back into the kitchen to find her mother calmly setting down paper grocery sacks.

"Peggy Jean Weaver." Bea stared at her daughter blankly. "What on earth have you been into? You look a mess."

"Mom." She took her into her arms. "Oh my god, Mama, I thought you were gone."

"I just went to the store," she said. "Your father's going to be starving when he gets home for lunch." She began to unpack her groceries. "Who's that young man behind you?"

"That's . . . Mike Yeager. He came to help me find Samantha."

"Mike." She smiled. "So nice to see you again."

Peggy looked closely at Mike. After a moment's confusion, he smiled.

"Always a pleasure, ma'am." He turned to Peggy. "I'm going to get some people over here, okay?"

She nodded. As he left, her mother absently closed the refrigerator door.

"What were you and Mike just now talking about?" Beatrice continued to unpack her groceries. "Is there something you need to tell me?"

"I'm sorry. I was just really worried about you."

"And here I was, worried about you and your father." She looked at her daughter soberly. "I guess it doesn't matter what you might have said a moment ago. I know I haven't been myself lately. I never was the strong one in this family."

"Yes, you are, Ma."

"No, I'm not. But that's neither here nor there." Bea's dark brown eyes settled on her. "Go take a shower, hon. And then I'll bandage that cut properly. Mike will look after me while you get cleaned up."

She spoke in a voice that Peggy had long since learned not to disagree with. "Okay, Mama. I'll do that."

"Good. And then we'll have a nice lunch." She smiled. "Rusty's going to get quite a surprise when he sees his future son-in-law is here."

**A short while later, Mike** found them in the kitchen. Beatrice Weaver was just finishing her application of Neosporin on Peggy's cuts.

"There, now. All pretty again." Bea smiled up. "Doesn't she look pretty, Mike?"

"She always does." He smiled—but there was some lingering tension in his eyes.

"Thanks, Ma." She followed Mike into the living room. "You don't look happy, Yeager. What is it?"

"It's good news, mostly. New stuff's been coming in on Slayton ever since you made the ID on him. Interpol has him on a watch list of known sex traffickers living in the Eastern Bloc. Apparently he befriended some of his KGB interrogators during his stay with the Pathet Lao."

"So that's how he knew the Cookes."

"Not directly. But you know that Brandon DuBose character we're looking for? That alias you gave me . . . DaBiz?"

"That's what it says on his rhinestone necklace," she said. "What about him?"

"I've seen that name," he said. "Adam Cooke's a member of one of those networking sites on the Internet. And there's a 'DaBiz' on his buddy list. As soon as I can get Yoshi to answer his phone, we're gonna pull the message log . . . find out what these kids have been saying to each other lately."

"So why so grim about it? That's a fantastic break."

"We also found Adam Cooke," he said. "In a North Philly crackhouse. Both wrists cut straight to the bone." He took a breath. "I'm sorry Peg. It was the one thing you asked me to do, and I fucked it up."

Her immediate impulse was to tell him he was right—then she just as quickly relented.

"I've been throwing a lot at you guys this week," she said. "Maybe that's my whole problem. I keep looking for the answers in too many directions. But the truth's been staring at me since I was ten years old."

"What's that?"

"Slayton wants me," she said. "I don't know why, but he always has. And it seems like everyone else he's hurt is just a way of getting to me."

"He'll have to get past me first," Mike said. "And he's got to be pretty damn stupid if he wants to lock himself in a room with a badass like Peggy Weaver."

"I don't feel like such a badass," she said. "Whatever my father taught me isn't working anymore."

"What did he teach you?"

"Strangely enough, how to protect myself from guys like Slayton." She sat in Rusty's armchair. "And all the while . . . he knew it was Slayton who was after me. And he never said a word. What kind of father does that?"

"The father of Peggy Jean Weaver." Mike half-smiled. "You and your dad both seem to operate on a need-to-know basis."

"Like how?"

He sat on the arm of the chair beside her. "Like everything about you since the day we met. First we had to keep our romance this big secret at work . . . and yet somehow I was the last to find out we'd broken up. And let's not even mention that bozo you hooked up with while I was in Nevada."

"Let's not, okay?"

"Fair enough. All I'm saying is that I've known you for seven years . . . and you never once told me what happened here when you were a kid. I still don't know the whole story." He stroked her forehead. "No wonder you've got so many blocked memories. You start keeping secrets from people . . . sooner or later, you'll be keeping them from yourself."

"Like when you never told me about your mother?"

"Yeah." He looked away. "Like with her."

She reached up to touch the back of his neck.

"I'm sorry, Mike. That was low." She sighed. "But we can't get angry at each other now. We don't have time." She looked up at him. "Are you sure you're not still pissed off about what happened with Sean at the hospital?"

"I really would have killed that joker." He dropped his eyes. "I can't believe you ever *slept* with a creep like that."

"Hey, that was just a hormonal decision of my youth."

He half-smiled. "I thought I was a hormonal decision."

"Not like that one." She tilted his chin down. "Please don't get jealous. I was a different person back then. I used to . . ." She sighed.

"Used to what?" He waited. "Come on. Whatever you were about to say can't be half as bad as what I'm imagining. What did you use to do?"

"I used to think he was too good for me." She opened her eyes. "I'm not with him anymore, Mike."

"You're not with me, either, though."

"I'm more with you than I've ever let myself be with anyone," she said. "Unfortunately, we're in the same profession. I can't make love to you today if I might have to order you on a suicide mission tomorrow."

"*That's* the problem." He laughed. "You just like giving orders too much."

"Damn straight." She kissed him lightly on the mouth . . . then again, a series of soft touches that gradually warmed her to him. The sensation wasn't glorious or overpowering; it was simply him, an old and familiar warmth. Mike tasted of strong coffee and mouthwash, and he still smelled like the burning embers of the Whitelaw stable. But he was close, and his arms were around her. And for an instant, she felt entirely safe.

Then he started to draw her toward him, muscles hardening. And Peggy could feel herself straining to breathe.

"Ow," she said. "Fresh bandages, Yeager."

"Sorry."

They touched foreheads in silence.

"It's just . . . you know, mother in the next room," she said. "It's a little weird."

"I guess I owe you an apology," he said.

She stood up. "No, you don't."

"A confession, then." He paused. "While you were in the shower, your mom showed me that scrapbook she's making . . ."

"The one for our wedding? Mike, you're insane. She's been working on that thing since the day I was born. And it's never finished. Don't even bother with the damn scrapbook, okay? Even *I've* never seen it."

"You're kidding," he said. "But I thought . . ."

"You looked at it?"

He nodded slowly. "And you haven't."

"No. It's my own life. Why would I need to?"

"Because it's your life," he said. "I think you'd better come take a look."

Throughout her life, the scrapbook had always been on her mother's worktable—evolving, growing, but never complete, halfway between a flawed masterpiece and a running joke. And yet not once had Peggy ever been tempted to look inside.

There were backyard barbecue photos of her at the Whitelaw house when she was two years old. And five. And six. Swimming in an inflatable pool, or blowing a stream of bubbles from a wand. The most recent picture was taken when Peggy was eight years old, happily astride a pale gray pony.

Lester Tidwell was holding the reins.

"I . . . remember the pony," she said. "But I don't remember him."

"Well, he wasn't a stranger to your family. There's at least half a dozen pictures of you on this farm. Tidwell's somewhere in every one of them." He pointed to a group shot.

"So what happens now? Do I start to recover buried memories of Slayton and Tidwell abusing me in the basement?"

"Peggy, please."

"I'm serious, Yeager. Believe me, I'd rather find out something shitty happened. At least then I'd know. It's starting to feel like everyone's got the dark secrets of Peggy Weaver's childhood—except me." She turned around. "Mama?"

"I'm in trouble, aren't I?" Her mother stood in the doorway behind her. "I know I shouldn't have shown Mike the scrapbook. It's just . . ."

"It's all right." Peggy held up the photograph of Tidwell. "Do you know who this is?"

"A friend of your father's." She stared blankly. "At least . . . he was before we married. I never much liked him."

"What about this one?" She took the picture of Kevin Slayton from her jacket.

"Dear Lord," her mother said.

"These are the people who took Samantha," she said.

The phone rang.

"I'll get that." As Mike left, Beatrice reached to the stool behind her for support.

"Is Sammie . . . going to be all right?" her mother asked.

"We don't know, Mama. It doesn't look good."

"I'm so sorry." Bea took a closer look at the picture. "It's a terrible shame what they did to that poor girl. And her with a baby inside. Don't you think it's terrible?"

"Yes, I do."

"People call themselves Christians. They don't know the meaning of the word." She shook her head. "On our wedding night, he told me . . . oh, everything. The shameful things those boys did. I would have left him—but he swore to me and God above that he wasn't involved. But that Kevin . . ."

"Mama," she said. "You're getting confused again."

"I'm not. I swear."

"I don't mean to upset you," she said. "But Samantha was just a newborn baby when you and Daddy got married."

Bea looked up, confused. "Who's talking about Samantha? That wasn't her name."

"Peggy." Mike stood in the archway, holding the phone receiver. "You'd better come take this."

"One second." She turned back to her mother. "Who are you talking about?"

"The girl who died," she said. "And her baby. Her name wasn't Samantha. It was . . . Mary? Laura?"

"Mara," Peggy said. "Mara Cumbaa."

"That's it. Mara Cumbaa. She was the sweetest girl anyone ever met. And none of these fine people ever shed a tear for her."

"Peggy." Mike held out the phone.

As she took the phone from Mike, she could see the deep warning in his eyes. He gestured to indicate he was going to pick up the extension.

"Hello?"

"Hello, bright eyes." It was the voice she'd heard on her father's cell phone, quiet and confident. "I tried calling your mobile, but you wouldn't pick up."

"I got the message." She stepped away. "Why did Gretchen have to die, Slayton? She was just a kid."

"I did her a favor. Ten years from now, she'd have been a truck-stop whore with AIDS and a meth habit. And she was a traitor to boot."

"And traitors die, right? But their children always die before them."

"You read the manifesto. Good." There was an odd pride in his voice. "Listen, I know you've got your Kraut Yankee boy on the other phone, so don't think I'm going to be stupid enough to let you track me down."

"Pal, when I'm done tracking you down, you'll wish you'd swallowed that RPG."

"You've got the wrong idea. I'm a highly moral person. I know the parameters of my mission. If you'd been a good girl last night, nobody would have gotten hurt—not even your limp-dick daddy."

His voice was maddeningly peaceful—like the host of a children's show, elated and yet touched with a strange gentleness. It seemed to soothe Peggy against her will.

"I think I know something about your sense of morality," she said finally. "There's nothing you can say that will frighten me."

"I don't want you to be afraid, sweet pea. I want you to listen. You said you wanted to finish the negotiation?"

"Yes. And?"

"It's finished," he said. "You can have the antivenom. You should be able to save Little Blondie if you move fast."

"In exchange for what?"

"We'll discuss that in person," he said. "Incidentally, we didn't fuck you in Aunt Martha's basement, all those years ago. I thought you might be a little worried about that."

"Thanks, I guess."

"All the same, you would have let me if I'd asked nicely," he said. "That's how it works between boys and girls. Just like your girl there. You should have heard her begging me to cut that little mongrel baby out of her womb."

It took all her strength to stay calm. "Where's the serum?"

"You'll figure it out," he said. "You're a smart girl. Even if you never could remember my face. Or that license plate number." He laughed. "Know what's so funny about that?"

"What?"

"He really did need that number. Honest to God, he did."

The line died.

"Can we get a trace, Yeager?"

"Not a chance." He joined her in the living room. "You handled that well."

"I don't think so." Her hand was shaking as she set the receiver down. "What's his next move? Why's he doing this?"

"Well, it's not because he suddenly grew a conscience. He's got to be setting a trap." He looked at her. "He really pushed your buttons, didn't he?"

She nodded. "I want to know where my father is."

"Okay," he said. "Right now?"

"I need answers," she said. "Gretchen said he tricked me *and* my dad into killing Tidwell."

"Tricked you how?"

"With a radio." She nodded. "When I asked my father how he set the incendiary device . . . he told me I should check the audio from that microphone I planted on him."

"So where's the recording?"

"At the sheriff's station," she said. "Let's wait until the squad car gets here, okay? Then we'll go."

"Sure."

He gave her arm a squeeze. As she returned to the studio, her mother was once again sitting with the open scrapbook—not working at it, but simply staring at its last blank pages.

"Mama . . . ?"

Beatrice looked up. There were tears in her eyes.

"I'm starting to wonder if I'll ever finish this," her mother said. "There's too many things I can't remember anymore."

# FIFTY-NINE

Sheriff Powell met them inside the media room.

"How old is this coffee?" Peggy pointed to a carafe beside the door.

"Any older and it could run for Congress." Powell poured out three cups. Peggy swallowed hers in one gulp. It scorched her like singed bark, but she figured it had what she needed.

"How is it?" Mike asked.

"Awful. You'll love it." She refilled her cup. "We need to get Logan Aldridge into custody, Sheriff. Send an ambulance if you have to. But make him tell us who bought that horse."

"Horse? You mean—the mare with the sored hooves?"

"That's right. Slayton said I'd figure it out, and I have. The serum's produced by injecting horses with minute quantities of venom, until it builds up antibodies. And that perlino is the only one of Slayton's horses known to be alive. He was there at the auction on Monday. He made sure I saw the mare up close—so I could identify her, and her new owners, when the time came."

"And he said he'd tell you the price for it in person." Mike swirled his coffee.

"Yeah." She drained her cup. "Come on. Let's give that audiotape a listen."

Powell nodded grimly. "There isn't much to hear, apart from what you already know. The static gets real bad once he walks into the lockup."

"Static?" Peggy raised an eyebrow. "It's a wide-range transmitter. There shouldn't be any static."

"Take a listen." The sheriff nodded to his technician. Seconds later, they were looking at video of Chief Weaver approaching the interview room.

The guards walked away and he put his hand on the door. Then the loop began again. Through it all, Peggy could hear noise—a pulsing sound, high-pitched sine waves that grew shorter with each step her father took.

"It's not static," she said. "It's radio interference. The closer my dad gets to the source, the faster it pings back. Like sonar." She turned to the technician. "Never mind the loop. Just keep playing the audio forward."

"Okay, but I gotta warn—"

Suddenly there was a loud whine over the speakers.

"What the hell was *that*?" Mike asked.

"Feedback from the explosion." Peggy waited for silence. "Did you catch that, Mike?"

"It happened before he even touched the door," Mike said. "He grabs the door handle—and then he instantly pulls away."

He stared at the screen for several seconds.

"The door's warm to the touch," Mike said finally. "You can see his pain—and surprise—when he feels the heat."

"He didn't know it was going to happen," she said. "You know, I must have watched this tape a dozen times . . ."

"Too bad your number one photo analyst was off sulking when you needed him." Mike tapped the screen. "Your father couldn't have carried in the incendiary device. And the room was clear, right? So it had to be something planted inside Tidwell. A magnesium capsule, maybe."

"Just like Gretchen," she said. "They both burned up from the inside. Sheriff, did your examiner recover any fragments of metal or plastic from Tidwell's body?"

Powell shook his head.

"We'll leave a list of indicators for a radio-activated fuse," she said. "It'd have had to be very small—low-wattage, with a short battery life. And almost certainly triggered by proximity to the transmitter in my father's boot."

"Peg," Mike asked, "you do realize what that means?"

"It means the fuse had to be preset to the same frequency as the transmitter," she said, "before Tidwell ingested it. And before I planted the wire on my dad."

"I've been meaning to ask you," Powell said. "Where did you get that thing from, anyhow?"

"Blaine said Sean gave it to him," she answered. "I have a pretty good idea who gave it to Sean."

Peggy walked into the hallway.

"Where are you going?" Mike followed her out.

"I'm looking for some cold water. The coffee's not working anymore." She looked back at him. "You were right, Mike. My father was trying to protect me. And it still doesn't prove a damn thing. It doesn't explain why he wanted to keep the truth from me."

"Obviously he considers that a form of protection," Mike said. "What exactly was he keeping from you?"

"Strangely enough—only this." She handed him the crayon drawing from her bag. "Apparently I drew it right after the first time Samantha went missing."

"It's not bad." Mike looked it over. "Where's the other drawing?"

"What other drawing?"

"There's crayon smudges on the back." He turned it over. "From what I can tell, you were using a lot of gray and midnight blue. And a little bit of gold and periwinkle."

She took the drawing back. There were impressions in the paper— shapes and swirls of color, too faint to make out clearly.

"You're right," she said. "What can we do with this?"

"Show me to the nearest scanner," he said. "I'll have the lab bring it back to life for you."

He took it from her. A moment later, Peggy met Sheriff Powell on his way out the door.

"We got a lead on the folks who bought that horse," he said. "Some veterinarian in east Sherburn got called in this morning about a sored mare. They were about fifteen minutes from having her put down."

"You're sure it's the right one?" she asked.

"From the description you gave, yeah. Want to come along and find out?"

"I've still got to take statements from Sean and his people," she said. "Bring the horse directly to the hospital. And the vet, too. I'll coordinate with Dr. Santos on this end."

"Will do." He gave a wan smile. "I do believe I'm close to crappin' out. Old age sure ain't for sissies."

"Don't quit on me yet." She watched him walk away. "Sheriff? Can I ask you something else? It's about my father."

He stopped. "Sure, darlin'."

"Years ago . . . the first time you were all looking for Samantha . . . do you honestly think it would have made a difference if I'd remembered the tag number on that black T-Bird?"

"Peggy, you know that wasn't your fault."

"Honestly." She looked at him. "Please. I need to know the truth."

He looked at her for a long time before answering.

"Early on, he thought he might be pretty close to findin' that Thunderbird. But he couldn't get a warrant without runnin' a title search. And for that he needed the tags."

"I see."

"I hate tellin' you that," he said. "I know how Rusty got on you about that license plate. Truth is, it wasn't a tenth as hard as he was on himself when Sammie turned up in that dumpster. The way he carried on, you'd have thought it was his own child who'd disappeared."

She found herself unable to speak.

"You couldn't be expected to know that about him, Peg."

"No," she said. "But then, I never asked."

# SIXTY

The enhanced image took nearly twenty minutes to come back from the FBI Crime Lab. Peggy didn't dare look at it until she was alone in the sheriff's private office. Finally she set down her handheld computer and called the hospital.

"Dr. Santos," she said. "I won't keep you. I just wanted to find out how our patient's doing."

"We've entered the critical stage," the doctor said in a low voice. "She's lost virtually all voluntary motor response. Brain function's minimal . . . probably in deep coma soon. We could use a little good news right about now."

"I might have some for you," Peggy said. "If we bring you a livestock animal carrying the proper blood serum . . . could you use it to extract the antivenin?"

Santos was briefly silent. "I've never tried anything like it before," she said. "If that's how it's coming to us, I guess I'll have to find a way."

"Do it. And don't let Sammie get away from us. Not until I . . ." Peggy stopped. "Sorry. I'm having a little trouble keeping my concentration."

"You don't sound good," the doctor said. "I wish you'd let someone examine you after your run-in with Sean."

"The pain's about all that's keeping me awake," she said. "You don't seem too surprised by Sean's behavior."

"I'm afraid not. Sean is . . . well, he's careful not to leave marks. That's about all I can say for him."

"I never knew him to be so violent. When did it start? After Caden was born?"

"Oddly enough, no. From what I gather, it wasn't until Samantha actually showed signs of completing her book."

"You knew about that?"

"Not much. Sammie asked for my help a few weeks ago. She'd taken blood and tissue samples from some local people she'd interviewed, and she was trying to assemble a . . ."

"Mitochondrial DNA profile," Peggy said. "By 'local' you mean Chillwater Cove?"

"I believe so, yes. I got the feeling it was all very hush-hush. Unfortunately, we don't have facilities for that kind of analysis here. I referred her to a colleague at Vanderbilt University, but I don't know if she ever called him. I can give you his number."

"Thank you." As she wrote the number down, Mike came into the room. He seemed very eager to get her attention. "Do you happen to know where those samples are now?"

"She took them back," the doctor said. "Apparently Sean went ballistic over them. I think he was afraid they'd be used in some kind of paternity test on Caden. Which is, of course, scientifically impossible."

"How so?"

"Mitochondrial DNA can't be used to identify the father," she said. "It's passed solely through the maternal line. I suppose you could use it to prove who Caden's mother is . . . but that's hardly necessary, is it?"

"No, but . . ." She stopped. "Was one of the DNA samples from Samantha herself?"

"Yes." Santos paused. "Yes, it was. Why?"

"Don't you think it's strange that Samantha should be trying to prove her own matrilineal descent? Wherever Olivia Stallworth grew up . . . I know it wasn't Chillwater Cove."

"I don't know if there's any connection," she said. "But several months ago, Samantha asked if any unidentified children were treated at this hospital in nineteen sixty-nine."

"Really."

"As it turned out, she was right. In April of that year—according to my predecessor's records—we had an infant girl, parents unknown, left anonymously in the emergency room. She was diagnosed as suffering from exposure and minor trauma. Unfortunately, all other records are missing. We don't know what happened to the child—or even if she lived."

"Is there anything to suggest that Samantha might have been adopted?"

"All I can tell you is that Olivia's never allowed me to examine her," Santos said. "But I suppose there could be more than one explanation for that."

"Thank you, Dr. Santos." She hung up.

"Mike?"

"We've got Brandon DuBose," he said. "One of your dad's cops hauled him in. From baccalaureate service, if you can believe it."

"Where is he now?"

"In the infimary, getting a drug test. Kid's high on something."

"I think that's just the way he is."

"Well, he's ready for you." Mike pointed to her handheld. "What do you make of what the lab sent? Does the drawing look more familiar now?"

Peggy shook her head.

On a cursory examination, the FBI Crime Lab had concluded that sufficient crayon impressions had been left by contact with the other drawing to reconstruct approximately 46 percent of the image with a 75 percent degree of accuracy. The picture on Peggy's screen was the image-analysis computer's interpretation of what it had to work with. It contained six different fragments of what appeared to be a single drawing: a log cabin, leaning crookedly against a forest hill; a line of trees with a view of a tiny red house; an arrow-shaped mass of gray, covered with blotches of orange and green; a child's lavender sneaker. None of it made sense. Only the final image was unmistakable: a human skull, fringed with dark hair, grinning with a single gold tooth.

"Is this mine?" Peggy asked. "Did I draw this?"

"It's consistent with a drawing made by a ten-year-old child," Mike said. "Someone whose right hand was shaking. Just like yours is right now."

As soon as he said it, she realized the computer was trembling in her hand. She instantly took it into her left.

"Is it that obvious?"

"You're covering well," he said. "If that sheriff's any indication—I think everyone's so exhausted, they probably wouldn't know if you sprouted feathers." He sat across the desk from her. "What else has been happening to you?"

"Cold," she said. "It started last Thursday when I saw the photographs. It got a lot worse last night. Everyone else is walking around in shirt-sleeves . . . and I'm freezing my ass off."

She passed the handheld to him.

"I don't remember making this drawing," she said. "But Gretchen said that Slayton wanted to keep me from finding the bones of Mara Cumbaa.

And he's willing to kill to protect that secret." Peggy turned off her hand-held. "You've seen Slayton's file, Mike. You've heard his voice. What does this guy want?"

"Like the man said—he's a soldier on a mission," he said. "He was gentle with that horse he tortured. You saw how careful he was with his aunt, even while he was killing her. And he told you that you'd have let him molest you—if he'd asked nicely. I think he needs to believe he's got his victims' permission."

"Then, he's not the guy in charge. Otherwise he wouldn't need anybody's permission." Peggy dialed her cell phone. "Can you get over to Logan Farms and deal with the Aldridges?"

"If you can get me a ride, sure."

"I'll lend you my Jeep. If Slayton's not running this, then Logan has to be." She listened to a recorded message. "Damn it."

"What's wrong?"

"This phone number Dr. Santos gave me isn't working." She tried again. "Maybe it's a different area code."

"Let me see." He took the Post-it from her. "I think you might have written this down wrong. It's not a phone number."

"Of course it is."

"Three-R-L-seven-six-P-five?" He raised an eyebrow. "It's been a long time since I've seen a telephone exchange with letters in it. How did you even manage to dial that?"

"I don't know." She took it back. "I think I must be losing my mind."

"You haven't slept, Weaver. You're bound to mix up a few numbers."

"I didn't mix this up," she said. "And you're right. It's not a phone number."

She took the number back, terrified by the low tremor in her voice.

"It's Slayton's license plate number," she said.

# SIXTY-ONE

"Twenty-five years I've been pounding my skull, trying to remember that damn tag number." Peggy accompanied Mike to the parking lot, under a cloud-heavy sky. "And now it comes flying out of me for no reason."

"Probably just a delayed reaction to everything you've been through lately," he said. "You've seen it happen to trauma victims before."

"That's my whole point, Mike. That's not me. I wasn't the victim."

"Okay, fine. You're not the victim." He watched her fish for her car keys. "All the same, maybe I should stay."

"Right now, you're the only person I trust to bring Logan Aldridge in." She handed him her key ring. "Don't worry. I'll be okay."

"At least you're starting to remember things. Maybe the tag number's something we can use." He climbed behind the wheel. "Go knock Brandon around a little. You'll feel better."

"Mike?"

He turned back to her.

"Do you really believe my dad was looking out for me? That he wasn't just trying to save his own neck?"

"All I know is that my old man never would have thrown himself between me and a bomb. And he claimed to be a man of God."

"Some day you'll have to tell me your whole story," she said. "I'd like to hear it."

"Apparently, it's all in my psych workup," he said. "Just be glad you have a mother to put Bactine on your cuts."

"I am," she said. "Listen, there's places around here where your cell phone won't work. If you hit a dead zone—"

"I know, I know. Use the federal radio in the trunk."

"And watch out for Logan Aldridge," she said. "He only looks like a feeble old man."

"I think the Kraut Yankee boy can handle him." Mike smiled. "Somebody needs to remind these crackers who won at Gettysburg, right?"

Before he could start the engine, Peggy leaned up and kissed him again.

"Don't fade away on me again," she said. "That's an order."

Peggy stopped for a body check at the lockup—mildly unnerved to recall that her father had passed through the very same procedure on his way to meet Lester Tidwell. *We used to call him Lester the Molester*, she thought with disturbing clarity as she passed the scorched-out interview room, still redolent of Tiny's burning flesh. *And Uncle Fester. Because he was fat, pale, and bald. And spooky. Kids can be so damned cruel.* She could picture him perfectly in those white swim trunks, smiling and sweating through a weekend barbecue at the Whitelaw farm. Or was that only something her imagination had crafted from old scrapbook photos—the way the FBI's computers had reconstructed that drawing?

If Peggy's memory was capable of keeping secrets from her . . . wasn't it also capable of telling her lies?

"Agent Peggy!" Brandon sat alone in the infirmary's examination room, grinning at her with unabashed joy in spite of the handcuffs. He still wore the clothes he'd been arrested in: a school blazer, a blue-and-crimson bowtie, an overwashed Oxford shirt, and a pair of khaki cutoffs. Not to mention the flip-flops.

"You don't look so good." He watched her as she sat down across from him. "Whatever shit you were into last night, I hope you saved me a gram."

"Your girlfriend's dead," Peggy said. "Somebody implanted a chemical explosive inside of Gretchen while she was unconscious. Any idea who did it to her?"

"Shit, there's so many guys with a working knowledge of that ho." He held out his cuffed hands. "One drink and she's got round heels . . . next thing, she's cryin' date rape."

She waved the guard over with her left hand, keeping her briefing folder in her right.

"Ma'am?"

"Could I get a cup of coffee, please?"

"I'll take a Heineken." Brandon snapped his fingers. "Shit, it was just a joke. Relax."

The deputy scowled at Brandon as he left.

"I don't care what kind of lawyer your family's got," Peggy said in a low, steady voice. "You keep talking that way, I'll make sure you await trial at federal pen. Maybe then you'll know what it feels like to be somebody's 'ho.'"

Brandon smiled.

"I've got your school records here." She opened the file. "It seems like you were pretty much flunking out this term—until you got a special dispensation last week from the vice president of administration, Sean Aldridge."

"Well now, that is mighty white of him." He winked. "So you wanna know why Sean did me a solid?"

"I want to know what you gave Sean in exchange for that favor," she said.

"What makes you think he had a choice?"

She closed the binder. "You need to understand that this thing you're involved in—Krypteia, or whatever it's called—is falling apart. I don't know what your plan was, but it's failed."

"Guess I'm screwed," he said. "So how come your hand's so messed up?"

She gripped the folder tightly.

"I bet you don't even know why." Brandon stretched out. "*I* do. Slayton told me your whole damn story. You know, he's not such a bad guy, once you get him talking. He blew my sorry ass away on PlayStation."

Peggy found herself wondering where the deputy was with her coffee. The woolly feeling in her head wasn't going away.

"So why don't you ask me the real questions?" Brandon played with the chain holding his cuffs together. "Don't you want to know how we found Adam Cooke? Or who Mara Cumbaa is?"

"All right, Brandon. Tell me about Mara Cumbaa."

"Fuck if *I* know. I'm the guy who flunked Southern history, remember?" He laughed. "I only know what Slayton told me to do. He says, go make friends with some guy named Adam, I make friends with some guy named Adam. Dunk this in Gretchen's beer—I dunk. He wants me to make sure you find Dr. Aldridge's book . . . that's what I do. That's how it works between guys."

"Maybe so, Brandon. But the fact is, you're in here with me. And until you give me what I want . . . here with me is where you'll stay."

"See, that's the problem with you women. All you do is ask for shit. You never offer anything in return."

She folded her arms. "So what are you looking for in return?"

"I'm good," he said. "Right now, I've got just about everything I need."

He spoke with such ease that it took Peggy a moment to realize how totally his behavior had changed in the past few minutes. Much of Brandon's fake homeboy act had evaporated; so had his goofy adolescent smile. He stared at her with frank awareness, taking her in completely.

And that wasn't all that was changing. She'd been fighting so long to stay awake that she'd barely noticed the numbness gradually flooding her body—ever since she, Mike, and Powell drank that last cup of coffee together. The knowledge came to her with a murderous tranquility.

"You're a real smart lady. But you've got it all wrong." Like a magician performing a trick, Brandon hooked his thumbs behind his handcuffs . . . and deftly unlocked them both. "*I'm* not trapped in here with you. *You're* trapped in here with *us*."

He threw the handcuffs down. And Peggy could already hear the door opening behind her. Officer Martin. She tried to stand; her legs buckled beneath her. Martin gripped Peggy by her forearms, probing her eyes.

Peggy kicked at him. It was in the right spot—squarely between the legs—but too weak to do any harm. Martin barely winced as he let her fall. She struck the concrete floor, feeling the room retreat from her at blinding speed.

"Tight-ass bitch," he said. "She asked for this."

"Screw around with her later." Brandon was circling the table. "We have to move fast before . . ."

He continued to talk—but nothing else he said was making sense, and to Peggy it hardly seemed to matter anymore. Some part of her was still fighting the drug. But the light on her face was cool and peaceful, and the pain in her body was entirely gone. All she could feel were grains of dust against her cheek, and the smooth surface of the floor beneath her. Sleep and quiet pressed her down. A moment later, someone was lifting her up into darkness.

# SIXTY-TWO

"What's the matter with her?" The lockup deputy's voice.

"I dunno. She just collapsed." Martin was speaking several inches from her ear. Carrying her over his shoulder. "Don't worry. We're taking her to the hospital."

"Infirmary's back the way you came—"

"It's okay," Martin said. "There's an ambulance waiting. Thanks anyhow."

"Listen, if there's any more like her lyin' around—save one for me, okay?"

The men shared a laugh.

"It's raining," Samantha was saying. "Can you hear it?"

Peggy *could* hear it: staccato droplets pinging the metal roof, sharp as gunfire. She wasn't exactly sure when Samantha first began talking to her, but it seemed like she'd been there for hours. A bump in the road shocked Peggy halfway back to waking. She could feel canvas straps binding her to a vinyl-covered mat. She sensed the bob-and-weave of the ambulance, heard its siren blaring past slower vehicles. Somehow Samantha always stayed close beside her, just beyond her field of vision.

"It's not really an ambulance . . . is it?" Peggy's tongue was heavy in her mouth. "The driver's smoking a cigarette. Real EMTs . . . don't smoke."

"You're in a lot of trouble, honey." Samantha's voice was at once soothing and strangely distant. "I guess we both are."

"And you're . . . not even here, are you?" Peggy tried to lift her head and couldn't. "It's just that drug they gave me . . . making me see things."

Samantha didn't answer.

"Where are they taking me, Sammie?"

"To Slayton," she replied. "He won't be gentle with you, Peggy. He knows you've seen Mara's bones."

"Bones? I . . . don't know about them."

"You do, Peggy. You just won't let yourself remember." Samantha leaned in close; Peggy could practically feel her warm breath. "You have to keep him away from Mara and the others. Just for a little while longer. It's important."

"Why? How could I—?"

"Shut the *fuck* up back there." Martin was barking at her from the driver's seat of the ambulance. "Can't even think with all that moaning. What the hell's she saying, anyhow?"

"It's just the drugs," Brandon said from the passenger's seat. "Stop scopin' the rearview. Watch the road."

"I keep waitin' for someone to come after us," Martin said.

"*Chill*," he said. "We got away clean."

The ambulance was beginning its ascent, winding up around the base of the mountain. Each hairpin turn threw waves of sickness through her. Peggy was regaining consciousness, and with it came the pain. One of her restraints' metal buckles was chafing her wrist.

"Suicide Run," Peggy said. "Sammie, where are you?"

No answer.

"Samantha!"

"That's *it*," Martin said. "I'm stopping right here."

Brandon groaned. "Fucking slow *down*, asswipe! Or we'll be the ones needing an amb—*shit*."

The vehicle suddenly jolted sideways, and Peggy's eyes opened wide. They were skidding in the rain, hydroplaning, the wipers going full blast.

"Peggy." Samantha's voice, vanishing away.

Peggy turned her head. And finally she could see Samantha: a ten-year-old child in a white jumper. Young and smiling and entirely unharmed.

"You're the one keeping secrets," Sammie said to her. "You're the one hiding the bones."

Peggy opened her eyes: Samantha was gone. She pulled at the metal buckle. The belt loosened but didn't give. One more tug . . .

"She's getting loose." Brandon had taken off his safety belt and was climbing back toward her. "Give me your piece."

"My what?"

"Your gun, man. Your thirty-eight. She's trying to get up—!"

Brandon was holding the revolver with one hand, bracing himself with the other. Peggy drove her knuckles sharp and hard between his eyes. He fell backward.

"What happened?" Martin turned to look over his shoulder. "Is she— son of a *bitch*—!" His cry was cut off by the blare of an eighteen-wheeler's horn. Martin swerved, missing the truck by inches. The ambulance rolled sideways, flipping once, then again. A long, terrible scraping of metal against the roof of the vehicle. They were sliding past the guardrail to the edge of the ravine.

*I'll say this for ya, Peggy Jean.* As she tore off her leg restraint, her father's voice rang in her head. *You always know when to jump ship.* And even as the van ached toward its tipping point, she was crawling to the rear door. *Fastest reflexes in the business . . .*

Cold air and hard rain struck Peggy's face as she pushed through, shocking her fully awake. She leapt onto the gravel shoulder, coming face to face with the frightened young driver of the tractor-trailer.

"Hang on, lady! It's okay. You're gonna be—"

"Don't let her get away!" The ambulance had slowed to a halt, and Martin was pulling himself free. "She's injured. You gotta help us get her to the hospital."

"Don't—listen to him." Peggy's voice shuddered. "They're trying to kill me."

"She says—" Before the driver could say another word, a bullet tore through his shoulder. As he fell, writhing, Peggy turned to see the .38 in Brandon's hands.

"Lie down." Brandon was aiming for her, but his grip was unsteady. "This shit is going to happen. Deal with it."

She half-dove, half-fell behind the tractor cab as a second round glanced off the hood. The driver's side door was still open . . . but the keys were gone. As she looked over the fifth wheel coupling, she could hear Brandon laughing.

"Can you *believe* this wench? Hey, Martin—!"

She took hold of the locking handle and pushed it outward.

A terrific squeal erupted as the trailer broke its hitch and rolled back down the hill. Martin barely had time to leap from the ambulance before the trailer swept it over the bluff.

Peggy was already running downhill.

The rain was falling in sheets now—what her mother used to call a real frog-strangler. Peggy knew her best bet was to make for the forest trails. She forced herself up an outcropping of sandstone, aiming for the treeline. One of her shoes fell off, and her bare foot tore against the rough edge. Brandon was a dark shape in the rain, circling to her right.

Her breath came hard and shallow as she pulled herself to the top. She looked down the hill: nobody there.

"Hey."

She turned to see Brandon standing beside her.

"God*damn*, but you're hard-core. Didn't you see the fucking *path*? Now come on and let's—"

She dealt him a side-thrust kick with her bare foot, straight into his rib cage. He struck his head against the rocks and fell. Peggy took the gun from him. Then she opened his cell phone. No signal.

*Chillwater Cove.* Peggy heard another vehicle pulling to a stop: a black SUV. Kevin Slayton stepped down from the passenger's side. He frowned as he examined the wreckage of the eighteen-wheeler, and the wounded driver trying to crawl away. Then he looked up and saw Peggy staring down at him.

She had the gun. She nearly fired. But her hand was shaking too badly . . . and she had no idea how many men Slayton had with him. Peggy shrank back into the trees. As she followed the narrow path into the woods, she heard an echo of gunfire: a killing shot, ending the truck driver's life. And the roar of the truck's engine. They were clearing it off the road.

*They'll try to cut me off,* Peggy thought as she forced her way through the underbrush. *They know I can't get to the fire trails without crossing the highway. And they can move a hell of a lot faster than I can right now.* She'd have to keep working her way deeper into the forest.

Peggy began to shiver: her adrenaline was wearing off. The need to lie down and close her eyes was overwhelming. She found herself following a stream bed down into the hollow, tripping over every step. She knew she was leaving a blood trail. There wasn't a damned thing she could do about it.

At last the stream broke over a line of flat rocks: a fifty-foot chasm yawned beneath her, surrounded by tall oaks. She'd reached the heart of the Cove.

A radio crackled about ten yards to her left.

"I've got her." Martin held the walkie-talkie in one hand, propping his twelve-gauge against his hip with the other. "She came this way, just like you said."

He was bleeding from the temple; from the way he listed, she could tell he'd torn a ligament jumping from that ambulance. His aim would be off. Then again, with that shotgun, he didn't need to aim.

"Stand still." He grinned. "Stay quiet."

Peggy raised her gun. Not fast enough—

A thin jet of blood broke from his neck, knocking him backward. The recoil scattered birds through the rain. Peggy turned to see a lean young figure crouched in the lap of an oak tree—holding an old fowling piece, as if he'd been waiting for hours.

"Fletcher," she said.

He smiled at her wordlessly. As he climbed down, others emerged from behind the trees. Then Elias Collins stood forth, calmly bending down to retrieve the dead man's rifle.

"Hello again, Weaver's daughter." He nodded to her. "Welcome back."

# SIXTY-THREE

"Thought you was gonna leave the guns behind this time." Zanda poured Peggy tea from a kettle. Half a dozen men crowded around her in the small kitchen. From the way they held their rifles, Peggy couldn't tell if they were guarding her—or protecting themselves from her.

"I know I'm bringing trouble to your doorstep." Peggy laced up a borrowed pair of boots. "Just let me stay till the rain stops and I'll be gone."

"Honey, you best hope that rain lasts till Judgment Day." Zanda sat beside her. "The minute the weather clears, Slayton's gonna be comin' for you. Elias, you got any word from Coffey and the others?"

"They're still out there at Mason Bluff." He took a quick peek through the window. "They'll high-tail it back at the first sign of trouble. I say we get the children up to Eva's cabin. We can protect 'em better there."

"I can't let you shelter me here," Peggy said. "It's me they want, not you."

"It is us they want." Elias's eyes shone crystal-blue. "These fine people have been trying to wipe us out for the past four hundred years. And they won't stop till the job's good and done."

"To get you off the land, you mean. So the Aldridges can build their million-dollar homes?"

"They're keen on the land, sure. And they wouldn't mind using us to fertilize it." Elias paced over to her. "But what they really mean to kill is our memory of who we used to be. The minute we forget that we once owned this mountain . . . that we were here before the others, that we used to be more than just human fleas . . . that's when we really start to die."

As he said this, Elias placed a hand on Abe Bunch's head, gently stroking what remained of the old man's white hair.

"That's our boy." Abe smiled. "Talks almost like a Cumbaa, don't he?"

"Is it true, then?" Peggy asked. "Krypteia murdered someone named Mara Cumbaa?"

Everyone in the room seemed to tense at the name—as if saying it might bring something evil into the room.

"And others besides," Zanda said. "Why do you care?"

"Sammie told me I knew where the bones were," she said.

"She told you?" Elias stared at her. "When?"

"In a . . ." Peggy was suddenly aware of everyone staring at her. "I didn't really hear it from her. It was in a dream . . . a hallucination, maybe. While I was half-conscious."

"What else did she say?" Elias asked soberly.

"She said I told her about the bones." She thought. "And that I was hiding them—whatever that means."

Zanda and Elias exchanged meaningful looks.

"The fact is, I don't remember," Peggy said. "If I ever knew to begin with. I don't even know who Mara Cumbaa is."

Zanda raised an eyebrow. "Do you *want* to remember?"

"If it's important, yes."

Zanda nodded.

"Take her to Eva," she said.

The rain was beginning to ease up, and Elias was deeply watchful as he led Peggy through the woods. Finally they came to a small timber cabin, tilted against the hillside, as if leaning for support. It matched Peggy's drawing precisely.

"We should be trying to find a way to get back to town," Peggy said. "If I can get word to my partner . . ."

"No way out now." He shook his head. "Slayton's trap sprung the minute you swallowed that coffee. Even the ones who might want to help you don't know the trouble you're in. They've got too much of their own trouble now."

She didn't answer, remembering that Mike—and Powell—had drunk nearly as much of that coffee as she had.

"You go in alone. Eva's waitin' on you."

"Who's Eva?"

"My grandmother," he said. "The only one of our people who saw Mara Cumbaa die . . . and lived to tell about it."

He pushed the door open. As Peggy walked in, he shut it behind her.

It was a single room, lit only by a Coleman lamp, heavy with smoked meat and tobacco . . . a rank and yet strangely honest smell. The walls were covered with rusted highway signs. WELCOME TO AVALON MOUNTAIN, read one of them, POP. 3,000 AND "CLIMBING." Peggy smiled, dimly remembering it from childhood. Then she noticed a much older one beside it:

**AVALON, TN, POP. 1700**

**WHITES ONLY WITHIN TOWN LIMITS AFTER DARK**

She'd never seen that one before. Finally, next to that, a third sign— carved from wood, elaborately painted in letters almost too faded to read:

**THE FREE CITY OF CUMBAA, TN**

**EST. 1600**

**POPULATION 5,012 SOULS**

"Ain't much to look at, is it? Still, it covers a few holes in the wall." The voice behind Peggy was ancient but strong—deeper than any woman's, yet too warm and rounded for a man's. Peggy turned to face her.

Most of the Melungeons Peggy had met could have passed for white if they'd cared to. Not Eva. Her skin was copper, her features broadly African, her hair dark and tightly curled . . . and yet her eyes were the same brilliant blue as Zanda's or Elias's. Eva was nearly as wide as the table she sat behind, solid and unmoving. The hem of her long skirt reached all the way down to the packed dirt floor. Peggy felt as if she were in the presence of someone who was not merely from the Cove, but somehow part of it.

"You're Eva," she said.

"What's left of her." The old woman twisted the top from a fruit jar full of clear liquid. "Whiskey?"

"No, thanks. I've had enough intoxication for one day."

"Bet you have." Eva grinned, showing a wide gap in her teeth. "It's good corn, though. Your daddy tried to have me arrested once for makin' it. But those boys couldn't stand to lift me, let alone get me out the door."

Peggy sat down. "So there really was a 'Free City of Cumbaa.'"

"Honey, you grew *up* there. It just goes by a different name now. But it was a real enough town—streets and houses and everything—back when your Avalon was only a bad dream."

"What happened, then?"

"Oh, the States' War came in eighteen sixty-one—and then old Lycurgus up and decided he wanted to settle in, right close to where all his boys died in Shagbark Ravine. Trouble was, we was here. So him and a bunch of them hooded bastards burned us out. Called themselves the Grand Old Order of Krypteia, or some such shit." She pointed. "You can still see scorch marks on the sign."

"And the deed of sale?"

"People signed that paper because they were afraid to die." Eva drank deep from the jar. "The only name you *won't* see on it . . . is Cumbaa. The Cumbaas never sold out their birthright. And theirs was the biggest claim by far."

"And with the developers coming, that land's worth a fortune." Peggy nodded. "So if you can prove legal title to Avalon . . ."

"*I* can't. Only the Cumbaas can." She folded her arms. "And all the Cumbaas are legally dead."

"What would it take to make them legally alive?"

Eva took Peggy's measure carefully.

"You remind me in a way of your daddy," she said. "He was bright as a penny, before he became a copper. Rusty'd come sit where you are now, and take a drop with me, and be like folks. Now why do you suppose he did that?"

"He's always been friendly enough. When he wants to be."

"He was friendlier to Mara," she answered. "Her picture's there on the chifforobe, if you want a gander."

Peggy studied it closely: an old snapshot of a lovely but strangely forlorn girl in a print dress. Something about the way she twirled her long hair made Mara seem at once pensive and playful—as if she were on the verge of telling a well-kept secret.

"Your daddy took that picture," Eva said. "It's the only one left of her. Now what do you think that child's got to say for herself?"

"I don't—" Peggy suddenly wished that Mike was with her. He could have sorted it out in two seconds flat. Then Peggy realized what was going on in the picture. *It's my father she's smiling at.*

Mara was touching her belly . . . just as Ripley's girlfriend had done at the hospital.

"Her child," Peggy said.

"That's right. She never would say who the daddy was. But Rusty *stopped* showin' right about the time she *started* to. Guess he was ashamed to bring a dark girl home to his folks. Mara was heartbroken. And the rest of us thought—well, that's all we're gonna see of Rusty. But then . . . I don't know exactly how or why . . . he got messed up with Slayton's boys at the college."

"What happened?"

Eva stared quietly at the lamplight.

"Oh—lotta commotion in those days, I guess. Mara's brothers got to thinkin' they was Martin Luther King, and this here was Selma. They up and decided to go to court to prove their claim . . . and somehow word of it got back to Kevin Slayton. So he and a couple of his buddies got them some white sheets and knives . . . made themselves a new Krypteia."

Eva paused—then took another drink.

"Mara's brothers were ready to stand up and die," she said. "They never stopped to think that maybe some other folks might want to live. Like Mara and her baby."

"What happened to Mara?"

"She died. You already know that." Eva squinted at her. "Ask the *real* question."

She took a breath. "Was my father there?"

"If I tell you," she said, "then you'll have to know it for the rest of your life. Do you understand?"

"Yes," Peggy said.

"Rusty was there," she said. "It was a spring evening like this one . . . most everybody was asleep. But I never could sleep too well on the warm nights. And I'd been havin' the awfullest feeling that trouble was in the wind. So it was that I happened to be lookin' out that window on the first night of the full moon . . . and I saw 'em. With my own eyes, I saw Krypteia."

"What did you see?"

"Scared boys with knives," she said. "One went straight past me, close enough to smell the liquor on him. And they was whisperin' to each other—'Hurry up.' And, 'Keep quiet.' There weren't that many of 'em . . . maybe three or four . . . but they all had white hoods on. And they all carried knives and guns—like for huntin', you know. And for cleanin' and guttin' the dead."

The old woman paused to breathe.

"And then I saw the Cumbaas," she said. "Bein' marched in a line, with their faces under burlap. Tied together like a chain gang. And when I saw Mara's big belly . . . you know, she couldn't have been more'n a week from givin' birth . . . I just couldn't help myself. I started callin' to her."

"And that's when they saw you."

"Oh, yeah. And Slayton—I knew it was him from them yaller eyes—he was all set to stab me. Then another boy stopped him. Hood or no hood, I knew that was Rusty. Well, they set to arguin' . . . and finally two of Slayton's boys took hold of me. And pushed me into that walkin' line."

"They didn't plan on finding you, did they?"

"No, I was not part of their plan. But they used me in it anyway. Took us all down to the cave . . . stripped every last one of us naked as the day we was born. And then . . ."

Eva's voice broke, a sound like stone falling from a cliffside.

"They pushed Mara down in the cave dirt," Eva said. "Each one of the boys was to take a turn with her."

Peggy found it hard to breathe. "Did . . . did my father . . . ?"

"He just stood there," Eva said. "And I was beggin' him to remember that he loved Mara . . . and finally, he said he wouldn't do it. And he told Slayton that they was only supposed to scare us a little, and they should let us all go home before they broke laws that would get them hanged. Well, that got Master Kevin mad. He took the butt of his rifle . . . beat your daddy till he was bloody . . . broke his leg. Broke the rifle, too. I thought they might kill him. But then Slayton yanked off Rusty's hood, and smiled, and said—'You don't get to die, Russ. Tonight you get to watch.'"

"And they made him watch," Peggy said.

"Child, it went on all night," Eva said. "We had to watch 'em . . . sweatin' on that poor girl. And by the end, she was just cryin' out—'Please, my baby. I only want to have my baby.' So finally Slayton said, 'Then go ahead and have it now.' And he cut her right open. And yanked that baby out, bloody and alive."

Eva drank the last of her whiskey.

"That was only the way it began," she said. "There was a lot more of the night yet to come."

"When did they . . . finally let you go?"

"They never let me go," Eva said. "I had to be the one to live with the memory. So I could teach the young ones what happens when niggerinjuns like us try to stand up to pure white men." She took a long breath. "Slayton was ready to kill me . . . and Rusty, *and* the baby. But he'd already set explosives to close down the cave entrance. So they had no choice but to run."

"How did you get out of the cave, then?"

"I didn't get out," she said. "Not all of me, anyway."

As she spoke, the old woman lifted her skirt halfway up to her knee. Peggy gasped.

Eva's feet had both been severed and cauterized at the ankles.

"Slayton made a joke about it," she said. "He told me he was gonna have the taxidermy man stuff my feet for a gun rack."

She let her skirt fall.

"It was Rusty who got us out, seconds before the cave-in. Him with his broke leg . . . me with my bloody ankles . . . and the baby."

"What happened to the baby?"

"Oh—she lived, of course. As you well know."

"Samantha." Peggy nodded. "That's why she used DNA swabs from herself and Caden. She was looking for a match. Only she never found the bones for a compare." Peggy breathed. Her head was clearing. "And if she can prove she's the daughter of Mara Cumbaa . . ."

"Then she and her baby boy own the whole damn mountain." Eva smiled. "Maybe that's why Slayton's folk weren't too keen on Sammie havin' babies."

"And that's why Sean wanted her back. She's the key to his fortune." Peggy looked back to Eva. "Where is this cave?"

She pointed to the door. "Follow the trail from here down to where it runs into the creek. It's all just rocks and mud now. But it holds the truth. And you're the only one who knows the way in."

"And if I can't remember?"

"You don't need to remember. You just need to know that you did it." Eva waved her off. "Now go on with your ways, girl. I like you fine . . . but you've got Russ Weaver's eyes. And I can't stand to look at 'em no more."

Peggy stood.

"Eva . . . do you hate my father for what he did?"

The old woman was silent a long time before answering.

"He did a bad thing, leavin' Mara in her time," she said. "He could've warned us, and he didn't. But in the end, he didn't hurt Mara . . . and he suffered for that. And he did rescue that baby." Eva looked at her. "I guess he had at least some of the raising of you, too. Seems you turned out all right."

Peggy was halfway to the door when she heard Eva ask:

"Do *you* hate him, child?"

"I don't know," she said. "Maybe you're right. Maybe he wouldn't do what Slayton told him to." She stopped. "But he was there. How do I go on being his daughter, knowing that?"

She left without another word, afraid to see what answer she might find in Eva's eyes.

# SIXTY-FOUR

Peggy walked ahead of Elias down the winding path from Eva's cabin. The rain had largely subsided, replaced by a cold clinging mist.

"The Cove's a honeycomb of little caves," Elias said. "Most of 'em close in after fifteen feet or so. You could spend all your days lookin' and not find the right way . . . and most ways will get you killed. Evil things attract death. And if there's a dead center to evil on this mountain—"

He suddenly stopped and pointed to the hillside.

"There it is," he said. "Stiller's Cave."

It was no more than a loose fall of rubble, partly covered with moss. For a moment, Peggy was tempted to think he might be pulling her leg.

"It's nothing," she said. "How do you go in?"

"You tell me," he said. "You were here. I wasn't."

Peggy looked around. "We can't stay here. If you're right about an attack coming—"

"This is why the attack is coming," Elias said. "We have to find it before they do. Now for chrissakes, think."

She stared at the rock fall—a mass of sandstone, impenetrable. Then she turned to look at the line of trees behind her.

"The view's wrong," she said. "The way I drew it, you should be able to see a red barn through the trees. The entrance has to be—"

She looked up. Mottled gray rocks jutted from the cliff wall, keen as shark's teeth.

"Give me your flashlight," she told him. "And stay here."

"I'm coming with you. It's my people buried down there."

"If two of us know the way in, then they'll have to kill us both. Right now I'm the only one in jeopardy." She took the flashlight. "If anyone comes, don't wait for me. Run."

She scaled up the hillside, following a narrow deer path. With each step, the sense of déjà vu grew more intense . . . until she was close enough to see the green and orange moss growing on the underside of the rocks. She turned to look into the valley: the trees had grown a few feet since she made the drawing, and the red barn was a little faded. But it was still there.

"Weaver." Elias was about twenty feet below her, hidden by the curve of the hillside. "What do you see?"

Peggy was about to answer when she felt a breeze on the back of her neck. Below the rocks, safely hidden in the shadows, was a narrow cleft— just wide enough for a child to slip through easily.

"Weaver!"

She took a deep breath and forced herself in.

Peggy had never liked the smell of caves, and now she knew why. It was more than earth and rock: it was dead leaves and dead animals, it was corruption and sulfur and rot. Peggy was barely more than a few feet in when she began to feel herself sliding down into darkness.

*Can't breathe.* The walls squeezed against her. Peggy was losing her bearings. Then an outcropping of rock knocked the flashlight from her hand. It fell, echoing against stone as the light faded away. And she fell with it. For a moment, the sensation was almost like floating. Peggy had images of herself breaking against a rock—skin flayed from muscle, tendons torn, fingers crushed like dry sticks. *Keep your feet together,* she commanded herself. *Stay upright.* Then there was a hard shock of cold, so intense that it forced the wind out of her: Peggy had fallen into water.

She floated on the underground stream for a moment, gasping in complete darkness. The water was steely tasting, iron needles against her skin. Peggy swam, feeling her way, until she made out a pale shape against the darkness. The flashlight bobbed on the surface, still shining. She waded toward it, trying not to guess what soft things her feet might be digging into. Then, as she clutched the flashlight, she saw what the light was reflecting against: a jawless white skull.

It was about the size of an upturned cereal bowl—resting on the lip of a narrow alcove, as if someone had carelessly kicked it out of the way. The rest of the skeleton was a few feet away: splayed out, ribs to the ground, legs spread wide apart. It was a child—a boy, judging by the width of his pelvic bone. His spine was knotted and twisted from malnutrition, his limbs thin and badly formed. He seemed to have died trying to crawl away from something. He couldn't have been more than fourteen.

Beyond him was a wide chamber, beehive shape, maybe fifteen feet at the highest point. There were five skeletons in all. One of them, a grown man's, still had barbed wire strung around his neck . . . and down between his legs. Another lay fetal, knees to chest, a mass of fractures. A fourth had wedged himself beneath a shelf of rock, like a wounded mouse trying to crawl away from a cat. His fingers still clutched the earth, leaving a trail of marks. His left leg was twisted back at a crazy angle, rudely hacked in two—cut, and left to bleed.

And then Peggy discovered Mara.

If they had only brutalized her, Peggy thought, it would have been enough to evoke pity. But someone had evidently been moved to look for humor in Mara Cumbaa's degradation. After crushing her flat, they had arranged her—hand behind head, knee out, in some grotesque parody of seduction. They had placed an empty beer can in her right hand.

And Mara still smiled, open mouthed, even though nearly all of her teeth had been broken out. One gold tooth remained.

Peggy stooped to examine the body. Mara's pelvis was crushed: even if she had lived, the baby would surely have died in childbirth. Her skull had been split wide open by a star-shaped contact wound, probably from a hunting rifle. Peggy could still see traces of powder imbedded in bone. And strands of Mara's wine-dark hair, forced into the mud.

There wasn't much else to see. Rotted clothing piled in a corner. Pabst cans and plastic six-pack rings, the splintered wood of a rifle stock. And a child's sneaker, periwinkle blue. Peggy's favorite color. The letters PJW were neatly written on the insole.

*I didn't just stumble in here,* Peggy realized with a clear rush of memory. *I knew the bones were down here. I looked for them until I found them. And then I made myself forget.*

Peggy was startled by a sudden noise from behind. She turned to see an opossum scurrying for cover: evidently she'd invaded its home. It stared at her with its doll's eyes, baring rows of teeth as it swung round its naked pink tail and disappeared behind the young boy's bones. As it did so,

Peggy ran her flashlight up the smooth rock face. There someone had written, in letters of blood:

**EXITUS ACTA PROBAT**

"Krypteia," she whispered.

With only a second's hesitation—an awful sense of having intruded, like a grave robber, in the halls of the dead—Peggy took a bone from the left hand of Mara Cumbaa. As she plunged back into the water, Peggy realized with strange detachment that what she had in her pocket was Mara's fourth metacarpal: the ring finger.

Peggy began to shiver almost as soon as she pulled herself from the water. The climb back up was difficult, especially with the flashlight in her bad hand. But she seemed to know her steps now. She cast one final glance back into the darkness—breathed a silent prayer—then forced herself back through the cave opening. Back into the fading light of dusk.

"Elias!" She took a deep gasp of air, feeling her body seize with the chill. "We have to go—Elias!"

She looked up. The rain had stopped.

"Elias!"

As she descended she saw a lone form, half-hidden in mist and twilight. He looked back at the sound of her approach.

"Daddy . . . ?"

Rusty Weaver hobbled toward her. He wore a leather jacket over green hospital scrubs. There was a look of defeated sorrow in his eyes.

"Peggy," he said. "For God's sake. Run."

"Daddy, I . . . thought they'd gotten you."

"They did get me," he said simply. "I'm so sorry, hon."

Then she heard a rifle bolt draw back. And even before she turned round to face him, Peggy knew who was standing behind her. She could feel his yellow eyes on her.

Kevin Slayton.

# SIXTY-FIVE

The post she hung from was about the height of a telephone pole, smelling of old pitch and gasoline. It still bore the sign that had been nailed into it: HUNTING AND FIREARMS NOT PERMITTED. The ligatures on her wrists and ankles didn't hurt nearly as much as when they first bound her. Peggy's extremities had long since moved beyond pain into a kind of red numbness. But her ribs were on fire. Her arms were tied behind her with a chain—forcing her to hang forward, so that simple breathing was impossible. Another rope was looped twice around her neck. She couldn't turn her head without blacking out.

As far as she could tell, they were at the intersection of two fire roads, close to the bottom of the Cove. Some kind of command post. Now and again, she saw lanterns moving through her field of vision, or heard the noise of ATV engines, or scattered radio static. Once, she thought she heard her father's voice. Peggy's mouth was sealed with gray tape. The air was cold and moist; mist coiled around her nostrils with each agonized breath.

Her eyes opened with a shock: Someone was teasing her legs apart, fingers tickling up her thighs. She looked down to see Brandon DuBose grinning up at her. He laughed, shaking his head, as if to say, Ain't it funny how things turn out?

He reached for the zipper at the top of her slacks. Then a snap of fingers brought him suddenly to attention.

Kevin Slayton watched her, calm and curious, with that same maddening tilt of his head. He lifted her chin, then let it drop. He seemed about to walk away—then turned, as if recalling some trivial matter.

"Little Blondie's dead," Slayton said in a plain voice. "They didn't get the serum to her in time. Pretty ugly, the way she crapped out. Sorry about that."

Then a slow smile crept across his face.

"Just kidding," he said. "She's fine. God knows how they did it, but they did. Pulled her right back from the jaws of death." He waited. "Come on, would I lie to you?"

He laughed.

"Or would I?"

Then he was no longer smiling.

Brandon waited until Slayton was gone before turning back to her.

"Milf," he said with a gentle smile.

"Shh," Slayton said. "Listen."

It was fully dark. Peggy heard explosions.

"You know what that is?" Kevin Slayton threw cold water onto Peggy's face. "The sweetest music in the world. That's the death-rattle of Stiller's Cave. The last remaining entrance . . . all those bones . . . the hopes of the great Melungeon nation, blown to dust. Never could have done it without you."

There were more sounds . . . a tremor that she could feel straight through the post she hung from. Leaves shook down from the poplars overhead.

"And you really thought we wanted to keep you *away* from there?" He calmly lit a cigarette. "Child, I've been waiting twenty-five years for you to show me the way back in."

He reached up to her, cigarette in hand—then roughly yanked the tape from her mouth.

"You always were the smart little tyke." Slayton rubbed her lips. "I guess you must've listened at a few too many closed doors during one of those family barbecues. Maybe it was Tiny who blabbed, maybe your daddy. Who knows? You just wouldn't give up looking until you figured out where those bones were. Then one day, little Peggy came home . . ."

*Without my sneaker*, Peggy realized. She'd told Samantha where she'd been. And the two of them were on their way . . .

"And the two of you were on your way back to find that cave the day you met me." Slayton smiled with strange pride. "That's why I went to all this trouble to lure you back. I knew you'd have to come after me, with Little Blondie in trouble again. Just had to right that one last wrong so you could . . . get on with life."

She stared at him for several seconds.

"It *was* you," she said, voice strained. "I remember you now."

"And now you remember." He took a long drag of his cigarette. "Du-Bose!"

A moment later, Brandon appeared behind him.

"Cut her down." He dropped his cigarette and stubbed it out. "Let's get this over with. We've all got a long night ahead of us."

He led them up a steep and narrow trail to the top of the bluff: difficult for Peggy, as her hands were bound behind her. Brandon kept his rifle muzzle against the small of her back.

"What happens now, Slayton?" It took all of Peggy's strength to speak. "Even if you kill me . . . and everyone on this mountain . . . this isn't eighteen seventy-six. You can't just form a lynch mob and disappear into the shadows. Your world died forty years ago."

Slayton turned, as if noticing her for the first time.

"Nothing happens now. You die. That's what happens."

He made a small flick of his eyebrows. Brandon struck the back of her legs with his rifle butt, sending her to her knees.

"This ain't about turning the clock back." He crouched down to her eye level. "It's about the future, sugar pie. *Our* future. Took me a couple years in a KGB prison camp to figure that out, but I finally did. Krypteia is not a thing stuck in the past. It's a grand, entrepreneurial dream. Hell, the day may even come when we let the niggers in. As long as they're open to our way of thinking."

"Know what I think?" She looked him straight in the eye. "I don't think there's anybody back at that command post. And those voices on the radio sounded an awful lot like police chatter to me. I don't think there is any 'grand entrepreneurial dream.' Or any organization called Krypteia. I think it's just you and a few other losers. Most of whom are dead now."

"Most. Not all." He stood back from her. "Weaver!"

Her father stepped into the clearing. He wouldn't meet Peggy's eyes. Slayton pressed his .38 into Rusty's hand.

"One round," Slayton said. "Make it count."

Her father stared up in confusion.

"You promised . . ."

"I promised *I* wouldn't kill her," Slayton answered. "I never said she wouldn't have to die."

"You cocksucker," Rusty said. "You know I won't."

"No, Russell. I know you *will*. Or we'll do it to her. And it won't be quick and pretty, like what happened to your Covite bitch. By the time we're done tearing her open, she'll be begging for that bullet. And you'll be watching every second, I shit you not."

He said it with all the emotion of a fisherman describing lures. Even Brandon seemed a little spooked.

Rusty numbly took the gun into his hand.

"Daddy." Peggy turned to her father. "You don't have to listen to him. No matter what you did in the past."

Rusty pulled back the hammer, a grim certainty in his eyes.

"All I ever wanted . . . was to hide you away from this," Rusty said in a hollow voice. Finally, he was looking straight at her. "You ready for this, Peggy Jean?"

"Yes," she said.

"That's my girl." Rusty pivoted the gun at Slayton and squeezed the trigger. The hammer fell on an empty chamber.

"Stupid dumb hick." Slayton shook his head. "Shoot 'em both, Brandon. We're behind schedule as it is—"

Rusty hurled the pistol straight at Brandon: The rifle went off as it flew from his hand. At that same moment, Peggy swung both legs at Slayton. He was already rolling away when she struck him—not in the solar plexus, as she'd intended, but against the shoulder. He grabbed her ankle with both hands, pulling her toward him. A hunting knife was in his hand.

"*Bad* girl," he snarled. "Brandon—!"

A second shot rang out. Peggy turned to see Brandon rolling off her father, half his face blown away. Rusty was holding the rifle.

Slayton pulled her up to his chest. Peggy felt his knife at her throat, ice cold. And his hot breath on her neck.

"Let her go, Kevin." Rusty pulled himself to his knees, drawing the bolt back again. "Hands up. Easy, now."

Slayton opened his mouth to speak: Peggy shut it with a backward headbutt. He rolled away, toward the edge of the bluff. Cornered and crouching, like a bobcat. Blood ran from his nose and mouth.

Kevin Slayton laughed.

"We're fighting for the same side, you know." Then he threw himself sideways, and disappeared over the cliff's edge.

"Shit." Peggy crept to the bluff, stared through the tree branches. There was no sound of anything striking the ground.

"Peg . . ."

"He dropped his knife. Get me loose." She waited as Rusty crouched down to cut her bonds. Then she brought herself back to her feet. "We're gonna have to go down there. I don't think we can count on the fall to kill him . . ."

She heard the knife fall against stone. Peggy turned to see her father slump to the ground. As she reached for him, Rusty yelled. Her hand came away from his stomach slick with blood.

"Kid got off . . . one lucky shot." Rusty opened his eyes, frantic. "Where'd it hit me?"

"Upper abdomen." She bent over Brandon's body, ripping cloth from his shirt. "We've got to get you some help before sepsis sets in."

"You . . . just leave me here. I'll only slow you down."

She wordlessly pressed the cloth against the wound, improvising a pressure bandage.

"I . . . know what you think about me." Rusty's breathing was quick and shallow: he was going into shock. "I never wanted you to find out . . . who your old man really was . . ."

"We'll talk about it later." She began cutting strips with Slayton's hunting knife. "There's no safe way back to town, Dad. We're gonna have to . . ."

"Transmitter." He stared at her.

"Transmitter," she said. "The one I planted on you? Daddy, we can't fight about this now."

"Under the trailer." He shook his head. "Still . . . working."

"The one Martin planted under Zanda's trailer. I understand." She reached under her father. "Take a deep breath, okay? Jesus, this is gonna hurt."

Her father bit his lip hard enough to bleed as she lifted him up.

# SIXTY-SIX

The way down into the hollow was agony for Peggy. She could only guess what her father was going through. Most of the way she had to support him, and twice he fell. As they reached the bottom of the ravine, Peggy listened for gunfire. She heard nothing; and that was the most terrifying sound of all.

"Slayton landed there," Peggy whispered, pointing to broken pine boughs above her head. "There's ATV tracks leading away—four-wheel, good for narrow passages and rough terrain. Heading straight for Zanda's house. Can you tell me if—"

Her father had fallen again. She went to his side, shook him. She slapped his cheeks. Finally his eyes opened.

"Tell me what we're up against," she said. "Is it just him?"

He nodded. "Slayton . . . wanted to fool people into thinkin' he had an army. Get everybody's hands full chasing . . . Aldridge's security team. Even Logan don't know . . . it's just a couple of guys they been dealin' with." He coughed. Blood spattered his fist. "Jesus. I'm a mess. Peggy . . ."

"Shh." She touched her father's forehead: it was ice cold. "Don't talk, okay? We don't know who's listening."

"You listen." He looked up at her. "Listen to your old man for once."
She waited.

"I was ashamed of loving Mara," he said. "I was a stupid, pig-headed teenager . . . didn't know what love was. But I knew fear. And all I could think was, if my people found out about her . . . what would they do to me? What would folks call me? What kind of . . . man would I be to them?"

"And you helped him," she said. "You went with them."

"Slayton . . . made it sound easy. He said . . . we'd scare 'em, that's all.

They'd be good and scared. And Mara wouldn't ever have to know it was me." He exhaled. "That's how ignorant your old man was."

"Did you know he was the one who kidnapped Samantha before?" She waited. "I know the truth about the license plates. Could you have caught him without the tag number?"

His eyes went wide. Then he simply shook his head.

"When you showed us that drawing . . . I knew right away it was him." He shivered. "But I couldn't track him down without the tags. So finally I had to . . . take the bargain he offered. He'd send her home . . . I'd keep my mouth shut. It was the price for letting Mara's baby live."

"For Samantha, you mean."

"What?"

"She's Mara's daughter," Peggy said. "Your child."

"That's . . ." Then he simply stared away. "Oh my god."

Gunfire echoed in the hollow.

"Come on." She tried to prop him up. He pulled away.

"What are you gonna do with, Peggy? Arrest me? Testify under oath to what I just told you? Hold my hand while I die by some . . . needle in my arm?"

She didn't answer.

"I'm dead already," he said. "You remember that button I told you about? The one that shuts off your feelings?"

"Yes."

"Push it now," he said. "You won't make it if you try to save us both."

"I can't. I . . ." She stood up. "What am I supposed to tell Mama if you die?"

"The truth," he said. "She deserves it."

"Dad, I—"

"Go."

Now there was returning fire: shotguns.

Peggy took the rifle and ran downhill.

There was enough noise ahead to cover the sound of her approach, and Peggy found cover behind a screen of new trees. Firelight reflected on the shallow pond. Zanda's cabin was a smoking shell; the rest were dark and empty. A body floated face down in the water: Abraham Bunch. He lay on his side, staring sightlessly through clouded eyes.

"What happened here?"

"Slayton happened." Elias strode toward her, face streaked with blood. "The firebomb was just to distract us from his real target. He's holed up with our kids in Eva's cabin. Where we thought they'd be safe."

"He must have been listening in on police frequencies." She looked back over her shoulder. "Where are you going?"

"My mother and half my family are bein' held at gunpoint," he said. "Where you think I'm goin'?"

"Look, it's what he wants. You try to take that cabin back by force, Slayton will shoot everyone. He doesn't care."

"Christ on a cross." Elias wheeled around. "You got any better ideas?"

"Help me get under the trailer," she said.

They had to cover their faces to breathe through the smoke. Elias stood guard while Peggy crawled along the mud beneath the trailer.

"Transmitter." Elias's eyes widened. "Goddammit, I knew it. All this time, you had us bugged?"

"It was my father who reminded me of it." She scanned the floor with Elias's flashlight. "We can adjust it to broadcast on federal frequencies. It may be our only—there we go."

There it was: a white box, about the size of a paperback novel, with an antenna and contact microphone attached. The red LED told her the unit was still working.

"A chance is exactly what we don't have," Elias said. "I know what happened at the caves. All that trouble was for nothing. Maybe you get to die with us, if that's any reward."

Peggy didn't answer immediately. The unit was still picking up her voice.

"They didn't destroy all the evidence," she said. "I managed to take a finger bone from Mara Cumbaa. It should be enough to validate the DNA profile." She opened the box and carefully retuned the frequency. "I don't know how long I'll get to talk. My colleagues are going to want to know how many civilians are inside."

"Six kids. Plus my mom and grandma." Elias's voice tightened. "For God's sake, hurry."

Peggy took the microphone into her hand. "All federal personnel receiving this transmission. This is Special Agent Weaver, FBI. Code Thirty. We have an eleven-sixty in the Chillwater Cove region, approximately half a kilometer south-southeast of Avalon Highway Bypass. One subject, armed and dangerous. Send air units and emergency medical teams. Repeat: Code

Thirty. We are unable to receive transmission. Lock in on this signal and proceed with extreme caution."

"What's a Code Thirty?" Elias asked.

"Officer wounded." Peggy crawled to him. "Requiring emergency assistance."

He helped her up. "You're not wounded."

"I'm not the officer," Peggy said. "Okay. We repeat the message at intervals until—"

"No, we don't," Elias said. "We don't have time."

Peggy raised her head. A searchlight beam cut back and forth through the line of trees.

"Somethin's happening at the cabin," he said. "Come on."

Slayton's ATV lay on its side in front of the cabin, half-buried in dirt. A dozen men stretched flat on the ground or hid behind trees, holding their rifles steady. Now and again, the beam of Slayton's searchlight would pivot through the front window, casting a wide arc across the ground.

"Gotta take him out," one of the men was saying. "Lookit him. Bastard's practically beggin' us to shoot him."

"Hold your water." Elias pushed the barrel down. "Can't you see that's a child's hands on that lamp? He'd like to make us shoot our own, wouldn't he?"

Peggy crawled forward, angling for a better firing position.

"Weaver!" It was Slayton's voice. "I know what you're trying to do, girl. I've got a radio, too. Now cut this shit out and show yourself before I blow these little mongrels wide open."

Peggy squinted through the light. She could make out perhaps a dozen silhouettes: no telling which was Slayton. And one shot was as much as she'd get before he started killing.

"If you're listening, Slayton, then you know you're screwed." She shouldered the rifle. "You shoot even one of those kids, you're dead. And five minutes from now you'll be the one caught in a standoff."

"Five minutes from now, it won't matter." He was, as ever, insanely calm. "What makes you think I plan to get away?"

"That's your pattern, isn't it? You abandoned your men to die in Laos. Just like Lycurgus Stallworth abandoned his men at Shagbark Ravine. You like a good lost cause . . . as long as you don't have to die for it."

There was a nervous silence. Peggy saw several of Elias's men fidgeting with their weapons.

"Now if that ain't the pot calling the kettle black." Slayton's voice was gently mocking. "Seems you know all about running away from trouble . . . don't you, girl?"

She waved Elias to her. "You want to talk, Slayton, or do you want to deal?"

"Deal," he said. "You can have your pickaninnies back."

"In exchange for what?"

"You, of course. And that finger bone, if you please."

A hand on her shoulder: Elias. He shook his head slowly: Don't do it.

"All right," she said. "Deal."

She passed her rifle to Elias.

"Wait for a clean shot," she whispered.

Peggy stood up into the light, hands raised.

# SIXTY-SEVEN

Peggy's heart caught fast, and as she approached the cabin her world seemed to freeze. She could hear the children's anxious breathing inside the cabin, the tense shifting of armed men at her back. She could smell black powder and gasoline smoke. And a night breeze brushing her hair across her face. She was less than six feet—a grave's depth—from the open cabin door.

"That's close enough." Slayton's gunmetal voice. "Show me that bone. Prove to me you've still got something left to trade."

"It's in my boot." Peggy started to bend down when she heard the telltale sound of an assault rifle bolt: Kalashnikov, on semiautomatic.

"Careful," he commanded. "Slow."

She glanced up. He was a dark shape against the open door. His other hand held a child's pale face—Zanda's girl—pressed against his leg.

"Let her go," Peggy whispered.

"In time," Slayton answered. "First we—"

"Slayton!"

It was her father's voice. Peggy turned as the searchlight found him: staggering toward the cabin in blood-soaked hospital scrubs. Alone and unarmed.

"Dad, stay back!" She couldn't help the terror in her voice.

"Yeah, Dad." Slayton chuckled. "Stay back."

"This ain't between you and her." Rusty shouted, though it must have cost him his last breath. "You and I got one last score to settle."

"Done."

Rusty spun to the ground as if he'd been whipped. A spray of blood danced in the circle of light. Peggy heard an empty shell from Slayton's rifle hit the ground.

Many things seemed to happen at once. Children screamed. Several men rushed forward. The searchlight struck the ground and tumbled away. And Kevin Slayton's eyes glowed like fireflies as he turned the muzzle of his AK-47 on the group of children cowering around Zanda on the floor.

Peggy reached into her boot, gathered up what she'd placed there.

"Slayton," she said. "Turn around."

There was just the trace of a smile on his face as she plunged the Bowie knife deep into the soft flesh between his neck and shoulder. The rifle fell from his hands. He choked—a bubble of blood—then tried to pull the blade out with both hands.

Zanda turned her body to cover the children's faces.

"Didn't . . . hurt." A strained whisper. Slayton sank to his knees. The blade came out, leaving an open well of blood at the base of his throat. "Why didn't it . . . kill me?"

"It will soon," Peggy said. "Give it time."

Others were coming forward to the cabin, their voices lost in the noise of approaching four-wheel vehicles.

"*FBI!*" Mike Yeager's voice, amplified on loudspeaker. "*You are surrounded. Do not fire on us or your hostages. Do not—*"

A group of federal agents, FBI and ATF, were moving into position. Peggy walked between the swinging arcs of flashlights to her father. He lay in the dirt, blood spilling over his chest and arms. His skin was blue-white, stone cold.

"Hang on," she said. "Help's here."

"It's fine," he said. "Don't need it."

"Dad . . ."

"Don't . . . regret." He looked at her with bald simplicity. "Not about today . . . or what happened before. You understand?"

She nodded.

"You did good, darlin'. You're ready." He looked at her. "Good shot. Did you . . . ?"

"Yeah," she said. "Slayton's dead. We got him."

He took her hand.

"That's my girl," he said. "And . . . you *are* my girl, hear? Never . . ."

Then he let go. Peggy was dimly aware of Mike standing close to her.

"I won't forget it," she said.

# SIXTY-EIGHT

Peggy waited until the last of the emergency vehicles was gone—EMTs with the wounded and other witnesses, morgue wagons carrying the dead, the evidence teams taking photographs—before making her own preparations to leave. By then it was almost dawn. Chillwater Cove was dead silent.

Then, just as she was about to climb into her Jeep, she saw him: a lone figure on a flat rock overlooking Eva's cabin. Fletcher Collins, holding his .22, crouched beside his three-legged Doberman. His blue eyes shone pale and clear in the dim light. It took her a moment to realize that his lips were moving. Then he smiled.

"Peggy." Mike's hand on her shoulder. "Let's get you to the hospital, okay?"

She nodded, then looked back at the ridge. Nobody there.

"What is it, Peg?"

"Nothing," she said. "Just saying good-bye."

Sunrise greeted Peggy with the news that Dr. Santos wanted to meet her at the ICU.

"We administered the serum late yesterday afternoon," the doctor said. "It was tricky extracting the antivenin—fortunately, I had plenty of assistance. First time I've ever shared my operating theater with a veterinary surgeon."

"How is Samantha?" Peggy asked.

Dr. Santos smiled.

Peggy found Samantha in a private room: pale and drawn from her ordeal . . . but breathing normally, and without the respirator. As Peggy sat beside her, she could feel tears coursing down her face.

"Not that . . . ugly . . . am I?" Samantha's dry lips barely moved.

"You're the prettiest thing I've seen all week." Peggy stroked her dark blond hair. "God, are you ever."

"Funny. *Feel* like . . . death warmed over." Samantha cleared her throat. "Where's Caden?"

"Outside in the waiting room. We'll bring him to you whenever you like." Peggy took a breath. "Sammie, I killed Kevin Slayton. He's gone."

"Oh." Samantha closed her eyes. "Okay."

She was silent for a long time. Peggy was about to leave when Samantha turned her head.

"Was I asleep . . . ?"

"For a while, yes. You should rest some more."

"I've had the worst dreams lately," she said. "Did you . . . find what was buried down there?"

"I did, Sammie. I found everything."

"I figured you would," she said. "You always do."

Then she was truly asleep.

Peggy returned to the waiting room to find Mike tossing a green nerf ball back and forth with Caden. The child was giggling happily as he bounced it off Mike's forehead.

"Who's winning?" Peggy asked.

"Caden's definitely mastered the art of the beanball," Mike said as he rolled the ball back. "You ready to go?"

Peggy nodded. Then she noticed Olivia Stallworth sitting by herself on the waiting room sofa. She held a cardboard box in her lap, starting emptily into the middle distance.

"Olivia," she said. "Where's Harrison?"

"I sent him on to the trustees' meeting," she said. "It's very important for him to manage things. Can't let our troubles interfere with . . ." She looked up. "I shouldn't rattle on like this. We heard about your father. Harrison and I are . . ."

She suddenly seemed to despair of words.

"Please tell your mother how very sorry I am," she said finally. "I'll try to come by later this afternoon."

"I haven't told her yet," Peggy said. "But thank you."

"Mrs. Stallworth." The nurse put her head out. "You can have a few minutes."

She stood up. "Caden. You go with the nurse, now."

Caden stood up and obediently—though reluctantly—took the nurse's hand.

"What's in the box, Olivia?"

"Oh—pictures from home. A few other things. I thought, since she's moving to a private room, my daughter might like a little prettiness . . ."

"Is she?" Peggy asked.

"Is she what?"

"Your daughter," Peggy said. "Or was she adopted? Forgive me for asking . . ."

Olivia pursed her lip, suppressing tears.

"I suppose she's often wished she had been," she said. "She's the child of my body, though. And I've had the pains in my body to prove it." Her eyes flew to Caden, who was trying to fetch his ball. "Caden, come! Leave it alone!"

Mike pulled himself up. "Here, Mrs. Stallworth. I'll—"

She reached for the child's shoulder. Caden yanked away, causing the box to fall from her arms. Several framed pictures hit the floor.

"Oh, *no.*" Olivia sank to her knees, crying. "They're *ruined* now. I can't *believe* this child."

Mike was about to kneel down to help when Peggy warned him away. "I'm sure they're fine, Olivia. In fact . . ."

As Peggy picked up a framed portrait of Harrison, she caught Caden's reflection in the broken glass.

There was no expression in the child's face. But Caden crossed his arms over his chest—just as he had the morning after Samantha disappeared.

"Z'ake," Caden said. "Z'ake."

"I wish he'd learn to *speak.*" Olivia took the picture from Peggy and gingerly placed it back into the box. "What is that child trying to say?"

*We're fighting for the same side, you know.* Slayton's voice echoed in Peggy's mind as she watched Caden trace the shape with his finger—a simple S-curve, coiling in the air.

"Snake," Peggy said.

# SIXTY-NINE

By tradition, the Avalon College trustees always met on the second floor of Culloden Hall—an oak-paneled room, carefully appointed, with portraits of long-dead presidents staring down at the men and women seated around the polished mahogany table. Harrison Stallworth stood at the head of the room, clad in his black academic gown and hood, his back to Peggy as she entered.

"... veterans of the bloodiest conflict this nation has ever known," he was saying in an earnest voice. "My great-great-grandfather, General Lycurgus Stallworth, found his bedrock not in hatred or force of arms, but in the greater good ..."

One by one, the trustees looked up at Peggy in alarm.

"... of the community." Harrison hadn't seen her ... but he seemed increasingly aware that his audience was no longer listening. "And the wisdom to look beyond the tyranny ..."

Then he looked back. For the briefest of moments, he actually smiled.

"... of failed ideas." Harrison closed his notebook. "Ladies and gentlemen, would you excuse us a moment?"

He drew her into his office—the scene of countless tutorials and private conversations between them over the years. Harrison sat. Peggy didn't.

"Peggy, I was so relieved to know you're all right. I would have stayed at the hospital, but ..."

"I realize today's a big day for you. The hundred and thirtieth commencement at Avalon. And your reappointment as president."

"Only on an interim basis." He shifted. "Are you all right? You have a very strange look in your eye."

"Get used to it," she said. "Cui bono."

"What?"

"Sean's in jail . . . Logan's still at home, of course, but nobody seems to think he'll live long enough to serve time. So ends the last threat to your administration. Slayton's dead with the rest of his crew . . . and my father, of course. Meanwhile, Samantha's still alive . . . and you're still president. So I guess all your problems are solved."

"Peggy, I don't understand. I know you've been under a lot of stress . . ."

"You do not know what kind of stress I've been under." She took a deep breath. "Please, for the love of God. Tell me how it's possible you can look so damned . . . *good* . . . after everything Samantha's been through."

He took a careful step back. "I love my daughter, Peggy. More than anything. And I resent the implication that . . ." He stood up. "You'll excuse me. I have work to do. Come to the house when you've gotten some sleep, and are feeling . . . more like yourself."

"Not more than anything," she said.

"Pardon?"

"You never said that you loved Samantha more than anything. You told me that she was one of two things you loved most. The other being the presidency of Avalon College. I never stopped to consider which of those came first."

"Peggy . . ."

"You took me to the archives at the *exact minute* Sean showed up to create a diversion, didn't you? And that paper Slayton wrote. You were so careful to make sure I knew he had a grudge against you . . . so careful that I never stopped to wonder how it was you were able to put your hand right on a document you supposedly hadn't seen in forty years."

"This is the grossest kind of speculation," he said. "To insinuate that I might have conspired with Kevin Slayton . . ."

"I know, I know. You can't prove a negative." She watched him. "Anyway, I never said you conspired with him. I can see now that Slayton was too much of a loner to take orders from anyone but himself. Still, twenty-five years ago, you knew he was the one holding your daughter."

He paused. "And how would I know that?"

"Because you saw the picture I made of him when I was ten. 'When you showed *us* that drawing'—that's what my father told me, just before he died." She waited. "I never thought to ask how you were able to identify a snake belt buckle you'd never seen before. But you had. Because I drew it for you."

"Ah, Peggy. Peggy." And he looked at her. "Well done."

Then he settled down behind his enormous desk.

"You were always my best student," he asked after a long silence. "What do you want?"

"I just want to know why," she said. "Why you didn't tell me his name right away. Why you let him come so close to succeeding. Why you let him—do unspeakable things to your only child."

He merely looked up as the door opened. One of the trustees, a middle-aged man, put his head in.

"Harrison," he said. "Are we—?"

"You carry on without me." He smiled, ever gracious. "I think my financial proposal is self-explanatory."

The man gave a curious nod and withdrew.

"Financial proposal?" she asked.

"We've decided to go ahead with Sean's real estate plan," Harrison said as the door closed. "With one key difference. The profits won't be lining Logan Aldridge's pockets. They'll be plowed back into scholarships, learning centers, endowed chairs . . . programs for racial and gender diversity. Avalon won't merely be saved from ruin, Peggy. It will finally become what it should have been all along."

"And the Cumbaas?"

"Ah. Well, it is true that there's no record of the Cumbaas' selling their claim to the mountain." He held up his hands. "But then, there's really no record of the Cumbaas, period. And the caves are gone. Dust, as the poet said, has no memory."

"Whatever happened to 'truth is never destroyed'?"

"Truth." He pondered that for a long time. "The truth is, when my daughter told me about the photographs, I suppose I had some inkling that Slayton might be about to return. And when that ransom note appeared, I was convinced it was him. I came very close to warning you. But by then . . ."

"By then you'd read Samantha's notebooks," she said. "And you realized that you and Slayton . . . and the Aldridges . . . all wanted the very same thing. To prevent anyone from ever finding proof of the Melungeons' claims to Avalon Mountain."

He glanced up, as if sensing a trap.

"Hypothetically," he said, "if such proof existed, it would destroy this institution. You must understand, my heart bled for my daughter's suffering . . ."

"But it was the price you had to pay for the greater good."

"Yes. Always for that." He stood up. "We can continue this discussion later. But now I must return to the meeting."

"Harrison," she said quietly. "Do you really think you're going back into that room? Ever again?"

He thought about it for a moment.

"I suppose not," he said. "But it doesn't really matter what happens to me now. Avalon is safe."

The clock chimed once: nine thirty.

"I'd considered waiting until after graduation to arrest you," she said. "But then I realized . . . you were probably counting on that, too, weren't you? You figured I'd be honor bound to give you that last moment of glory—favorite pupil, and all."

"It would have been nice." He laced his fingers. "But I won't be disappointed if you decide otherwise."

"I'm going now," she said. "My partner will be here in fifteen minutes to take you into custody. I think you should prepare yourself for what's coming."

"Peggy, please . . ."

"Don't."

She reached into her jacket . . . and placed a .38 on the table.

"This was Slayton's revolver," she said. "There's one round in it. Don't worry, it's clean of prints. The gun's like the dust. It doesn't have any memory, either."

She went to the door, then turned. He was still staring at the gun.

"My father wasn't a perfect man, Harrison. But he died for that greater good of yours." She opened the door. "If you really want to avoid bringing shame to the college . . . maybe you'll find a way to die for the greater good as well."

He didn't answer as she left. But as she shut the door, she saw his fingers close around Kevin Slayton's gun.

# SEVENTY

Mike pulled up to the driveway of Peggy's house.

"How much time do you need with your mom?" he asked.

"I don't know," she said. "I'll call you."

"I'll be done in . . ." He looked at his watch. "Yikes. I should probably go arrest that professor of yours, huh?"

"There's no rush," she said. "By the way, when's your flight back to Philly?"

He shrugged. "It's an open ticket."

"Maybe you'd like to drive back with me? It'd mean staying a couple more days . . . for the funeral, and the rest of it. But I could use your company. And we'd have time to talk on the way home . . . tell each other stories."

"I'd like that," he said.

"I wish I could promise more than that, Mike. But . . ." She stepped down from the Jeep. "We're still in the same profession. Nothing's changed."

"Nothing except that you're about to get promoted—again." He smiled. "And I notice your hand's not shaking anymore."

As she raised the folder in her hand, she saw that he was right.

"What's that you're holding?" he asked.

"Preliminary Mitochondrial DNA report on the bone sample from Mara Cumbaa," she said. "No match to Samantha. Or Caden. It's difficult to believe that all this . . . was for nothing."

"Not for nothing," Mike said. "I mean, that kid of Mara's . . . she's got to be still alive out there somewhere. And whoever she is, she's stinking rich. She's gonna want to know about that, right?"

"Maybe there's more to life than being stinking rich," Peggy said. "Maybe this kid . . . whoever she is . . . would rather get on with her own life."

She kissed him. Then she went inside.

The house was the same as it always had been. Her father's coat slung over a kitchen chair. The permanent impression he'd left in a sofa cushion. Countless rings on the coffee table. Broken corn chips on the floor. The photographs and certificates on the wall. Echoes of Rusty Weaver, abandoned, unaware of his passing.

Her mother was still asleep in the master bedroom, reaching out for the empty place beside her. Peggy was about to go in and wake her up. Then she caught the smell of scorched pine. *Sometimes she falls asleep over the damn wood-burner,* her father had warned her. *It's like to set the whole house on fire.*

Peggy went into the studio to unplug the cord. Then she stopped to look at her scrapbook again.

It had never really occurred to Peggy just how few pictures there were of her and Beatrice together. It was always Peggy and Sammie. Peggy and Rusty. Peggy and Harrison. And—disturbingly—Peggy and Tidwell. But her mother always seemed to find her comfort behind the camera, observing her little girl from a safe distance. Even in her earliest baby pictures, Peggy and her mother were never together. But still, it was a beautiful scrapbook Beatrice had made for her. She hoped it would be finished some day.

Peggy was putting the scrapbook back onto the easel when something fell out of its leaves, onto the floor: *CERTIFICATE OF ADOPTION,* it read.

*Sometime I'll tell you about the day we brought you home,* her mother had told her. *I knew right then my Peggy Jean was gonna be a fighter.* There were no pictures of Beatrice Weaver during her pregnancy. None. Peggy always figured her mother was simply modest. But . . .

"I am his girl," Peggy said. "I am."

For a bare instant, she actually found herself wishing she hadn't made the connection. It wasn't the money. It was knowing that with the knowledge came the responsibility to decide. Not just what Avalon would become . . . or what even she would become . . . but what her entire world would become, once the truth was upon them.

There would be time for that decision in the days to come. And a long ride home with Mike to figure out what would happen next. But first she had to see to Beatrice.

She took a moment to breathe and compose herself. Then Peggy Weaver carefully replaced the adoption certificate in her childhood scrapbook, and the scrapbook in the bookcase. And went in to wake her mother, and tell her how her father's story had ended.